How (NOT) to Date a Pop Star

Jada Trainor

wattpad books

wattpad books **W**

An imprint of Wattpad WEBTOON Book Group

Copyright © 2023 Jada Trainor

Published in Canada by Wattpad WEBTOON Book Group, a division of Wattpad WEBTOON Studios, Inc.

36 Wellington Street E., Suite 200, Toronto, ON M5E 1C7 Canada

www.wattpad.com

First Wattpad Books edition: July 2023

ISBN 978-1-99025-986-9 (Trade Paper original)
ISBN 978-1-99025-987-6 (eBook edition)

Library and Archives Canada Cataloguing in Publication information is available upon request.

Printed and bound in Canada

1 3 5 7 9 10 8 6 4 2

Cover design by Lesley Worrell

Images © ghrzuzudu © Nella via Shutterstock

For Julian, Carter, Lincoln, Weston, my husband,
my mom, and Onika: I hope you never stop dancing!

One

The Time Has Come

The line started in the Village Square Mall and ended in the parking lot, growing longer by the minute. The signing was nearly over, but cars were still spilling out of the lot and parking on the side of the road, bumper-to-bumper. My best friend and I had been standing in that line since before the mall opened at 8:00 a.m. When the mall finally closed, Tyler Moore would get back on his tour bus or his private jet, and the world would drown in oceans of teenage tears. Truth be told, I still held on to the days when the only pop stars I knew were the ones on my wall.

Quinn danced on her tiptoes in a fruitless attempt to see above the crowd. "What's in the water? These eighth-graders are *huge*."

We were in middle school hell—most of Tyler's fan club had pigtails, braces, and concert merch.

"You're just short, Q." I grinned. "Remember when we first met, and you had that giant poster of Tyler's face on your bedroom ceiling? I'm sure he'll get a kick out of that. I know I did."

I would never forget the way I'd laughed when I saw his big, stupid face floating over her bed. Or the way Quinn had freaked out, galloping around the room when I told her he and I were once friends.

"I used to listen to the radio and pretend he was singing me to sleep . . ." Quinn played with a glossy lock of hair, staring dreamily into the distance.

I followed her gaze, disgusted. "Girl, I am unfollowing you."

The line ahead moved slowly. We caught glimpses of Tyler here and there, sitting at a glass table, flanked by rows of security guards. Tyler signed pictures and T-shirts and records, snapping selfies with his fans. The only time he didn't smile was when the beautiful brunette hovering at his side would lean down and whisper in his ear. She was young, practically college age—put her in a plaid skirt and school sweater and she'd fit right in. But in that sleek black pencil dress and matching stiletto mules, she looked like the kind of person who knew how to get shit done.

I could tell Quinn was nervous by the way she fiddled with the necklace her dad had given her. She slid the locket up and down its chain, biting her lip. I would have told her to relax, only I was nervous too. It had been a long time since Tyler and I had seen each other. What if he pretended not to know me?

Up ahead, a teenybopper with a mass of curly red hair burst into tears as Tyler took his CD from her hands. She howled and covered her face when he signed it and gave it back. Her mother steered her away as she sobbed uncontrollably. It was then, as I watched them go, that I realized Tyler wasn't just Tyler anymore. He was a god.

A grown man stepped out of the way, clutching his signed collectible figure, and suddenly Quinn and I were face-to-face with the platinum pop star. Gone was the tall, gangly kid with acne and braces and social anxiety whom I had once known. The boy sitting in front of me was confident and arrogant and . . . hot. The jawline, for instance—where the hell had that come from? And the tattoos on his hands, those were new. Tyler was only seventeen, but time on the road had matured him.

I had never seen that much money up close until I saw it on him—the Colgate grin, the chains, the iced-out watch on his wrist. His ash-brown hair was cut in a curtain of shiny, tousled waves that touched his leather jacket. The haircut suited him. Everything about Tyler looked expensive, like he would cost you in more ways than one.

Tyler's smile widened. "'The time has come,' the walrus said . . ."

That famous line from our favorite poem danced in the air between us.

"Someone's been busy," I teased, reaching out to give him dap.

"Maybe a little." Even his modesty was a flex. "Happy belated birthday, by the way. I'm sorry I missed it."

"Me too." But being the upstanding Libra that I am, I smiled to let him know it was okay.

Tyler turned his attention to Quinn, and my stomach flip-flopped as I wondered what he was thinking about my stunning best friend. Quinn drew you with her looks and kept you with her charm. Her cool blue eyes, dirty blond waves, and beach model frame turned heads wherever she went. And when she sang onstage, there was no looking away. Quinn knew how to work a room.

I cleared my throat. "Um, Tyler, this is Quinn. Quinn, meet Tyler. Quinn's been to five concerts in three different states. She's kind of your biggest fan."

"That's awesome. Thank you." Tyler went for a fist bump, chuckling as she grabbed his hand and shook it. Quinn blushed, laughing the way she always did when she was embarrassed.

"Q's a songwriter too," I said, giving her shoulder a nudge. "Your girl can hit a solid B5."

"Mostly in the shower." Quinn's eyes widened. "Not like that! Y'know what I mean."

Tyler and I both laughed, earning a dark glare from the woman hovering off to the side.

"Well, actually, it's Aaliyah who's your biggest fan," said Quinn, pulling me into the spotlight. "Of course, we both *loved* your last album, but she was absolutely *obsessed* with dissecting the lyrics. Weren't you, *Aaliyah*?" The accusation came with a swift elbow jab.

"I wasn't obsessed," I replied, pretending to inspect my black Doc Martens. "I was . . . curious."

"You know what they say about curiosity, Ali-Cat." Tyler winked.

The sound of that old, familiar nickname threw me off guard. To regain my bearings, I unzipped Quinn's backpack, grabbing the T-shirt stuffed inside.

"Would you mind signing this for Q's cousin? He's seven. He wants to sell it on the black market for a million bucks."

"Sweet." Tyler chuckled and accepted the shirt, fingers brushing against mine. I played it cool, tucking my curls behind my ear, ignoring the fluttering in my stomach.

Tyler scribbled his name in the bottom corner of the picture on the shirt, pausing as he recognized the photo—a candid shot of an onstage performance. His back was to the camera, posed against a bright, faceless crowd of thousands, his mic raised to his fans. The picture was black and white, but you didn't need color to see how brilliant the spotlights were, how they shone on the audience, illuminating Tyler in a halo.

He gave the shirt a half grin of approval and tried passing it to Quinn, who stared at it like she'd found a pot of gold at the end of the rainbow. Of course, I'd lied for her—the shirt was never intended for her cousin. Thank goodness I had talked her out of wearing concert merch.

"So, um, did you just come by for the T-shirt, or . . ." His green eyes were as mischievous as ever, and perhaps I was only seeing what I wanted to see, or perhaps I was seeing nothing at all, but he looked hopeful. Like maybe I wasn't just embarrassing myself in a mall full of people. Maybe he was happy to see me too.

Before I could invite him back to my place for spaghetti, Quinn boldly interjected, gripping the edges of her white cropped sweater in both hands.

"Tyler, can you sign my—"

The brunette lady ditched her Bluetooth and entered the chat.

"I will have you removed in two point five seconds," she warned Quinn, who immediately let go of her shirt. "Tyler, we have a six a.m. flight, then two radio interviews, a session with your vocal coach, and a meeting with the label to prepare for. So let's not keep the rest of our fans waiting, shall we?" I didn't know which was more impressive—Tyler's schedule or the boredom in her voice as she announced it with a smooth Aussie lilt.

Tyler wasn't pleased. "Aaliyah's not a fan, Astrid; she's my *friend*. Can we cut the business talk for five minutes?"

"Time is money, Tyler."

"Not everything is about money, Astrid."

"Then you're in the wrong industry." Astrid dusted her immaculate skirt. "Why you would trade a performance at Madison Square for a two-bit signing in a town you refer to as the armpit of the USA, I will never bloody know. But we're here now, so let's make the best of it, hmm?"

Tyler's nostrils flared, his chest swelled, his mouth opened wide—and then the wind left his sails the moment he saw my face. Did he really think our hometown was an armpit? Wasn't there one good thing about Harbor Village that he had taken with him on the road to fame?

"Astrid, embarrassing me in front of my friends isn't part of the contract," said Tyler, jaw clenched, smoke pouring from both ears.

But behind that perfect, no-makeup makeup countenance, not a single Chanel fiber was out of place. Astrid couldn't have had more than a decade on us, but like Tyler, something about the industry had aged her. Beneath Tyler's withering scowl, her large brown eyes remained impenetrable, her heart-shaped lips turned up in amusement. She didn't seem to care that Tyler was upset and throwing a tantrum, which would only piss him off more. Classic move. Since Tyler and I were little kids, the "I don't care" button was usually the first one I pushed, because I knew I would get a reaction.

"Tyler, it's my job to keep you on track," said Astrid. "I'm your manager."

"Well, I don't pay you to make me look like an asshole."

"You do that on your own. So put on a smile, act happy, and soon enough we can put this sad little experience behind us and get back on a plane to civilization. Mm?" And with that, she went back to her Bluetooth.

"I'm *taking* a *break*." Tyler left his seat, storming away from the table to a chorus of boos and cries. His bodyguards followed, the impassable wall between his world and mine. His manager hardly noticed when he left, but I did.

He never said goodbye.

On the second floor of my aunt Katrina's cozy Victorian home, I burst through the bathroom door into the hallway. My aunt was blasting The Weeknd, just in time for me to sing Ariana's solo. Towel on my head, I sang off-key into my comb, pointing at my imaginary audience. Planting a kiss on the picture of my mom hanging on the wall, I danced my way downstairs and into the bright, sparkling kitchen.

My aunt stirred a giant pot of sauce simmering on the stove. She'd replaced her hospital scrubs with gray shorts and a matching oversized hoodie, and her hair was in a pineapple as she danced around and sang the words into a spatula. I joined in, finishing the song with a little fancy footwork.

"You dance better than yo' mama did." Laughing, she slapped hands and gave dap, then asked Alexa to turn down the volume. I frowned, rolling my eyes at Alexa, who'd had the nerve to follow up with a Tyler song.

"You look tired," I said, taking the spatula and stirring the sauce. "I'll take over from here."

For once, Trina didn't argue, just took a seat at the kitchen island, watching as I served spaghetti onto our plates. "I've been running low on energy lately. Must be all those overnights at the hospital. How'd it go with Tyler? I thought the plan was to get him back here for dinner?"

Dropping into the seat next to her, I rested my chin against my fist and sighed. "Oh, you know what they say about pop stars . . ."

"What do they say?"

I shrugged.

Trina laughed. "Underneath all that hair and ice I'm sure he's still the same old Tyler who played *Minecraft* and ate Pop Rocks."

"Well, it's a lot of hair and a lot of ice." I sighed, twirling spaghetti on my fork. "Boys suck, even the pop star variety."

"Tyler used to drive your mama *crazy*." Trina grinned. "But you were a good influence on him—Amelia knew that."

I ducked my head, sheepish, guilty. The way our old house had creaked with every other step, maybe my mom *had* known all those times Tyler snuck through the window. I imagined her sitting downstairs in her old rocking chair, drinking chamomile tea, smiling as she listened to our footsteps overhead.

"Well, none of that matters anymore. He's probably on a plane back to civilization by now."

"Oh, I'm sure you two will patch things up in time to dance at my wedding," she replied, taking an innocent sip of her ice water.

I nearly choked, coughing in surprise—death by garlic bread.

"Ew. Never." I took an extra-long sip from my own glass. Dance with Tyler Moore at my aunt's wedding? How embarrassing! I would never live it down. But if that sly smile was any indication, Trina had her own ideas.

☆ ☆ ☆

Quinn knew how disappointing the signing had been, so the next day I drove to her place, and we prepped for a night at the local roller rink, Stellar.

Autumn nights were cool in Harbor Village, but your outfit had to be bold if you wanted to make a splash under the black lights at the rink. We snagged biker shorts and crop tops from Quinn's walk-in closet, then Q did our makeup. I flipped through the latest issue of *Cosmo*, enjoying the feeling of being pampered.

"Which one says, 'Girls Rule, Pop Stars Drool'?" she cooed in Valley Girl, popping her gum as she advertised two hangers like Vanna White. I chose the gemstone jean jacket; Quinn went with the varsity pink. Downstairs, we dodged her mom's drunken invitation to watch *Euphoria* as she guzzled white zinfandel, then headed outside and piled into Q's Jeep. I leaned through the window, hands up high, letting out a whoop as Quinn honked and headed for the highway.

A few laps around the rink and my weekend was salvaged. I jammed with a group of students from the local dance studio, eating up a hip-hop routine that translated even better on skates. We were Day-Glo stars under Stellar's neon lights, showing off and loving every minute. Dancing is a carnivorous art. Part of the rush of being a performer is knowing the audience worships you, and the hunger never stops.

We finished the dance amid cheers and whistles that carried me from one side of the rink to the other. Sailing backward, I caught up with Quinn, and we linked arms, hair flying as we spun in giddy circles. Dizzy and breathless with laughter, we were twins dipped in glitter and pink body paint as we took a lap, then headed to the counter for refreshments.

Legs wobbly, we lounged against the wall as we sipped spiked slushies from giant Styrofoam cups. We were cracking up at a boy who had lost his footing and dumped his nachos when a beautiful girl with smoky eyes and pink space buns skated past us. She performed a graceful one-eighty, blowing me a kiss, while blatantly ignoring Quinn.

"Dude, that's so weird. I don't even know why she hates me." Quinn took a frustrated sip from her drink.

"I know, right? You're, like, the coolest person ever."

"And yet, half the cheer squad treats me like toe jam." Quinn slid her straw up and down, looking slightly murderous. "And since Dani's captain now, I somehow got demoted to the bottom of the pyramid."

I turned aside, covering my laugh as Quinn scowled. "It's not funny, Ali! I worked hard to make it off the base."

"Boooo, who cares what a bunch of cheerleaders think?" I threw my arm around Quinn's neck and drew her in for a cheek-to-cheek side hug. "You're Quinn Josephine Davis. You're going to Vegas to write music and sing on the strip. And, one day, you're gonna be totally famous and write a hate-song about the high school experience."

"Cheers."

Quinn raised her cup, tapping it against mine with a smug, no-teeth grin. I smiled back, even though it hurt to think our time together was coming to a close. I never would have guessed that being so alike could take us down such different paths.

But we still had senior year. Arms linked, we left the roller rink, pausing for selfies under Stellar's neon sign—a rocket ship blinking in the stars. Just as Quinn was lamenting about Tyler and vowing that she would never again meet one of her idols, a white Hummer stretch limo pulled along the curb, like a spaceship with rims. We glanced at each other in awe while random passersby stopped to stare as a uniformed driver stepped out, opening a door to another galaxy.

The platinum pop star was crashing on the top floor of La Maison du Champagne, an extended-stay hotel where you could have a five-star meal in the restaurant, get pampered in the spa, or pick a room and party with rich kids. More than once I'd pretended to be a guest just so I could have an excuse to read in the lobby. Here, the shiny marble floors gleamed, and the potted palms peeking between gold and silver columns looked like something out of old Hollywood. The air, always clean and fragrant, was warm and inviting on cold winter nights and cool and refreshing on hot summer days.

Quinn and I followed the driver's directions, heading for the golden elevators across the lobby. Mesmerized by the crystal canopy of chandeliers overhead, I walked backward, apologizing when I bumped into someone.

"You don't belong here, little girl." A woman stared at me, her Cleopatra gaze narrowed with a hate I had grown to recognize. I froze as the older woman walked off in a huff.

The accusation stung, but I would never stop being me—even with glitter in my curls, body paint, and sparkly Doc Martens.

"Don't listen to her." Quinn steered me away, her arm wrapped protectively around my shoulders. "One day, Aaliyah, you'll be dancing on tour, performing your own choreography, and the only ones telling you what to do will be self-absorbed pop stars. Like Tyler."

We hugged each other tight, laughing as the elevator doors closed.

☆ ☆ ☆

Using the key that the driver had given us, we let ourselves into Tyler's penthouse suite. As I stood in the foyer, the first things I noticed were the floor-to-ceiling windows, elegant red drapes open, revealing a breathtaking view of the evening sky.

"Whoa." Quinn whistled, her blue eyes wide. "Your boy is *loaded*. Look at this place."

"Tyler?" I closed the door behind us then called for him again. "Hello?"

A security system on one of the foyer's two supporting columns beeped, and when Tyler didn't come to shut it off, I strode forward, quickly entering his birth date.

"How the hell did you know the passcode?" demanded Quinn.

"I know Tyler."

We stepped from the foyer into a glamorous open-plan sitting room. An electric fireplace was set to a low flicker, and a Drake song played on an intricate stereo system. There was a bar in the corner, a flat-screen opposite, and a gourmet kitchen to the left. Tyler had come a long way from sack lunches.

"I still can't believe he lives like this now." I ran my hand along a Victorian accent chair, then paused, noticing a gold folding table by the fire. A heart-shaped box of Godiva chocolates lay on top of it. My favorite.

Quinn circled a sleek pool table and grabbed a pool cue. She racked a new game as I plopped down on a champagne settee, wondering where Tyler could be.

"Something's wrong with me. He was a total brat at the signing, yet I'm still crushing. Is it the money?" she asked.

"Definitely the money." I had watched his net worth skyrocket over the years, stunned by Tyler's ascension. I spread my arms overhead, stretching luxuriously.

"Has he always been a jerk or is that a recent thing?" asked Quinn, rubbing chalk on the cue. "Granted, his manager has major control issues." She straightened, inspecting her work, then circled the table for the next shot. "Still, how could Tyler just walk out on his fans? After that, I really don't feel bad for screwing up this excruciatingly obvious date."

"Date?" I rolled my eyes. "This is *not* a date."

"Fire, chocolate, music," said Quinn, ticking off the evidence on her fingers. "C'mon, baby girl, keep up."

"Date Tyler? The guy who shoved French fries up his nose and once asked if girls could get pregnant from French kissing? No thanks."

Quinn cracked up, leaning on the pool cue so she wouldn't fall over. It took her a few attempts to speak. "Then why are we here?"

"He did put some effort into this," I said, turning on my side to face Quinn. "He knows he messed up at the signing. I'm willing to hear him out."

"Yeah? But what if you don't like what you hear?"

There was a loud ding, followed by voices from down the main hall, none of which sounded like Tyler.

"Who is that?" Q whispered. "How did they get in the apartment?"

We both thought for a minute, and I'm sure she was thinking what I was thinking—they had taken a private elevator.

The voices were getting closer; something about their tone made me not want to be around when they arrived. Quinn must have felt the same because she backed away from the noise, bumping into a small end table furnished with a regal Tiffany lamp. I sat up when it fell, clapping my hand over my mouth at the sight of the lamp in pieces on the floor.

Naturally, we panicked. I bolted from the settee; Quinn threw down the pool cue. I grabbed her arm, and we dashed into a closet on the other side of the room. Sitting on the floor, clutching each other in the darkness, we held our breath and waited. The door was shuttered, so we had a perfect view of the three men who entered the sitting room.

"It's Tyler's dad!" I whispered.

"Shit! Are we gonna die?"

"Yes!"

I held my breath, listening to Tyler's dad, Pete, address the two men who had followed him inside. One was a balding giant, the buttons straining on the business suit stretched across his massive frame. The other man wore a turtleneck with gold and silver jewelry. He was tall and thin like Tyler's dad, with blond hair pulled into a bun, loose hairs framing his devilishly handsome face.

"I have it, it's right here. I'm telling you—it's worth a fortune. My son's grandmother left it to him. Tyler doesn't even know how much it's worth. Kids these days . . . he won't miss it."

Just from the fact that his father said he wouldn't, I knew that Tyler *would* miss it.

"Just give us lamp," said the giant in a curt Russian accent. "Then we are circle."

"The word you are looking for is *square*, Bortnik." The thin man was also Russian. He lit a cigarette, casting a meaningful glance around the suite. "Your son has provided you with a comfortable life, Mr. Moore. And you repay him by stealing? Is there no honor among thieves?"

"Don't use my son against me, Aleksandr. You want your money, don't you? Then take the lamp. After that, you tell your father I'm *done*."

Aleksandr flicked his ashes and took another drag. "Circles and squares."

Pete skirted the couch, heading for the end table. Goosebumps rippled across my skin as I watched his gaze travel in slow motion from the empty table to the lamp fragments under his feet to Aleksandr's unflinching face.

Pete cursed.

"Problem, Mr. Moore?" Aleksandr's lazy drawl was heavy with amusement, but there was no mercy in his dark eyes.

"It—it's broken. The *goddamn lamp* is *goddamn broken!*"

Aleksandr sighed.

The giant flexed.

Quinn and I shared a horrified glance.

The giant shrugged at his partner. "*Vy khotite, chtoby ya pozabotilsya ob etom*, boss?"

"*Terpeniye, Bortnik. Otets dal strogiye instruktsii,*" he replied. He turned to Mr. Moore. "You are a very unlucky man. You should quit gambling."

I could almost hear Pete swallow. He raised his hands, pleading. "I'll get you the money, Aleksandr. You have sway, tell your father I'm good for it! Please—"

Bortnik grabbed Mr. Moore by the shoulder, and I swore I felt the vibration when he punched him in the gut. Pete doubled over, and this time Bortnik hauled him up by his collar before headbutting him to the ground. I couldn't see him, but I heard him grunt as Bortnik kicked him over and over, using the couch for leverage.

I don't know when Quinn grabbed my hand, just that suddenly it was in hers, and she was squeezing so hard I couldn't feel my fingers. I lunged forward, and she yanked me back, shaking her head.

"They're gonna kill him, Q!" I whispered.

"If you go out there, we're dead too!"

I swallowed the lump in my throat. We were cowards.

The thin man was the only observer unbothered. He thumbed through the magazines on the coffee table, continuing to smoke as Bortnik brutalized Mr. Moore. When his gaze swept across the apartment and landed on the closet door, that's when I knew it was curtains for us too. I froze, feeling only the bite of Quinn's nails as Aleksandr stared right at us. His eyes narrowed. Head bent, drawing on his cigarette, he took a few steps toward the closet.

"He knows we're here." I shrank back from the closet door, pressing myself to the wall.

"What is he, Superman?"

Aleksandr winked.

If Pete hadn't yelled at that exact moment, I'm not sure what would have happened. But I sighed with relief when Aleksandr turned away.

"*Khvatit*, Bortnik."

Bortnik stepped aside at the command. Sweating, he brushed away the thin strands of dark hair that had fallen in his face, then removed a handkerchief from his pocket. I felt sick watching him blot his forehead and wipe his bloody knuckles before tossing the cloth on Pete.

The giant folded his arms; his scarred, ugly face twisted in hate as he glared. I couldn't see Pete, but I heard his long, ragged breaths as he wheezed at Bortnik's feet.

Now I understood: Bortnik was the muscle, just a dog on a leash. Aleksandr was the one to be afraid of, not just because he was dangerous but because he wouldn't get caught.

Aleksandr was a criminal, but with those blond waves falling across ice-blue eyes, he looked less like a thug and more like a movie star. He was young and suave. He had manners, he was undoubtedly rich and probably educated. That's what scared me the most—Aleksandr's evil actions weren't reflected in his face.

Aleksandr tossed his cigarette on the carpet, grinding it under the heel of one shiny Ferragamo shoe.

"My father is running out of patience, Mr. Moore. He's not as forgiving as my friend Bortnik." He sighed. "Speaking as a son to a father, you're a disgrace, Mr. Moore. You do not provide for your family; they provide for you—and you take advantage. My father built an empire on weak men like you. They're so desperate, they are willing to sacrifice everything, even their own families."

I stifled a gasp, biting my lip at Aleksandr's not-so-subtle threat.

"The next time we meet, you will have my father's money. Or your family will bury you in a closed casket." Aleksandr walked toward the door, pausing as Bortnik shuffled around him. "There is someone hiding in your closet. I hate loose ends, Mr. Moore. Tie them." He smirked at the closet one last time then closed the door behind him.

I exhaled as soon as he left, eyes squeezed shut in relief.

"Tyler?" Mr. Moore was panting. "Tyler, get out here!"

Quinn's eyes were saucers in the dark; she motioned at the door—*Should we go out?* I shrugged back—*What other choice do we have?* I left the closet with Quinn close behind. We circled the couch at a distance, Quinn's hand on my elbow as we approached the bloody pulp on the floor. Pete was a crumpled, battered mess, his nose still streaming as he clutched his side in obvious pain. He groaned when he saw us.

"Tyler . . . where's my son?" Mr. Moore's voice sounded the same way he looked. Broken.

"W-we don't know," I said as Quinn took a silent step back, edging toward the door, fingers tugging at mine. "Tyler wasn't here when we arrived."

"What the hell did you do to my lamp?" He rose with a pained grimace, using the couch for support. His swollen, bloody face was more like ground beef, his silk shirt and dress pants ripped and soiled.

"I dropped the lamp," I said in a rush. "I did it, it was me."

Quinn hissed at me. "Aaliyah, don't!"

I silenced her with a sharp glance.

"Do you know what you've done!" Pete bellowed, holding his side as he limped forward. "You little bitch! You just cost me a hundred and fifty grand!"

"Y'know, something as expensive as that should really be insured." Quinn never missed a chance to add more fuel to the fire.

Mr. Moore seized a lamp from the coffee table, chucking it at the wall in his anger.

"I always knew you were never good enough for Tyler, Aaliyah!" His voice was an angry roar. "Get the hell out! And if you say one word to my son—"

Quinn and I didn't stick around to find out what would happen. Right before I slammed the door, I heard a tinkle as something else broke.

☆ ☆ ☆

We ran into Tyler on our way down the hall. He stepped from the elevator, a nursery of roses in his arms, oblivious to the chaos awaiting him in the apartment.

"Aaliyah, hey!" His smile faded midbloom as I darted past him. "A-are you leaving?"

Quinn jammed a bunch of different buttons, pacing back and forth, trying to breathe as she shook her hands.

"I'm sorry, Tyler. I can't do this."

Even the roses seemed to wilt as he watched me get in the elevator.

"Can't do what?" he asked as the doors closed in his bewildered face.

☆ ☆ ☆

Our small town has an upscale vibe, but Harbor Village isn't skyscrapers and city lights. There's no bumper-to-bumper traffic, you can't take the subway to school, and the concerts are usually local bands or karaoke night with your friends. Every sunrise and sunset is a painting, the perfect backdrop for boat rides on the ocean or hikes through Gentle Forest. And every summer, along with the tourists come all my favorite attractions. But the most important thing is that you can always smell the sea.

I was eight when I moved to the Village. I missed New York; I missed my friends; I missed falling asleep to the sounds of trains at night and waking up to rush hour in the morning. But at least in the Village the gray skies were clear of smog, and there were no toll booths or boom gates to block the shady, winding streets.

In those first few years, it was just Mom and me. We window-shopped in the town square and took pictures by the fountain, where the trees were strung with lights. We drove to the beach, watching seagulls dip in and out of the blue-green waves as they searched for fish. And sometimes we took a drive down Peach Street, where the Victorian-style homes were painted exquisite shades of cotton candy.

Mom's younger sister, Katrina Lewis, would often drop by for a family meal. Trina would take me whale-watching at Pointer's Bay or shopping at the square, where she secretly bought all the things Mom refused to let me try on. Eventually, Trina introduced us to her boyfriend, Hudson Espinosa. Born and raised in the Dominican Republic, he now ran the best auto repair shop in the Village. In the summer, Hudson was there for snow cones on the pier, and during the winter we ice-skated. When I dropped French for Spanish, I learned more from Hudson than I ever did from Profesora Barnes. And because my dad was a deadbeat, Hudson showed up for every father-daughter dance, every tournament or major event. What can I say? Life was predictable, until I met Tyler Moore.

One day, my mom decided to take up weekly yoga lessons. A retired dancer, she had been the first Black prima ballerina in her company. She stopped dancing a few years after I was born, but she always made time to stay active. I thought yoga was boring—too much sitting and standing in one place, but when Monday and

Wednesday afternoons rolled around, I was always the first one at the car, a yoga mat tucked under each arm, and a backpack supplied with towels and water bottles. We would pick up Aunt Trina, stop for green tea smoothies, and make it to yoga just in time.

Eventually, my mom made friends with a fellow yogi named Madilyn who could bend and contort her body like she was made from elastic. Madilyn invited us to take dance lessons at her studio, Perfect Form. I was sick of yoga, so I figured why not learn something new?

Under Madilyn's strict but never harsh guidance, I dabbled in ballet and hip-hop and absolutely fell in love with contemporary. Madilyn always said you didn't truly learn a song until you had shed blood, sweat, and tears. She was right—and I was *good*. But I hadn't put much stock in other people's opinions until I saw her son watching me one afternoon.

I was in the studio, practicing to Paramore. It was a freestyle dance—there wasn't rhyme or reason to it, except for my obsession with a flawless attitude and the grand jeté. This particular studio had blue and purple lights, with floor-to-ceiling walls of glass. It was like dancing in a kaleidoscope. My croisé devant would have been perfect if I hadn't been taken off guard by the boy leaning in the doorway.

I had seen him around. His name was Tyler; he was rude and obnoxious and brooding, and he got away with it because his mom ran the studio. He acted like a jerk and only spoke to me when I had food to share. None of that mattered at school, however, where he checked off all the boxes for popularity— he was cute and funny, and he played a guitar named Lola. Tyler was magnetic without trying to be, and that day in the studio he was my first real audience.

"You're pretty good," he'd said, lifting his guitar into position. "Can I play while you dance?"

Pretty soon, Tyler wasn't just popping up at the studio, he was dropping by my house with his mom for dinner. Lola came wherever he went, and we'd spend entire afternoons in the backyard, dancing to the songs he wrote. From our mutual interests bloomed a years-long friendship I thought could survive anything. But when fame knocked on Tyler's door, he left the same year as my mother. Colors faded, time slowed, but the world didn't stop. While it continued to turn, I continued to dance, but nothing was ever the same.

Quinn pulled her Jeep along the curb in front of my aunt's home. We'd had to call a taxi to go get her Jeep from the rink, and she hadn't stopped panicking since we'd left the hotel.

"Aaliyah, I was just kidding when I said I didn't wanna live to see the SATs!" She shook her head at the steering wheel, tears clinging to her mascaraed lashes. "I broke that stupid lamp, and now Tyler's dad can't pay those men." Her voice rose higher with each word, ending in a squeak. "If Tyler's dad dies, it's all my fault. Oh my god. I have to step down from the fan club—"

"Quinn? Relax." I put my hand on her shoulder, breathing with her. "Nothing that happened back there was your fault. Okay? Whatever that was, it's on Pete, and it's his problem—not ours."

We stared through the windshield in silence.

"Are you gonna tell Tyler?" Quinn asked finally, twisting her lip between her teeth.

I nodded.

"He's gonna hate me. Just like everyone else does."

"Not everyone hates you, Q. Tyler's not gonna hate you either." I exhaled. "He's gonna hate his dad." More than he already did.

"Well, what do we do?" said Quinn. "Do we tell the parentals? Do we go to the police?"

"We'll let Tyler decide. C'mon. You should eat before you drive. Everything's gonna be okay."

We got out of Quinn's yellow Jeep, and I slung my arm around her. Quinn's head rested on my shoulder as we walked up the driveway. She stepped through the front door, but I paused, letting my gaze travel behind me, down the dark, manicured lawn, across the quiet, shaded street. As the storm door closed behind me, I couldn't shake the feeling of being watched.

Two

On the Run

Once Trina had realized dancing was more than just a hobby for me, she'd had the spare room in the basement converted into the perfect workout space. The walls were lined with mirrors, the carpet replaced with hardwood. She'd added a stereo system, had a barre installed, and bought a treadmill for cardio and rubber mats for yoga. Most importantly, she was front and center at every recital, wearing her sparkly T-shirt with my face on it. For a long time, Mom and Tyler had been the ones sitting in her place, waving cheesy signs while I crushed the competition. Tyler wasn't really interested in dancing until I dragged him to the studio. His mom taught her students to be the best, which was why the only person Tyler couldn't out-dance was me.

Down in the basement, I pressed Play on a hip-hop mix, stretching as my skin tingled from the pre-workout. An entire album passed before I emerged from the basement, tired and sweaty from dancing. In the shower, basking under waves of warmth, every time I closed my eyes, I saw Tyler's dad bleeding on the floor. I had grown up with the Moores: I babysat their daughter, celebrated birthdays, and was with them on family vacations. Anyone close to their family knew Tyler's dad wore a mask in public. Today it had slipped. I would never forget the image of Bortnik using him as a punching bag, nor the way Aleksandr had smiled at the closet.

Towel wrapped around my head, I took a seat at my vanity, blotting toner half-heartedly against my face. Normally I felt at peace within the peach-painted confines of my room. The walls were plastered with pictures of friends and family, and the shelves were lined with trophies from dance and gymnastics. There were lamps and candles to brighten the room, and purple string lights dangling down one wall. The bed, fitted with pink and olive bedding, covered in matching pillows, was where Bernard, my favorite teddy bear, lived his days in comfort. Tyler used to sprawl on those same pillows, munching popcorn while I sat at the computer desk in the corner, translating his English paper into actual English. He wasn't famous back then, and we didn't act like total strangers.

My phone buzzed. I picked it up and checked the notification: an update from Twitter.

Party with a rockstar read the tweet, followed by a stream of emojis. Tyler was tagged; underneath was a Boomerang video of him kissing his ex on the cheek. As the resident queen bee of Harbor Village High, Daniela Vega was his by default. She was even entitled to that rose in her hair, which I just knew was from Tyler's bouquet. My blood was simmering, but using Tyler to clout-chase wasn't the lowest Daniela could sink. She was known for stealing boyfriends, suckering adults, and crushing souls under the heels of her Aquazzura pumps. It was Saturday night. As the only senior not getting faded at Daniela's party, I had officially replaced the school mascot as the lowest rung on the social ladder.

My fingers itched to dial Tyler's number, just to see if his old one still worked. Who knew how long he was back in town for? I chewed my thumb, debating. I felt stupid blowing him off at the hotel, but if the only reason I called him now was because I didn't like seeing him with another girl, what kind of person did that make me?

My phone rang. I picked it up, frowning at the unfamiliar number on the screen. Was it Tyler?

"Hi. Uh, I mean—hello?"

"Is Aaliyah Preston on the line?" I didn't personally know anyone from Australia, but that impatient clip in her tone was pretty recognizable.

"Yep, I would say my neck is definitely on the line." I switched the phone to my other ear, unwrapping a Twizzler from the candy jar on my vanity.

"I'm Astrid Chapman, Tyler Moore's manager," was her curt reply. "We've met. I'm currently standing in the middle of Tyler's *empty* suite at La Maison. He's switched rooms and refuses to give me the pseudonym he's staying under. We've an early-morning flight that I'm positive he's going to ditch. He never listens, because of course that would require compliance on his part, and common bloody sense."

"He has issues with authority. In eighth grade, Tyler locked our art teacher in the supply closet until she cried." I nibbled the Twizzler. "You're his manager—why would Tyler leave without telling you?"

"Because he knew I would stop him. Tell me where he is, and I'll write a check with your name on it. Better yet—convince him to go back to New York, and I'll add another zero."

I took a seat on the edge of my bed, lip between my teeth, wondering just how many zeroes it would take to get Tyler to go home.

"What makes you think I know where he is?" I held back

telling her his new room number. Clearly, Tyler had kept Astrid out of the loop for a reason.

"You're the first number on his emergency contacts. And in his very first interview he referred to you as his best friend. Unless that's changed?"

I sighed and bit a large chunk of candy. "It's your job to protect Tyler, right?"

"I'm his nanny, his chef, and his parole officer. Now, where is he staying?"

"I don't know, but I'll find him—*if* you promise to keep an eye on his dad. Mr. Moore is stealing from his son."

"I'm not surprised. And I won't ask how you know, but I'll handle it." Astrid exhaled. "And should Tyler run into any further trouble—"

"Don't worry, Evil Poppins. I got your back."

The Vega family manor featured a decorative pool that flashed rainbow colors, a sophisticated stone fountain Daniela frequently pushed people into, a garden with the perfect bench for kissing, and a circular driveway lined with foreign cars—and that was only the front yard. I pressed the doorbell and stepped back, gazing in envy at the elegant porch bathed in moonlight. Daniela's parents were hotshot lawyers who'd moved from California when we were in the sixth grade. We used to be friends. Now, she threw parties and forgot to invite me.

Daniela opened the door and stepped out on the porch, adjusting the oversized jean jacket draped over her shoulders. Half of her pink and brunette waves cascaded down her back, while the rest was gathered in a messy topknot decorated with a rose. Her upturned brown eyes narrowed when they landed on mine. She was gorgeous, the kind of devastatingly pretty that made you self-conscious about your own flaws. The olive skin under her airbrushed makeup was perfection, not a blemish in sight, aside from the fake beauty mark at the corner of her lip. Her skinny jeans and gray cropped T-shirt were offset by gold rings and necklaces. Arms folded, one velvet ankle boot balanced on its toe, Daniela scoffed at the loser on her doorstep.

"Hey, girl. Shouldn't you be, like, studying or something?" She took a sip from her red plastic cup, licking the moisture from her strawberry-pink lips.

"Just thought I'd crawl out of my cave and come talk to Tyler," I said, lifting my arm in a half shrug. "I'll wait outside."

"Then you'll be waiting till the morning." Daniela's one-note laugh was more verification than I needed. I winced, trying not to think of the two of them together, alone in her gauzy bedroom.

I turned to go, pausing when Daniela stopped me.

"Ali, stay," she urged. "Come hang out by the pool. Have a drink. The water's warm."

How easy it would have been to fall into the old rhythm of our friendship . . . I sighed.

"Quinn would never go somewhere I wasn't welcome. Neither would I." As the reigning queen of Harbor Village High, Daniela would never know what it felt like to be excluded.

"Loyal to the grave . . ." Daniela gave her pretty head a slow shake, descending the porch steps to meet me. "So loyal you never went out for the squad because you knew you'd overshadow Quinn. You know what they say about those who can't do." Daniela smirked.

Admittedly, teaching Cheerleading 101—working with the second team and watching the rest of the squad from the sidelines—was often bittersweet. Most of the students who tried out for the B-Team were freshmen, hoping to impress the coach,

Robin, long enough to make it through the season and maybe get promoted up to the Angels. Not everyone would enjoy it, but I did, and one day, I hoped the B-Team would outshine Dani and her crew.

"Quinn walks around thinking you need her, when really, it's the other way around. Don't you get sick of it, Aaliyah?"

"Don't you get sick of dissecting everyone else's life but yours? I know you're not familiar with the concept, but Quinn and I are *friends*, Dani. And some of us have real-world problems on our hands."

"You think I don't have problems?" she demanded, the blue glitter on her eyes shimmering as they narrowed.

I took a pointed look at the Vega residence, tracing the petals on a red chrysanthemum bush lining the stone path.

"None that I can think of, princess."

Turning on my heel and strutting away didn't feel half as good as the sound of her front door slamming closed. It was stupid and embarrassing that I had even gone there tonight. The truth was, I just wanted to be alone with the one person who would understand what it was like to be trapped in Pete Moore's shadow.

I walked through the manor gates. As they closed behind me with a definitive clang, I followed the sidewalk to where I'd parked my silver Honda on the empty roadside. Digging in my purse for the keys, I halted, shielding my eyes against the oncoming glare of LED headlights. Was I paranoid, or were they slowing down? Knowing it was dark, knowing I was alone on a quiet road, I shrank against the door as the dark SUV passed.

Whoever it was behind those tinted windows, they were looking at me too . . .

Dawn on Sunday mornings is the best time for a jog down the misty, winding streets of Harbor Village. My breath puffed in thin, transparent clouds as I sprinted down the sidewalk. It was September; the wind was sharpening her cold edge, and the maple and oak trees were shedding their leaves. As my feet slapped the pavement, I kept my eyes trained on the green-gray hills in the distance, using them as a focal point while I concentrated on my breathing. Thoughts of homework, graduation, prom, the wedding—all were interrupted by *him*.

I reached a stop sign and slowed, jogging in place as I waited for a car to pass. Tired of thinking, I turned up the volume in my headphones, letting Rina Sawayama take it away. It was obvious that too much time had passed—Tyler and I weren't friends anymore, not really. Speculating about him only made the truth that much harder to accept. If I wanted to move on, I had to get him out of my head.

I jogged through the neighborhood until sunrise erupted in the east. The sunlight filtering through the cloud cover was weak, providing beauty but not much warmth. Lowering the hood of my sweatshirt, I stopped by an empty meadow to stretch. Purple wildflowers covered the field during warm months, and fireflies swarmed at night. *My first kiss was in this field . . . soft, slow, and minty . . .* Arms stretched overhead, I groaned. So much for cooling down.

Returning to the sidewalk, I headed toward home. Absorbed by the pop metal flooding my earbuds, I jumped sky-high when a vehicle pulled alongside me. Even after I realized it wasn't that weird SUV from last night, my heart still beat like a couple of bongo drums. This was an obnoxious Rolls-Royce stretch limo with tinted windows and a fresh wax. The back seat window was rolled down; Tyler hung out the side, a giant smile gleaming under a pair of Ray-Bans.

"'Friends, Romans, countrymen, lend me your ears!'" he bellowed, arms wide, a bottle of Dom in one hand. "'I come to tell Cabbage: I am her king!'"

He had some nerve. That at least hadn't changed.

"Go home, Roger," I said.

"Aww, don't be like that, Preston."

I crossed the street, nose in the air, the Rolls's tires crunching slow and steady.

"Can we talk?" His voice had that smoky charm you just couldn't resist. "Let me take you to breakfast," he coaxed. "You wouldn't have come to the hotel if you didn't have something to say."

I came to a stop, and so did the Rolls. Tyler stared back, dark brows raised, lower lip in a seductive pout.

"*You're* Cabbage. *I'm* king."

"Your Majesty." Tyler bowed. "Get in."

There's a speakeasy-style diner on Platinum Street with a decadent omelet bar. I love how the counter servers act like detectives, lapels of their trench coats pulled high, fedoras low as they scribble your order in a notepad. Everything, from the fake boxes of gin stacked along the walls to the shiny jukebox to the table bussers dressed like bellhops, gives the Harley Sunset an underground vibe perfect for a celebrity undercover.

Tyler pulled his navy ball cap over his shades, sinking lower in our cozy, tucked-away booth.

"I physically cannot," I said, pulling the sunglasses from his face and setting them on the table. "Ten seconds ago, you were shouting at the top of your lungs. I thought you were used to people staring."

"I *am*. I just wanna lie low while I'm here."

"You mean 'here' as in here in the restaurant."

"Yeah. Right."

Ravenous from my workout, I inhaled the steam rising over my omelet, grabbed my fork, and dug in. Our plates were filled to the max, while glasses of OJ and small mugs of piping-hot coffee sat on the side. Tyler needed it. He reeked of Swisher Sweets and alcohol. It was barely nine in the morning, and he was still in last night's clothes—blue jeans and a gray sweater with the hood pulled over his hat. There was a chain tucked into his shirt and silver rings on his fingers. The boy notorious for food stains and Kool-Aid mustaches had left the Village and become an icon.

Tyler stared as I dug into my food. I froze, fork halfway to my open mouth.

"What?"

"Nothing." He gave his head a quick shake, frowning as he smiled at the table. "It's just good to be home."

"*Are* you good?" I asked, remembering the scene Quinn and I had left behind in his apartment.

"I'm always good, Preston." A bald-faced lie, but the grin was charming enough for me to accept it. For now.

"Then eat."

"Yes, ma'am." Still smiling, he grabbed his fork and obeyed.

After breakfast, we went our separate ways to shower and change, then agreed to meet back up at the Sapphire Boardwalk. "This is not a date, this is not a date, this is not a date," was my mantra as I primped my curls, applied makeup, and spritzed my favorite perfume.

As I crossed the parking lot, Tyler waited at the boardwalk's edge, his grin spreading wide as I approached. He was taller than he used to be, and one ear was filled with hoops. His hair was longer too, brown waves that lightened in the sun falling over vivid green eyes. Everything, from his black zip-up sweater to his gleaming high-top sneakers, was upscale, but those bright, intuitive eyes connecting with mine were the real luxury. Was he as impressed with me as I was with him? After all, I hadn't gone deep-sea diving in my closet for the cropped wrap top, my best skinny jeans, and the vintage Mary Jane pumps *not* expecting a compliment.

"Are you competing with me?" he said with a teasing grin.

"Excuse me? I always look this good."

Tyler chuckled as he fell in step, hands in his jeans pockets as we walked along the pier. In the summertime, the Sapphire had an arcade and amusement rides; this October it would host a haunted house and a Halloween carnival. For now, it was mostly empty, the majority of shopping venues and street vendors waiting for warmer days. Tyler and I walked along the rail, sunlight glinting on the water beyond. We weren't too far from the shoreline. The first buoy bobbed far out in the distance—a red point nearly swallowed in a vast expanse of gray that matched the sky.

"We should come back here," said Tyler, hands still in his pockets as he motioned with his head at the boardwalk. "Y'know, when everything's open. Catch a movie at the drive-in, ride the Ferris wheel. Kick it—like we used to."

"They have funhouses in New York," I said quietly, studying the disappointment in his handsome face. Why was he suddenly making long-term plans? "Tyler, why did you come back?"

"Do I need a reason?"

"You said you wanted to talk, remember?"

"Right." He nodded, giving in with a short exhale. "I guess I just need a break from my life. I had to use the signing as an excuse to come, otherwise I never would have convinced Astrid to let me get on a plane. Then I show up and embarrass myself in front of you and my fans. Pathetic, right?"

"Well, I wasn't gonna mention it, but . . ." I laughed at his guilty grin, nudging his arm as he ducked. "I'm really sorry I ran out on you the other night. It was a shitty thing to do." I could tell by his sly side glance he had been waiting for that apology.

"Well, I know seeing my dad all banged up wasn't what you expected. He said you stopped by. I'm sure he wasn't pleasant. I had no idea he'd be there. He just shows up—out of the blue— gets in a car accident, then smashes this heirloom my grandma left me."

"Is he okay?" I asked, chewing my lip in anxiety.

"Yeah. He said it was a car accident, but I feel like he's lying, y'know?"

"A car accident? Seriously?"

"He didn't want the police involved—who drives a Corvette with no insurance?"

"Beats me." I swallowed.

Extra touchy, I jumped as a boy with deep brown skin and a dark, mischievous gaze blasted past on a skateboard, laughing maniacally over his shoulder. I didn't realize Tyler's arm was around me until he let go.

"Eat shit, Eric!" My heart beat faster than his wheels could turn. Why had I ever dated him? Eric Williams was more than a player, he was a menace.

"Never trust a dude in a letterman jacket." Tyler scowled, watching Eric catch up with his buddies down the boardwalk. "You know him? He was a pain in the ass at Daniela's party."

"He's my boyfriend—*ex*-boyfriend. He *thinks* he's clever." I took a deep breath, inhaling through my nose as I repressed memories of the SUV. Last night's nightmare about Aleksandr and Bortnik hadn't done much for my composure or my sense of humor.

"Aaliyah." Tyler's voice shattered my concentration. "The look on your face when Eric scared you was the same look as when you left my apartment. I know when you're scared . . ." He waited, but I couldn't bring myself to answer him. The words were there, but they were stuck in my throat.

But Tyler wasn't one to give up so easily. "Last night, I ran into these guys as they were getting out of the elevator," he said. "They kept looking at me—and not the way my fans look at me. And one of them had blood on his sleeve. Then I get upstairs, and you're a wreck . . . and then I get into my apartment, and my dad's a wreck. Ali." Tyler stepped close, lowering his head so he could look me in the eye. "What really happened last night?" He repeated my name when I didn't answer.

"Your dad owes those guys a lot of money. And Pete was going to steal the heirloom to pay them back, but . . . I broke it."

"So they beat him up."

I nodded, a lump in my throat. My heart was racing just talking about last night.

"I was hiding in the closet—I saw everything. And I feel terrible, Tyler. If I hadn't broken the lamp—"

"Then my dad would have stolen it. Now he can't."

"I'm so sorry. I—I'll pay you back—"

"Ali, I don't care about the lamp, I care about you."

"I just hope you don't change your mind when I tell you that Astrid offered to pay me to convince you to go back to New York. I don't like her very much, and I didn't take the money, but maybe she's right. Maybe you should go back to New York. It's not safe here, Tyler." I knew that if I told him about my fear that I was being followed, he would never leave the Village.

"Things weren't any better in New York." Tyler leaned against the rail, both hands clasped as he looked at the sea. "Gambling." Tyler shook his head with a bitter smirk. "Figures. But I can't pretend I didn't make my own mistakes while I was gone. I did some dumb shit I can't take back. Eventually, I realized that if I had been home with my mom, Emma, you—I never would have gotten away with it."

"Damn right," I said, knocking his shoulder.

Tyler straightened. "I don't know if I can keep doing this, Ali. I used to sing because I enjoyed it. Now, most of the time, I just do it because I have to. People act like I'm so fucking important, but how can you be important if you always feel invisible, y'know?"

I nodded. I knew what that was like—constantly wondering if people saw the real you, and if the real you was good enough.

"I'm sorry I was a dick at the signing," he said. "That's why I invited you to the hotel—so I could fix things. I live there now. And I'm not running away from the only place that's ever felt like home just because my dad is a piece of shit. He can figure out his own problems."

"Tyler—"

"Look, I know what you promised Astrid, but I really need this, Ali. The Village is where I fell in love with music. Maybe if I stay, I can find that spark again. So I won't leave . . . unless you ask me to." Tyler waited, hands in his pockets.

Telling Tyler to leave now would have been like Bortnik kicking Pete while he was down.

"C'mon," I said, walking backward as I tugged on his sleeve. "Let's hit the food stand."

We bought our snacks, arguing over the bill until I tossed my debit card over Tyler's head. Then we resumed our stroll along the boardwalk, enjoying the smell of the ocean in the air and the seagulls wheeling overhead as we ate our ice cream cones—mint chocolate chip for Tyler, pistachio for me.

It had to be magic when toward the end of our stroll, the light bulbs tracing the colossal WELCOME sign flashed to life over the Hall of Mirrors. Most likely, it was just the technicians running maintenance. Still, it was our lucky day.

Tyler egged me on with a meaningful glance over his shades. "Shall we?"

"We shall."

Dumping our trash in the wastebasket, we crossed the boardwalk, sneaking through the entrance to the Hall of Mirrors. Grabbing Tyler by the sleeve, I led him through the darkened tunnel, emerging into a glass world of swirling lights and wacky reflections. Swept away by the bright lights and pop music, we chased each other through the twists and turns of the maze. I lost track of Tyler for a few seconds—until he grabbed me from behind, whisking me away to dance with the lights.

We triple-stepped and did the bow tie as we sang, a thousand Tylers and Aaliyahs moving in unison. Alone, we were as ordinary as heat and sand. Together, we were something amazing, like sparks coming alive in the dark.

The sun was beginning to set over the Airwalk skate park.

Later that day, after my date that wasn't a date, Quinn and I sat on the edge of a deep bowl, feet dangling. We were sharing her AirPods, listening to music as we watched skaters cruise. The fading sun was a red ball shooting laser streaks of pink and orange across the blushing sky. Sunglasses in position, Quinn leaned back on her palms, catching the last rays of the sun. Her blond waves were tamed into a messy bun, but a few locks had loosened to frame her pretty face. She wore her dad's old ABU jacket rolled at the sleeves, the large hoops in her ears silver like the dog tags dangling around her neck.

"I can't believe you told Tyler it was you that broke the lamp—what the hell, Aaliyah!"

I pulled the straw from my drink and tipped my head back, depositing a few drops on my tongue. "Well, I *thought* I was doing you a solid. I mean I could have told him you're vice president of his fan club . . ." I laughed as Quinn raised her fist, pretending to swing. "You should show him your songs. I'm sure he'd love to give you some feedback."

"I dunno." Quinn sighed. "I mean, Tyler's a great guy, but . . . I just never thought meeting him would lead to . . ."

"Aleksandr and Bortnik?"

"Don't say their names," Quinn hissed, glancing around like we had summoned Voldemort. Frowning, she popped her shades back in place.

Legs swinging back and forth, I gazed at the world through pink heart-shaped sunglasses. "I think I have PTSD."

"Who doesn't?" she replied, sighing as she laid her head on my shoulder. "My dad said when you have PTSD, it's like bringing the war home in your head. Maybe that's what Tyler did. I used to wonder why he dodged questions about his family in interviews. I thought he just wanted his privacy—now I know. It's not like you can tell your fans your dad owes money to gangsters."

All three of us had lost a dad in some way, but unlike Tyler and me, Quinn had grown up with a father who cared. In some ways, that was worse.

"Before I met Tyler, I used to wish my dad never left," I said. Quinn's head was still resting on my shoulder as I leaned back on my palms, studying the sunset. "I changed my mind after I met Pete."

Tyler was sitting on my front steps when I came riding up the driveway. I hopped off my skateboard, scooping it deftly beneath my arm. He stood when I approached, lowering the hood of his sweatshirt as I joined him on the porch.

"I'm on the run," he said. "I don't know how they found me

so fast. There's a whole crowd outside La Maison waiting for me to walk in."

"I can get them to leave. I'll just show them a picture of you crying because Emma *destroyed* you in *Mortal Kombat*."

"Zip it," he said, poking at me.

It was funny until I remembered that cold feeling of being followed all the way home. I had taken a few alleys and side streets just to escape the paranoia.

"Do you think you were followed here?" I asked, glancing anxiously up the street.

"I hope not." Tyler shrugged. "Back in New York, I can't even go for a coffee without my picture being taken. At least here I have somewhere to hide."

How could I say no to that?

We snuck inside—down the hallway and up the stairs, creeping past Trina's cracked bedroom door.

I closed my door behind us, watching in amusement as Tyler took the grand tour of my bedroom. A Grammy award–winning star was poking through my GigaPet collection while pretend-drumming to "Celebrity Skin." *What?*

"Nice room, Ali-Cat." He picked up Bernard and tucked him under his arm. He left the bear on the edge of the vanity when he saw what was leaning against the wall.

Tyler grabbed my ukulele then took a seat on the bed.

"You kept playing?" he asked, tuning it by ear.

"I may have taken your MasterClass." I sat down with a grin.

"Show me what you got," he said and passed it over.

Feeling shy, I tucked my hair behind my ear and put my hands in the play position.

"After you left, I learned my mom's favorite song," I said. "Do you remember?"

"Think I'd forget?"

Grinning, I strummed the opening chords of "Closer to the Heart," watching his eyes come alive as he sang. He belted the lyrics, his melodic voice in perfect harmony as my fingers danced with the strings. Jamming with Tyler took me back to the old days, when things felt normal and hanging out with him didn't feel like sneaking around.

We finished strong; I gripped the ukulele with my finger to my lips, waiting for Aunt Trina to bust us. I sighed in relief.

"I think we're good." I set the uke aside and sat back on my palms, grinning when I realized Tyler was staring. "What?"

Tyler's lopsided smile held the leftover notes of sadness that had twanged in the ukulele.

"It's too bad we didn't keep in touch," he said. "I know it's been hard since I left."

"My problems didn't start when you left the Village, Tyler." Tyler left home to chase his dreams when we were fifteen. But my dad left when I was three, and my mom died two years ago. There was no big solution for that, and no one to blame, except maybe my dad.

In the silence that followed, something passed across his face, like a rippling curtain hiding a secret. But I didn't press him. Instead, I grabbed my backpack from the hook on the wall and took a seat on the rug, my back against the bed. Spanish homework had fallen by the wayside, and tonight was my last night to catch up. Maintaining a steady grade-point average was key; anything lower than a 3.7 and I would be sweating. With college applications due in January, I couldn't afford to get off track. Not if I wanted a spot at the Boston Conservatory.

Tyler was lounging on the bed, his head hanging off the side as I highlighted my Spanish notes.

"Do you ever think our lives would have been different if we had both won that talent show?"

Tyler winning *Epic*, a national talent show, had changed both our futures. Tyler had gone on to become a famous pop star, while I stayed behind and dreamed of dancing in college. The night we were meant to perform was the night my mom's battle with breast cancer had put her in the hospital. Tyler had gone on to win, while I'd lost everything.

"Maybe if we had both performed, we both would have won," I said slowly, twisting the highlighter in my hand. "Or maybe we would have lost." Sometimes things happen for a reason. Sometimes they happen for no reason at all. Wondering why just leaves you with regrets when you're old.

Tyler flopped on his stomach, chin resting on his arms. I wanted to trace the vibrant tattoos that mapped his golden skin. Starting with the colorful, detailed rose that had bloomed on his left wrist. My fingers would tiptoe across the water droplets on the petals, following the vines and thorns winding up his arm . . .

I cleared my throat, returning my focus to the notebook in my hands. "I'm glad things happened the way they did—for you anyway. Your life is pretty sweet now, right? Everything's been decided. You don't have to worry about SATs and college applications—or whether dating the captain of the basketball team is where you peak . . ."

I'd thought I was ready for graduation, but the closer it got, the more I felt like the walls were caving in. I thumped my head against the bed and sighed.

"Ali, having your life mapped out doesn't mean everything will go according to plan—trust me. And there is just no fucking way dating some jock is the best your life is gonna get. Are you kidding? We have to get you out of here."

I shrugged, waiting for him to explain.

"If you're gonna have a dance career, you have to leave the

Village. I mean, you can't stay here, right? So? What's the plan, Stan?"

"Well, if the Boston Conservatory doesn't pan out, Quinn invited me to go with her to Vegas."

"The Conservatory?" Tyler mulled that over. "Isn't that where your mom went?"

I nodded.

"Well, there are some pretty fire campuses up north," he agreed. "We're talking Columbia, Barnard, NYU . . ."

I chuckled. "Those are all in New York."

"You don't say."

I smiled back. "It's not like I have an acceptance letter. I'm still figuring things out." Who could say what would happen after graduation? All I knew was that I didn't want to look back one day, resenting the life I had chosen.

"Wanna know what I think?" he said.

"You're an Aries. I'll pass."

I had forgotten how much I enjoyed laughing with Tyler— as much as I enjoyed laughing with Quinn. Just in different ways.

Tyler fell asleep waiting for me. By the time I finished my Spanish essay, he was passed out spread-eagled on the mattress.

I got ready for bed, turned out the lights, and slipped between the cool sheets. This wasn't the first time Tyler had slept over, but it was the first time that Tyler being in my bed had ever felt . . . tempting. I lay still in amazement, taken aback by the sight of his handsome face, carved in moonlight and darkness. He reached out and pulled me in; I fell asleep, tucked close like an extra pillow.

Tyler was gone when I woke up, but he had left Bernard in his place and used my lipstick to draw a walrus on the mirror.

After staying up late and waking up extra early, I should

have been exhausted. But there were parts of my conversation with Tyler running through my head. He would never know, but falling asleep in his arms had been electrifying.

The girl in the mirror wasn't a wreck from lack of sleep. Her amber eyes were bright and alert, and her warm brown skin was even toned and blemish free. Today, her curls were in French braids that dipped past her shoulders, a hairstyle that accentuated her heart-shaped face and pointed chin. Being biracial, identifying as Black and white, was like walking a tightrope between two worlds blindfolded. The only time I felt truly centered was when I danced.

I raced through the last of my morning routine and flew downstairs to the kitchen. I grabbed an apple, a Pop-Tart, and a water bottle, kissed Trina goodbye, and was out the door.

Quinn was already parked at the curb. I ignored when she honked, apple clenched between my teeth as I locked the door behind me. Halfway down the sidewalk, juggling my food, keys, and backpack, I spotted the black SUV creeping along our street. Paralyzed with fear, I watched as the SUV rolled past Quinn's Jeep. It inched along at a slow, steady crawl until it turned the corner and finally disappeared.

"Dude, you always take *forever*." Quinn was too busy checking her lip gloss in the sun visor to notice that I was a mess.

"*Drive drive drive!*" I urged, buckling my seat belt with shaking fingers.

"Okay, okay! Why are you always in such a rush, geez."

First the SUV had been outside Daniela's house, today it was outside mine? This was more than a coincidence. But I was scared of making Quinn panic, so I kept my mouth shut and spent the ride double-checking the rearview mirror.

There was still an hour before the first bell when we arrived.

Quinn parked in the student lot, then we made our way across the grounds. Harbor Village High wasn't like any school I had ever been to, which was really saying something considering the flashy institutes in New York City. HVH was an old renovated castle straight out of a gothic romance. The patterned masonry was punctuated by mullioned windows and a stately mansard roof. The campus was lush and green, with a garden entrance leading to a courtyard with a bubbling fountain. Small groves of apple trees dotted the campus. Students trampled the red, orange, and yellow leaves underfoot, but otherwise the villainous gardeners kept the sweeping lawn immaculate. They were on constant patrol, waving their shears, cursing nearby students when trash and butts were discovered.

Inside, the airy, prestigious halls—lined with trophy cases and portraits of principals past—were nearly empty. But within the hour, students would be traveling in clumps, lingering at the bottom of the stairs or sitting against the banks of lockers with their legs sticking out.

The gym was usually hogged by athletes at this hour, but when it came to arranging events, Chinara Tijani, from the East End of London, took no prisoners. As the new class president, planning the homecoming dance was her first hurdle of the year. Chinara approached us with her clipboard in one manicured hand, Starbucks coffee gripped in the other. Half of her blond butterfly locs were pinned in Mickey Mouse buns, her brown, upturned eyes outlined in crystals. Her smooth brown legs and curvy figure were emphasized by a red split-hem skirt and black cropped cami. The ripped jean jacket draped over her shoulders was the perfect accessory.

Dancing in her ankle-strap heels, Chinara caught the beat the pop music injected through the speakers. Quinn and I joined in, shouting the lyrics to a Tyler Moore original.

i feel fine until i'm alone
wish you'd call and say hello
you kiss him and i kiss her
wanna play some truth or dare
do you dance for him while i sing for her
can't say it out loud
'cause i'm insecure
so if i ask you to dance with me
you know what i really mean

"It's our tenth-grade formal all over again," Quinn wheezed, clutching her side.

"I don't care what you say, fam, that song is still a banger," said Chi. "Half the set list for homecoming is Tyler's bloody music. I heard he's in town, staying at La Maison. Aaliyah, didn't you used to date him or something?"

"Ew, absolutely not," I said, taking a peek at the clipboard. "Really, Chi? I wouldn't have volunteered if I knew you were only gonna have three of us on balloons—"

"The Heathers are at it again, I see." Quinn pointed with her chin. Across the gym, at the art supplies table, a teary-eyed Daniela was being consoled by half the squad.

"Daniela's whinging on." Chinara tsked. "Her hot date was a no-show last night. Smart bloke." As fellow cheerleader, Chinara was one of the few Angels Daniela couldn't control. Chinara lived to see Daniela put in her place.

"The ghost was finally ghosted." Quinn flipped her hair in satisfaction. "Chi's got me on streamer duty, but I'll help you with the balloons instead," Quinn whispered, linking arms as we headed for our station.

I made the mistake of glancing over my shoulder at Daniela, and I realized she wasn't crying from sadness. Daniela was crying because she was *pissed*.

This year's theme for the homecoming dance was Disney; I told Quinn that Aunt Trina had already ordered my Princess Tiana dress—a stunning blue gown with a sash at the hips—and long white gloves.

"My mom was the first Black prima ballerina in her company." I smiled. "And seeing as how Tiana was Disney's first Black princess, I *had* to represent."

"My lady." Quinn vogued.

Laughing, dancing, we tied giant helium balloons to the sign-up desk just outside the cafeteria's double doors. Starting today, students would man the desk where you could buy your tickets for the dance between classes. The hallway was lined with sparkly posters and banners we'd made for Chinara, along with dozens of silver and white balloons; a few lucky freshmen would find their lockers tagged and decorated. With only fifteen minutes until the first bell, activity in the halls was rising.

I was tying the last balloon when I heard a commotion behind me. I turned, watching Quinn and Dani in the middle of an argument.

"Not today," I muttered, wincing as Daniela tipped the paint can in her hands, dripping white paint on the black lace-up boots Quinn had borrowed from me.

Quinn retaliated by lunging for the paint. The girls wrestled for it, and Quinn lost her footing, dumping more paint down her front.

Daniela cackled, covering her mouth as she backed away from Quinn. Her short pink overalls and white crop top were spotless. The entire hallway gave a collective gasp, staring at Quinn, whose arms and legs were spread like a scarecrow.

Students scattered like chickens, giggling as Quinn rushed past them. My bestie was strong, but even Hercules had his off days.

I caught up with Quinn in the girls' room, rinsing her head in the sink. She straightened when I entered, makeup ruined, her clothes a sopping mess. There was water running down her face, but I could tell she had been crying.

I didn't care about the paint or water. I held out my arms, and Quinn walked into them, resting her head on my shoulder.

A few minutes later and we were both standing at the sink. I was late for astronomy, but helping my friend seemed a lot more important. Quinn was scrolling through her phone as I used a comb to remove the paint from her long, wet locks.

"Are you kidding me—the whole thing is already on Insta?"

"Don't look at that stuff," I said, taking the phone from her hands. "You know how this works. They'll be laughing at someone else next week." I paused. "You know that Battle of the Bands competition the school hosts every year?" I asked, turning the comb in my hands.

"The competition Daniela and her band have been bragging about all year? What about it?"

The door to the bathroom swung open. A mousy freshman clutching her books to her chest quailed under our sharp gazes and left.

"Well, for one, there's prize money," I said. "And for two—"

"We could wipe the floor with that bitch." Quinn smiled back at me in the mirror.

Daniela Vega was going down.

Three

From Bad to Worse

I spun the combination on my locker and opened the door. Words of affirmation were taped between pictures of Aaliyah and Normani. I was trading the textbooks in my backpack for second-period anatomy when the book was plucked from my hands.

"*The Map of the Human Body*," said Eric, reading the title aloud. "Pretty edgy material for a straitlaced girl like you." He grinned, pretending to flip through the pages.

Smelling like soap and cologne, he leaned his tall, athletic frame against the lockers, turning the pages with feigned interest. Eric wore tan twill joggers with spotless white Nikes and a matching half-sleeve hoodie. His fade was fresh like he'd just left the barber.

"Every day is a *wonderful* reminder of why we broke up."

"Please, Aaliyah. You wanna eat me for brunch and you know it."

Breakfast *and* lunch? Smartass. That would be false if it hadn't happened once or twice.

Eric closed the book with a snap. "So, are you and Tyler Moore a thing now?"

I rolled my eyes.

"Then we're still on for the dance?" He leaned against the lockers, dark-brown eyes narrow with mischief.

"Maybe," I replied, snatching my book.

"Saturday at seven—be ready." Eric winked, walking backward as he gave dap to a passing member of the team.

I made my way to anatomy, daydreaming about my dress and dancing in a certain someone's arms.

World lit with Mr. O'Sullivan was the highlight of the school day. There were a million reasons to like Mr. O, and not just because he was young, handsome, and brought sexy back to the sweater/dress pants combo. If the day was wrong, he turned it right. If you asked for extra time on an assignment, he might call you a *sleeveen*, but he'd still say it was grand. Mr. O was the kind of teacher who made you want to show up for class. He was always full of energy, striding between the aisles of desks, tossing a candy if you got the right answer or if you fell asleep. Sometimes, if we bullied him enough, he would tell us what it was like growing up in Ireland. We scrambled to please him.

"I mean, you have to bloody admire a man like Don Quixote. He wanted to be a hero; he wanted to *save* people. The poor sod was an idealist—and what's wrong with that?" Book in hand, he leaned against his desk, blue eyes agleam as he waited.

I glanced down at my notes, second-guessing the word I had written and circled—*romantic*—because that's what he seemed at heart.

Daniela raised her hand high. "The problem with Don Quixote is that he was a fool. He wanted to be something he could never be. And at the end of the day . . ." She smirked down the row at Quinn, who was in her gym shorts, wearing the T-shirt Tyler had signed, her hair still wet from the paint. "He was a total *loser*."

The class erupted in snorts and giggles.

Daniela's glossy lips spewed venom at Quinn. *"Pero ni Don Quixote fue tan patético como tú, perra."*

Face red with embarrassment, Quinn glared back at Daniela, twisting her pencil until it snapped. She didn't have to speak Spanish to know when Daniela was pressing her.

"Un día, serás tú quien esté cubierto de pintura," I warned, smiling warmly at Daniela.

"Ahem, ladies—" Mr. O's intervention was cut short when the classroom door swung open. "Ahh, Mr. Moore—what's the story? I presume you've a good reason for being late to class. Were you attacked by a swarm of hormonal teenage girls? Chased down the hall by paparazzi, perhaps? Or did a dog with a pipe and an old-fashioned vest happen to eat your school map?"

Tyler hoisted his backpack higher on his shoulder, replying with a good-natured grin. "I overslept."

Whispers and gasps flew across the room. No thoughts, head empty, I blinked in shock at Tyler.

"Find a seat, Mr. Moore. Next time you're late it'll be detention. Just because you've a great head o' hair and can bang a guitar doesn't mean you can break the rules."

There were more chuckles as Tyler picked his way through the desks. Mr. O threatened to make phones disappear if they didn't stop filming. Students who hadn't been surprised into silence recited Tyler's most popular lyrics in loud singsong voices. A girl who normally barely lifted her voice above a whisper squealed outright. Even I held my breath in anticipation as Tyler walked down my row, choosing the empty seat in the back. My gaze traveled to Daniela, who was scowling at Quinn, who was staring at Tyler in awe.

If he was tired from staying up all night, you couldn't tell—he was fresh as the morning rain. Tyler's leather jacket was perfectly worn, the black V-neck underneath stamped by Gucci, his white-toothed grin flashy as his chain.

"All right, you muppets—eyes on the board!"

My phone vibrated. When I was sure Mr. O wasn't paying attention, I checked the alert, opening a text from Tyler. *Surprise*, it read, followed by the zany face emoji. I turned and shook my head at Tyler, who waggled his eyebrows in return. So much for lying low.

This was no longer a high school. We had now entered the Twilight Zone.

The halls were buzzing with the news that Tyler Moore had enrolled at HVH. Classmates tagged me on social media; likes, comments, and followers came flooding in. I turned off my phone so it wouldn't die. I showed him to his classes and helped him find his locker, doing our best to hide from the hordes of teenage girls tailing him everywhere.

"Psst." Quinn peeked from around a bookshelf in the library.

I waved, and she approached, stopping dead in her tracks when she saw Tyler, sitting on the floor eating an egg salad sandwich. They both glanced at the shirt knotted at her stomach. Quinn hadn't expected Tyler to catch her wearing the signed T-shirt ever. I stifled a giggle, mouth full of sandwich.

"This is *not* what it looks like," she said.

"Of course not," said Tyler, staring at his sandwich, trying hard not to smile.

"Feeling better?" I asked, making room.

"I'm on YouTube," she replied miserably, taking a seat against the bookshelf. "They're doing remixes—with *paint*." Quinn glared as Tyler and I snorted with laughter.

"Don't sweat it," said Tyler. "I fell off the stage at a concert once; I was the next meme overnight. Thought I would never live it down." It was endearing, the way he tried to reassure Quinn, who was such a super fan you could see the stars in her eyes when she looked at him. I sat back, watching them bond over music and mayhem until the five-minute bell rang.

"Well, that's my sign, folks," said Quinn, balling up her lunch bag and tossing it in the nearest trash can. "I've got chemistry—which is basically across the quad."

"Better start jogging," I teased, watching her go.

Tyler and I took our time strolling through the bookshelves, falling into a comfortable silence. He blushed when I caught him sneaking a peek, recovering with an easy laugh.

"Something on your mind?" I smiled, brows raised.

"Yep," he said, popping the *p*. Just before we left the sanctity of the bookshelves, he darted in front of me, calling my attention with a lopsided grin. "What if we go out, Saturday night? We could have dinner then drop by the dance. Look, I've already been asked to homecoming a thousand times today. *Please*, put me out of my misery."

I blinked. "Tyler, are you asking me to the dance?"

"Sure. I just figured, since I don't have anyone to go with, and *you* don't have anyone to go with—"

"That I would go with *you*—because poor, lonely Aaliyah couldn't possibly have a date, right? *Wow*." I walked past Tyler, shaking my head.

"Is that a yes?"

"Find your own way to calculus," I called back.

That night, I decompressed at my vanity, wearing a bright green face mask and studying the techniques of other dancers on YouTube. It was either that or obsess over the blogs contemplating Tyler's silence, wondering where he was hiding out—and who he was with. Chewing a Twizzler, distracted by the video on my phone, I wandered to the window seat to grab a pink velvet pillow. As I scooped it in my arms, I caught sight of a dark figure striding across the lawn, masked by the shadows of a full Libra moon. I panicked—until a text from Tyler came through and set me at ease.

Knock knock.

I wiped off the mask, gargled mouthwash, teased my hair, then spritzed perfume. It occurred to me that I was putting in a lot of effort for someone who wouldn't notice in the first place. A few moments later, I opened the front door and peeked outside. Tyler waited with a smile and a white teddy bear made of roses.

"I shouldn't have assumed you don't have a date to the dance." Tyler shrugged his shoulders. "You've always been there when I needed you. I guess I just figured you'd do what I asked, like everyone else. But you're not everyone else." Tyler smiled. "That's what I like about you."

I smiled back, the last of my irritation drifting away like the tide.

"Whoever your date is, he's a lucky guy—who probably can't dance." Tyler ducked, shielding himself with the bear as I cuffed his shoulder. "Sweet dreams, Preston." Tyler handed over the bear; hands in his pockets, he turned to go.

"We can't go to the dance," I said, smelling the top of the teddy's soft, fragrant head. "But you can stay. If you want." Cuddling isn't against the rules, right?"

Something about his knowing grin sent a secret thrill up my spine.

"I like your hair," he said, fingers brushing my curls as he slipped past me.

Knowing secrets never last long in the Village, I closed the door, biting my lower lip as I smiled.

☆ ☆ ☆

The next morning, I thundered downstairs and into the kitchen. Trina's fiancé, Hudson Espinosa, was already whipping up breakfast, grooving to merengue. I joined him, laughing as I twirled my way to the sink, hands and feet a flurry of rhythm.

Hudson danced at the stove. Singing in Spanish, he stirred the scrambled eggs he had mixed with chorizo, onions, and bell peppers. His skin was a warm sepia, harmonious with his bright, toothy grin and the black ringlets that fell in his dark-brown eyes.

"*¿Para aquí o para llevar?*" he asked. Scooping chorizo and eggs on a plate, he added a slice of buttered toast and passed it over.

"*Por aquí, gracias,*" I replied, taking a seat at the kitchen table.

"*Yala.* Then you have time to discuss the boy who snuck from your room at six a.m."

I choked on my toast. "On second thought, I'll just take this to go—"

Hudson raised his brows, and I planted my ass right back in that seat.

I winced. "Are you going to tell Trina?"

"Your aunt is feeling under the weather," he said, pouring me a glass of orange juice. "I see no reason to bother her. This time." Hudson winked.

I sighed in relief. "Tyler's just a friend—he needed a place to crash. People keep showing up at his hotel."

"Sounds like a problem—for him."

But last night had been rated G compared to whatever Hudson was imagining. I had fallen asleep in Tyler's arms, catching up on the past, basking in the moments where the music took over. But rolling over that morning, seeing the bed empty again, had been as disappointing as finding a bare safe. Was this the way Daniela felt when Tyler skipped out on her too?

"What's wrong, *cariña?*" He sat down at the table, plucking an apple from the fruit bowl. "This boy—has he made you unhappy?"

"Not on purpose. Before Tyler left, things were . . . simple. But now . . ." I shrugged.

"You're a dancer, no? You learn to be balanced—*strong*—even when you are spinning in chaos." Hudson smiled. "When you are unsure, your heart will guide you—just as your feet guide you when you dance. You will find your center; give it time." He kissed the top of my head, then went back to the merengue.

At school, classes functioned on block scheduling—each week split between black days and silver days. Today was a silver day, which meant my final class was a free period.

Some free periods I went home early, others I volunteered at the hospital with Aunt Trina. Today I was working with the B-Team—the students who were hoping to improve enough to become full-fledged Angels.

If I had known Tyler had PE at the same time I was coaching, I would have had the girls meet me at the football field
and not inside the gymnasium. Mr. Newton's fourth-period class
was running on the second floor; Tyler was on his second lap,
sprinting past classmates still jogging the first round.

I wasn't the only one who had noticed the pop star flying
overhead. As captain of the squad, Daniela ran a tight ship. The
group wasn't normally this chatty, but nothing superseded the
sweaty, gorgeous singer jogging circles around them. I clapped
my hands, vying for the attention of the ragtag group of students
assembled in front of me. Some were tinkering with their PE
uniforms, rolling the waistbands of their black gym shorts, tying
their gray T-shirts with scrunchies.

I brought my finger to my lips and whistled. "If you want to
join the other Angels at nationals one day, then quit looking at
Tyler's ass and keep that same energy for these back handsprings!
Get in line. And I'll know if you didn't stretch . . ." The grumbles
began, but at least I had their attention.

Finally, after the B-Team were warmed up, we gathered for
the two-two-one pyramid. We assembled on the mat, performing the routine's opening steps.

We're angels
We're proud
We're gorgeous and we're loud
Go black!
Go silver!
Our team will deliver!

Still chanting, the squad assembled for the hard part, hoisting
the first two members in the air. Since I was the only one ready
to top the pyramid, I was lifted next, stomach jumping with the

usual butterflies as I was raised up high. Pom-poms to the ceiling, I joined the squad, reciting the final words of the chant.

They're vicious
They're mean
They're who you came to see
Goooooo Ravens!

We had practiced the routine religiously; it should have been foolproof. But I knew things had taken a turn when the two people holding my legs began to wobble.

Screams ricocheted across the gym as the pyramid came tumbling down. It wasn't my first fall—I knew how to land. But I hit the mat hard, ears ringing, vision fading to a pinhole as pain and darkness threatened to swallow me . . .

"Aaliyah, are you okay?"

"Ohmigod, she's dead!"

"Brent and Candice killed her!"

"Shut up, Gina, damn!"

I pushed onto my knees, accepting the hand stretched before me. Lifted to my feet, I took a moment to catch my breath, bruised but breathing.

"Throw in the towel, Aaliyah. I would say you could land on your feet, but alas . . ." Only Daniela would pick you up just to kick you down. "And this is why A-Team is so high above you basic little bitches." The B-Team shrank beneath her narrow, withering gaze. "Wash the stink in the showers—*vete*," she said, dismissing the squad with the swat of one manicured hand.

"They're distracted," I said, one wrist pressed to my forehead. "The B-Team is getting better. They just need more time."

"Or *maybe* they need someone who can actually teach them."

Considering how I was literally going to school for choreography, that stung. "It's only been a few weeks, Dani."

"We both know what it takes to win nationals. If the B-Team doesn't have the routine down by then, next year they'll be handing out water to the football team."

"You're mad at me for being friends with Quinn, so you're taking it out on the B-Team—admit it. Why do you hate her?"

Dani's high ponytail bobbed as she shook her head. "Tyler left the Village, then suddenly you were too good for the rest of us. But you had all the time in the world for Quinn."

I met Quinn at a grief workshop the school counselor forced us to attend. We bonded over donuts and mandated therapy. Quinn understood me in ways my other friends couldn't.

"Imagine choosing Quinn over me. That's like trading a luxury model for a Pinto—yikes." She strutted past me, spinning on her Nikes when I called her name.

"That's not how it happened, Dani."

"Tyler dumped me, then you dumped me next—for the bitch who used you to get on the squad."

"Quinn's not like that."

"Let's be clear, I only keep her around for you, Aaliyah. Same for the B-Team."

"Don't try me, Dani. I can train the B-Team to sweep your spot at nationals. And that would be pretty embarrassing. For you, not for me." Anyone else would run for the hills, but Dani smiled back.

"Oh my gods, are we having a moment?" An OG Angel, Chinara looped her arm around my neck, cheesing in Dani's face. "Girl, you got paint all over the necklace Quinn's father left her. She said she's going to handle you at Battle of the Bands. I think she's going to whoop you for real, sis."

"Today is not the day, Chinara." Dani raised one long,

manicured nail in warning. "You better level up, Aaliyah, because when it comes to competitions, I don't lose."

Daniela's hair nearly whipped me in the face as she passed.

I scoffed, watching her go. "Chi, Coach Ashby gave me special permission to put 'manager of the B-Team' on my transcripts," I said in a low voice. "If Daniela cuts them, this could seriously mess with my applications."

"And I'm sure the B-Team won't mind, yeah?"

"Of course they would," I said, biting my lip in shame.

"Well, if you're looking for your answer, maybe it's already found you." Chinara gave me a teasing nudge, then nodded up at the balcony, where Tyler was stretching against the rail.

I was still simmering when I left the gym. I hurried down the concrete flight of steps leading to the courtyard, pausing in frustration when my phone started to sing. I dug it out of the duffel bag hanging off my shoulder, but my irritation vaporized when I read the text from Quinn.

look who i found toots

I clicked the link under her message, my jaw dropping at the Instagram page. Aleksandr Vitali had over a *million* followers. I bit my lip, mulling it over before clicking Follow.

I was startled, then annoyed, as someone loud and obnoxious cleared their throat. Tyler's gray Ravens T-shirt was still damp from his run, his hair wet like he'd just stepped from the shower.

"I saw you fall earlier. Anything damaged?" Tyler took my duffel bag, sliding it over his shoulder as he fell in step beside me.

"Only my pride." I grinned, suddenly shy as I tucked my hair behind my ear. "I'm training the B-Team."

"Ah, yes, the B-Team—because I completely understand what that means."

"Think Remedial Cheerleading 101."

"There's nothing remedial about the way you dance."

"That means a lot, coming from someone with real experience."

Was that an actual blush spreading across his face?

"You're talented, Aaliyah—don't sell yourself short." *Le sigh.* His green eyes were as soft as the ivy tendrils swaying in the stone arches overhead.

I took comfort in the silence as Tyler walked me to my car. When his arm slid across my shoulder it felt more natural than breathing. Things felt okay again, until I saw the commotion ahead in the school parking lot.

We froze.

Daniela was surrounded by a mob armed with cameras.

"You've gotta be kidding me." Tyler's grin held no trace of amusement. "Dani's giving an interview."

"That's not good, is it?"

Tyler turned his back, hands on his head as he exhaled.

After school security booted the paparazzi, I gave Tyler a lift to his hotel. We cruised down the highway, the wind in our hair, enjoying the last rays of the autumn sun. There was a moment when Tyler glanced over and smiled at me, and it felt like I had found my center, like I would never lose my footing as long as he was around.

I drove into La Maison's parking garage, where a concierge waited at a special side door for incognito guests. An awkward moment passed when I stuck out my hand and Tyler went in for a hug; we settled for a fist bump.

"See ya later," he said, which was a lot more disappointing than "see you tonight," which was probably for the best.

At home, I had just enough time for a shower and a snack. I left a sticky note on the fridge for Aunt Trina—*don't wait up, love you*—then headed back to campus for tryouts. I met up with Quinn outside the auditorium, where she was pacing frantically back and forth.

Our outfits were color-coordinated—black biker shorts and cropped hoodies, with checkered shirts tied around our waists. We had matching oversized earrings; Quinn wore a backward snapback. Looking the part is one thing, feeling it, another.

Hands on her hips, Quinn took a few deep breaths. "We got this, right?"

"You got this, Q."

She squealed and grabbed me, hopping with excitement. "I love you, thank you so much for being here!"

"Of course," I said, rounding out the hug with a high five. "We've danced to your song a million times. The only thing I can't help you with is the part where you sing. We'll lose."

Quinn laughed. She knew I couldn't sing; I was awful. I'd probably sing better with a sore throat.

We scribbled our names on the sign-up sheet tacked to the door and ducked inside. The auditorium was buzzing with students. A few dozen were already gathered, wandering through the seats, milling in the aisles. Several more were onstage, tinkering with the lights and performing sound checks. Mr. Woods, the choir teacher and overseer of each year's auditions, was chatting with a group of students, who, judging by their instruments, belonged to the school band's brass section.

We found an empty row of seats near the back, still close to the aisle. Right away, Q was approached by a tall, skinny senior with sparkling brown eyes and a messy-cute mop of brown hair.

With his affinity for hippie sweaters and boat shoes, Declan Westbrook belonged at the Airwalk or on the beach, mojitos on tap. He swung his backpack to the front, removing a sparkly pink binder that he passed to Quinn with a sheepish smile.

"Thanks for the chem notes, Q." He sat backward in the row ahead, arms crossed over the top of his chair. "To show my undying gratitude, I promise not to one-up you in the talent show."

"Bring it on, Skater Boy." Quinn's cheeks were so pink I couldn't resist sticking my elbow in her ribs. Declan's head was stuffed with cotton, but there was a reason girls and guys knocked at his door.

"Um, Dec, are you sure you're in the right place?" I chuckled, coating my lips with a fresh layer of gloss.

"With pride, ladies." His puffed-out chest promptly deflated. "The Lip-Sync King at your service," he said, bowing with a flourish.

"Yo, Dec!" A senior football player jumped in the aisle. Hands behind his head, he swung his hips in lewd circles. "P-push it real good!"

"Fight me, bro—I pushed it on your mom last night and she *loved* it!" Declan took off after his friend, the two of them clowning their way toward the stage.

"I'm so pumped he asked me to homecoming." Quinn leaned forward wistfully, resting her chin on his empty seat. "He asked Dani first, and she said no because he's second-string. Can you believe that?"

"Yes."

My gaze floated down the seats and across the aisle, where Daniela sat with the two Angels who, with her, dominated the talent show every year. Piper Gordan and Sonam Kumari were having some heated conversation Daniela wanted nothing to do with. She sat back in her seat, studying her nails, her gaze drifting across the auditorium. She caught me staring, as I so often caught her, and for a minute I flashed back to the sleepovers, the birthday parties, the friendship we used to have.

I flicked my wrist, mouthing the old phrase. *Period.*

It took a moment, but Daniela smiled back and went through the motions.

"Speaking of naughty boys, you know who strikes me as a gone-by-morning kinda guy?" said Quinn, nudging me with her elbow.

"You just described half the boys in our school."

"Well, Aleksandr's one of a kind," said Quinn, whipping out her phone. "Check this out: one-point-five *million* followers, and he's only following a dozen people."

"It was eleven last time I checked."

"Congratulations, baby girl, you're lucky number twelve." She showed me the proof on her screen. "Whatcha gonna do?"

I didn't need Quinn to egg me on—I had already made up my mind. I pulled out my phone and sent Aleksandr a DM.

The lights in the audience darkened as Mr. Woods took the stage, clipboard in hand. Trailing behind the middle-aged, balding man with disheveled clothes was a living, breathing star. A hush settled over the auditorium as they ascended the stage, and the last of the students scattered to find seats.

Quinn spoke through the side of her mouth, eyes wide. "Aaliyah, if Tyler is entering the contest, *I will kill him with murder.* Did you know about this?"

I shook my head in disbelief.

Mr. Woods issued an ear-splitting whistle with his fingers.

"*Guten tag!* Welcome to this year's audition for Battle of the Bands!" He paused, earning a polite round of applause. "I want to thank each and every one of you for signing up. Unfortunately, due to budget cuts, we have limited spots for acts, so please don't be offended if I grab a broom and sweep you offstage." The students chuckled. "Before we begin, I'd like to remind you there will be no performances involving nudity, cursing, or fire—that goes for you, Mr. Westbrook." This earned more laughs from the audience. Even Tyler, radiant in the spotlight as usual, seemed to enjoy himself.

Mr. Woods tapped his mic. "And let's give it up for our three-time champions—Motivation!"

Daniela and her girlfriends stood, dancing, amping up the crowd. I gave a few perfunctory claps, more invested in the way Daniela blew Tyler a kiss and the way he smiled back.

"And last but not least—what I know you'll really be excited to hear—Tyler Moore is this year's opener!" The choir director waited patiently for the deafening applause to subside. There was a thin layer of hate beneath the cheers, a smattering of boos and jeers.

"As most of you probably know, the five acts selected from tonight's audition will go on to duke it out against three other high schools. In the past, the winning band received ten thousand dollars." Students howled and pounded their seats. "This year, thanks to Tyler, the winning band members will receive ten thousand dollars . . . each."

The auditorium went wild.

Eyes round, Quinn gripped my arm like a vise. "That's *twenty Gs!*"

Make that thirty grand for Daniela, Piper, and Sonam. So much was on the line here. This time, when I caught Dani's gaze, neither of us smiled.

"Tyler will also be joining our panel of judges. Let's show our thanks to Tyler!"

The auditorium erupted once more. Everyone else was celebrating; Quinn was jumping in her seat. But all I could think about was what would happen if we won—it would be because of Tyler. And if we lost it would be because of him too. At the end of the day, who would he vote for? Us or his ex?

Tyler and Mr. Woods took their seats at the judges' panel, and Audrey Hannah was called to the stage. Over the next hour, Quinn and I sat through a variety of acts—solos, duets, concert ensembles, bands. And Declan was a total liar—he wasn't lip-syncing. I think we were all picking our jaws off the floor when he got onstage and sang an outstanding rendition of "It's Not Unusual."

Personally, the doubt didn't creep in until Daniela and her Angels took the stage. They danced to an original hip-hop song that Sonam had probably written. Dani could sing, but with a body like hers, in that backless jumpsuit, I doubt anyone noticed. Years of cheerleading and tumbling gave the girls flawless, synchronized rhythm and an athletic edge that was unmatched. Their performances always featured a stunning array of acrobatics—backflips, somersaults, running aerial cartwheels—but this time, whenever Daniela's feet left the stage, my stomach dropped.

We were screwed.

The song ended to thunderous applause. Daniela waved like a pageant girl, twerking in celebration.

"I'm gonna be sick." Quinn gripped her seat so hard her knuckles were white.

"Q, your high notes can shatter glass. You wrote a badass song, and my choreography is sickening. Tonight, we're unstoppable. We're top five."

Quinn nodded and took a deep breath. "Top five, baby."
She gave me dap, looking queasy.

When Mr. Woods finally called our names, Quinn handed
her CD to one of the theater techs, and we took center stage.

"Aaliyah Preston! Quinn Davis! Great to see you!" Mr. Woods
nodded in friendly encouragement. "And what will you be performing for us?"

As Quinn took the microphone and answered his question,
Tyler's steady gaze reeled me in. He licked his lips, and I was
shocked to realize that I wanted to be that pen he was twisting
in his hands.

The auditorium darkened, and spotlights lit the stage as
Quinn's song began, her striking voice commanding all eyes on us.

i'm too much woman for you
don't have money but you wanna gamble
tried to ball and broke your ankles
square in the mirror, i'm solid angles
i'm too much woman for you

As my body moved to the beat of the music, I made the
decision, in a room full of people, to dance only for him.

☆ ☆ ☆

I was backstage in one of the nicer, private dressing rooms
reserved for the real stars (the drama students), about to change,
when someone knocked.

Half-dressed, I poked my head out the door. "Tyler?"

"I know this is a bad time," he said, glancing anxiously up
and down the hall. "But I am legitimately in fear for my life, bro.
These freshman girls are *intense*."

Right on cue, I heard the sound of giggles as someone shouted his name.

"Help me," Tyler begged.

"All right, all right, get in."

Tyler darted inside the small, dimly lit room. He locked the door behind him, sagging against the frame in relief. I lifted my shirt over my head, pretending not to notice when he did a double take.

"You never mentioned judging Battle of the Bands," I accused, stepping out of my shorts.

"You didn't mention auditioning."

I grinned. Turning my back on Tyler, I grabbed my jeans from a vanity desk covered in fabric and jewelry and took my time putting them on.

"I really like that we're hanging out again," he said. "Fair warning though, the more we're seen together, the more questions the media will have."

"They wouldn't *actually* think we're together, would they?" I asked over my shoulder.

"Would that be such a bad thing?"

I faced Tyler with a smirk. "All publicity is good publicity, I guess."

"Your dancing speaks for itself, Ali." Tyler's head was flush against the door as he studied me. "You killed tryouts. You're better than my backup dancers, and that's saying something."

"Well, I did learn from the best," I replied, pulling my sleeveless T-shirt over my head. "I hope I'm not putting you in an awkward spot—y'know—with the judging . . ." I gathered my curls, pulling them from the neck of my shirt.

Tyler's smirk widened. "I'll be fair. Scout's honor."

"You were never a Scout."

"And I never had honor."

We grinned.

Tyler grabbed my jacket from the vanity and stepped behind me, sliding it over my shoulders. I could have leaped from a cliff and my stomach wouldn't have jumped nearly as hard as when his fingers brushed my neck. In that moment, there was nothing I wanted more than to be seated on the vanity and kissed like our lives depended on it.

I exhaled. "Tyler? Can I ask you something?"

"I would literally say yes to anything you asked me right now."

"Anything?" I gave him a crafty smile, tapping my fingers together like an evil mastermind.

"Please. How can I say no when you smile like that? See, it's like sunshine in a bag."

Suddenly bashful, I tucked my hair behind my ear.

Focus, Aaliyah, focus.

"Well, since you're voluntarily volunteering . . . would you help me coach the B-Team? Choreography is one thing, but teaching it is another. The B-Team deserves a real shot at the Angels, and I figure, with all your experience, maybe you could show us a thing or two." I winced, laughing in embarrassment. "That last part sounded different in my head."

"I like the way it sounded. Honestly, Aaliyah? I'd do anything for you." I shivered; he took the signal to step closer. "But you already know that." He cupped my face in both hands, lowering his forehead to mine. Our noses brushed, lips skimming like seagulls on ocean waves. I closed my eyes, basking in his warmth, like a flower turning its petals to the sun. My jacket sleeves had fallen; he kissed my shoulder, releasing tension like he had pressed a magic button.

I drove Tyler backward against the door, fighting tooth and nail against the temptation to rip the leather jacket from his frame.

"I know what you're craving," he whispered. "You try to hide it, but I can see it in those pretty brown eyes." He ran his thumb along my jaw, tracing my lips with his finger. "Why do you keep torturing yourself?"

Kissing him now, knowing one day I'd never be able to do it again, would be so much fucking worse.

"Everything would change," I said quietly. "I don't know if I'm ready for more." I stepped back, lifting the shoulders of my jacket. "Besides, I saw this magazine that had ten reasons to never date a pop star. A very compelling read."

"You know what you and the author have in common— neither of you ever dated a pop star." Tyler winked, popping his sunglasses in place before sliding out the door.

Touché.

☆ ☆ ☆

I left the school, meeting up with Quinn and a few friends at the Harley Sunset. Under the diner was a hidden nightclub, the kind a real speakeasy would offer. I gave the girl at the counter this week's password, and she led me around the back, through the secret door, and down the steps to a glamorous, dimly lit lounge. Here, the music was sultry and secrets were on tap with the drinks.

I made my way through the crowd, passing Tyler sitting with friends. He understood my nod and left the table. Taking my hand, he followed me deeper onto the dance floor, and this time I didn't push him away.

Dancing with Tyler? It was like having a sentence finished by someone who knows you better than you know yourself. His body fit mine like a glove, and he had all the right moves, keeping up with me in ways others couldn't. We danced with our hands raised, fingers clasped. His forehead resting against mine was the sweetest torture.

Tyler brought his lips to my ear, his breath warm on my skin. "I'd ask you what you want, but I don't think you even know," he said.

"I know what I want," I replied and drew him closer.

Later that night, I pulled in to the driveway, parking alongside my aunt's silver Range Rover. I got out of the car, biting my lip with a secret smile, riding the high that came from dancing with Tyler. I had only taken a few steps before the sudden crank of an engine tore through the stillness.

I turned with a gasp, hand on my heart as I watched a dark SUV parked across the street. The headlights clicked on, banishing the shadows it had hidden within. I waited, praying for it to drive off. But it stayed put, engine idling. I knew in my heart the driver had been waiting for me.

Trembling, heart pounding in my chest, I power walked to the front door, digging frantically in my purse. When I dropped the keys, it was like that moment in a horror movie—except this was real. I pushed the door open and dared to turn back, watching the SUV roll away from the curb and drive slowly up the street. Like the driver was taunting me.

Once, when I was five, I'd lost my mom in a crowd. I got lucky—she was only gone a few moments, and she found me right away. Until now, I had forgotten that terror of feeling alone, like you were lost forever and no one was coming to save you.

Eyes closed, I took a few strangled breaths, listening to the fire alarms screaming. Between the two of us, it wasn't unusual for someone to slip up and burn something.

"Aunt Trina? I—I'm home." I removed my jacket, hanging it on the coatrack as I wrinkled my nose—something was definitely burning. "Aunt Trina? Is everything okay?" I listened for the sound of my aunt's voice over the din of the smoke detectors. I knew something had to be wrong when I called her name and again no one answered.

That's when I noticed the thin layer of smoke clinging to the air. Adrenaline kicked in once again, and I sped down the hall and to the kitchen. Coughing and choking, eyes burning, I batted at the smoky air, pinpointing the orange light flickering on the stove.

I darted forward, shrieking Trina's name when I tripped over my aunt. She was sprawled on the floor in a growing puddle of water. Meanwhile, a pot of spaghetti was in flames on the stove, and the sink was overflowing. Racing into action, I grabbed the fire extinguisher from the cabinet, killing the flames with white foam. Then I traded that mess for the one at the sink, water spilling on my sneakers as I shut off the taps.

You just never know when things will go from bad to worse.

I dropped to my knees at Trina's side, relieved when I stuck my finger under her nose, feeling her breath on my skin. She was alive but wounded, a trickle of blood running from her scalp to her forehead. First, I called the paramedics, then I called Hudson.

Four

The Heat Is On

I was still pacing when Hudson finally walked through the waiting room doors of St. Cyprian Hospital. His face and coveralls were splashed with grease and motor oil, but I didn't hesitate to fly into his arms.

"*¿Estás bien?*"

"I'm fine, it's Auntie. I came home, and she was unconscious. Sh-she woke up in the ambulance, and she was really confused. I—I haven't seen her since we got here."

Hudson placed his hands on my shoulders. "She woke up. That's good news."

I swallowed. "Hudson, I can't lose her like I lost my mom. Trina can't die, she *can't*—"

He cupped my face in warm, rough hands, wiping the tears that fell. "*Mi querida*, no matter what happens, *you will never be alone*. I promise."

"Aaliyah? Mr. Espinosa?" Dr. Stetter stood off to the side, clipboard in hand. Even surrounded by crow's feet, her clear blue eyes and gentle features brought a warmth that so many doctors seemed to be missing. Her white coat was as clean and crisp as her blue scrubs underneath. Her brown hair was pulled from her face by bright, youthful clips. As Trina's friend and coworker, I trusted her when she told me she would do everything in her power to help.

Dr. Stetter smiled. "Katrina can see you now."

It was a relief to find my aunt sitting up in bed. Her hospital gown and the IV in her wrist had demoted her from doctor to patient. Her hair was a mess, and she looked exhausted, but her brown eyes lit up as soon as we entered the room.

Hudson walked to the bed, kissing his fiancé on the forehead. "*Mi amor*—how are you feeling?"

"Alive—thanks to my *hero*." Trina reached across the bed and squeezed my hand. "Lay it on me, Doc. How long do I have to live?"

"Katrina, you aren't going anywhere anytime soon." Dr. Stetter lifted her clipboard, flashing her easy smile across the room. "But you do need rest. You got dizzy and fell while you were washing dishes. You hit your head on the sink, which is probably how you got the concussion. And your blood pressure's slightly elevated, so we're keeping you overnight. As for the hyperemesis gravidarum—we'll give you medication that's safe for the baby."

Trina's eyes grew large; she sat up straight, rigid as a board. "Abby, you're *joking*."

"I'm not joking, Trina. Congratulations, you're pregnant."

Trina's pregnancy was a cause for celebration, but I've seen roadkill more festive than me. As Trina and Hudson debated baby names and when to tell the rest of the family, I was thinking back to the black SUV.

When Hudson gave me a ride home, I really wanted to tell him about Aleksandr and being stalked, but the more he gushed about the baby, the less I knew what to say. I mean, it sounded ridiculous—gangsters, money, and blacked-out SUVs. So I put on my dancer's face, smiling and nodding, when all I really wanted was to disappear faster than the car lights flashing past. Tyler's worst problems had followed him back here, and now we were both on the run.

Hudson pulled into the driveway, lowering the passenger window as I got out of the truck.

"*No te metas en problemas. Pero*, I'm here if you do. I'll call soon to check in."

"Don't worry. I'll be good, *lo prometo*." I held up my pinkie, and he held up his.

Hudson waited for me to unlock the door before reversing down the drive. Soaking in the last few dregs of feeling safe, I watched his truck lights fade through the window. Shadows from headlights washed over the walls; I stepped back, rubbing the goosebumps on my arms.

At two in the morning, I was on my hands and knees, wearing yellow rubber gloves and scrubbing the floor tiles. The kitchen was covered in powder from the fire extinguisher, there was water all over the floor, and the charred pot of spaghetti that was still on the stove had left the house smelling like an ashtray. I stayed up and cleaned the mess because the thought of falling asleep alone was terrifying.

I nearly slept through my alarm the next morning. Hungover from exhaustion, I rode the bus for the first time since freshman year. I took an empty seat in the back, FaceTiming my aunt. She was still in her hospital gown, Hudson sleeping on a cot beside her bed. I didn't care that she chastised me for working too hard and not staying home, I was just glad she was well enough to do it.

I got off the bus, wondering about Aleksandr's plans for Pete and me. I was a thousand percent sure that Pete couldn't come up with that much money on his own, not legally anyway. It wasn't fair that Tyler should have to pay his father's debts, but I was afraid of what would happen if he didn't.

Pushing through the double doors leading into the gym, I made a beeline for Daniela, who was running cheers with the Angels. Ignoring the football players catcalling as they ran drills, I tapped my ex–best friend.

"Dani, we need to talk."

"Later, loser." She barely spared a glance over her shoulder before returning her attention to the squad.

"No, *now.*" I grabbed her arm, dragging her to the girls' locker room.

"What, bitch? It's homecoming week, I don't have time for drama."

"You *survive* off drama, Dani. That's why you had that little chat with the paparazzi in the parking lot."

"What paparazzi?"

I rolled my eyes.

"Oh, *those* paparazzi." She chuckled, bangles sliding down her arm as she planted one hand on her hip. "What about it?"

"Tyler came home because he needs a break. How's he supposed to get one with you giving complimentary interviews?"

"Relax, okay? His manager already hit me with the cease and

desist. What's it matter to you anyway? Whatever it is, it better not distract you from the B-Team." Daniela folded her arms.

I took a heavy seat on the bench. If I told her about Aleksandr and my suspicion that he was having me followed, the old Dani would have understood. Aleksandr already knew where I lived. The more he knew about our personal lives, the more he could use it against all of us.

Daniela interrupted me before I could speak. "You're into him, aren't you?"

I gave an uncomfortable chuckle, nearly falling from the bench. "Wh-what makes you think that?"

"You didn't answer the question," she replied, eyes narrow. "He was with *you* the night he was supposed to be with *me*, wasn't he?"

I slowly rose to my feet. "Look, Dani—"

"You should know—this isn't the first time Tyler and I've broken up. We even dated while he was on the road. He always comes back to me." Her lips spread into an awful smirk. "Little tip—Tyler likes the kind of girl who goes for what she wants. You're not a fighter, Aaliyah. Save that energy for the competition. You're gonna need it."

Daniela strutted from the girls' locker room and didn't look back.

Tyler showed up to world lit right as the final bell rang. He took his seat and offered a stoic nod. I turned around when I realized Daniela was staring. Quinn shrugged her shoulders high; we spoke through facial expressions.

Uh-oh, what happened?

Nothing, I'm good.

But Quinn didn't look so convinced.

Tyler caught up with me in the hallway after class. He didn't say a word as he tugged me into a nearby janitor's closet. The dim light of a single bare bulb illuminated a small, cramped space that smelled like mildew and cleaner. Pretty hard to outrun the truth when you're nose to nose with the person you're hiding it from. Daniela's accusation rang inside my head.

You're into him, aren't you?

"I texted you last night. I wanted to be sure you got home okay," he said. "I know we're just friends, Preston, but I'm still gonna check up on you."

"I know. I'm sorry I didn't text back. Things were kinda hectic after I left . . ." I inhaled. "Trina's pregnant."

"Holy shit, that's awesome!" Tyler held up his hand, lowering it when he realized I wasn't in the mood for high fives. "I mean, that *is* awesome, right?"

"Of course . . ." I just wished I hadn't found out in the worst way possible way. I cleared my throat, changing the subject. "Um, so why are we in a closet exactly?" I poked the handle of a mop in a bucket, pushing it the other way.

"Privacy," he said, thrusting his hands in his pockets. "I wanted to warn you: there might be a few stories about me in the media soon. Maybe some pictures."

"It's because of Dani's interview, isn't it?"

"Astrid shut it down pretty quickly, but she didn't plug every leak. The label thinks it might be good for my image."

"As long as it's the right girl." They had probably vetted her, and no doubt Daniela had checked all the boxes—wealthy, popular, intriguing . . . beautiful.

"Would that bother you, if I dated other girls?" Tyler stepped close, ducking to catch the smile I hid. His cologne, mingled with the scent of his body wash, was an invitation hard to ignore.

"There will always be other girls."

"Not when it comes to you."

Pretty words, but at the end of the day, that's all they were.

"Don't fool yourself." I gave his shoulder a playful push. "Did you drive to school today? I could use a ride."

"I, uh . . ." Tyler hesitated. "I don't drive."

"You're Tyler Moore. Don't you have a car?"

"I have, like, six. But I don't drive. I mean, I *can't* drive." Tyler's face reddened. "I don't have a license. Or a permit."

"Seriously?" I bit my lips, failing to muffle the chuckle that escaped. "Why not?"

"Because I have drivers? And . . . I never really had the time to learn." He rubbed the back of his head, flustered. "Not having your license is pretty embarrassing, right?"

"No, not at all, mm-mmm." Lying was second nature these days. "It's not too late to sign up for driver's ed. Or I can teach you. If you want."

"Really?"

"Yeah. Under one condition—there's practice after school with the B-Team. Can you make it?"

"I'll be there."

"Good. Because I'm gonna need you to take over."

"*What?*" Tyler raised his hands in disbelief. "C'mon, Aaliyah, I can't teach the B-Team without you!"

"I have to be somewhere. It's just one afternoon, Tyler. You'll be fine."

"Yeah? And where will you be?"

If I told Tyler where I was going, I had no doubt he would try to stop me.

"None of your business," I said, flicking the strings on his hoodie.

"What are you hiding?"

"Nothing I can't handle. *On my own.*" I walked past him, pausing at the door. "Look after the B-Team. Don't let Daniela get in their heads, okay?"

"You're in my head, Preston." Tyler smirked. "What am I supposed to do?"

"Have you considered being a good boy and listening for once?" And I slipped away before he got in my head too.

The parking lot at the Harley Sunset was a ghost town; the neon lights that always said WE'RE OPEN were dim. The bell jangled overhead as I entered the diner, walking between two men in suits and sunglasses who were standing guard.

A server crouched to the side, peeking cautiously over the counter—the other waiters must have been hiding in the back. Aleksandr was the only customer, waiting in the same seat where Tyler had been just days ago. I took a seat across from him. As much as I was concerned about being killed, I was just as worried about looking childish. Seeing Aleksandr while hidden in a closet was one thing. To be in his space, watching him eat blueberry pie with whipped cream and fresh fruit, acting like a normal human being, was even weirder.

"Americans have such good desserts."

I stared down at the butterscotch sundae in front of me. It even had sprinkle-frosted whipped cream and two maraschino cherries—just the way I liked it.

"How did you know I like butterscotch sundaes?" I asked.

"Instagram."

"Oh." I grabbed my spoon and took a small bite, frowning around at the deserted diner. "The last picture on the 'gram said you were in New York. How did you get here so fast?"

"Private jet." He took another bite then set his fork down. Balling up the napkin tucked in his collar, he dabbed his mouth. He leaned back in his seat, studying me through shrewd eyes. Part of me wanted to run. The other part wanted to climb across the table, pour whipped cream in his mouth, and kiss him.

"What do you want from me, *pchelka moya?*"

"I know you've been following me. You, or maybe somebody you hired, like Bortnik—driving through my neighborhood, past my house at night. *Why?*"

"You know why." He smiled. "Go ahead. Say it."

I rubbed my knees under the table and took a breath.

"Because you know it was me—I'm the one who was hiding in the closet in Tyler's hotel room."

"*Da*, the girl who broke the lamp." Aleksandr looked around me, chuckling with his bearded friends like I was a running joke. "I know who you are, Aaliyah. So nice to finally meet you. And what about your little friend that was with you—what is her name?"

Aleksandr was like an evil TV supervillain. He liked to pretend he was harmless, but a serpent is always prepared to strike.

"You already know her name," I said. "You're just screwing with me." Like a cat playing with its dinner. "Are you following her too?"

"Why would I do that? She's not the one affiliated with the Moore family. She is not the important one."

"She's important to me. And so are the Moores."

"Even Tyler's father? The man who steals from his own son?" Aleksandr grinned, sipping from a small coffee mug.

"If you know the real Pete Moore, then you know stealing isn't the worst thing he's ever done. But that doesn't mean he deserves to die." I licked my lips, waiting for Aleksandr to dismember me right then and there.

He smiled, showing all his straight white teeth like a shark. "The blogs may not see it yet, but you are clever."

"Wait—blogs? What blogs?"

"You are a seventeen-year-old girl. You do not read magazines?"

"I've been busy."

"Tyler's life—it is like a soap opera. My girlfriend finds it entertaining. She gives me details."

"Look, I—I didn't come here to talk about my friends. I came here to tell you to stop following me." No more cringing like a little mouse. I sat up straight.

"I'm afraid you have no room to negotiate, *pchelka*." Aleksandr pushed his pie aside, folding his hands on the table. Suddenly, I felt trapped, like I was cornered in a cage. "I'm a bit of a collector," he said in a low, slow voice. "But I don't like tangible things, like my father—he collects body parts." Aleksandr shrugged at this, like the notion of ears floating in jars was common. "I like to take things—invisible things that I know will cause people horrible, excruciating pain. Would you like to be my next volunteer, Aaliyah?"

Mouth dry, I shook my head.

"Good." He chuckled. "Then you will play ball. I will keep my eye on you until Pete Moore's debt is paid. And he *will* pay, one way or another." His blue eyes glinted as he sipped his coffee. The conversation was over.

I grabbed my purse and slid from the booth. "Tyler's dad is worth more alive than dead. If you kill his father, you won't see a dime."

"I would have more fun dropping Pete Moore in the ocean than I would taking his money," he replied.

I believed him.

Friday afternoon, I performed a halftime routine with the B-Team at the homecoming game. Whatever magic Tyler had used on them worked—the crowd was amped. Being up nine points might have had something to do with it, but it was also our best performance yet.

We waved our black-and-silver pom-poms one more time then left the field. Daniela was waiting on the sidelines. With the black ribbons in her hair and the sparkles and face paint, she didn't *look* vicious, but . . .

"Cute." She smirked. "Ready for a real show?" She sauntered past me, joining the A-Team on the grass. I had a sinking feeling watching Daniela lead the Angels—the B-Team had a long way to go.

☆ ☆ ☆

"We won!"

Quinn joined me in the school parking lot, pom-poms still in hand as she threw her arms around me. The Ravens had creamed the away team—everyone was celebrating. The tailgating in the parking lot would last only so long before the parties branched out to the places where you could drink.

Q primped, pretending to speak into a microphone. "This just in, folks: the B-Team slayed the game. Bad bitches are indeed on the rise. Back to you, Tom."

We fist-bumped, miming explosions.

"Declan invited us to a party at La Maison," said Quinn, passing me a stick of gum.

"Good. They have hotel security, right?" I rubbed my arms, bending my knees up and down to stay warm. The thin sweater I had thrown over my cheerleading uniform was useless against the evening chill. But the weather was only half responsible for the goosebumps on my arms.

"Um, yes? Why are you acting like a teenager in a *Scream* movie?"

"I was sitting in the stands after halftime, watching the game—and I saw Aleksandr. Q, he was *sitting behind me*. Eating popcorn!"

"Okay, just . . . I dunno, try to relax," she said, hands on my shoulders, blue eyes wide with fear. "Look, he's messing with you. He's not gonna kill you in the middle of a football game."

"I don't want him to kill me at all!" I said a little too loudly.

"Calm down," she muttered, grabbing my arm, leading me away from curious onlookers. "Babe, you met up with a *psychopath* in a *coffee shop*! What did you think would happen?"

"I don't know! Okay?! But you're right—it was a dumb idea."

"The dumbest—which is a lot, coming from me! And just to be clear, when I gave you his Instagram, I thought you were just gonna make a fake profile and troll him or something. If I had known you were gonna meet up with the dude, I would have put sugar in your gas tank!" Quinn shook her head as she marched past me.

"Exactly why I didn't tell you or Tyler," I said, scrambling to keep up with her. "Aleksandr's not going away until Pete gives him the money."

"You don't need a crystal ball to see that's never gonna happen." Quinn grabbed my arm. "If Pete had access to that kind of cash, he wouldn't have to steal from Tyler. I think it's time we tell Tyler about Aleksandr. And by 'we' I mean 'you.'"

"Q, I dunno."

"Pete put everyone's lives in danger—Tyler should know what he's up against. Seriously, Aaliyah, Aleksandr is not a secret you wanna keep from him."

I sighed. "You're right."

"What was that?" she said, hand cupped around her ear.

I rolled my eyes. *"You're right."*

"Come again?" She switched ears.

"Don't push it."

Quinn patted my arm in sympathy. As we headed for my car, I caught sight of Tyler across the parking lot. If I told him the truth, he would have to leave the Village and kiss his fresh start goodbye.

The next morning, I awoke to a string of dance emojis from Tyler. I should have been excited—this was my last homecoming dance, and his first one. It was supposed to be an unforgettable night for us both, and it would be—especially after I told Tyler the truth about Aleksandr. I tossed my phone aside and threw my arm over my eyes, lounging for another hour before making my way downstairs. Aunt Trina was in the kitchen, whipping up breakfast. Apart from the morning sickness and the weird cravings, she was her old self—with more than enough energy to perform her parental duties. Unfortunately.

"Baby, do you know they are *blogging* about you now?" she asked, placing a heaping stack of pancakes before me.

"Apparently, hanging out with Tyler has a few downsides. Are you mad?"

"Mad?" She sat down next to me. "Not at all, kiddo. With the career you're aiming toward, this could actually be great exposure for you. I just don't want a *blog* to be the way I get the scoop on your life. So keep it real with me—ya dig?"

"I dig." But I found it hard to swallow my pancakes. There was no way I would ever tell her about Aleksandr. Especially not in her condition.

I took over cleanup duties so Trina could rest, then made my way to Quinn's house later that afternoon. Most of the crew had already beaten me there. We put on our faces and curled our hair, gossiping in Q's bedroom as we passed around a bottle of peach schnapps. It was fun, even when Quinn's mom dropped by, wasted from habitual day-drinking, asking if we needed any condoms.

"Was she serious?" asked Chinara after Quinn's mom closed the door. Chi had a head full of large pink rollers to curl her braids.

"As a heart attack," I said, flipping through the pages of *Canceled*, a popular rag mag known for exposing celebrity drama. "Holy shit," I said, staring at the page. Blogs were one thing, but the last thing I expected was to see a picture of *me*.

"Oh. My. Gods. Is that you on your doorstep?" Chinara ripped the magazine out of my hands. "And is that *Tyler*? With a *teddy* made of *flowers*?"

"Let me see that!" Quinn yanked the magazine from Chinara's hands. Her jaw dropped. "Aaliyah, the person who wrote this article thinks you and Tyler are dating!"

"His name is the poop emoji in my phone—I am *not* dating him!"

"Well, that's a relief, since he asked *me* to the dance." The room filled with a chorus of oohs and ahhs as everyone congratulated Chinara.

"Chi, I'm happy for you, I really am," I said, lying through my teeth. "But this picture was taken out of context and without my consent. It's creepy."

"It's the paparazzi, love." Chinara dropped onto the bed, one arm on her forehead as she pretended to faint. "I'm ready for my close-up, Mr. DeMille."

Our friends laughed, but I didn't see the appeal of people

lurking outside my house, snapping pictures from the bushes as they watched me.

As afternoon turned to evening, our dates arrived, one by one. Most of the guys lacked imagination, showing up in varying versions of Prince Charming. At least Eric's costume came with a plastic sword. Tyler was the last to show up, rap music blasting as he danced through the roof of a white Hummer stretch limo with neon lights attached to the undercarriage.

"Um, maybe we should just take your car," I suggested, extending one white-gloved hand for Eric to slide the blue orchids onto my wrist. They matched his boutonniere perfectly. "It might be . . . romantic." I gave a twirl, lifting the hem of Princess Tiana's iconic blue gown.

"And miss the free minibar?" Eric scoffed. "If he's buying, I'm drinking. Period."

Rolling my eyes, I followed him into the Hummer.

I joined my friends with a half-hearted effort as we toasted with shots from the minibar. I wanted nothing more than to forget about Aleksandr and the paparazzi for one night, but the less I thought about them, the more I thought about Tyler. More specifically, how good he looked with his hot date.

Today, the sun shone for Chinara and Chinara only. Her Ariel costume was a work of art—the gown had a blue-and-green-sequined skirt with a fishtail hem at the bottom. The upper half of the dress was sparkly flesh-toned mesh with a seashell bra and pearl chains. But Ariel was nothing without her Prince Eric. His gold, white, and blue dress uniform was authentic down to the shiny brass buttons and the golden tassels on his shoulders. Tyler looped her pearls around his finger, completely taken by the pretty girl who passed him another shot.

After a beautiful candlelit dinner at La Maison—where Tyler and I sat across from each other and didn't say a word—we returned to the Hummer for more pre-dance drinks. It felt like I was alone in the eye of a storm, watching my friends from the outside looking in. Things like the calla lily corsage on Chinara's wrist or the way she and Tyler shared drinks had my stomach twisted in knots. Deeper and deeper, I sank into my jealousy like quicksand. Eric didn't notice I was bothered until I tossed back a shot and immediately prepared another.

"Whoa, slow down, girl!" Eric took the shot and poured it back. "We haven't even made it to the dance. Chill!"

"I need some air." I pushed past him, climbing to the opposite end of the Hummer. I flopped into my seat, dragging my fingers through my curls in anguish—my stomach felt like hot, swirling soup, kind of like the thoughts in my head.

"Don't mess up your tiara," said Quinn, brushing my hands away. "Here, drink this." She passed me an orange Gatorade, and I took a grateful sip.

Quinn was ravishing. Her sparkling black gown, with its plunging neckline and thigh-high slit, was so risqué she would have to cover up with her cloak to make it into the dance. Maleficent's historic horned crown was the perfect touch. Declan, her date, had decided to break the mold and come as Rumpelstiltskin, flashy in a gold floral tux.

"Why does it seem like you and Tyler picked the wrong dates for homecoming?"

"He didn't, but I did."

"Ali, are you *into* Tyler?"

I covered her mouth with my hand, frantically shaking my head. "Quinn, you can't say a *word*—"

"Forget Aleksandr, Aaliyah—Daniela will *murder* you."

There was no way Tyler could hear our conversation over the rap music pumping through the speakers, but I could tell by his reaction to my face, he felt the danger too.

I had to give Chinara her props. Practically overnight, she and the dance committee had transformed the gymnasium. To enter, you walked through a canopy of trees strung with fairy lights, emerging into an enchanted forest. Cascades of brightly colored flowers hung from the ceiling and bloomed on the tables; vines dripped down the walls. Lanterns flickered, lighting the path to the refreshment stand, where punch fountains flowed between giant platters of finger food. The DJ played a fast song that had everyone dancing in the fog.

A beautiful white pumpkin carriage had been converted to a photo booth. After taking a few stiff headshots, Eric finally confronted me.

"Why does it seem like you don't wanna be here?" he demanded, hanging back from the others. Behind him, Tyler and Chinara were having an intimate conversation at a small, cozy table. His laugh, and the way she reached out and tucked his hair behind his ear, made something *burn* inside me.

"Trust me, there's no place I'd rather be." I took Eric's hand and led him to the dance floor, breezing past Tyler's table. If Tyler could have a good time, so would I.

My feet were still buzzing when Eric and I left the dance floor. We joined our friends at a candlelit table for refreshments while we waited for the announcement of this year's homecoming court.

"I voted for you and Tyler, by the way," said Chinara. She sat beside me, licking the frosting from a mini cupcake as she waited for her date to return.

"You did? Really?" Guilt ate at me from the inside, like worms. "Why would you vote for *us*?"

"Well, I'm not voting for Dani, am I?" She chuckled. "Honestly? When Tyler showed up in the Village, and I saw how close you are, and how fetching you look together . . ." She jabbed me with her elbow, brows wagging up and down. "That's when I made up my mind. Shame you don't like him. He's been gabbing about you all night. Bloody annoying, innit?" Laughing, Chinara excused herself from the table, in search of someone with a flask.

It would have been an awkward conversation to overhear, had Eric been paying attention. But my date was two tables over with a few of his teammates, discussing draft picks—how romantic. Arms folded, I sat back in a huff. A song ended, and suddenly the gym exploded in clapping and whistles. Chinara's date had taken center stage at the mic stand. The gymnasium grew dim, and a blue spotlight shone on Tyler, the star who had fallen from the night sky. I sat up straight, mesmerized as he held the mic like a lover and sang the blues.

not quite the outcome I expected
i'm still a work in progress
someone asked me if it was worth it
did i get everything i wanted
it feels selfish when i tell the truth
'cause the only thing i can't have is you
i learn my lessons the hard way

scraped knees and impending heartbreak
not quite the outcome i expected
baby, i'm still a work in progress

My view of the stage was suddenly blocked, but I was used to Daniela popping out of nowhere.

"Who the hell do you think you are, Aaliyah?"

Quinn wasn't the only one who had chosen to come as Maleficent. Daniela didn't need the horns or the fierce makeup or the long black stiletto nails—her glowering stare was deadly on its own.

"I'm Princess Tiana. You can't tell from the dress? Girl, why are you being so messy?"

"Why are *you* being so *shady*? Where do you get off telling *me* not to give interviews, when you're taking photo ops with Tyler?"

Daniela had clearly seen the picture in the rag mag and believed the article, which I had to admit looked damning.

"Dani, that wasn't planned. It's just a picture—the article isn't *real*."

"Then why was he giving you *flowers* at your *house* in the middle of the *night*?" Daniela waited, watching me stutter. "That's what I thought, *clout-chaser*."

She snatched my drink, pouring the punch right over my head. For a moment, I saw how pathetic I looked.

I jumped up with a gasp. Punch streamed down my face, stinging my eyes, staining my dress. Princess Tiana? Who was I kidding? I should have come as Cinderella. The filming and the laughter began. But the worst part was how Eric just sat there with his fist against his mouth, giddy, like he was watching ladies mud wrestling.

"You think *I'm* messy?" Daniela scoffed, one elbow propped

on her hand as the empty cup dangled from her finger. "Take a look in the mirror, bitch."

I would have given the contents of my purse for that to be the end, but the confrontation didn't hit its peak until Quinn shoved Daniela. Then Daniela shouted and pushed Quinn back. As the two girls began to tussle, there was feedback from the mic as Tyler's song was cut short. Chinara rushed forward, trying desperately to separate the two. The fight couldn't have been more than a few seconds, but my brain speed was set to slow motion. It was an out-of-body experience, watching Quinn and Daniela trade blows. Over me. When teachers finally noticed the commotion, hair had been pulled, dresses were ripped, and there was no dignity to salvage.

The three girls were escorted from the dance floor. I was already on my way out when Quinn sent an SOS from the parking lot. My bad luck was confirmed when Tyler and I entered the tunnel at the same time; there was a stack of napkins in his hand, which I reluctantly took. We worked together, blotting and wiping as much punch as we could.

"Aaliyah, what *happened?*"

"You happened. As usual."

Tyler was wounded. "Okay. That's fair."

"No, it isn't," I said, exhaling. "I shouldn't have snapped at you. I'm sorry."

"Don't be," he said, dabbing at my dress. "Someone showed me an article from *Canceled*. Now your picture's being blasted all over the Internet. I didn't mean to drag you into my mess, Ali."

His green eyes lingered a few seconds too long. I cleared my throat and took the napkins before he said something sweet and romantic that would only get us in more trouble.

"I'll get rid of these," I said. "You should go. Your date's probably waiting."

Tyler nodded, gave my arm a squeeze, then headed reluctantly up the tunnel.

I made it to the parking lot in time to watch Chinara shoo Tyler back inside the dance. Meanwhile, I tended to Quinn, who was already being nursed by Declan. Her dress was torn, her hair was mussed, and she had a decent nosebleed. But it still wasn't as bad as Daniela's black eye was going to be.

"Declan, can I borrow your date?"

"Sure. Looks like Q and I are hitting the after-parties early." Ever the optimist, he passed me Q's purse. "I'm gonna go grab my jacket."

"Bring me some shrimp cocktail!" Quinn cried. "And some weenies!"

"Don't tip your head back," I commanded, bringing Quinn's hand to her nose. "Pinch here."

"Is it broken?"

"You'd know if it was broken. But you are gonna need ice." I opened the glittery clutch at my side, digging out a few leftover napkins. "Look, Q, I appreciate you sticking up for me, but I can handle Dani. Seriously, don't get yourself in trouble for me."

"She deserved it." A grumpy Quinn brushed my hands aside. "She treats people like shit and wonders why she doesn't have real friends."

"Well, she might have had a good reason to be pissed at me—this time."

"That doesn't mean you deserve a drink to the face, Aaliyah!"

"*Miss! Davis!*" Quinn and I both jumped at the sudden harp of Mr. O's voice. "Monday, eight a.m.—you, Daniela, in the principal's office. Clear?"

"Indubitably." Quinn's smile was stiff, like a ventriloquist's dummy. "Um, Mr. O, I just wanted you to know that, um, Chinara didn't have, like, anything to do with this. She was just trying to be a good friend."

"Aye. I can't let her back in the dance, but that'll be the extent of her punishment. Though I can't say the same for you and Miss Vega. As for you, Preston . . ."

I gulped, waiting on him to bust me for sipping that Everclear from Declan's flask.

"What are you standing around looking at me for? Get your arse onstage!"

Like a goof at the chalkboard, I was still trying to figure out what the hell was going on as Mr. O ushered me back into the school. It didn't start to click until we arrived at the gym. The hushed crowd parted like the Red Sea, allowing Mr. O to escort me across the dance floor. Straight ahead, Tyler was center stage once more, the homecoming crown askew on his forehead.

A teacher took my hand and helped me up the steps. Onstage, another teacher slipped a sash over my head, thrusting a bouquet of roses in my hands. Someone else held a glossy pillow beneath my nose, offering the choice between a fancy crown or a top hat embroidered in the HVH colors. I switched my tiara for the new crown, then took my place at the head of the younger students already gathered.

Side by side with Tyler, who gave his attention to me instead of the crowd, the music and the lights slipped away as I was announced senior homecoming monarch. Confetti burst over the crowd, falling like silver rain as Tyler slipped his hand in mine.

Over the years, I had danced with Tyler a million different ways, but slow dancing in the center of the gym, wearing monarch sashes, was definitely a first. It was weird having a literal spotlight on us, but I guess that's the whole point of homecoming, right?

"Is this awkward?" Tyler flashed his famous grin, the one from all my favorite fancams.

"No, not at all."

Tyler raised his eyebrows.

"Well, maybe a little," I admitted.

"I can't believe they're playing one of my songs," he mumbled.

The song was a ballad, and it was beautiful. Still, Tyler wasn't just being modest, he was genuinely embarrassed.

"You should be proud of it," I said. "It's in a movie, so you know it's good."

"I was in a different place when I wrote this song. It's about the pain of loving people who are gone. I wrote it specifically for the movie . . . and your mom."

Optics be damned. I stood on my tiptoes, throwing my arms around Tyler. "You never said anything."

"I didn't know how." Tyler stepped back, his green gaze searching the crowd. "Tonight, plus the article . . . everyone's gonna take this the wrong way."

"Let them." I took his hand again, placing the other at my waist. As we swayed in a few breezy seconds of silence, my gaze traveled from our interlaced fingers to the curls brushing his forehead to his sultry lips. It was a relief when other couples began to join us on the dance floor; the spotlight disappeared, but the heat was still on.

"I hope your date told you how beautiful you are tonight, and that you look like a sexy Victorian princess."

"Not as eloquently as you." I smiled. "I knew you'd look nice tonight. Everyone's seen you on the red carpet." His Met Gala looks were always flamboyant and highly praised.

"Maybe one day we'll walk the red carpet together."

I bit my lip. "Maybe."

Tyler cleared his throat in the heavy pause that followed. "Chi told me about the fight."

"Yeah? Did she tell you that the reason I'm standing here is because she, Dani, and Quinn got kicked out?" This was the first time I had ever been nominated for homecoming court. I should have been thrilled to see my name on the ballot. "I didn't even vote for myself. I voted for Chinara."

"Chinara's awesome." Tyler stopped dancing and lifted my chin. "But you deserve to be on the stage too. Your name was on the ballot. People voted for you, Aaliyah."

"They only voted because they see me with *you*. It's all because of you, Tyler. *Everything*." I stepped back, aware of the many pairs of eyes that followed.

"Aaliyah—"

"I have to go." I was wrong. The optics always mattered.

I was halfway up the tunnel when the Darth Vader ringtone sounded. I fished the phone from my clutch, stifling a long-winded exhale. She was calling outside of billable hours—it had to be an emergency.

"Astrid. Let me guess, this has something to do with Tyler."

"Aaliyah, what are your sources? Who are you talking to?"

Sources? "Um. Well. Mr. O says Wikipedia isn't reliable, so—"

"Thank you, Aaliyah, but that's about as bloody useful as a third armpit. I have to admit—you surprised me. I thought you were someone Tyler could trust, someone he could rely on. I didn't think you were the type of girl to make money off your friends. Either you're very good or I'm losing my touch."

"Oh, you've definitely lost something, lady." Pacing the tunnel, I switched the phone to my other ear. Most of what Astrid was saying still didn't make sense, and the parts that did were starting to freak me out. "I don't know what's going on, Astrid." I glanced around, lowering my voice as couples passed by. "But I would *never* use Tyler."

"You haven't been in contact with any media outlets? You haven't exchanged money for information about you or Tyler?"

"Of course not!" I hissed. "Is this about the *Canceled* article? Because I had nothing to do with that—"

"The *Canceled* article? It's only the beginning, Aaliyah. The person who took the picture that night—did you ever stop to wonder *how* they found you? No? Well, I'm afraid we have a very big problem on our hands."

I came to a halt, closed my eyes, and tried to focus on my breathing. For a dancer, balance is everything—from the physical to the emotional, even the spiritual—and I was off center in every way. Lately, there was a wrecking ball around every corner.

"Astrid, you're talking money, information, media outlets—and I still have no clue what the hell is going on!"

"There's a bloody leak. Aaliyah, *someone* is selling your story!"

I woke up the next morning in Tyler's guest room, autumn sunlight filtering through the elegant space. The bed was so large and luxurious I swam in sheets of gold and white, struggling just to reach the other side. Quinn snored at the foot of the mattress, still clutching a bottle of Dom.

I grabbed my phone from the dresser and padded across the room. Throwing open the balcony doors, I stepped into the sunlight to enjoy the view. Seeing the Village from this height, with a clear shot to the mountains and the sea, was opulent. My first introduction to the upper class had been on Wicker Hill, not far in the distance. From the outside, the wealthy gated community, with its pristine mansions, seemed untarnished by sin. But once you looked past the big Georgian and colonial homes, with rambling lawns long as racetracks and green as the summer sea, you saw the truth.

Daniela's enormous, neutral-brick home was nestled on a quiet shoulder, the shaded street most certainly lined with foreign cars. Last night, when Wicker Hill was just a series of yellow dots on the horizon, I had gazed at the lights from this same spot, wondering if it was Daniela selling our story to the press. Now, I wondered the same thing. I hated the thought of being betrayed by someone close to me.

I left the balcony, closing the doors quietly behind me before tiptoeing across the room, past Quinn. Last night, until the early morning, Tyler's penthouse had been filled with music, laughter, and weed smoke while the apartment's LED lights flashed every color of the rainbow. The usual crowd had arrived for the homecoming after-party—a mix of juniors and seniors, with a few underclassmen playing pretend for the night. And if you didn't have a date, at least you had a red plastic cup. But I hadn't needed distractions to stay afloat. Secret glances from across the room and the brushing of our fingertips as he passed had been more than enough. Watching him dance with other girls, pretending I wasn't into him, had been like trying to ignore a toothache.

After one too many glasses of Dom, Tyler had helped Declan carry a plastered Quinn to the guest room, where I'd covered her with a blanket.

"Is Q . . . okay?" Declan gazed at his drooling date with concern.

"What do you mean?" I asked, casting Tyler an anxious glance.

"She drank a lot, even for her. And she kept trashing this dude named Aleksandr something?"

"Well, Q is a little . . ." I twirled my finger around my ear. "She was probably just wound up after the fight," I assured him, patting his arm.

Declan gave me a dubious nod and left.

"Y'know, Preston, Declan can't tell when you're lying, but I can," said Tyler, arms folded.

"Why are you still dressed like Prince Charming?" I retorted.

"Your manager called me tonight. She says someone's talking to the media. A lot. We should probably figure out who that is."

Or more stories would keep rolling out. Stories that could impact our future.

"Wait, wait, wait. Since when is Astrid calling you and not me?"

"Since she figured out who the mature one is," I said, breezing past him and out of the room.

Declan, Tyler, and I kept a close eye on Quinn for the rest of the party. It was pretty obvious she wasn't going home that night, so she and I both stayed.

"Don't worry, Dec, I'll make sure she gets home safe," I promised.

"Take it easy, bro." Tyler bumped Declan's fist then closed the door. Without the music and the people, only the empty bottles and plastic cups they'd left behind, the penthouse felt almost . . . normal. Although, passing the spot where Pete had nearly died gave me the chills every time I walked by.

Tyler and I grabbed a couple of trash bags and worked in

silence, cleaning up the debris and sorting out the furniture. In the living room, when we reached for the same empty bottle, a tug-of-war ensued until he let me win.

"Wanna watch a movie?" he asked. "There's, like, a million Marvel shows I have to catch up on."

I glanced behind me at the giant flat-screen TV. It was tempting, the image of curling up with a blanket and popcorn, the lights dim as I fell asleep, safe and sound, in his arms.

"What about Chinara?" I asked.

"What about Eric?"

I shrugged. "Eric who?"

Sometimes Eric forgot we weren't dating. After we'd argued about me dancing with Tyler, my homecoming date had disappeared halfway through the night, reappearing on my Instagram feed in a group shot with Daniela, who had covered her black eye with bangs and makeup.

"Chinara and I decided we're better off as friends," said Tyler, taking a seat on the arm of his couch. "Actually . . . Chinara decided. She said she has more chemistry with my music."

"Ouch." Chinara was infamous for her brutal honesty. "Bummer."

"No, Chi was right—she deserves better. She said she wants to find a guy who looks at her the way I look at you."

I stood up straight, then sat down on the couch, defeated. "Why would she say that?"

"Why do you think? Look, Ali, I know you and Astrid aren't thrilled about the rest of the world thinking you and I are together. But . . ." Tyler shrugged one shoulder, like it wasn't a big deal that we were about to be exposed. "Maybe that's not such a bad thing."

"You're right—it's *terrible*!" I jumped to my feet. "If people start thinking we're together, they'll never take me seriously again. I won't be Aaliyah Preston anymore, I'll be 'Tyler Moore's girlfriend.' And if I do get into a good school or maybe open my own studio one day, they'll say it was because of you."

"That's not true."

"Can you promise me it won't happen?"

Tyler opened his mouth, thought better of it, and glanced away.

"I wish someone had told me that getting everything you ever wanted means you can't watch a movie with your best friend," he said.

"Me too."

"I hear what you're saying, and I get it." Tyler stood up, then took a seat next to me on the couch. "But when I look in your eyes, why does it feel like you want the opposite?"

"Because I do." I slid my fingers through his, enjoying the way he squeezed my hand. We stole these moments like thieves, knowing they wouldn't last.

I grinned. "It's less boring when you're around."

Tyler tucked a strand of hair behind my ear and smiled. "Then I'll be waiting."

We exchanged wistful good nights in the hallway. I closed my bedroom door, thumping my forehead head against the wood, wondering how I managed to keep screwing things up. Tyler was right—I always said one thing while wanting another.

After Q rose from her coma, Tyler called his driver and asked him to have the limo ready.

"Dibs on the minibar," said Quinn, diving into the back seat.

"Thanks for making breakfast." I smiled. "And by making,

I mean ordering from the restaurant and having it sent to the penthouse."

"You just love to torture me, don't you?" Tyler smiled wide, clearly enjoying it.

"Ah, yes, one of my many pastimes." I smiled too, until I remembered I had to tell him the truth. "Can we meet this afternoon?" I asked. "They don't allow pictures under the Sunset. We'll be safe there. Safe-ish."

"Well, that sounds adorably ominous." Tyler placed his chin on his arms, balancing on the car door as he smiled at me from the other side. "I am intrigued."

"That's not all you are," I said, smiling back, smitten with the way he gazed at me even though I was wearing sneakers and last night's punch-stained dress. "Just be there, okay? There's something *really important* I have to tell you. Like, life or death."

"Y'know what's important?" Quinn poked her head out, holding up mini bags of treats. "Chocolate. Covered. Peanuts."

I pushed Quinn out of the way and stepped into the limo.

"I'll be there," said Tyler, closing the door behind me.

"You're gonna tell him about Aleksandr, aren't you?" Quinn's mouth was full of peanuts as she broke the seal on a sparkling water. "Once he knows, he has to leave."

"He'll go back to New York . . . where he belongs." I turned, watching Tyler through the window for as long as I could.

Quinn glanced up from her snacks with a frown. "Where the fuck is the driver going? We didn't even give him our addresses yet."

"I'll check," I said, rapping on the glass partition. There was a low, mechanical buzz as it lowered halfway.

"Excuse me, my friend and I—" The evil gaze reflected in the rearview mirror completely derailed my train of thought. His sunglasses couldn't disguise everything.

Bortnik turned and smiled—he had a new gold tooth.

"Circles and squares!" he announced, cheerful as a Christmas card.

Quinn screamed, and chocolate-covered peanuts went flying.

Five

Wild Nights

Bortnik asked where we wanted to go, cracking a stupid joke about giving us little girls some money for ice cream at the mall. Was Bortnik there just to rattle our cages, or had Aleksandr sent him to finish the job? I sat back in my seat, hyperventilating, wondering if this was it. I made a mental checklist of all the things I would never accomplish—meet the baby, stomp Daniela, graduate, dance at the Conservatory . . . tell the only boy I'd ever loved how I really felt.

"Just take us home, psycho!"

"*Quinn!*" I grabbed her arm, preventing her from throwing more peanuts at Bortnik, but he only laughed.

"*Da*, I know where you live," he said.

"Then take us there!" I pressed a button, raising the privacy screen.

"Is he really taking us home?" asked Quinn.

"You wanna find out?"

Quinn frantically shook her head.

"Then here's what we'll do . . ."

The plan was simple—escape.

"Ready?" I whispered.

Quinn gave a silent nod, both hands positioned on the door . . .

"*Go!*"

At the next red light, we threw the doors open and jumped into traffic, running for our lives down Salinity Boulevard.

We didn't stop to look over our shoulders until we collapsed at my aunt's house. As we lay in the grass, breathless and sweating, I floated up into the blue autumn sky and let the wind carry me away. It was moments like this when I wanted to leave the Village and see the sky from somewhere new. Right now, all I could see now was how ridiculous we must have looked, climbing over fences and running down the street in our homecoming dresses. The lowest point was when a squad car had whooped, flashing its lights as we ran past. Quinn and I had hidden in an alley, ducking behind a dumpster until it was gone.

"Bortnik was gonna kill us and wear our skin!" Quinn wheezed, clutching her chest.

"We don't know that." I sat up, wiping the moisture from my forehead. "Nice day, Mr. Schulze!"

He was checking his mail. I waved; he gave me a strange look and hurried back inside. I looked down at my dress—torn, stained, and ripped—and wondered how I would explain it to my aunt.

"C'mon," I said. "Trina's waiting."

She hailed us from the living room before Quinn and I could sneak past her and up the stairs.

"Wow." Trina was sitting at the couch, eating from a pickle jar as she watched TV. "That must have been a wild night, ladies—congrats!"

Quinn gave a knowing laugh and pulled a leaf from my hair.

Later that afternoon, I ordered a coffee and waited for Tyler in the lounge under the Harley Sunset. I was thankful they'd even allowed me back in the place after my meeting with Aleksandr, but that's the great thing about the Sunset—no one asks questions.

More nervous by the second, I sat for a while, listening to the pop music on the speakers, hoping that I hadn't been followed by Aleksandr, Bortnik, or paparazzi. As I sat there, I realized that had Aleksandr really wanted us dead, we would be. He'd wanted to scare me, probably to punish me for setting up that stupid meeting—and it had worked.

I received an alert from my phone. It was a text from Eric—a candid picture of me and Tyler standing in front of the limo that morning. I didn't need a blog or an article to see the insinuation behind the photo—I was standing outside his hotel in last night's dress.

My fingers shook as I dialed Eric's number.

"Hello?"

"Eric, tell me you did not take that picture!" If he was the leak, I was going to explode.

"Hell no!" He sucked his teeth at me. "You and Prince Charming are all over the Internet."

"That picture—it's not what it looks like. So don't go around telling people I'm with Tyler, okay?"

"All right." He sounded relieved. "Where are you?"

"At home. If you weren't spying on me from the hotel this morning, where were *you*?"

"Oh yeah, I, uh . . . I was at home."

Liar.

"So wassup with you and Daniela?" he asked, with an innocence too rare to be real.

"Nothing," I said and hung up, knowing full well he was probably in her bed as the two of them listened to me on speaker. I checked my watch, realized Tyler was late, and shot him a quick text.

i'm at the sunset where r u bonehead

Then I ordered another coffee.

It was almost closing time when I settled my tab and slid my jacket over my shoulders. *Tyler wouldn't blow me off without a reason, and it better be a damn good one.* Before I could leave, an all too familiar figure slid his way into the booth.

"Mr. Moore . . ." I froze under the spell of his cold, contemptuous gaze. The last time we'd met, he'd been bloody and battered. Today, he was suave and put together. His bruises were fading, but I knew the reminders of what had happened never would—for either of us. Pete's veneer of cologne, jewelry, and luxury apparel had forever worn off. Whether I liked him or not, Aleksandr had done us both a favor that day when he peeled back the layers, showing everyone who Pete Moore really was.

"Expecting someone else?" He gave me a familiar smirk and interlaced his fingers on the table. "Whiskey, neat," he said, winking at a passing waitress. "How are you, Aaliyah?"

"I . . . I . . . I . . ."

"You look nervous. Is something wrong?"

"I . . . I . . . I . . ."

"Got your nose," he said, giving it a wiggle; my skin crawled at the feeling of his hand on my face. All I could do was sit there, shaking in my seat. "Tyler used to love it when I did that," he said. Maybe it was just the shock, but his voice sounded faint and distant, like he was speaking underwater.

"Y'know, I once had to have a similar conversation with your mother, god rest Amelia's soul." He shook his head in pity, but his eyes lacked any true remorse. "Thanks, hon," he said with a shark's grin, sipping the whiskey the waitress left on the table.

"I haven't done anything wrong," I said stonily.

"Of course not," he replied in his usual patronizing way that made you feel small and alone. He could suck out the air from the room and turn the sky black with a single look. "Your mother meant well too, even though she was always poking her cute little nose where it just didn't belong." He gave a long, drawn-out exhale and drank from his glass again. "She got in over her head. So are you."

"She loved your family," I said through gritted teeth. A hot rush of anger coursed through me; my body shook like guitar strings. "All she ever wanted was to help."

"Eh, that's not *all* she wanted." Pete's smirk slipped away, and I relished it, because I knew he was thinking of my mother, remembering her in ways that made him feel small and alone too. "Amelia tried to take my son away from me. Just like you. I've seen the blogs, Aaliyah."

"I would never—"

"Acht!" He cut me off with his finger. "Tyler has work to do, which he can't focus on if he's thinking about you. It took some . . . *convincing*, but I managed to get him on a plane. Tyler's on a flight as we speak."

"Y-you sent him back to New York?" For once, something good had come from Pete Moore's selfishness.

"*Yes*," he hissed. I flinched. "And I'm going to repeat what I told you when Tyler first left the Village. This time, I want you to remember it: Let. Him. Go. You're a distraction, Aaliyah, and Tyler doesn't have room for those. Are we clear?"

I didn't waste time with words, I grabbed my purse and slid

out of the booth. Pete's hand whipped out, snatching my wrist in a hard, icy grip.

"Stay away from my son, Aaliyah."

"Tyler's emancipated. You don't get to make decisions for him anymore." I nearly pulled my arm from its socket trying to get away from him. Then, blinded by angry tears, I stumbled from the lounge and sat in my car, crying, until I was okay to drive.

That night, I danced in the basement, flowing from one song to the next. Times like these, music was all that kept me from falling apart at the seams, and when I was numb, it was the only thing that made me feel alive. I put every thought and emotion on display until I was on my knees, exhausted and panting.

Trina leaned in the doorway, wearing her purple bonnet, a fluffy white bathrobe flowing over her pajamas.

"When did Tyler decide to go back to New York?"

"This afternoon," I said, rising to my feet. "How'd you know?"

"The Internet. He's everywhere. The fans and paparazzi were waiting as soon as the plane touched down. It was practically a mob."

The paparazzi were always one step ahead. I wondered how Tyler had felt when he stepped off the plane, and whether he felt alone, like me. I hadn't even had the chance to say goodbye.

Tired but still glowing, Trina cocked her head to the side, exhaling in empathy. "It's too bad he left so soon. He seemed pretty excited for graduation."

"He was," I said, my quiet voice tempered with a loud sigh. "But he's better off in New York."

"Really?" Trina put her hand on her hip and smiled. "I would have thought he was better off with you. It's late. Get some rest, kiddo."

I took my aunt's advice and went to bed, but I tossed and turned all night and couldn't remember my dreams the next morning.

With pictures of Tyler at the airport circulating, school was buzzing with theories about his disappearance. Everyone had questions, including the B-Team. A handful of them cornered me at my locker, demanding to know why Tyler had left and when he would be back.

"Just when we were starting to get good!"

"He dumped us! Hit it and quit it, just like my ex!"

"Please, Aaliyah, you have to tell him to come back!"

"Guys, guys, guys!" I held up my hand. "Tyler isn't coming back. We're on our own. But we can do this. Right?"

They walked away grumbling, shaking their heads.

"We don't stand a chance," I heard someone say, and I wondered if that was true. Tyler would be safer in New York than in the Village, so why did it still feel like the fate of the world was resting on my shoulders?

After school, I made my way down to the football field. Mr. Woods had just posted the results of the Battle of the Bands, and I was buzzing with the news that Quinn and I had made the final cut. But so had Motivation, which, given their track record, was only to be expected.

I took a seat on the bleachers, two Styrofoam cups of coffee in hand. Daniela hesitated, then took the cup I offered. Together, we watched the basketball team run drills on the field as the wind tousled our hair, urging us toward the sea.

"Are you here to gloat?" she asked, studying me from behind large Gucci shades. But the sunglasses couldn't hide her bruised face. "Principal Hall gave me and Quinn detention for two weeks, and I'm now on probation with the squad. One more screwup and my parents are going to kill me."

"Am I supposed to feel sorry for you? I'm only here because Mr. Woods made a last-minute announcement—they're pushing the contest back a few months. Apparently, one of the judges from the other schools got mono."

"Ew," we said at the same time.

"Actually, *me importa una mierda*, okay?" She rolled her eyes in annoyance. "My parents force me to do the contest *every* year."

"What about cheerleading?" I asked. "Do they force you to do that too?" I couldn't help but wonder if I'd love dancing the same if I were forced into it like Daniela and Tyler.

But Dani didn't answer; she simply cast me a dark look from behind her shades and said nothing. For a while, we just sat and watched the players on the field, silent when we used to laugh and joke so easily.

"Just because my parents force me to do the talent show doesn't mean I don't want to win," she said in icy tones of resentment. She pushed her glasses on top of her head. The gems accenting Daniela's smoky gaze flashed in the sun as she glared down at the field. "I've been under a lot of pressure lately. The pressure to get into a good school, maintain my GPA, leave my name stamped somewhere in HVH's dusty halls. But that's not the real problem. My problem is *you*, Aaliyah." When she finally turned and looked at me, her fierce stare was sharp enough to cut. "Because of you, my captainship is in jeopardy, and the B-Team is upside down. And I wouldn't be surprised at all if *you* were the reason Tyler left."

I stood, grabbing my backpack and sliding it over my shoulders in disgust.

"I don't even know why I try to be nice to you. Quinn was right, Dani—you *don't* have real friends, and this is why I'm done trying."

I thought I would feel better, standing up for myself, but all I felt as I walked away was a sinking feeling, like I had lost something important.

Tyler still hadn't responded to my texts, and creeping on his socials didn't give me much in the way of answers either. But on the second day, I knew he was reaching out when he posted a few lines from "The Walrus and the Carpenter" on his Instagram. I tried to go on like normal, to pretend that things were the way they had been before Tyler came back, but I was . . . lost. While everyone else was grounded, I was stuck on the ceiling with no gravity.

I was still distracted at dance practice at the studio that Friday. Self-pity had me faltering on even the simplest steps. My rhythm was off, my timing was terrible, and don't even get me started on my grand adage. After being slow on the uptake for the umpteenth time, Madilyn finally cut the music.

When Madilyn entered the room, you saw where Tyler had inherited his good looks. But like his dad, there were differences between Tyler and his mom that you could spot a mile away. Madilyn's green eyes were wiser, her words more careful, and her course always steady. Madilyn was responsible for the best parts of her son. Sometimes I worried about her, because my mom wasn't around to remind her how amazing she was.

Tall and slender, she wore black dance leggings and a matching high-collared leotard. Her long, brown waves were tied in French braids, and she wore fresh-faced makeup accented by winged liner and bright red lips. Today, the eyebrows were raised, the lips were pursed, and the arms were folded.

"Aaliyah, last week I would have said you were ready for your online audition for the Conservatory. But after the dancing I've seen today . . . I'm not so sure."

My head hung in shame.

"You have your mother's gift, Aaliyah, and that kind of talent deserves a real stage. But that also requires real focus—which you'll need to get into the Conservatory. You're clearly distracted—that kind of dancing has no place anywhere."

"I know. You're right. I'm sorry, Maddie." I slid my arm across my forehead, removing the sweat. "I guess I am having trouble staying focused. Have you heard from Tyler?"

Madilyn's eyes lit with understanding. "He's . . . okay. I think he's more concerned with everyone else."

"Did he happen to say anything? Like, why he left?"

"He only gives me vague answers." Madilyn's face darkened. "But I think his dad had something to do with it." She shook her head. "Tyler came home to clear his head. I was really hoping he'd stick around this time."

She pressed her lips together in disappointment. "Maybe it's summer fever or senioritis—Tyler's pretty distracted these days. I wish I could keep a closer eye on him, but ever since his father and I divorced, Tyler thinks he'd be choosing sides if he moved in with one of us, so he stays at La Maison."

"Sounds lonely."

"I don't like it, but Tyler's emancipated. Us parents don't have much say in what he does anymore—maybe that's for the best. At least I still get to boss you and Emma around." Madilyn winked and clapped her hands. "Now, from the top?"

I nodded, rolled my shoulders back, lifted my chest, and raised my arms in position as Madilyn counted the tempo.

Saturday morning, I walked through the high wrought iron gates of the Village cemetery, following a small, winding path by heart. I found my way through the sea of headstones, past familiar mausoleums and monuments. There were names inside my head belonging to faces I had never seen, but certain graves stuck with me over the years, comforting as old postcards.

My mom was buried on a little hill underneath a crown of cedar trees. I swept aside the dirt and leaves collecting at the base of the headstone. *Here lies Amelia Jane Preston, loving mother, beloved sister, angel in flight* were the words engraved beneath an etching of ballet slippers. Frowning at a fresh bouquet of white stargazer lilies on her grave, I removed the old flowers from the vase, adding a spray of roses sprinkled with water. I rose, glancing from side to side as if the visitor might still be lingering. My question was answered as I descended the hill to find Aleksandr waiting, smoking a cigarette.

"It's rude to talk to people at cemeteries," I said coldly, walking past him.

Aleksandr fell in step with a grin, striding with me down the winding, shaded path.

"I'm just out for a stroll," he said, the lapels of his navy peacoat turned up against the autumn chill.

"In a cemetery? Please. What are you even still doing in the Village?"

"I like to keep a close eye on my investments," he replied, taking a drag on his cigarette. "And I enjoy being at sea in the fall. Would you care for a ride?"

"I don't want anything from you. *Ever.*"

"Well, there is something I want from you." Aleksandr's penetrating blue gaze swept across the horizon then returned to stop me in my tracks. "Pete must think he's very clever, sending his son to New York. Annoying, but this line of work is not without its challenges."

"I'm sorry, is there a point to this conversation, or did you just come here to threaten Tyler?"

"Two birds, one stone." Aleksandr stepped closer. "Tyler will go where he pleases, but I want you to stay in the Village, *pchelka*. No flying away where I can't find you." He lowered his voice, ducking his head and looking closer when I refused to meet his gaze. "I sent Bortnik to make a statement—*I'm always watching.* So if you leave, I will know. And there will be consequences." He flicked his cigarette in the grass, giving me a last icy nod before he left.

My fear spread like a poison, rooting me to the spot as I watched Aleksandr continue up the path, whistling.

☆ ☆ ☆

When Chinara texted me later that afternoon, I jumped at the opportunity to get out of the house. Even constantly checking the rearview mirror for phantom SUVs was better than peeping through windows at home like a sitting duck. Helping Chinara take down decorations after a school function I wouldn't have attended under pain of death was a welcome distraction.

"Only the mathletes would rent a ballroom at La Maison for a competition no one cares about," said Chinara. We were halfway across the hotel parking lot, the last of the decorations stuffed in the boxes we were carrying.

"Thanks again for volunteering," she said, fishing out the

keys in her pocket to unlock the trunk of her Toyota Camry—the birthday present she'd received for aiming high and applying to the law schools her parents had suggested.

"It's no big deal," I said, setting my box in the trunk. "Plus, I still feel bad. Y'know, about homecoming . . ."

"You mean, stealing my crown?" Chinara laughed, setting the boxes in the car. "Don't worry, mate. The crown won't get me into law school." She closed the trunk, then snapped her fingers in exasperation. "Bollocks! I left the pamphlets in the ballroom. The mathletes had fifty leftover invitations to the next meeting, imagine that."

"Don't worry, I'll get rid of them."

Chi grabbed my arm in relief. "Thanks, love. Swing by the Sunset later if you have time. A bunch of us are meeting for coffee—and *proper* English tea."

I chuckled, waving goodbye. "We'll see."

La Maison was well-known for the luxury experience. But the hotel had something even better than fine wine and dining in the restaurant, mud baths and massages in the relaxation center, tennis in the courtyard, and champagne by the pool—La Maison had room for an audience.

The first time I'd set foot in the ballroom at La Maison, I'd seen a shining future across the rows of empty seats—one with stages and audiences, tiaras and tutus. Bouquets and long-stemmed roses and programs with my name inside—and the bittersweetness of another curtain falling on a grand performance.

Floating dreamily down the aisles, I imagined the vast field of seats fully occupied and claps and whistles from the balconies after a flawless show. The accompanist would rise from his seat behind the grand piano, and together we would bow . . .

Spotting Chinara's stack of pamphlets at the edge of the

stage, I scooped them up and crossed the ballroom for the last time. As I reached for the door's giant silver handles, the slow, arresting timbre of piano keys called out with their haunting tune. I turned toward the hall, awed by the captivating voice that filled it. Spotlights above Tyler shone down in a perfect halo of light as he sang his ballad.

the walrus and the carpenter, they took us by the hand
and somewhere by the boiling sea, they left us in the sand
our love was hot, she was burned
the sand had turned to glass
feed my soul to the starving waters
with the oysters, hand in hand

The piano carried on where Tyler left off—a delicate projection of notes, ascending like a tidal wave, rising higher and higher until the final note, a beautiful, resounding crash, like the sea rollers from his song.

"It's not finished," Tyler said as I approached. He stayed put, examining the keys. "The chord progression is off; I'm better at guitar. And the ending . . . I don't know it yet."

"Maybe it doesn't have to have an ending," I replied. "Endings suck."

I climbed the stage, admiring the big, glossy instrument, intimidated by the piano and its keys—tiny black-and-white complexities I would never understand. Doing that was a far less daunting task than asking where Tyler had been and why he had butterfly stitches across his eyebrow.

"You never showed up at the Sunset," I said, watching Tyler from across the piano. "I thought I wouldn't see you again."

Tyler patted the bench, sliding over to make room. "Do you really think I'd leave you without saying goodbye, Ali-Cat?" He took my hand, his warm fingers curling around mine. "I'm sorry I didn't reach out. Dad lost his shit and took my phone."

"Why?"

"He said there's nothing for me in the Village and that I'm holding myself back. Then he hired a bunch of bodyguards to make me get on a plane back to New York."

"Is that how this happened?" I brushed his stitches, imagining Tyler defending himself against a room full of security. I saw him, surrounded at the airport, taking his seat, forlornly, on the plane.

Tyler inhaled, staring silently down at the piano.

I tapped one of the bright, smooth keys. And then another. Where Tyler's notes were sweet sounding, mine came out high and clunky, so I put my hands in my lap, where they belonged. I glanced around the empty ballroom, imagining rows of round white tables filled with white china plates and bouquets of white roses. And there was more than enough room for the cake table, a band, and the first dance, right here where Tyler and I were sitting. I could see it perfectly. But when I tried to picture dancing with Tyler at the wedding, everything went dark.

"It's not safe for you in the Village, Tyler. That's what I tried to tell you before you left."

I took a deep breath then finally admitted everything I had meant to say at the Sunset: how Aleksandr had been following me and had warned me to stay in the Village. Tyler's face collected anger like storm clouds brewing on the horizon. I knew Aleksandr pissed him off, but he didn't lose his cool until I told him about his dad showing up at the Sunset, warning me to stay away from his son. Tyler slammed the keys on the piano, then slammed the fallboard too.

"What else?" he demanded, chest heaving, his fierce green gaze lasered into the distance.

"Honestly, I think I've probably said too much—"

"*What else*, Aaliyah?" I didn't have a choice when his gaze pinned mine.

"This wasn't the first time your dad warned me to stay away," I said, looking down at my lap. "After you won *Epic*, he turned me away at the airport when I tried to say goodbye. You were both leaving, and I didn't know when or if I'd ever see you again. Well, he pretty much decided that for us both when he told me to let you go. He said now that you were famous, you didn't need any 'distractions' while you were on the road."

"What the hell, Ali? Why didn't you *say* anything?"

"You know what he's like, Tyler."

In Tyler's eyes, I saw the replay of every time Pete had ever yelled, called him stupid, or struck him. The countless times he had slept over and we'd lain in bed listening to my mom pleading with Madilyn on the phone, urging her to call the police. Alone in the dark, gazing at the ceiling, I think we both knew there were reasons Amelia and Madilyn couldn't get rid of Pete. Adult reasons we were too young to understand . . . but I was starting to.

"I shouldn't even be here," I said, jumping to my feet in a sudden panic. "I—I shouldn't even be talking to you." I grabbed the pamphlets from where I had abandoned them on the piano.

"Ali! Aaliyah, *wait!*"

But I walked offstage and hurried down the steps, seeking refuge in the center aisle.

Tyler called out from the stage. "You can't keep running away, Aaliyah."

I turned around reluctantly, watching Tyler jump down from the stage and walk, slowly, up the aisle.

"I came back for you," he said. "Sometimes I think it would be easier if I just gave in, let my dad have what he wants. But if that means losing you . . ." Tyler stopped a few feet away, shaking his head. "I did it once, and I won't do it again."

"Tyler . . ." I shrugged, searching for the right words to make him leave without hating me.

"I know you're scared, Ali." Tyler approached, peeling one of my hands from the stack of paper I clutched like a lifeline. "And if I were you, I wouldn't risk my career for me either. But I want you to know that what you and I have is *real*. I've felt this way for a long time, these feelings aren't new for me. And I can prove it."

"Really? How?" I swiped at the tear that had fallen, collecting myself before more could follow.

"Let me show you." Tyler bit his lip in a crafty grin. "Come with me. To New York."

"Tyler, New York is, like, a thousand miles away."

"Actually, it's forty-five minutes by plane. I mean, if we go now, I can have you back in time for dinner. *Or*, you can ask Quinn to cover for you and spend the night—with me."

"No. No way. Are you kidding me? Forget it!"

Tyler darted in front of me when I turned away.

"Why not?"

"*Why not?*" I repeated. "I can't leave the *state*! I can't even drive on the highway without asking!"

"That's why we're flying." Tyler was not to be deterred—he lived for a challenge. "You always talk about how much you miss New York—"

"Yeah, I *do*, but—"

"Then what are you waiting for?"

"I can't leave the Village, remember? Not until your dad pays Aleksandr! He's been a little vague on some things, but he was pretty clear about that!"

"Ali, it's one weekend, okay? And I promise I'll keep you

safe." Tyler followed my jawline with his thumb, returning my wandering gaze to his. "No one will ever know."

It was hypnotic, watching those honeyed words drip from his perfect lips. It made me feel stupid . . . and invincible.

"But what about your song?" I asked, finally giving in. "It's not finished."

"Neither are we." Tyler grabbed the papers and tossed them in the air. He took me in his arms as they fell and spun me around, like a prima ballerina in a snow globe.

Six

Under Water

We bought black baseball caps and matching zip-up hoodies, then changed into our new clothes at the airport. Tyler was waiting for me outside the bathroom, where he pulled the hoodie over my hat, concealing my curls. If the paparazzi captured my picture tonight, the world would know me only as Tyler's mystery girl. He bought two first-class round-trip tickets to NYC, we boarded the plane, and there was no going back. Sure, I felt bad lying to Trina, telling her I was crashing with Quinn, but Tyler's smile overshadowed the guilt.

We sat across from each other, in seats designed like cozy cubicles, a foldaway table planted between us. Tyler sweet-talked a flight attendant, and moments later they brought us something to celebrate our freedom. We toasted with champagne as pink as the vibrant sky beyond the window.

"This is really beautiful," I said, gazing out the window.

"So are you," Tyler replied, sitting back to enjoy the view.

My heart was still hammering when the flight touched down. Tyler took my hand and led me through the tunnel. Without any bags to slow us down, we picked up the pace, moving faster and faster as we navigated the crowd. Tyler had warned me on the plane—if we stayed in one place for even two seconds, our cover would be blown before we even left LaGuardia. Running toward the exit, we dodged security and burst through the doors, slipping away into the bright lights of the city.

I hadn't realized how much I'd missed NYC until I was immersed in the steady beat of its traffic. Wheeling under a navy horizon interrupted by soaring skyscrapers, I inhaled the nostalgic combination of street foods and exhaust—and thought of my mother. The sunlight in her hair, and how wide she had smiled every morning as she walked me to school.

Tyler and I bought street food from a vendor, dashing away before Tyler was recognized. We window-shopped, pointing out eye-catching landmarks as we strolled down the sidewalk, eating hot dogs.

"This is definitely the best part," said Tyler, licking his fingers.

"The hot dogs?"

"I mean getting away from everything and being here—with you. But the hot dog is a nice touch. A-plus on the hotdog." Tyler slowed down. "Ali, before I left, you made it pretty clear that we can't be more than friends. Is it really about your career, or are you scared of something else?"

I came to a stop, fidgeting with my hot dog as Tyler waited.

"After your dad showed up at the Sunset, I had a few days to accept that you were gone. And I started to think about my mom, how she gave up her career for my dad—because she loved him. She mostly thought about him when she was dancing, and that scares me, because I think about you too."

Tyler ruined the moment, taking a sloppy bite from his hot dog, grinning as he chewed with his mouth open. "I knew it."

"You know what, Tyler, I am *so done* with you. Taxi! Taxi!"

Fifteen minutes later, Tyler pulled me close in the back seat of a cab en route to Central Park. He gazed out the window, his arm around my shoulders, our fingers intertwined as I lay against his chest. The streetlights washed over his chiseled face, making his green eyes darker than ever between the shadows. I felt his heartbeat under my hand and knew that it was mine.

By the time we made it to the park, the sun was just a thin slice of orange on the horizon. Tyler scooped up my hand as we headed toward the gate. He walked backward, the brightness of his polar-white smile rivaling the evening stars.

"It's amazing, Ali. You're gonna love it."

"I already do."

We rented a pair of bikes at the park entrance and set off. The sweet-smelling air that whipped past my face was more refreshing than coffee as we rode beyond the sky-high trees waving just beyond the gate. In no time, the cobbled paths gave way to smooth pavement littered with golden-brown foliage. Towering trees with yellow-green leaves lined the avenue, their branches meeting overhead, canopies intertwined like lovers. Streetlights stood guard underneath in stately, uniform rows, their golden-white glow in lovely contrast to the navy twilight. Tyler rode ahead at a fast pace, leaves scattering in his wake. He didn't get very far before he turned back, falling in line behind me, tracing my movements in lazy loops that eventually closed and became a circle.

We followed each other until I was no longer ahead and he was no longer behind—we were simply two spokes caught in the same wheel. Around and around we went, long enough for me to close my eyes and let intuition be my guide. I raised my hands up high in the air, the wind on my skin as I fell into the sound of the tandem movement of our bikes—the whir of the tires and the *tick-tick-tick* of the chains turning, effortlessly, like they would never ever stop.

Suddenly, Tyler broke free and zoomed ahead. Rising from his seat, he threw his head back and let out a whoop. I chased after, gliding so fast my hood flew off, the ball cap staying snugly in place. My curls streamed in the wind, the same color as the leaves that swirled around us. I caught up, sailing past Tyler, letting the speed of our adventure carry me farther and faster than I had moved in a long time—with anyone.

We raced until he caught up, then coasted the rest of the way.

☆　☆　☆

Tyler and I walked our bikes along a grassy trail framed with trees the likes of which I had never seen in the Village—or anywhere. The branches were veiled in clusters of purple-white blossoms that floated free with every shift in the wind. They drifted on the air like cotton balls, leaving their perfume on your clothes and skin before fluttering to the ground.

Tyler veered right, and I followed. We left our bikes at the base of a tree, and once more my hand disappeared in his. I followed him a short way, stepping through a bed of purple-white foliage as densely packed as snow. He stopped at one tree that was smaller than its brothers and sisters but whose leaves were oddly bright. Tyler took out his phone, shining the light on the bark, and there it was, surrounded by a heart no bigger than my palm:

Tyler + Ali
4 ever

"When I first left the Village, it was rough for a while." Tyler paused, lifting his face to study the flowers in the moonlight. "One day, I woke up and decided to come to the park. I skipped every appointment I had—I even skipped breakfast. Astrid and my dad were pissed. They called so many times I broke my phone and threw it off a bridge. But I didn't care. I just needed some time away to *think*. Because I had this *fear*, y'know, that, like . . . everything was falling apart. Amelia died, my parents were getting divorced, everyone had all these expectations and *you* . . . you were . . ." He trailed off, leaving me to fill in the ugly blanks. "And then I saw this tree, and I wanted to leave *something* behind. I had to. In case the dream really was dead."

"Doesn't look dead to me," I said, running my fingers across the rough, uneven bark. The words were brighter than the surrounding wood, the cuts thin but deep. Over time they would fade, but the message would never completely vanish. It was here forever.

"I'm sorry if I ever made you feel alone when you were gone." I sighed; my fingers dropped. "I guess it was just easier for me to believe that everyone else was doing a better job at being there for you."

"Ali, your mom was sick—I *knew* you couldn't be there. But you're right about one thing—Dad took care of me, all right. But just enough to take care of himself, because the *only* person Pete Moore really cares about is himself." Tyler turned and sat down against the tree, thumping his head against the bark. "The whole time we lived here, it was like *he* was the one on tour. Sometimes that asshole thought he was my manager too." Tyler ticked off the abuses, one by one. "It was late nights, early mornings, drunk dad in between. I did everything he asked me to, everything, and he repaid me by taking you away. He's a bastard. He and Aleksandr deserve each other."

The rest of the world was in the dark, but it was no secret to me that Tyler had clashed with his father growing up. I still had vivid memories of the two of them shouting at each other in the front seat of their car, Mr. Moore so furious he'd swerved into oncoming traffic.

"Sounds like you really hate him," I said.

"Maybe I do."

"I get it. Sometimes I hate my dad too." I wrapped my arms around me, shielding myself from the loneliness he inspired. "After my mom died, he didn't even show up at the funeral. We haven't spoken in *years*. He might not even know she's dead."

"He knows," said Tyler. "He's just a coward."

I reached out, pulling Tyler to his feet. "The point is, sometimes we have to make our own families." I smiled. "You've always been part of mine."

Tyler reached down and grabbed a blossom, smiling as he tucked it in my hair. His green eyes were full of magic as he brushed his fingers along my cheek. Gripping his sweater in both hands, I stood on my tiptoes, pressing my lips gently against his. Tyler pulled away with a half grin, then dived back in, lifting me off my feet.

Our little tree shook in the breeze as we kissed, spilling its petals over us.

It was after midnight when we made it back to the Village. Tyler walked me back to my car, where it had sat in the hotel parking lot all day. We could take our time saying good night. Aside from the cars, the lot was deserted, with no one around to tell our secret.

"You could come up," Tyler suggested, hands in his pockets, smiling bashfully as I opened the door.

"Or, you could come in . . ." I crooked my finger, and he followed me into the back seat with a devilish grin.

Tyler, who was stubborn, arrogant, and used to getting his way, fell under a spell at my fingertips. He sat back in his seat and pulled me closer onto his lap, his soft, full lips tangled with mine. After the first taste, I wanted to devour him, to learn and master him like a new dance routine. Kissing Tyler, it was easy to believe in a future where I could have him and the music.

"What's wrong?" I asked, pulling back from his half-hearted kisses.

"Not you, you're perfect," he said, tucking my hair behind my ear. "But I started thinking about your parents, how your mom gave up everything for your dad. Maybe at the time she thought she was doing the right thing, but it was only good for him, not her. That's why I'll never put you in a position where you have to choose me over everything else. If I screw up everything else, this'll be the one thing I do right."

I held his face, smiling as he kissed my hand.

"I know I'm safe with you," I said. "We'll protect each other. Okay?"

Tyler nodded, staring back at me. "Okay."

I wrapped my arms around him, snaring his lips with an eager kiss—until yellow headlights washed over the windows.

Dread turned my blood cold as I rubbed fog from the window, peering into the night. I watched a door slam a few rows down. When I saw the owner's cold blue eyes sweep across the parking lot, I gasped, sinking back into the shadowy depths of the car.

"It's Aleksandr."

"You mean, Aleksandr Aleksandr?"

"Yes, *that* Aleksandr!" I scrambled to adjust my clothes. "None of this was smart. If he catches me here, he's gonna have questions. And he *cannot* find out about New York."

"So he finds out you went to New York for a night. What's the worst that could happen?"

I covered Tyler's lips before he could utter more blasphemy. "You don't know him like I do."

Twenty minutes later, I slid into Quinn's bed, clutching my phone. I breathed a sigh of relief when he texted me a thumbs-up. He had made it back to his penthouse safely. I held my phone to my chest.

"Your aunt called—I covered for you." Quinn's sleepy voice reached out in the dark, and her arms followed. "Did you have a good time?"

"Yeah, I did." I chewed my lip as I stared at the glow-in-the-dark stars on the ceiling. Like maybe if I looked hard enough, the answers would reveal themselves in the constellations. "Q, I think I really screwed up," I whispered. "You were right, it was reckless. I shouldn't have gone to New York."

I turned on my side to hear her smart-ass reply, but Quinn was fast asleep.

The following Monday was Tyler's first day back at school. The buzz of his sudden reappearance wasn't as overwhelming as the first time around. For one thing, we ate lunch in the cafeteria together. And during free period, while I was leading choreography with the B-Team, Tyler ran up and kissed me in the middle of the gym. The rest of his class ran past, cheering with the squad. In that moment, wrapped in his arms, all the things that had seemed big and important were suddenly small in comparison.

"Go Ravens," he said then slipped away, running backward with a grin.

I was so inspired by the kiss that I gathered the courage to plan a full-on coup. While the rest of the school was gathered in the gymnasium for assembly, the B-Team and I crowded outside the double doors. I peered through the dusty glass, waiting for Quinn's signal. When Tyler began singing "The Star-Spangled Banner," I knew the time was near.

"God, his voice makes me wanna melt," said one of the spotters, clasping his hands as he listened to Tyler.

"You and Daniela are so lucky, Aaliyah," gushed one of my flyers. "What's it like taking turns with a pop star?"

"Uh, well, we're not dating, actually."

"Then . . . what are you?"

They might as well have asked a question about quantum physics or rocket science. Before I could even contemplate the answer, the gym went dark.

Q's signal was to turn on her LED necklace.

"There's the signal!" someone said.

"Okay, guys, you know the drill." I took a deep breath. "We're going out there, and we're showing the whole school we're not just as good as the A-Team. We're better."

We threw open the doors and stormed the gym, taking our positions across from the Angels. This was supposed to be their show, but not anymore.

"What the hell do you think you're doing?" Daniela demanded.

"Taking what's mine," I said.

We struck the first pose as the music began.

"Fam, that was *wicked*!" Chinara threw her arms around me; the B-Team shot high fives as they passed. After the cheers from the performance, I knew the B-Team was finally being taken seriously.

"No hard feelings if we take your spot at nationals?"

"Are you mad? You got my crown and my homecoming date; I'm not letting you take that. You'd better leave room for me."

"Always," I promised, hooking my pinky through hers.

"I'm a feminist, so I support you—but have you ever considered that Daniela's your karma?" Chinara motioned at Daniela, who was across the gym having a heated discussion with the principal. The assembly was over, and kids were filing from the bleachers. I was standing on my tiptoes, trying in vain to see over the crowd, when a strong poke to the side nearly tipped me off balance.

Tyler grabbed my arms to keep me steady, then he tapped one of the stickers near my eyes.

"My place. Seven. Bring a bathing suit . . . or not." He flashed me his sexiest grin then caught up with Declan as he was leaving the gym.

"*Now* I get it." I turned to see Dani standing behind me, arms folded. The black-and-silver ribbons in her hair matched the pom-poms in her hands. "This isn't about proving yourself to the B-Team. It's about proving yourself to *him*."

"I don't know what you're talking about."

"All this trouble for a boy who's incapable of loving you back." Daniela cuffed my arm as she passed, smirking over her shoulder.

That night, instead of studying for my American history test, I swam laps in the heated pool on Tyler's balcony. Neon lights turned the warm, crystalline waters a relaxing shade of green, and rap music played in the background. I shouldn't have had a care in the world, floating in a penthouse in the sky. But something had followed me home from New York, something I couldn't shake, not even in the arms of a gorgeous pop star.

Tyler wrapped my legs around his waist, nuzzling my neck for attention. I traced his lips, enchanted by the pool lights reflected in his eyes, the water droplets sliding down his olive skin. If this was intoxication, no drug would ever compare.

"Would you like a distraction?" Tyler murmured, sliding his fingers through my curls. "I happen to be very good at them."

"That's the problem," I said, laughing. "I can never get anything done."

"You're welcome." Tyler turned me in circles, pulling me in where the water was deeper. Fingers in his hair, I tasted the water on his lips when we kissed, craving more.

"Is this enough for you?" I asked, draping my arms around his neck. "Are you sure you wouldn't rather be in New York? Or with your ex?"

"In New York, all I did was drink and party. And with Daniela, well, let's just say we didn't do much talking. It wasn't like with me and you." Tyler traced the strings of my bikini where they marked an X on my chest. "I don't count our time together, Aaliyah. Even if I did, it wouldn't be enough."

Tyler wrote lyrics for a living—he knew how to tell a girl what she wanted to hear. But when he looked me in the eyes so intently before he kissed me, that part was easy to ignore. We were so wrapped up in each other, we didn't notice the buzzing sound at first. I opened my eyes, immediately covering myself when I saw the drone hovering above. Tyler cursed and swam for the Super Soaker, shooting it down before it could fly away.

I didn't move the first few seconds, half expecting there to be more as Tyler tossed the toy aside and picked up the drone.

It looked like a small, dead spider in the moonlight. I wondered how long the owner had been enjoying the show, and whether he still was . . .

"Make sure it's broken," I said.

Tyler obeyed, holding it under. Leaving the drone at the bottom of the pool, he swam back to me and asked if I was okay.

I shook my head, shivering, even though the water was warm.

"Nowhere is safe," I said. "If it's not your dad or Aleksandr or the paparazzi, it'll be someone else who gets in the way."

Tyler pressed his forehead to mine. "I should have stayed in New York."

"So your mom and Emma and I could be miserable without you?" I shot back, pushing water at him.

"No." He pinned my arms to my sides so I couldn't splash him again. "So I can *protect* you, Aaliyah. I know you think there's hope for people like my dad and even for Aleksandr. But there isn't. You're just fooling yourself."

His sudden coldness felt like a betrayal. I wriggled from his grip, and Tyler waded backward, eyes flashing.

"You've always tried to see the best in everyone, Ali. Grow up. People don't change."

"Really? Then I guess that would make you a lost cause." I pushed more water in his face then swam to the other side of the pool, ignoring Tyler when he called after me. I heard him curse and strike the water as I grabbed a towel from a sun lounger and left the balcony.

Tyler's bedroom was straight out of a *Vanity Fair* spread. A large, luxurious bed shrouded by a gauzy canopy was complemented by ornate furniture with a modern Victorian aesthetic. Lola, his trusty guitar, leaned against the wall. An electric fireplace glowed, and a silver tray sat nearby with the covered remains of the beautiful candlelit dinner Tyler had ordered. The room's lights were set to dim, so the shadows of the flames jumped and flickered on the walls.

I had pulled my jeans on over my bikini and was drying my hair by the fire when Tyler walked in with a towel around his waist.

"I'm sorry about what I said earlier," he said, taking me by the hand. "I was a dick."

"Yeah, you were," I replied, loosening in his arms, even though I was still annoyed.

"I was upset, and I shouldn't have taken that out on you. Look, Ali, I didn't wanna tell you this, but Declan says some guy followed him, asking questions about you and me. He had a camera. First him, now the drone. Maybe it's connected, but maybe it's not."

"Well, was he paparazzi?"

"Maybe. Dec blew him off, but he said the guy gave him a bad vibe."

"Well, whoever he is, he can't do more damage than Aleksandr already has. I do see the good in people, Tyler, maybe more than I should. Like it or not, I *have* to believe that there's something redeemable in Aleksandr, because that's the *only* thing that stops me from running away every time I see him."

I stepped into Tyler's arms and closed my eyes, not caring if it was a lie when he promised me that everything would be okay.

Like a campfire in the dark, a week in Tyler's arms kept the night at bay. Whether we were sneaking kisses under the bleachers, studying in my room, or dancing at the studio, I savored every moment like it would never happen again. Who knew how long we had before Pete or Aleksandr found a way to ruin everything?

That Thursday after school, as Quinn and I shopped at the Village Square Mall, I spilled all the details.

"Look, Ali, the midnight swims, little adventure to the Big Apple, and teaching Tyler how to drive is super cute and all." Quinn poked a ringed finger at her mouth and retched. "But can we *puhlease* hurry up and get to the good part!" she squealed, taking an eager seat at the food court as we set our trays on a table. "He's a good kisser, isn't he? Ha! It's true! See, you're blushing! I knew it, I knew it!"

I smiled down at my tray, biting my lip as I twirled my fries in ketchup.

"Well . . . *and?*"

I shrugged. "And what?"

Quinn lowered her voice and glanced around. "Have you two . . . *y'know* . . ." She poked her finger in and out of her fist, whistling suggestively.

I shook my head, losing half my appetite and setting my cheeseburger aside.

"You turned him down?" Blue eyes wide, Quinn took an eager sip from her strawberry milkshake.

"Actually, *he* turned *me* down."

Clutching her fake pearls in mortification, Quinn said a prayer for fallen fangirls everywhere.

"Shut! Up!" I said, throwing fries as she ducked.

"Ali, he turned you *down*," she said, whisper-shouting the last part. "Aren't you, like, upset?"

At first, I had been more confused than anything.

I would never forget the night of our moonlight swim. Or the feeling of his cold, wet lips on mine as I kissed him into the pillows. I'd traveled inches of wet skin, marveling at his sculpted abs and defined chest, pushing damp waves aside for a better view of his emerald gaze. I sat up when I saw the hesitation in his eyes, kissing the freckles on his nose in concern.

"What are you thinking about?" I'd asked.

"How pretty you are, obviously." He grinned, chuckling over the soundtrack of the crackling flames. "I thought you didn't want things to move too fast."

"Yeah, *relationship*-fast. This part is just for fun . . . right?"

Tyler traded places with me, staying silent for a few moments as he traced my collarbone. "This *is* fun," he said quietly. "But that's not why I did what I did."

"What did you do?" I asked, trying not to make Tyler feel like I was jumping to conclusions.

"I saw how upset you were that night when you saw Aleksandr in the parking lot. So after you left, I followed him into the hotel . . . and I fucked him up." Tyler's jaw clenched; his eyes were hard and unforgiving. "I told him to stay away from you. I think he got the message."

"So that's how this happened," I said, running my fingers across some bruises I'd noticed on his knuckles. I sighed. "What did he do after you hit him?"

"He laughed. His mouth was bleeding, and for some reason that was *funny* to him." Tyler exhaled. "I don't care if I made it worse. He needs to know that he can't touch you, Aaliyah. I won't let him."

Being a pop star doesn't make you invincible. Taking a stand against Aleksandr was like David facing Goliath. And Tyler was doing it for me.

"Thank you for standing up for me," I'd said, drawing him close. Tyler had said nothing, just laid his head on my chest, watching the flames as I stroked his hair in silence.

And now I was at the mall with Quinn, trying to ignore the feeling that this could be my last meal before Aleksandr finally came for his revenge.

"Shit, I have to go," I said, checking my phone.

"What's up?" said Quinn, sampling my Coke.

"I don't know, but it doesn't look good. Trina never texts me in all caps. And she wants me to bring Tyler."

"Oh, shit. Well, good luck. You should probably take the fries to go—don't wanna get grounded on an empty stomach."

"Damn it, Q."

Thirty minutes later, Tyler and I sat side by side in my aunt's living room, hardly daring to breathe as we watched Trina pace back and forth, mumbling to herself.

"Um, Trina? Is—is everything okay?" asked Tyler, shooting me a nervous glance.

Trina laughed in outrage.

"*Page six*," she hissed, holding out a magazine rolled into a tube.

Tyler slowly took the magazine, unfolding a new issue of *Sugar*, a popular tabloid well-known for exploiting the lives of the rich and famous. He flipped to page six—and froze.

"*Fuck*," he said. "I—I mean, oops. Sorry."

I grabbed the magazine, staring at the picture displayed on its glossy, vivid pages. "America's Bad Boy Settles Down . . . Tyler Moore Finds the One!" Below that—a crystal-clear snapshot of a couple in front of a beautiful backdrop. The boy was on bended knee, his hands outstretched as she covered her face. I recognized the tree, the purple and white blossoms, the navy blue of the evening sky above . . .

"We were followed in New York?" I gasped. The magazine shook in my hands.

"You're getting *married*?" Trina retorted.

"Of course not! I was yawning, Tyler was bending down to tie his shoe! Aunt Trina, this is insane!"

"That's what I said when one of the doctors at the hospital showed this to me in the break room. Damn neurosurgeons . . ." Trina snatched the magazine, twisting it anxiously between her hands. "They're a menace."

"Trina, this is my fault," said Tyler. "Ali didn't have anything to do with it. Going to New York was all my idea."

Trina shook her head, walked away, then came back.

"What do you think Amelia would say if she were here?" she demanded, giving the guilt a few more seconds to eat away at us. "Tyler Andrew Moore, I don't care how famous you are now. You don't take my niece across state lines without my permission—*got that?*"

Tyler nodded, biting his lip as he lowered his gaze in shame. "Yes, ma'am."

"And as for you, Ms. Thing—"

I sat up straight, holding my breath as Trina jabbed her finger at me.

"How long did you think you could keep sneaking him into my house?"

"Hudson ratted me out?" I sat back in a huff, arms folded in annoyance.

"Well, he didn't have a choice after this," she snapped, brandishing the magazine. "Okay, sneaking boys in is one thing— but running off to *New York*?" Trina threw her hands in the air. "Honestly, what were you two *thinking*?"

Tyler and I both jumped in, but Trina knew bullshit when she heard it.

"Zip it!" She rubbed her forehead like she was getting a headache. "I just want my Cheez-Its . . ."

"I'll go get—" But Tyler sat down as soon as she peeked between her fingers. "Never mind."

"Listen, you two. You're seniors; you're almost eighteen, and Tyler has an almost unlimited income. I get it. But there have to be boundaries—and no more secrets." She inhaled, releasing her breath in a slow exhale. "Is there anything else I should know?"

"Nope!"

"Nothing. Absolutely nothing."

"Good!" Trina smiled. "You're grounded!"

"Wait, m-me too?"

"Yes, Tyler! Now go home. I don't wanna see you for two weeks—and I'm *calling your mother*!"

Sorry, I mouthed at Tyler.

"Me too." Tyler kissed my cheek, apologized to my aunt, and saw himself out.

Hands on her hips, my scowling aunt waited until he had left the living room. "Aaliyah, I am buying you birth control!"

"Auntie, please!" I wailed, covering my face in embarrassment.

"Uh, people get pregnant, Aaliyah, hello!" she said, pointing to her stomach. "It happens."

"Well, not to me," I replied, hands twisting in my lap. "We haven't gone that far."

"*Yet.*" Katrina softened, taking Tyler's seat on the couch. "But if you do, just be careful. Think about your future, Aaliyah. And his too." Trina patted my arm, then crossed the room, pausing in the doorway. "Oh, and when I say *grounded*, I mean two weeks, no going out—and no Tyler." Trina made a V with her fingers, pointing at her eyes and then mine before she left.

I grabbed one of the couch pillows and flopped back with a sigh, wondering how things could spiral so quickly.

That night, I ran a bubble bath, lit some candles, then stepped out of my clothes and sank deep into the warm water. I leaned back in the tub, closing my eyes as I imagined strong arms enveloping me from behind. My breath quickened just thinking about Tyler's hands gliding across my skin, pulling my hair back as he whispered in my ear. He slipped from behind me and called my name. But when I looked up, the eyes gazing back at me were blue, not green . . .

I sat up with a gasp. I was alone—the bubbles were just suds, and the water was lukewarm. I had fallen asleep in the tub. Hearing my phone sing from the bath mat, I scooped it up, answering Tyler's FaceTime with a cryptic smile.

Tyler was lying in bed, his arm under his head, smirking at his phone. "Thinking about me?"

"How'd you know?"

"Because I'm thinking about you." His smile faded. "I got you in a lot of trouble, didn't I?"

"Don't worry about Trina," I said. "I'm throwing her baby shower—she'll forgive me. And you too. Eventually."

"No offense, but I think Trina's the least of our worries. Especially if Aleksandr sees that spread in *Sugar*."

"Not if, when," I corrected, drawing my knees to my chest. "And if Aleksandr doesn't see it, his girlfriend will. She lives for this kinda stuff."

"Stuff?"

"You know, celebrity drama. She thinks you're cute—and is probably plotting our destruction with her boyfriend."

But Tyler wasn't in the mood to be entertained. He sat up with a heavy sigh, like there was something that needed to be said and it was weighing on him.

"What did your mom say when Trina called?" I asked. Whatever she'd said to Tyler, I knew she'd say it to me next.

"She squawked at me over the phone." His laugh was reassuring, even if it only lasted for a moment. "But it was actually kinda nice being yelled at today. Took me back to when we were kids, and our parents could still fix our problems." Tyler sat up, swinging his legs over the edge of the bed, finding it hard to look in the camera. "My mom said I put your life in danger, Ali. And she was right, I shouldn't have taken you to New York."

"Why are you and my aunt acting like I didn't have a choice? I *chose* to go with you to New York, Tyler. That was *my* decision."

"Yeah, because I asked you to go, Aaliyah." Tyler's face grew stony. "If Aleksandr retaliates for what I did, then that's on me too. This whole time, I've just been doing what's best for me. Not very good relationship material."

My heart skipped a beat then started racing. I could hardly say the words. "Tyler, are you *breaking up with me*? Over the *phone?*"

"Technically, we are face-to-face."

"Wow." I sat back in astonishment. "All that stuff you said in New York—did you even mean *any of* it?"

"You know I did." Even the performer in him couldn't hide that he was breaking. I was angry at him, but seeing Tyler struggle only made me feel worse.

"We also said we would protect each other. That's what I'm doing."

"Really, Tyler? Because it sounds like the only one you're protecting is you."

Tyler pushed his hair from his face in frustration. "Yeah, well, when fate consistently finds a way to keep us apart, the self-preservation kicks in."

"So you're just . . . giving up."

"No. This time, I'm following the rules. Trina doesn't want me to see you. And you said it yourself—we're not dating.

Remember?" There was the sound of giggles in the distance and Weezer floating in from the background as Tyler's bedroom door was opened. "Bro, this isn't the love shack! Get the fuck out!"

"Tyler, are you having a *party*?"

"Some people invited themselves over. I'm sorry, I'm not trying to be insensitive." Tyler's doorbell sounded in the silence. "I gotta go. Call me if you need anything, okay?"

Knowing I wouldn't, I didn't waste time with goodbyes. I hung up, tossing my phone aside with an angry sob. Tyler had hurt me, but the brunt of my anger was directed toward the people who said they were just taking pictures—when what they were really doing was stealing moments from other people's lives and never thinking of the consequences. And if getting punched in the face wasn't provoking enough, then finding out I had left the Village was just the incentive Aleksandr would need to punish me.

I sank beneath the water and screamed.

Seven

Dark Hearts

I avoided Tyler at school the next day, finding excuses not to sit next to him in class, turning the other way when I saw him in the hall. Seeing him laughing at his locker with his friends, I wasn't happy for me, but I was happy for him. We both needed time to focus on things other than trying to resurrect our cursed relationship. Even if being apart felt like I was drowning. I used to think walking the halls with Tyler's arm around my shoulder would be the scariest thing in the world. Now it felt like the only safe place in the storm, and I was locked out.

But I was able to keep my shit together—until Aleksandr texted me in the middle of class. Everyone else in world lit was tuned into Mr. O's discussion of *The Handmaid's Tale*, while my universe was imploding over an apple emoji.

I jumped up and grabbed my bag, mumbling something about needing to see the nurse. I rushed out of the room and didn't stop until I was underneath the stairs on the second floor. I pulled out my phone, dialing Aleksandr's number. I spoke before he could answer.

"New York was a mistake, okay? Are you really going to punish me for one night?"

I heard my heartbeat in the pause.

"Yes." It was the lack of anger in Aleksandr's voice that gave me the chills. "Unfortunately, my plans don't work without you, Aaliyah. We have to learn to rely on each other, you and I." In the short pause that followed, I heard the all too familiar beep of a heart monitor. "I am in Russia for a few weeks on family business. Enjoy your freedom—for now."

"Why? What are you going to do?"

"I'm going to take something away from you," he said matter-of-factly. "Perhaps then you will take me seriously."

"It's really amazing how you can still torture me from a million miles away. I *hate you.*"

"We all have to live with consequences, *pchelka.* Sins of the father and all that."

"Yeah, well, until then, enjoy Russia, asshole."

I could hear his smirk over the phone. "Don't disappoint me again, Aaliyah."

Aleksandr hung up. Shaky from anger and disbelief, I was still staring at my phone when I turned and walked into someone.

"Aaliyah!" Tyler grabbed my arm as I passed him.

"What do you want, Tyler?"

"Just the truth." He shrugged, one arm looped through the backpack slung on his shoulder. "Did you really mean what you said? Was New York really a mistake?"

Too much of a coward to be honest, I pulled my arm from his grasp and walked away.

Between getting ready for my upcoming midterms and the talent show, I spent the next few weeks consumed with studying and dancing. Everything in between was a blur. I had thought that finally performing my audition for the Conservatory would be a relief, but my stress doubled. I was petrified of losing my edge over the summer, showing up to college and dancing like a stage-frightened amateur. Some people had nightmares of walking into class naked. I dreamed about blanking on my routine in the middle of a performance. To prevent that from becoming a reality, I devoted myself to perfecting my schoolwork *and* my dance technique. The result was over-caffeinated, late-night study sessions and mumbling routines in my sleep. These days, I was exhausted just blinking.

At least the jokes about getting married to Tyler had slowed down, probably because people stopped seeing us together. My two weeks of punishment came and went, but the coldness between us remained, personified by the coming of winter.

One Saturday morning in October, I left the house in a rush, thanking my lucky stars for the heated seats in my car as I made my way to HVH. It was the annual career fair, the school's attempt to drill it into the students' heads that soon—very soon—the real world was coming, and we needed to be ready. I was beginning to question if that was even possible. I had seen glimpses of the real world. Some things in life you just can't prepare for.

Normally the career fairs were like ghost towns—strange groans of pain, the occasional tumbleweed rolling by. This year, the gym was packed. Every October, Madilyn picked a few performers from the studio to run the dance booth. This year, it was my turn. Running one of the more popular booths, Madilyn always came through with some famous dancer that nobody ever heard of but who could draw crowds with their demonstrations and knowledge. One "I danced backup for Britney Spears" and all eyes were on them. This year, Madilyn hadn't put anyone on the schedule, but once I reached the dance booth, I saw it wasn't necessary. The fair had just begun, and already our line was huge—and growing.

"It's her, it's her!"

"Aaliyah, over here!"

"Hey, Aaliyah, can I get your autograph?"

Everyone in the gym was looking at me. I made my way to the booth, dazed.

"Aaliyah! Good! You're here!" Madilyn and two of her dancers worked feverishly behind the table, passing out flyers and answering questions. I took the name tag she handed me, removing the sticky part and pressing it against my Perfect Form T-shirt.

Hello, my name is So Not Important.

"Uh, did I miss something?" I asked, motioning at the swelling crowd. Madilyn's mysterious smile widened as she took me by the arm, leading me off to the side.

"All of these people—they're here for you."

"What?" I laughed.

"You and Tyler, you two have *inspired* them, inspired the whole *community.* That's not just a bunch of bored high school seniors out there. Those are adults and children, fans of music— and love. And they want to dance with you. This year, *you* are the guest speaker, Aaliyah."

I heard the words and tried to compute them, but none of it made sense. I blinked.

"But, Maddie, I—I haven't done anything."

"Your videos on TikTok and Instagram are viral. And it's not just because people see you with my son. Your talent speaks for itself."

Occasionally, words failed me, and this was one of those times. I hugged Madilyn, who laughed and kissed my head.

"How is he?" I asked.

Madilyn didn't need me to clarify. "He misses you. I think he's beating himself up about New York. Is that why you two still aren't speaking?"

I let my gaze drop to the floor. "A little."

"Things between our families have always been a bit . . . complicated, to say the least. But I know you and Tyler will sort it out; you always do. Now, c'mon, your fans await." Madilyn winked then returned to the table.

I turned my back for privacy, chewing my thumb as I pulled out my phone and opened Instagram. I had turned off my notifications weeks ago, when the influx of comments and follows became overwhelming and drained my battery. My follower account had surpassed a hundred k, and I'd gained influencer status. I got offers for modeling, traveling, and advertisements, but I turned them down. Well, most of them anyway. I did do a photo shoot with Chinara, Quinn, and the B-Team, just because.

There had been one email that had felt different, so I'd called the number and spoken with an agent from New York who'd offered me representation. After talking things over with my aunt and taking some time to reflect, I'd called him back and told him I wasn't ready, but maybe I'd reach out after graduation.

"It's my senior year," I'd told him. "This might be the last time I ever have to feel . . . normal."

"I understand," he'd said in his Southern twang. "Call me when you're ready. With my help, you're going to do big things, Aaliyah."

Thinking about what he'd said, I realized that a career fair might not be a big thing, but it was a first step, and one I couldn't have done without Tyler. So I posted on Instagram—a candid shot of us, laughing, as we danced in grayscale. The photo was from an afternoon in Madilyn's studio, goofing around near the barre. In the background, the wall mirror reflected grainy images of the dancers who had stayed on task. But Tyler and I were clearer than ever.

It was one of my favorite pictures of the two of us. I knew he would get the message.

As my board hovered on the edge of the biggest bowl at the Airwalk, Quinn and Declan called out from behind, challenging me and cheering me on at the same time. I tossed them one last grin, then dropped in, bending my knees as I flew downward, collecting enough air for a simple backside kick turn up the other side. Sounds complicated, but I wasn't Tony Hawk. I could only do beginner tricks—tic-tacs, manuals, kick turns off the ramps, ollies. For me, it wasn't so much about the delivery but the experience—the wind in my hair, the world rushing by, the feeling of my feet *never* touching the ground. I would have been a happy drunk if I could've bottled that feeling.

Over time, the cement at the Airwalk had been overrun by graffiti—patterns and symbols and prose that covered the body of the park like sprawling tattoos. Shaped like a giant figure eight, the Airwalk was surrounded by a chain-link fence and orange streetlamps that drew the night moths like the park drew the restless. Skaters sailed in and out of sight, gliding along the snake run from one bowl to the next. They followed the arcs of the banked ramps, taking the snake to the next pool then flying out of that, using the pyramid for a smooth landing, gliding down the rippled sides on to the vert ramps or maybe the fun box. It was hard to keep up; not many were bold enough to try.

Those of us who were brave skated until the sun set. Quinn offered me a ride home, but I told my friends to go ahead. I would ride through town on my board, enjoying the freedom of not being grounded or stuck under Aleksandr's thumb—however long that lasted. I was cruising down the sidewalk past a popular outdoor restaurant when I spotted Tyler's dad having dinner with a beautiful girl barely old enough to drink. I stopped short as I debated crossing the street and minding my business or taking the rare opportunity to screw over Pete Moore.

I rode my board to their table, stopping so suddenly Pete's date jumped in fright. It gave me immense pleasure to watch Pete turn red, suddenly blustering.

"Hey, Dad!" Just to make it authentic, I reached out, sampling the scallops on his plate.

Pete's date frowned in confusion. "I thought you said Tyler Moore was your only kid?"

"You're right. Uh, this is just a misunderstanding, Kat—"

Her eyes widened in realization. "Wait . . . aren't you Aaliyah Preston?"

I nodded at Kat, smiling without teeth.

"But in that magazine, it said you were getting married to Tyler . . . and he's your *brother*?"

I nodded, my smile widening as Pete balled up his napkin, tossing it on the table in defeat.

"Okay, this is a little too weird for me. And I model in Hollywood. So . . ." She grabbed her Birkin, ordered Pete not to call her, and left.

"Sorry about that." I plopped into her empty seat. "I probably should have specified that Tyler is *like* my brother." I shook my head, pretending to check the menu.

Pete snatched it from my hands then lowered his voice,

glancing around the restaurant as he fumed. "You are playing a very dangerous game, Aaliyah."

"Which you started when you decided to gamble with Aleksandr's family—both literally and figuratively. *Wow*."

"Why do you think I sent my son to New York? I warned you to stay away from him!"

"And I have! For the most part." I exhaled, leaning back in my seat. "Trust me when I say, we learned our lesson about going on that trip to New York."

"And if you see him again, you'll continue to pay," Pete warned, dark eyes glinting.

"Enjoy your night alone," I replied, digging my fingers into his food before dropping my board and riding off into the sunset.

After dinner, I said good night to Trina and Hudson, pausing in the kitchen doorway to admire the two lovebirds. Trina was starting to show, and Hudson was thrilled at any chance to spoil her. The way he kissed her stomach and joked with the baby, I knew I wouldn't have to worry about my aunt while I was away at college. If I lived that long. No matter what I did, Aleksandr's timer was always ticking in the background, louder and louder as the clock wound down. He would be back from Russia any day now . . . and I would suffer the consequences. Until then, I would try to get some sleep before my math test.

My eyes closed as soon as my head hit the pillow. When my phone rang in the middle of the night, jolting me from the coma of sleep, I was so disoriented I thought it was my aunt.

"Trina . . . the baby . . . I got the keys . . ."

A laugh I was still too tired to recognize echoed down the line. "Wake up, Ali-Cat. It's me."

"I'm not asleep!" I insisted, sitting up straight, wiping the drool from my cheek. "I was washing the dishes . . ." I scratched my head, glancing at the green digital numbers displayed on my alarm clock. "At three o'clock in the morning." I yawned, loudly, as evidence. "Why are you calling at three o'clock in the morning?"

"Because there's something I have to say, and it can't wait." Tyler took a deep breath, and suddenly I was wide awake. "Aaliyah, these past few weeks have been torture without you. Every day, I wake up feeling like I lost something, and when I close my eyes at night, all I see is you. I tried parties, I tried booze, I tried *doing my fucking homework*—"

I chuckled, and Tyler laughed with me.

"There's something about you, Aaliyah Preston. I just can't get enough."

"That was so romantic, I might even be willing to forgive you."

"Good. Look out your window."

Puzzled, I got up from the bed, catching a glimpse of the wild-haired girl in the mirror. Horrified, I used my free hand to comb through my curls. At the window, I raised the lower sash, poking my head into the night air. When I saw the B-Team gathered on the front lawn, I bumped my head and nearly dropped my phone at the same time.

Everyone was in footie pajamas. Cats. Puppies. A unicorn. Lipstick kisses. Winnie-the-Pooh. A green dinosaur headed the formation. Tyler the T. Rex blew a kiss at my window. Someone pressed Play, and "The Cure" by Lady Gaga began. Tyler could have gone to the studio and rounded up more experienced dancers, but I think we both knew the flash dance would mean more coming from my friends. And they were amazing. Their hip-hop routine was funny, coordinated, and sloppy in all the right ways.

Tyler proved he could do the monastery and the moonwalk in a silly costume and still be drop-dead gorgeous. And he also proved Madilyn right.

The world could pull us apart, but the music would always bring us back together.

Tyler booked a session at a recording studio just so we could have time alone—and on the label's dime. Here, within these soundproof walls, no one would question what he was up to or dare to interrupt.

"Finally." Tyler closed the door and leaned against it, tugging on the hem of my shirt.

"Finally," I agreed, luring him in with the temptation of a kiss, then walking away with a smile as he laughed at my dirty trick.

I was genuinely interested in the limited-edition vinyl records lining the walls, but Tyler was impatient. There was something different about him as he walked me backward, undoing my half ponytail, running his fingers through the curls that framed my face. He sat me down on the edge of the soundboard, messing up the dials as he mashed his lips against mine. But he was gentle when he pushed down the straps of the tank top and covered my shoulder with butterfly kisses.

"This feels too good—have you been practicing?" I teased.

"No," he murmured, his lips against my ear. "I've been holding back." In two swift motions that made me gasp, Tyler pushed my legs open and pulled me closer.

"Do you know what a double aria is?" he asked. Nose to nose, Tyler gripped my waist as I looked into his eyes. "You're the cavatina, the first part. I get to take my time with you."

"And what's the cabaletta, the second part?" I smirked,

tracing the scar through his eyebrow. "Can I be that instead? It's faster."

"Ah, but the cabaletta is the grand finale." Tyler's smile made me shiver as he traced my lips in the shape of a heart. "It's where I ruin Aleksandr Vitali."

As part of his contract with his label (who weren't too thrilled about his hiatus in the Village), Tyler dropped a single out of the blue that hit the charts instantly. In honor of his favorite holiday, he made plans to shoot a Halloween-themed video to accompany it. The label rented an old mansion on the outskirts of the Village, and he spent a few days at dance rehearsal, preparing for the shoot.

The night before the big day, Tyler and I donned our dark sweaters and baseball caps and spent an evening at the Sapphire. The boardwalk's Halloween carnival was up and running, including our favorite rides—the haunted Hall of Mirrors and the Ferris wheel.

Tyler held me from behind as we navigated the blue-lighted maze together. Smoke puffed at our ankles, and ghastly images reflected in the mirrors as the actors did their best to scare us. Moans and screams filled the air as witches stirred bubbling cauldrons, nurses hacked at helpless patients, and prisoners reached for us through the bars of their cages. It was all fun and games until I got separated from Tyler.

Lost in the center of the maze, I rounded a corner into a tight space encircled by walls of glass. Knowing it was fruitless trying to be heard over the screams and Halloween music, I turned in a slow circle, calling Tyler's name. But it was someone else who stepped into view. I thought it was one of the actors come to scare me until I recognized the cold blue eyes and calculating grin reflected all around me. My gaze dropped to the Louisville Slugger in his hand, but before I could react, he had already taken the first swing.

I screamed and ducked, covering my head as glass showered down around me. Aleksandr struck more mirrors, raining down destruction in a symphony of chaos. The sound of his rage ringing in my ears was almost majestic, like thunder crashing in a valley of darkness. The screams from those around me mingled with the cries on the Halloween tape as people fled. But I was frozen in fear, forced to bear witness as Aleksandr stepped through the rubble, glass crunching beneath his Oxfords. There was not a wrinkle to be seen in his suit, the blond hair falling in his eyes the only sign of his exertion. He stopped short, looking down at the bat as he swung it in his hands.

"It's nice to see you again, Aaliyah."

I swallowed and took a step back. Bumping into a glass panel, I slid sideways to the edge, just to put some distance between us.

"A week ago, my company's stock was on the rise. Then your boyfriend gives an interview, says my cologne, my fashion line, my jewelry—it's not sustainable. Apparently, my brand isn't 'eco-friendly.'" Aleksandr bit his lip, smirking with rage. "Now I'm hemorrhaging points *left* and *right!*" Aleksandr took another swing. I jumped aside, falling to the ground as he smashed the mirror.

Aleksandr advanced, pointing the bat as I scuttled backward on my palms.

"Tyler cost me fifty grand, Aaliyah. I don't suppose you have that lying around?"

Eyes wide, I quickly shook my head.

"I didn't think so." Aleksandr squatted beside me, pushing the hair from his face with a sigh. "You know, my father has very high expectations. He's backed all my ventures. My company is the only thing that doesn't have his name on it." Tilting his head to the side, Aleksandr used the tip of the bat to lift my chin. "I won't let your boyfriend destroy what I've built. End this, Aaliyah." Fishing a lighter from his pocket and a cigarette from behind his ear, Aleksandr lit up and took a deep drag. He offered me a puff, but I shook my head. "The fifty thousand—I am adding it to Pete's debt."

"No, *please*—"

Aleksandr tucked my curls behind my ear. "I told you not to disappoint me again. Especially not when I'm on bereavement leave." He stood. "But don't worry, I still owe you for New York. I have a *big* surprise for you—lots of fireworks. You're really going to love it." He grinned.

Meanwhile, someone in a Ghost-Spider costume had been cowering in the corner the whole time. Aleksandr asked them which way was out, and they pointed, fingers shaking. Aleksandr, never one to forget his manners, thanked them as he walked past. I waited a few more seconds, then got up and ran the other way.

After reuniting with Tyler outside the Hall of Mirrors, we stood behind the yellow lines as police checked the maze. My gaze roamed the crowd in search of Ghost-Spider, but they were long gone. Ghost-Spider and I were the only witnesses to the damage Aleksandr had wrought, and we weren't talking . . .

Tyler put his jacket around my shoulders then bought two drinks and two tickets to the Ferris wheel. After the warmth of hot chocolate and a dose of his slow kisses, I eventually relaxed in his arms.

As we rose high in the air, safe inside our little cabin, I gazed beyond the bright orange lights of the Ferris wheel to the white and yellow lights of the town. Above, the sky was black as ink, but still not as dark as Aleksandr Vitali's heart.

"We could leave," said Tyler casually, one arm thrown along the back of the seat.

I stared at Tyler. "What?"

"We don't have to stay, Aaliyah—we don't have to play Aleksandr's game. Your aunt said it—we're almost eighteen, and I have money. We can go anywhere. I can take care of you."

"I don't *want* you to take care of me—I want to *graduate*. I'm supposed to dance at Trina's wedding. And the baby is due in May. I can't just *leave*." I pulled away from Tyler, turning my gaze toward the night. But I softened when I felt his arm slide around me. He guided my gaze back to his, kissing me as he held my face in his hand.

"I'm sorry I keep trying to save you. Bad habit." Tyler smiled. I was still wearing his leather jacket when he reached in one of the pockets. "But since we aren't leaving for a while . . ." He pulled out the key to his apartment and dropped it in my hand.

"This is a big step," I said. "Are you sure?"

"The only thing I'm sure about is you. Besides, I need someone to clean up after me."

I pushed his shoulder, then curled my hand around the key, holding it close as Tyler kissed my cheek.

"Will you come to the shoot tomorrow? Bring your girlfriends, we'll hang out at the after-party."

"You just want to keep an eye on me," I teased.

"I want to do so much more than that," he said, pulling me close.

Ghost-Spider was waiting when I arrived home. Maskless, Tyler's sister, Emma, was sitting on my doorstep, still in her costume. It was late—I was minutes away from my midnight curfew. But Emma was only fifteen—I wondered if Madilyn knew where she was. Though I had seen Tyler's little sister less and less over the years, every reunion was like we had hung out just yesterday. Like her older brother, Emma had a fondness for sarcasm and rule-breaking, but somewhere along the line, she had traded music for sports.

She tucked her short brown hair behind her ear and waved.

"Shit," I said, waving back and cutting the engine.

"Ali Ali oxen free," she said, just the way she used to. I could tell by the way she stood, nervously rubbing her hands, that Emma was still rattled from the Hall of Mirrors.

"Hey, Em." I drew her into a warm, tight hug. "I had no idea that was you. I am so sorry you saw that tonight. You must have been so scared—"

"I was," she said, stepping back. "But not for me, for you. I—I'm a coward—I just stood there while he did that . . ."

I sighed. "Em, please, there was nothing you could have done, okay? If Aleksandr had wanted to hurt me, he would have."

"Aleksandr . . . so that's his name." She stared down at her black Converse. "Why did he do that, Ali? What does he want from you?"

Hands in the pockets of Tyler's leather jacket, I glanced up the street and shrugged. At first, I'd thought it was just about the money. Now I wondered if Aleksandr didn't have other motives for keeping me close.

"Be honest with me, okay? I'm not that dorky little kid you used to babysit. I want the truth, Aaliyah—why was Aleksandr talking about my dad like he owes him money?"

"Because he does, Em. Your dad owes Aleksandr a *lot* of money."

"Okay. So why doesn't Tyler just pay it?"

"His manager put a lock on his income. Astrid's soul would leave her body before she let Tyler pay off Aleksandr. This is something your dad has to fix."

"Well, he's kind of shitty at fixing things, so . . ."

When Emma rubbed her arms, I took her brother's jacket and draped it over her shoulders.

"I thought things would get better after Mom divorced him, but . . ." Emma shook her head. "I know he's a bad person. He scares my mom. My brother doesn't say it, but I know he's scared too, scared that he'll be like him one day."

"He won't," I said firmly. "Your brother is nothing like your dad." I placed my hand on her shoulder. "Em, I know it's not fair for me to ask you this, but I'm gonna do it anyway: please don't tell anyone about this, okay? It's safer for you if everyone thinks you don't know. And Tyler will lose his shit if he finds out you were in the Hall of Mirrors."

"I know." Emma grinned. "Oh, by the way—Aleksandr dropped something." Emma pulled a key from the neck of her costume and tossed it. "It looks just like the one Tyler has."

"It's from La Maison," I said slowly, examining the key. "Room 837."

Aleksandr's room key.

Feeling like I had a bomb in my hand, I threw all the keys back to Emma. "Get in the car—hold on to that key for me," I said, trotting backward. "I'm just gonna let Trina know I'm taking you home."

Emma called out to me as she got in the car, rolling down the passenger window.

"I'm sorry about my dad, Aaliyah. You don't deserve to be caught up in my family's mess. We should use the key—teach Aleksandr a lesson."

"Okay, when I get back, we are going to have a nice long conversation about why that can *never* happen."

But when I returned, it was to an empty driveway. Emma was gone, and so was my car.

Eight

The Nightmare

It had started to rain when my Uber arrived. I had to wait down the block in case Trina happened to look out the window. She would have questions if I didn't have my car—questions I couldn't afford to answer. By the time I made it inside La Maison, I was drenched, running past the gilded front desk and into the elevator. Tyler finally called me back as I was pushing the button to the eighth floor.

"I'm here," he said. "I'm walking down the hall—you said room eight-thirty-seven, right?" His words came out in a rush—he was moving fast.

"Yeah, I'm pretty sure that was it," I said, breathless with panic. What if Aleksandr was in the apartment when Emma arrived? What would he do? What would *she* do?

"Ali, go up to the penthouse. I left the door cracked—please, wait for me in the apartment, okay?"

"What? Tyler, no! If Emma's in there with him—"

"Then I can't risk you getting hurt too," he said. "I'm going to get my sister—now wait for me." Then Tyler hung up so I couldn't argue.

Reluctantly, but knowing he was right, I pushed the button for Tyler's floor.

I let myself into Tyler's apartment then spent the next few minutes watching the clock as I paced around the living room. When I heard the alarm beep, signaling the front door had opened, I rushed into the entrance hall to see Tyler walk in after Emma. She was holding Aleksandr's bat, wielding it like a trophy.

"Thank god," I said, throwing my arms around Emma, who laughed and hugged me back.

"Wait in the living room, Smalls." Tyler motioned with his head, and I followed him outside the front door into the corridor. "I'm sorry I didn't answer sooner—I was in the shower. How'd you know she was going to Aleksandr's apartment?"

"She had my car and the key. I just did the math."

Tyler rubbed my shoulder. "You're always looking out for my family. I don't know what we'd do without you."

I don't know why I had a sinking feeling when Tyler hugged me.

"So, uh, tell me what happened," I said after pulling away awkwardly.

Tyler recovered from his disappointment, leaning against the wall as he spoke.

"Em left the door open, so when I get to his apartment, I just walked right in. He's got a nice place—well, *had* a nice place."

I gasped, covering my mouth with my hand. "She didn't!"

"Ali, she found his bat and *trashed* the place. The stereo system, the mirrors, the coffee table, the entertainment stand. I mean, Jesus, Aaliyah, I saw a flat-screen *in pieces* on the floor."

Tyler buried his face in his hands. "We're lucky he wasn't there—this would have been *so* much worse. He could call the cops, Aaliyah. If he finds out we're involved, Emma could be in some serious shit."

"Knowing Aleksandr, he probably has cameras all over the place—he's definitely gonna know," I said, folding my arms. "But he won't call the cops. He'll just get even." Which was most definitely worse.

"I don't get it, Aaliyah—what was she was *thinking*?"

"Why don't you ask her?" I replied gently, leading Tyler back to the living room.

Emma was sitting on the couch, scrolling nonchalantly through her phone when Tyler snatched it from her hands.

"Hey, give that back!"

"Zip it! Do you have any idea what you've done, Emma?"

Emma rolled her eyes.

"This isn't some high-school prank, okay? You stole Aaliyah's car, and you *destroyed* someone's apartment."

"Look, Aaliyah, I'm sorry I took your car—but I have my permit! I'm a good driver!"

"Yeah, and you're pretty good at swinging a bat," said Tyler, not the least bit impressed. "Seriously, Em, what do you have to say for yourself?"

"*No one* messes with my family."

Tyler stared at me, taken aback. I shrugged—who could argue with that?

Tyler sighed then took a seat next to his sister. "Look, Em, I know it was scary, watching Aleksandr go at Aaliyah like that. So if destroying his place was your version of justice . . . I get it. But you can't go off the rails like that. You have to *think*."

"I would do it again." Emma's pretty face hardened. "Give me that bat, and I'll go back and finish the job. Aleksandr's *not* a good person. Neither is Dad—this is *his* fault. So why are you yelling at *me*?"

"He's not yelling at you, Em. Tyler cares about you."

"And I care about you, Aaliyah. You're part of this family—I would have done the same thing for Tyler. Aleksandr deserved it. I don't regret what I did, and I don't care if I get punished. So go ahead, tell Mom and Dad."

"Are you kidding?" Tyler stood up in disbelief. "Tonight does not leave this room *ever*."

Emma smirked.

"I love you, punk. I'll call Mom and tell her you're spending the night. Go to bed."

"But—"

"Bed!"

Emma flipped the double bird at her brother but obeyed, once more rolling her eyes as she stalked from the room.

Tyler sank back into the couch, grabbing his head in his hands. "Ali . . . I don't know what the fuck I'm gonna do."

"Don't be too hard on her," I said, giving his leg a nudge. "She's just like you. She saw something messed up, and she decided to do something about it. Dude, Emma's a badass."

Emma was tough as nails. Maybe I could be more like her when I grew up.

Tyler groaned. "Ali, *please*, do *not* encourage her."

I winked. "It's late—and you have a big day tomorrow," I said, scooping my keys from the dish on the coffee table.

Tyler walked me to the door, his fingers lingering on the doorknob. "Let me walk you to your car."

I shook my head. "Stay with Emma. I'll be fine."

"*Are* you fine?" His vivid green eyes studied mine, searching for chinks in the armor.

"No." I shook my head. Some wounds are so deep you can

fall in them forever. "But I will be okay. Once we can finally put all of this behind us."

"We will." My skin broke out in goosebumps as Tyler placed his hand on the back of my neck. "I could have lost you and Emma. Tonight really helped me put my feelings in perspective." Tyler cupped my face in his hand, not afraid to charm me in the middle of the hall. "I don't ever wanna lose you, Aaliyah."

"Oh my god, just shut up and kiss her already!"

"Damn it, Emma!"

I grinned. "Well, she has a point."

Tyler used the belt loops on my jeans to reel me in. "Now, where were we?"

When it came to hooking up their artists, Tyler's label pulled out all the stops, as I found out when they rented a place for his music video. I had actual anxiety the next day when my friends and I pulled up outside the property's gates. They stood through the roof of the Jeep and hung out the sides to get a better view of the mansion on the hill. Whether by design or sheer luck, the dark, stormy clouds overhead made it the perfect backdrop for a Halloween shoot.

Jared, a junior on the B-Team, whistled from the front seat.

"Baby, look at this *crowd* . . ." He popped a sucker from his mouth, pushing short, rose-gold locks from his curious brown eyes for a better view. "Is it my birthday or *what*?"

Q navigated to a clear spot on the property's extended drive, where a sign pointed to the parking area for staff and VIP only. Dozens of fans were gathered outside the gates, where security monitored who came and went.

"This is *brilliant*," said Chinara, flashing her dimpled grin as we all left the Jeep. "Thanks again for inviting us to the after-party. Mum's wrong—I know a posh place when I see it, and I guarantee they serve *proper* shrimp cocktail."

"A woman after my own heart," gushed Quinn, sliding her arm around Chinara's shoulders.

My friends and I pushed our way forward, ducking the signs and posters waving in the air. We reached the gate, and one of the guards on our side tipped his hat at me.

"Miss Preston, welcome. Mr. Moore is expecting you."

The other guards kept the crowd at bay as the gate began to swing open.

"Aaliyah!" An out-of-breath, rumpled Daniela reached from the chaos, flanked by her equally winded friends, Sonam and Piper. They looked like they'd been fighting the crowd for a hot minute. "Aaliyah, would you *please* tell these *morons* at the gate to let us through? They don't know who I am!"

"And neither do we!" Quinn laughed and grabbed my arm, ferrying me along. I had to admit, it was satisfying, watching the gates close in front of Daniela's angry face.

Like Dr. Jekyll and Mr. Hyde, the mansion's mazelike interior was divided. While most of the manor retained its nineteenth-century style, pockets of the place had been transformed into an elaborate gothic labyrinth with Hollywood sets. A ballroom had been turned into a graveyard, there was a mad scientist's laboratory, and I saw a hallway lined with gory portraits and suits of armor that trembled when you walked past. Red velvet ropes cordoned off most rooms and hallways, a polite request to refrain from wandering through the rest of the mansion. The tour ended in a huge room, where the dancers and the crew gathered between sets, unwinding with music, studio chairs, and tables of fancy refreshments. The water alone was a mortgage payment.

"Bruv, what did I say—*what did I say!*" Chinara joined Quinn, worshipping one of several overflowing towers of shrimp.

"Miss Preston?"

A young woman handed me a long-stemmed rose with a smile. She wore a tailored suit and cardigan, her major accessories a clipboard and AirPods.

"Hi, I'm Valentine. Tyler's in hair and makeup. They've got two more scenes, a few quick shots, and then production will wrap."

"Wow. That's so fast."

"Tyler's a G. He's been at it since five a.m. with zero sleep, and yet I've *never* seen him this focused. Something's clearly inspired him . . ."

I glanced away, my face growing warm under her knowing grin. I felt more like a dartboard than someone's muse. Last night, Aleksandr proved I couldn't protect myself. Apparently, I inspired others to do their worst.

"You're a dancer."

"Yeah." I nodded.

"You're a quick study, according to your TikToks—and we always have room for more dancers . . ."

"Uh, well, y'see, I—"

"Aaliyah—do you mind if I call you Aaliyah—having you in the video would give you a lot of publicity—*not* that you need it," said Valentine with an airy laugh. "But it will give you a career boost, if you're interested in Hollywood or New York."

I blanched. In my heart, New York would always translate to Tyler.

"I'm not looking for a career boost," I said, glancing over my shoulder at my friends devouring the buffet. "But my friends are dancers too . . ."

My friends were whisked to hair and makeup, then fitted for wardrobe. Everything was so efficient and fast-paced that I knew they were in the hands of professionals. They got to dress up like dead cheerleaders, and after a quick practice session, they joined Tyler in the cemetery set. Sometimes I felt awkward standing alone—out of place and in the way at the same time— so I did my best not to be a distraction from the sidelines, watching my friends nail a flawless hip-hop routine. Lightning jumped in the background and fog rolled across their ankles as they danced for their lives between the headstones. Even though I wasn't part of the action, it was enough to see my friends having fun—and Tyler in his natural element, doing the things he loved.

It was early evening when the director wrapped the shoot. I'll never forget the way the crew and dancers clapped, popping bottles in celebration. It was magical, watching Tyler laugh under the falling spray. Music was part of him; it was in his DNA. It was the glue holding him together. He could never do anything else.

"Admit it." Quinn smirked, still dressed like a dead cheerleader as she balanced her arm on my shoulder. "You are completely, undeniably, one hundred percent in love with Tyler Moore."

I sighed. "Take me away, officer."

☆ ☆ ☆

Aside from tanking Aleksandr's stocks, throwing a party in a mansion, on his label's dime, was Tyler's biggest flex yet. The hundred-dollar bottles of champagne were "for the crew," but everyone turned their backs as Tyler and his friends celebrated. Security relaxed at the gate but confiscated cell phones and required NDAs from the guests. For one night, I decided to forget about Aleksandr and enjoy my first taste of Hollywood.

The food, drinks, and dancing never stopped. Camped out in an elegant marble bathroom, Quinn and I filled our water bottles with champagne.

"Cheers," we said, linking arms to take our first sip.

"I had *sex* with *Declan*," she said suddenly.

"You and Declan have been pretty tight lately," I said with a grin.

"Uh-huh." The color rose in Quinn's cheeks as she studied her water bottle.

"You had sex with Declan," I gloated, perhaps a little too loudly because she quickly covered my mouth.

"Yes, I had sex with Declan," she said solemnly. "And it was totally wicked!" she crowed, slapping double high fives. "He asked to come with me after we graduate. *And* . . ." Suddenly nervous, Quinn flapped her arm as she took a sip of champagne. "I said *yes*! He's coming to Vegas with me after graduation! Is that totally out there?"

"Out there is picking a fight with a gangster and thinking you can win." I tapped Quinn's water bottle with mine. "This is normal in comparison. You and Dec are really good together, Q. If the boy wants to follow you, don't stop him."

"Kinda hard to listen to someone who doesn't take their own advice," she replied with a crafty grin. "Tyler took on Aleksandr for you. He came back *for you*, Aaliyah. For a self-absorbed pop star, that's actually pretty selfless."

We fist-bumped, then I grabbed my friend and held on, hugging like I'd never let go. One day soon, after graduation, Quinn would head south and I would head north, and we would go our separate ways. But at least she would have Declan, and she'd be far away from the Village.

I had to admit, even without the Halloween sets and party decorations, the mansion was extra creepy at night. All I wanted to do was find Tyler, kiss the freckles on his nose, and tell him how I really felt. I was tired of spending all my time waiting for the other shoe to drop instead of enjoying every second that it didn't.

I had asked Declan if he'd seen Tyler, and he'd told me to check the hallway with the creepy portraits. If only I didn't have to cross the equally creepy graveyard set to get there . . .

Humming a song I'd heard on the radio, I fished a stick of gum from my pocket. I had nearly reached the end of the cemetery when Tyler finally texted back. I pulled out my phone and skimmed his message with an ugly curse. He was in the kitchen, which was in the complete opposite direction.

"Of *course*," I grumbled, turning on the heels of my ankle boots. I glanced up from my phone, did a double take, and halted. The world swayed like the sea as tunnel vision took over. My fingers went numb, and I was only vaguely aware of my phone tumbling away, lost in the swirling mist. As the world around him shrank to a pinhole, a figure appeared in front of me, growing tall as a giant. He was dressed in black jeans and a black hoodie, wearing a Halloween mask of Tyler's face.

My mouth went dry as the person entered the graveyard, crossing through the gravestones with slow, determined steps. I flinched, covering my ears as the ringing sound of shattered mirrors echoed in my head. Maybe it was just a dumb Halloween prank, or maybe it was Aleksandr beneath the mask—or someone else. But I didn't care. I was tired of being messed with.

"Fuck this." I scurried into the darkness of the hallway, where between the gory portraits was a door nailed shut with boards.

I returned to the cemetery. The person stopped in his tracks when I emerged from the darkness carrying a two-by-four.

"No more running," I said, but that's exactly what he did.

I was hiding in the closet when Tyler walked into the foyer. He was looking at his phone, a smile on his face as he sent me another flirty text.

The sound of him yelling "Oh, shit" when I grabbed his arm was satisfying as I pulled him into the darkness.

"Shh, it's me." I giggled, shrieking with laughter when Tyler tickled me in retaliation, driving me backward through a sea of forgotten, moth-eaten jackets and up against the wall.

"What the hell are you doing, Aaliyah?"

"I don't know." I smiled, running my fingers through his hair, imagining the color of the eyes that scanned me in the dark. "But I like it," I said, tracing his lips before I kissed him.

Tyler's video dropped just in time for Halloween, and for once, it wasn't about me. I was more than happy watching Quinn, Chinara, and Jared eat up the spotlight. There was only one person bitter enough to rain on the parade. The queen bee was in danger of losing her crown, and she never backed down from a fight.

Halloween afternoon, I was on my way to calculus when Tyler popped up. I could tell by his face he was already upset, but I couldn't stop the giggle that escaped my lips.

"What are you wearing?" I sagged against a bank of lockers, my stomach cramping as I laughed harder.

It looked like his track suit had been in the dryer too long—the sleeves barely came past his elbows, and the pants reached just below his knees. I wasn't the only one laughing and pointing. Cameras were already swiveling in our direction.

Apparently, Daniela had surprised Tyler in the locker room while he was taking a shower. When he'd turned down her advances, she'd left—taking his clothes with her. Tyler had had to break into Coach Radley's office, naked, just to find something to wear.

After the last bell, I caught up with Daniela in the parking lot just as she was opening the door to her keyless Chevrolet Malibu.

"Dani, I need you to stop."

"Stop *what*?" She rolled her eyes.

"Throwing yourself at Tyler. It's embarrassing."

"Why? Are you worried I'm going to steal him away from you, Aaliyah? Because I dated him first, remember?" With every word, she'd gotten closer and closer, until we were inches apart. "Why don't you ask him where he spent his first night back from New York?"

"Fuck you, Dani."

"That's what I thought," she said, laughing as she sauntered back to her car.

Tyler knew something was up when he followed me into Trina's kitchen after school. He hopped on the island, plucking an apple from the fruit bowl, peeling off the sticker and putting it on his forehead.

"What's wrong, Ali-Cat?"

"We're almost out of almond milk, but it looks like we still have enough jelly for the PB&Js . . . and that's not what you meant, was it?"

Tyler shook his head.

I would die before I revealed my jealousy over his past relationship with his ex. And it seemed so petty compared to everything else going on.

"What do you want me to say, Tyler? I mean, I wish all we had to deal with is your ex-girlfriend stealing your clothes. But the truth is, we're all living under Aleksandr's shadow. It feels like I'm just waiting for him to pull the rug from under my feet."

Everything could come crashing down at any moment.

"So?" Tyler waited, as if I actually had a solution to the problem.

"So, I am going to make myself a peanut butter and jelly sandwich with a nice, cold glass of almond milk, and . . ." I shrugged.

"Wait for the inevitable?"

"Bingo," I said, removing the bread from the pantry.

"Or . . ." Tyler hopped off the counter and swept me into his arms. "We can skip the Halloween parties and the trick-or-treating this year and just make the night about us—you and me."

"Just you and me?" I smiled, lower lip between my teeth as I looped his chain around my finger.

"Me and you." He tapped my nose, but the playful smile disappeared as he gathered my hands. "What happened to you at the Hall of Mirrors is on me—I'm *sorry*, Aaliyah. I got Aleksandr riled up, and he took it out on you. And then someone tried to scare you wearing my stupid face. I'm kind of over Halloween."

"Well, lucky for you, I'm not over your stupid face." I smiled, peeling the sticker from his forehead. "I have an idea."

Tyler and I stayed for dinner then said good night to Trina and Hudson on the doorstep. Hudson was dressed as Beetlejuice, and his fiancé was Lydia Deetz, wearing the iconic red wedding dress.

"Have a wonderful time, my loves." Aunt Trina balanced a large bowl of candy as she hugged us both. "Don't do anything I wouldn't do."

Hudson grinned. "Or anything we would do, for that matter."

They were passing out candy to the evening's first trick-or-treaters when we left. As Tyler slid his arm around my shoulder, I took one last look at my aunt and her fiancé. The soon-to-be parents looked so happy; it was hard to imagine anything could ever get in the way of that. Even Aleksandr would have a hard time. Tonight, we were all invincible.

Tyler's green eyes lit with surprise as we pulled into the local drive-in theater.

"They're showing old black-and-white horror flicks all night." I smiled and cut the engine. "But if this is too lame—"

Tyler silenced me with a kiss. "It's never boring when I'm with you. And sometimes . . ." Tyler slid closer, his fingers brushing my cheek. In the dark, his teeth were as white as the moon outside the window. "It's dangerous."

He kissed me again and didn't stop until the movie had started and the windows were fogging up.

"I'll get the popcorn," I said, peeling myself away like Velcro before the whole night slipped by in his arms.

"Hurry back," said Tyler breathlessly, his sly smile my last image as I closed the door behind me.

I found my way to the drive-in's outdoor counter and gave the menu on the wall a quick perusal.

"May I have two large popcorns, two boxes of Swedish Fish, and two large Cokes—oh, and extra butter on the popcorn, please?" I passed over the money and stood off to the side, waiting on my order. Arms loaded with drinks and snacks, I turned, nearly losing everything when I bumped into the person standing behind me.

"Extra butter is a silent killer, you know." Aleksandr steadied the snacks before they tumbled away.

"No," I said, shaking my head. "No, I just wanted one night—*one night*—"

"Before me, you must have thought you were untouchable," he said, tucking stray curls behind my ear with a delicate hand.

My breath tangled in my throat, choking the words I wanted to say, compelling me to silence.

"Your little world was so narrow. Has it opened up yet?"

I was shaking so hard the ice rattled in the cups. "W-was that you in the mask at the mansion? Did you come back that night to teach me another lesson?"

"I don't wear masks, Aaliyah." I swallowed, blinking hard when Aleksandr stepped closer. "I took mine off a long time ago."

"Then why are you here?" I demanded. "What do you *want* from me?"

"What do I want? I want you to *suffer* because that is the only way you will ever be strong."

"Strong enough for what?" I asked.

"You and your little friends made quite the mess in my apartment. I was wondering when you'd fight back." Did my eyes deceive me, or was that a twinkle in Aleksandr's wicked blue gaze? "Enjoy the fireworks, *pchelka*." Aleksandr snagged one of the bags of popcorn, munching as he walked away.

"*Strong enough for what?*" I repeated, but Aleksandr's only answer was a wry smile over his shoulder.

When I returned, Tyler was too distracted by the snacks to notice how out of it I was.

"You just missed it," said Tyler, sucking on the straw of his drink. "The bad guy chased the maiden into the cornfield—then she turned into a vampire and bit his head off. Long story short—it was awesome." He threw his head back, devouring a handful of popcorn, pausing when he finally noticed my face. "What's wrong?"

"Nothing." I brightened, forcing my lips into a smile. "They forgot the butter."

When Tyler hesitated like he didn't believe me, I pressed my lips to his, enjoying a salty kiss.

"She bit his head off?" I asked, leaning back in the seat, scooping up some popcorn. "I like her already."

The movie ended with fireworks. I watched them through the windshield as Tyler kissed my neck. His lips on my skin were the only reprieve from the nightmare unfolding around me. Aleksandr's signal was terrifying and beautiful . . .

The next morning, when I came downstairs for breakfast, I saw Trina sitting at the kitchen table. Hudson was standing behind her, rubbing her shoulders. Silent tears rolled down Trina's face, splashing the letter in her hands.

"Trina? What is it? What happened?"

She wiped her face and tried to smile. "To be honest, Hudson and I were considering moving in the future—to make room for the baby. But it looks like someone made the decision for us. We've lost the house."

Nine

The Fallen Angel

I banged on Aleksandr's door, waited a few seconds, then banged again.

"Aaliyah, I *really really really* don't think we should be here!" said Quinn, wringing her hands as she paced up and down the hallway.

"Quinn, he bought out an entire neighborhood just to take my aunt's house. I'm not going *anywhere* until he gives it back!" This time I banged harder.

"Okay, well, you might wanna consider knocking a little more quietly, before someone calls security. Actually, y'know what? On second thought, keep banging."

I still had Aleksandr's hotel key. I fished it from my pocket and stuck it in the lock, hoping it worked. I was so angry that I didn't care if it was good luck or bad luck when the door swung open, inviting me into the darkness.

"Just stay behind me," I said. Quinn took my hand, and I led the way . . .

Whatever mess Emma had left in Aleksandr's luxury hotel suite was long gone, along with him and his personal belongings.

I searched the suite, but the minute I stepped in the living room, I knew he wasn't there. All that he had left behind was a single piece of paper on the floor. There were no words, just a winking smiley face that I knew was meant for me. Growling in rage, I crumpled the paper in a ball and tossed it to the floor.

By the time I climbed back in the passenger's side of Quinn's Jeep, we were both cold and wet from the rain. It was November now, snowing here and there. The sea was gray, and the trees were bare. Without anything green, the Village was in a state of decay, kind of like my life.

Falling tears mixed with the rain. Quinn pushed damp strings of hair from my face and hugged me.

"It won't be like this forever, kiddo," Quinn promised, squeezing tight. "We'll graduate, and we'll leave this cursed fucking town, and we'll never look back."

"I don't get it, Q." I sniffed, wiping my face. "It's like he's barely interested in the money anymore . . . like he wants something else."

"I don't think it was ever really about the money, Ali. I think Aleksandr wants *you*." Quinn straightened and cranked the engine, throwing the Jeep in reverse. "We just have to figure out why."

But it might be a long time before we got answers, and we certainly weren't getting any from Aleksandr, who ignored all my messages. The best thing I could do was be there for my aunt, who had less than a year to have a baby and find a new home.

☆ ☆ ☆

"It's not the end of the world," Trina assured me one night over dinner. "By the time the due date comes, we'll already be in our new house. The chaos will be long gone by the time he's here."

"*He?*" I asked, grinning over my plate of steak and potatoes. "You weren't supposed to find out until *after* the baby shower! Hudson, how could you let it slip?"

"*Lo siento.*" He shrugged, taking an innocent bite of asparagus. "She dragged it out of me."

"No secrets in this house." Trina was pretty proud of herself. If only she knew . . .

Hosting Trina's baby shower was the distraction we all needed. Tyler and my friends came together to decorate one of the small ballrooms at La Maison. With their help, I strung green, gold, and white balloons with matching streamers and sprinkled confetti on green cloth-covered tables. Hudson ordered a special cake with a baby bear topper and supplied me with Trina's address book so I could invite her closest friends and colleagues. I watched my beautiful aunt spend an afternoon being cherished by the ones she loved, and I was grateful that Aleksandr had taken only the house and not her.

"I could buy Trina a house," said Tyler. We were standing off to the side, drinking champagne disguised as sparkling grape juice, watching Trina laugh as her drunk, blindfolded friends tried to put diapers on fake babies. "Consider it a baby-slash-wedding gift."

"Why would you do that?" I asked, continuously awed by his generosity.

"Why wouldn't I? I mean, isn't that the kinda stuff you do for the ones you love?"

Maybe it was the champagne or the sparkly rose-gold mini-dress I was wearing, but this was the closest Tyler had ever come to saying "I love you."

"You're right." I smiled, running my fingers along the tee beneath his color-block shirt. "Thank you for offering, but I think Hudson's actually looking forward to buying Trina a house."

"I get it. He wants to take care of her. Like I wanna take care of you."

In a weird way, all Aleksandr had really succeeded in doing was bring everyone closer. I doubted this was his version of strength, but during moments like these, twirling under bright chandeliers, dancing in arms that held me close, I was unbreakable.

The fun was over when I saw Eric hovering by the cake table, still in his jersey. Tonight was a home game. The A-Team was cheering, but Chinara, Quinn, and the B-Team were by my side in honor of Trina. I hadn't thought twice about skipping the game for the shower, and I'd kept the guest list narrow for a reason.

I asked Tyler to hang back, approaching my ex with growing concern.

"Eric? What are you doing here? Please tell me you didn't drive." The Ravens had lost to the Tigers, so maybe that's why he smelled like beer and looked so disheveled.

"I—I have to talk to you, Aaliyah."

"Okay, well, now's not really the time. It's my aunt's baby shower."

"It's important, okay?" Eric grabbed my arm to stop me from leaving. "Damn it, Aaliyah, I can't concentrate—I cost us the game tonight. I missed shots checking for you in the stands. Please, Aaliyah, just tell me what's going on."

"Eric, let go."

"Yeah, *let go*," said Tyler, shoving Eric back. "Don't touch her again," he warned.

"You think you're real tough, huh, pretty boy?" Brown eyes narrow, Eric stepped up to Tyler with an ugly sneer. "The whole town's been messed up since you got here. You're probably the reason Aaliyah was attacked in the first place—*get off me.*"

"Attacked?" I dived between Tyler and Eric, arms outstretched. "Eric, what are you talking about?"

"That night—at the Hall of Mirrors—I was there." Beneath the anger on Eric's face was regret. "I saw everything, Aaliyah. I haven't slept since."

"Wait . . . you were *there*?" I was stunned at the thought of Eric leaving me to face Aleksandr alone. Eric wasn't some scared fifteen-year-old girl. He didn't have to be a hero, but he could have done *something*.

"Are you *kidding* me?" This time, there was no holding Tyler back when he stepped around me. "You didn't help her? You just watched? As that maniac terrorized her? Congratulations on peaking in high school, you *fucking* coward!"

Eric shoved Tyler, who fell against a nearby table. Underneath the upbeat pop tunes wafting through the speakers, the sounds of chaos were spreading. Tyler charged past me and tackled Eric, the two of them wrestling their way right into the cake stand. I watched in horror as my aunt's three-tiered strawberry champagne cake went flying—right into my face. I heard the gasps as I reached up, wiping a layer of frosting from my eyes.

My aunt, mortified, pinched the bridge of her nose while Hudson fanned her, desperately, with a magazine.

"Hudson, I'm really, really sorry for ruining the party," I said for the thousandth time. We stood in the evening air at the top of the steps leading into La Maison. "I know she was looking forward to this."

"*Sí*, she was," he replied, removing a glob of icing from my stringy, crunchy curls. "I just hope tonight wasn't about more than two boys fighting over a pretty girl."

"It wasn't," I said, crossing my fingers behind my back.

"Good. That I can live with." Hudson grinned, patting my arm in sympathy, then gingerly wiped the cake from his hand. "Don't worry about all that stuff she said before. She's not actually disowning you or Tyler. She's just a little stressed. Having a baby—it is much harder than it looks. She's going to catch up on her rest—I'll take her back to my apartment tonight. She'll feel better by the morning."

"Thanks, Hudson."

He kissed the top of my head and said good night, then met Trina at the bottom of the steps, sliding his jacket over her shoulders. My aunt turned and waved one last time before Hudson helped her into the passenger seat of his truck.

I turned. Tyler waited for me in front of the hotel's golden revolving doors. When he took me in his arms, he didn't care that I was still covered in cake. I closed my eyes as we swayed back and forth.

"Do you think I'm still invited to the wedding?" Tyler asked.

"Oh, we're *definitely* off the guest list," I replied, then proceeded to cover him in frosting.

☆ ☆ ☆

Eric attempted to apologize for ruining the baby shower, but after a few days of being iced out, he got the hint that I wasn't interested. I had other things to focus on, like school and prepping for the talent show. With the competition just around the corner, Quinn and I began practicing every day. I asked Tyler not to drop by the studio during our practice sessions—it gave us an edge, and I didn't think that was fair.

Quinn and I were at the mall one cold afternoon, buying accessories for our costumes, when I happened to pass the phone store. Noticing who was inside, I paused and told Quinn I'd catch up at the food court.

"Don't cause trouble!" ordered Quinn, chewing her gum with a vengeance as she pointed her gold-painted nail at me.

"I'm a Libra," I said, popping my shades in place as I walked backward, bags in hand.

The bell rang, jingling overhead as I entered the store. Pete was standing at the counter, waiting as the clerk bagged up his purchase.

"Enjoy your new prepaid phone, Mr. Moore."

Just who was Pete Moore talking to that he needed to cover his tracks with a burner cell?

Tyler's dad muttered his thanks and grabbed the bag. He turned and froze, rolling his eyes when he realized it was me whom he'd nearly mowed down.

"Don't you just love how we keep bumping into each other?" I pulled down my shades with a crafty grin.

"What do you want, Aaliyah?"

"You don't hear the clock ticking? Aleksandr wants his money."

"What are you now, his little lapdog?" he snarled, marching past me. "He'll get it when he gets it."

I followed Pete from the store, not to be deterred.

"You and I both know that's not good enough," I said, darting in front of him. "You might think this only affects you, but it doesn't. I can't leave the Village until you pay Aleksandr."

"You?" Pete scoffed. "What does he want with you?"

"I was hoping you could tell me."

"You have a lot of nerve standing here asking me for anything after you and Tyler cost me an extra *fifty grand*." Pete sucked through his teeth, obviously torn between selling out Aleksandr and telling me to kick rocks. But when I folded my arms, he gave in, taking a wary glance around the mall like Aleksandr was waiting to catch us both.

"Look, Aleksandr's old man is a bigwig—his pockets run deep in New York. He's part of every inner circle there is. He's got friends in high places, especially the music industry. But he's got enemies too. Aleksandr's swimming in a sea of sharks, looking for any advantage. Looks like you're it."

"Me?" I asked, swiveling to face Pete as he walked past. "Why?"

"How should I know, kid? Whatever Aleksandr's problem is, you're gonna wanna steer clear. He's been groomed to run his father's empire. He's got this obsession with proving his chops to the old man. Combine that with his temper—and his *incessant* need for vengeance—and you've got matches and dynamite."

Or baseball bats and mirrors. I swallowed.

"I warned you, Aaliyah. I told you to stay away from Tyler. So whatever happens next, that's on you."

Mouth dry, I watched Pete leave, knowing he was right.

☆ ☆ ☆

Pete's description of Aleksandr and his father was so reminiscent of Tyler's relationship with his dad that it kept me tossing and turning in bed. Then dark thoughts about my own father started sneaking in, and I knew I was spiraling.

I turned on the light on my nightstand and left the bed, only to return and tuck in Bernard. Then I sat down at my computer desk and slowly opened the drawer, removing an old, worn Polaroid that hardly ever saw the light of day. But I liked to look at it from time to time, when I was homesick or feeling nostalgic.

It was one of the rare pictures I had of me and my father, and secretly, it was one of my favorites. My then four-year-old cousin Cody was hanging off my dad's leg as he smiled, bending to show the little pink buddle in his arms. I was only a few weeks old at the time, blissfully unaware of the difficult years to come, for which he was partly to blame. It was hard to imagine a man could look at you with so much love in his eyes, then completely abandon you.

I sat back in my seat, pushing my hair back with a frown as I studied the picture. Dots were beginning to connect, forming a picture I didn't like. My dad was a music producer based in New York. And if Aleksandr's dad was as prominent as Pete had said, then our parents might have bumped into each other once or twice.

I pushed the power button on my computer, taking deep breaths as I waited for it to load.

At school the next morning, I could barely contain my excitement until I found Quinn.

"Q, I did it!"

Quinn squawked when I grabbed her from behind, pulling her into the girls' restroom.

"Out," we said, shooing away the others gathered at the sink.

"Bitches," someone muttered, which I understood, considering one of their eyebrows was incomplete.

"So, what's up?" said Quinn. "I could use some good news, some good cheer, some good *anything*. Eric's been on one since we got whooped by the Tigers. That or he's severely depressed that you won't talk to him. Either way, he's taking it out on the whole team. He made Declan do so many push-ups, he couldn't lift his arms the next morning. This is severely impacting our sex life."

"Quinn, if you're asking me to forgive Eric just so you can get laid—don't hold your breath."

"Okay, that is not fair," said Quinn, twisting her hands. "I'm not asking you to forgive Eric, I'm just asking you to, y'know, put him out of his misery, gently, like a lame horse. Or Old Yeller."

I exhaled, shaking my head as I dug in my purse for a folded-up piece of paper. "No way."

"That's okay," she said stonily, snatching the paper from my hand. "It's not your fault. I know you'd have more empathy if you were getting laid. I mean, what are you and Tyler even waiting for, the second coming?" Quinn unfolded the paper. "What's this?"

"*This* is what I wanted to show you," I said, scrambling behind her to look at the picture over her shoulder.

"Okay. Who are the McHotties in the drip?"

"That's *my* dad having dinner at a charity function with *Aleksandr's* dad, Andrey Vitali."

"Holy shit, Aaliyah, you did it—you found the link. So? Are you satisfied?"

I shook my head.

"Of course not, and once again, no one can blame you." Then Quinn proceeded to tear up the paper it had taken me hours of research to find.

"Hey, what are you doing!" I demanded, following her into the bathroom stall and watching her toss the shredded remains in the toilet and flush.

"Aaliyah, it wouldn't do you any good for someone to find out your dad rubs elbows with guys like Andrey and Aleksandr Vitali. And I really think the more you keep digging, the less you're gonna like what you find."

"You think I don't know that? But Q, if Aleksandr is using

me, I have to know *why*. At least this proves that it's about more than just the money Tyler's dad owes him. It's about me too."

When had Aleksandr figured out our parents were connected? As soon as he met me? Before? After? Was it a surprise to him as well, or had he known all along? I had so many questions, but there was only one that kept me up at night. Aleksandr had said he needed me to be strong—to what end?

Quinn and I both jumped when one of the bathroom stalls opened. Daniela sauntered up to the bank of mirrors. We watched her outline her evil smile in red as her reflection smirked back at us.

"Everything's *always* about you, Aaliyah." Daniela swiveled to face me, popping her lipstick back in her Coach bag. "But if this is your show, and you're the star, I'll be happy to play the villain."

Stupefied, Quinn and I watched Daniela flounce from the bathroom.

I winced. "How much do you think she heard?"

"Take a wild guess," said Quinn, throwing her hands in the air.

☆ ☆ ☆

That weekend, with his parents getting drunk at a conference in Aspen, Declan threw open the doors to his family's lake house. I used GPS to navigate the winding roads through Gentle Forest. Chinara and Jared were in the back seat, and we all sang along to the hits on the radio. Tyler covered his face with his hands when one of his songs began to play, his ears red with embarrassment as we belted out the lyrics.

But it was a long drive to the lake house, and we didn't spend the entire time singing. After Jared plugged in his headphones and Chinara fell asleep on his shoulder, I gave Tyler a recap of my conversation with his dad and how I'd figured out Aleksandr's dad knew mine.

"That *is* kind of a weird coincidence," said Tyler, frowning at the dark blanket of trees flashing past us. "Have you thought about calling your dad?"

"All the time."

"Why haven't you?"

"I dunno." I shrugged. "Maybe because he hasn't called me either?" The GPS interrupted, reminding me to make a right in a half mile. We were nearly there.

"Let's try not to let our parents and Aleksandr ruin our night." Tyler laced his fingers through mine and kissed them. "I have a surprise for you."

I grinned. "Backstage passes and free concert tickets?" I teased.

"You wish." He turned up the radio with a smile, pretending he couldn't hear my questions.

☆ ☆ ☆

The Westbrooks' lake house was more modern than most of the other houses there, its three-story wooden exterior interrupted by giant windows overlooking the lake. There were lights strung in the trees and lanterns lighting the snowy path to the front door. Just a few feet beyond the home's massive wooden deck was the dock leading to the water and the boathouse, where the Jet Skis and the ketch were stored until summer. For now, the lake house was a winter wonderland—or at the very least the snowy getaway on the back of a holiday postcard.

The home's bright yellow lights stood out against the darkness, welcoming as a lighthouse in the night. Inside, it was just as warm and friendly. The cabin-like atmosphere wasn't overshadowed by the modern furniture nor the other luxurious features, like the spa room, the movie theater, or the warm towels hanging in the bathrooms. Not to mention, the kitchen was stocked, the beer was cold, and there were at least thirty miles between us and the nearest adult.

The party was already underway when we arrived. Tyler and I went our separate ways at the door, waving goodbye platonically as Chinara stood between us, rolling her eyes.

"You're both mad," she called after us. "Absolutely bonkers!"

I met up with Quinn and Declan at the giant firepit. We joined a handful of others drinking beer and making s'mores out back. This gang was from one of Declan's past lives and went to a different school, so the topic of conversation never veered toward pop stars, music videos, or if we could give them shout-outs on social media. I introduced myself as Ali instead of Aaliyah and practically reinvented myself.

Eventually, the chocolate dried up, the fire burned a little lower, and someone suggested we hit the hot tub. As everyone else was leaving, Quinn and I continued chatting on the stone bench, finishing the last of our s'mores.

"Hey, Ali."

I blushed when a cute boy named Christian tossed me a smile as he walked past, obviously taking his time.

"Uh-oh," said Quinn, dark brows raised as she licked her thumb. "Looks like Tyler's got competition."

"Hardly," I said, throwing my stick in the fire.

But I knew Christian was interested by the way he offered to open my beer in the kitchen, and then again when he asked to dance in the living room. But Tyler cut in after a few minutes, and my game of pretend was over.

"Don't be jealous." I turned and danced against Tyler, enjoying the warmth of his breath on my neck and the way he gripped my curves as I moved to the music. "It's not very subtle."

"Meet me on the third floor at midnight," he said in my ear, sending chills up my spine. "Is that subtle enough for you?" he asked, walking away with a smirk.

Lounging in a pool-sized hot tub, I tipped my head back and closed my eyes, trying to empty my head of the endless, swirling thoughts. I ran a cold beer bottle over the bikini strings crisscrossing my neck, letting the cold and the steam caress me like gentle hands. Here, under the stars, away from the drama and disappointment of the Village, my inhibitions slipped away. I inhaled and bit my lip, tasting air sweetened by the firepit, chasing it with a swig of beer. When I opened my eyes, Tyler and Christian, sitting on opposite ends of the hot tub, were staring at me like I had just danced topless.

"Imagine a Tyler-Christian sandwich," said Chinara, sitting at my right in a purple frilled bikini that had also drawn Christian's gaze.

"Can you run interference on Christian?" I asked in a low voice. "He's very . . ."

"Distracting?"

I blushed.

Chinara grinned. "Don't worry. He won't be able to resist my British charm." She tapped her beer against mine then crossed the hot tub, drawing Christian's attention.

I sat back with a sigh of relief. Across the water, Tyler sipped his beer with a knowing grin.

As the night wore on, I tried to pretend I wasn't distracted by the green eyes summoning me to a midnight rendezvous. I did my best to engage in conversation, but Tyler's magnetic gaze interrupted me. The heat between us was scorching compared to the warm water and tepid chitchat. But I didn't feel true flames until Daniela strode up in her ice-white Pleasers. Stepping gracefully from the heels, she descended the hot tub steps in her white cut-out bikini, her dark waves piled high. The bottle of Fireball whiskey in her manicured hand was half-empty, but full of trouble.

Daniela waded up to me, reeking of cinnamon candy, far more venomous than sweet. Gripping my arm like a vise, she brought her cherry lips close and whispered in my ear.

"Aleksandr sends his regards . . . *pchelka*."

Suddenly, the night was darker and the warm water less inviting. Fear and anger washed over me like the shallow waves from the hot tub.

"What the hell did you do, Daniela?"

"I did what you wish you could do—I called your daddy." A slow grin spread across Daniela's face as an uneasy silence fell beneath the rap music. Everyone was a witness as the queen turned her wrath upon me. "I told him *everything*, Aaliyah. How you got in over your head with Aleksandr, and how Tyler's dad owes him money." Daniela wasn't smiling anymore. Her dark eyes burned like coals. "I really thought he would care when I said how scared I was that you might do something reckless to try and save your boyfriend." Daniela pretended to swoon, her evil laughter ringing in my ears as I imagined the painful, embarrassing conversation.

"And do you know what he told me? After *all* of that?" Daniela lifted one of her brows, a stupid smirk on her face as she waited for me to take the bait. "Your dad said he doesn't *have* a daughter named Aaliyah, and to *never* call him again."

Whispers traveled around the hot tub. A few people laughed.

My eyes burned with tears; the only thing more embarrassing than my father refusing to rescue me was him pretending I didn't exist.

"I'm sorry, Aaliyah, I was just trying to be a good friend," she said with her voice raised. Those who didn't know her might think she actually cared. But when Daniela wrapped her arms around me and whispered in my ear, her voice was icy as the November chill. "Your life is so pathetic; I doubt Aleksandr will even enjoy destroying you . . ."

My stomach jumped; the cool night air felt hotter than a sauna in July. Suddenly, something in me snapped like firewood in the flames. I pushed Daniela, and she lost her footing, crashing backward into the water. As she sat up, choking and spluttering, I pushed her back down and held her ass under until Eric pried me away. The hot tub was in chaos. Declan was holding back Quinn, Christian had his arms around Chinara, and half the basketball team had Tyler in a chokehold just so he couldn't get to Eric.

Eric hauled me from the water, ushering me inside the lake house. He tried to coax me down the hallway, but I refused to move past the foyer, wrenching my arms from his grip.

"You couldn't save me, but you can save her?" I asked, rounding on Eric.

"That's not fair, Aaliyah. I know Tyler and I act stupid sometimes, but this isn't like you. You never used to let Dani get under your skin."

"Yeah, well, that was before—" I cut myself off so I didn't embarrass myself by saying Aleksandr's name aloud.

Things were tense when Tyler walked in, shirtless, brown hair dripping in his eyes as he and Eric sized each other up.

"*Don't,*" I warned, looking from one to the other. "I'm leaving."

"Aaliyah, *please*, come with me," said Tyler. "Everything Dani said was bullshit. The night doesn't have to end like this."

I shook my head. "I'm going home." The ghost of Daniela's taunts chased me down the hall as Tyler called my name.

Quinn found me in one of the second-floor bedrooms. I had already changed into basketball shorts and a T-shirt and was stuffing my wet bikini in a duffel bag. Quinn ordered me to stop, digging out my makeup bag and returning it to the bureau.

"I'm not staying," I said, zipping my duffel bag with finality. "I knew Dani was upset, but I didn't think she hated me enough to do something like this. And now my dad hates me too."

"*Stop.*" Quinn took me by the arms and gave me a little shake. "Sit," she commanded.

I took a seat on the edge of a large bed with ruffles, sniffling as I watched Quinn stride into the bathroom.

Her phone, forgotten on the bedspread, buzzed while she was gone. I paused, listening to the splash of water from the bathroom, then picked up Q's phone, reading the messages displayed on the screen. How long had Quinn been in Aleksandr's DMs?

I could only read the last two messages and didn't dare to scroll up for more.

what the hell am i supposed to do about dani???

you know what to do Quinn

I heard the water shut off, tossing the phone aside just as Quinn returned. I tried to keep my concern from showing as she used a wet cloth to wipe my face. The truth was, I didn't *want* to know what Aleksandr had convinced Quinn to do. Because the vengeful part of me wanted Quinn to go through with it.

"You're not going anywhere," said Quinn firmly, smoothing primer across my face. "Daniela is a jealous, venomous snake; if you leave now, she gets her wish—that you'll mess things up with Tyler. Because what you and Tyler have is real, and she knows it. Close your eyes, tilt your face."

I sat still, allowing Quinn to work her magic. She applied foundation with a soft, smooth brush, in careful, even strokes, then blotted my face with a sponge.

"Look, Ali, even if Daniela isn't a monstrous, lying bitch, and all that stuff she said in the hot tub is true, it doesn't matter—lift your eyelashes, hold still . . ." Quinn chewed her gum in concentration, applying mascara like a surgeon saving a patient on the table. "Only a piece of shit rejects their own kid. You're better off without him." Quinn finished up the last steps in her routine, then stepped aside so I could view the finished product. "And even if he doesn't love you, we do."

Quinn didn't have to elaborate on "we."

She stood behind me, spritzing and scrunching my damp curls as I turned from side to side in the mirror. The foundation made my skin glow, and my brown eyes popped from the cat-eye liner.

"Look, I wasn't gonna say this, Ali, but Tyler wanted tonight to be special for you. So if you leave now, it'll totally ruin the surprise." Quinn pulled a floral minidress from my duffel bag, holding it up against me in the mirror. "We both know you brought this for a reason," she teased, coaxing a tiny smile to my lips.

I nodded and took the dress. Little by little, I began to feel better as I changed clothes and stepped in my clean, white low-tops. A little self-care really does go a long way, I thought, admiring the backless, fitted dress, with its plunging neckline and thin, delicate straps.

"A bad bitch never stays down," said Quinn, adjusting my dress from behind. "Me and the squad will handle Daniela. Tyler's waiting."

I thanked my friend and left the room. I took the staircase to the third floor, entering the long, moonlit corridor with apprehension. A door at the end of the hall was cracked, and squares of light fell from the shadows beyond. I stepped tentatively inside, closing the door behind me. The light in the bedroom was dim, supplied by white candles flickering all around. Their soft, rosy light revealed the petals scattered across the room, the wine chilling on the dresser, and the flowers on the bed. How long had Tyler planned this, running after me while I chased Aleksandr?

Tyler was standing by the fire, listening to "Apocalypse" by Cigarettes After Sex. He turned and lowered the hood on his OAMC sweatshirt when I entered, striding across the room to draw me into his arms.

"Are you okay?"

"No, not really." I shook my head. "All these years I thought my dad just didn't care. Turns out, he hates me."

"That's not true," said Tyler, tucking my hair behind my ear. "When I look in those pretty brown eyes, I don't know how anyone could ever hurt you. Whatever it was he thought he could gain by leaving you, it wasn't worth it."

My eyes burned; I quickly wiped the tears away, grateful for the distraction when the white glare of headlights washed over the walls. I walked to the window, pushing aside the sheer, gauzy curtains in time to see Quinn leading the mob ushering Daniela back to her car. The only things missing were the torches and pitchforks.

When I turned around, Tyler was behind me with an envelope in his hand.

"What's this?"

"The world's sappiest love letter." Tyler grinned. "Maybe not as good as a promise ring—"

"It's better." I took the letter and threw my arms around him, pecking him with kisses.

"Ali, the next time you feel alone, and I'm not there, I want you to read this," he said, tracing the dress strap that had slipped down my shoulder.

"Tyler, I don't know what to say." An actual love letter? It was better than any surprise I could have imagined.

"You don't have to say anything." Tyler laid his forehead against mine, his lips tantalizingly out of reach as he pressed my arms to my sides. "The dress says it all."

Tyler picked me up, my legs around his waist as he kissed me and carried me to the bed. He tossed me against the pillows with a chuckle, lifting his hoodie over his head. I pushed back the hair that had fallen, admiring the clear view of his stunning face.

"Are you sure?" He tucked my hair behind my ear, smiling when I nodded.

The firelight reflected in his eyes dared me to ignore the risks and come closer.

"Why me?" I asked, following the curves of his handsome face in the moonlight. "You're Tyler Moore. You could have anyone."

"I want you," he said. His soft, full lips turned my world into a hazy dream I never wanted to wake up from. "Growing up, I thought the music was all I would ever need. But in New York, I was so fucking alone, Ali. And then I came back to you, and everything was different. I don't ever wanna go back to the way things were. I know we agreed to keep our distance in public, but I don't wanna be distant from you. I love you, Aaliyah. I always have."

Fingers threaded in my hair, Tyler kissed me again. He kissed me like the devil was after us and we were on borrowed time. I placed my hand over his, helping him slide up the hem of my dress.

"I love you too." And that was all I said for a while.

Tyler sat up and stretched late the next morning, his green eyes narrow from sleep.

"So, this time it *wasn't* a dream?"

"Lucky you." I sat on the edge of the bed in his T-shirt, looking down at the velvet box in my hands. "This isn't cuff links."

"Although you would look amazing in a suit." His skin was gold as honey in the morning sun. He spread his arms, and automatically I returned to them, sliding under the covers, where it was warmer anyway.

"Well, the plan was to give it to you last night, but y'know . . . kinda lost track of time." He smiled, brushing my hair from my shoulder. "Open it."

"I already did." Earlier that morning, I had discovered the jewelry box under my pillow and had fallen out of bed when I saw the necklace inside. "You sneaky little snake—when did you get this?" He'd never left the lake house, which meant he'd driven up here with it stowed away in his things.

"Q helped me pick it out." Leaning against the wooden headboard, Tyler folded his hands behind his head and smirked, immensely pleased with himself. "When the jeweler found out who I was, he insisted I choose from their private collection. At no extra cost."

I sighed. "It's beautiful, Tyler. But I can't accept this."

Tyler refused to take it back at first, then gave in when he realized I wasn't changing my mind.

"This isn't what we do," I said. "We don't spend ridiculous amounts of money on each other. *Especially* because you're rich, and I'm not." I smiled so he would know this wasn't an accusation, just a fact. "I can't keep up."

That necklace could pay someone's rent a few times over. It was an amazing gift, and the best I could do in return was spring for a movie and dinner for two.

Harbor Village is one of those old, wealthy towns where the same rich families have ruled for generations. It's not an easy place to find your footing or make your mark—especially if you're an outsider, like me. Back when it was just my mom and me, sometimes it was hard having wealthy friends while being the kid on a budget. But over the years I'd learned to work for the things I wanted. Despite my aunt's cushy job, I still saved money from summer jobs I took down at the pier, and sometimes I helped Madilyn around the studio when I wanted extra cash. Dazzling as his diamonds were, I didn't need a thing from Tyler.

He exhaled in disappointment. "I'll take it back—for now. But I have money, Aaliyah, and it's part of who I am. You can't expect me to hide that forever. Just like I don't wanna hide my feelings for you anymore. If I can't buy you fancy jewelry or fly you around the world, what can I do?"

I slid into Tyler's lap, nuzzling his neck and planting coy kisses on his cheek. "There's nothing more valuable than your time and energy."

"Then it's all yours, gorgeous. And so am I."

I gasped when Tyler flipped me on my back and laughed as he pulled the covers over our heads.

The dozen of us who had stayed at the lake house overnight had a lavish French toast brunch in the dining room. Tyler and I offered to stay behind and help clean up after the party, but Declan assured us he had tipped the family's cleaning service to leave no trace behind. With Chinara and Jared catching a ride back with Christian, Tyler and I had the car to ourselves.

Before we said our goodbyes, I took a walk to the end of the dock and watched the last geese fly over the nearly frozen lake. Tyler hugged me from behind, a green-and-blue-checkered camping blanket wrapped around the two of us. I would never forget how beautiful the lake had been at night, when the snow and the lights from the house reflected on its still, peaceful waters.

"I did a few shows in Switzerland," said Tyler, his chin resting on my shoulder as he held me close. "The snow was *amazing*. But it never made me feel like this . . ." He squeezed me tighter. "Must be because I'm with you."

I smiled. "Must be."

Tyler and I said our goodbyes to Quinn and Declan, then made the return drive to the Village. Once we were back in town, I sent a quick text to Trina, letting her know I was safe, then made a pit stop at the gas station. I pumped the gas while Tyler bought snacks. He returned a few minutes later, sliding into the passenger side.

"So, I know you only asked for two things, but, like, c'mon—how could I *not* buy you chocolate, right?"

I smiled.

"One bag of Flamin' Hot Cheetos," said Tyler, digging the treat from the bag, "and one non-bougie water, coming right up!"

"Fiji Water is non-bougie? Are you kidding?"

He passed me the water and winked. "Bottoms up."

"Thank you—for making the weekend special and for taking care of me. Seriously, Tyler, it means a lot."

"I got your back—always." He leaned against his seat, smiling as those Venus flytrap eyes lured me closer. "I mean, what are boyfriends for?"

"Boyfriend?" I sipped my water, pretending to be outraged.

"Ouch," said Tyler, grabbing his heart.

"But it does have a nice ring to it . . ." I grabbed his shirt and pulled him close. We kissed for a few minutes, blissfully unaware of the outside world, until another car parked alongside mine, forcing us hastily apart.

"Oh, fuck," said Tyler, taking a closer look at the car. "Is that . . ."

"Yep, it is."

Dragging my fingers through my hair, I watched Eric step out of the passenger side and walk into the store. Beside us, the driver's-side window of the Malibu lowered, and Daniela's furious face was confirmation—now that Tyler and I were officially a couple, she would make us pay.

That Monday, as I walked the halls of HVH, something was different. And it wasn't just my relationship with Tyler—which I couldn't downplay, not with his arm around me between classes. People had started to notice me when Tyler came back, but now that he was kissing me in the halls, they were awestruck. Boys opened doors for me and scrambled to carry my books, girls complimented my curls and asked me to do TikToks. My status had changed overnight. I was more than popular. I was practically royalty.

"About bloody time," said Chinara, shaking her head as she passed Tyler and me flirting on our way to the gym.

While my rank at HVH was on the rise, Daniela's stats were

on a downward trend. She trudged through the halls alone, minus her usual crowd, with high-waisted mom jeans and flat hair. I had to know what was going on, so I approached Quinn in the gym, just before the school assembly. The Angels were performing—everyone on the A-Team was gathered on the sidelines, warming up for the pep rally. There was a basketball game tonight, and we were still in recovery after a streak of crushing defeats.

"Something really weird is happening. It's like everything's backward, Q—Daniela's miserable, and I'm happy. What the hell is going on?"

"Karma," she replied, smiling mysteriously as she shook her pom-poms. "Daniela's reign of terror is *over*. Trust me."

But there was a sinking feeling in my stomach as I watched Quinn join the other Angels in the center of the gym.

"Do you know something I don't?" I asked Jared, taking a seat next to him on the bleachers.

"Yes—but I am sworn to secrecy," he replied, locking his lips and throwing away the key.

"Oh, no," I groaned.

"Oh, yes," he gloated.

The lights dimmed, and the Angels took their positions, Daniela front and center. But as the hip-hop music played and Daniela began to dance, it was like the Angels were glued in place. Daniela didn't notice and kept spinning; some of the girls threw down their pom-poms and folded their arms. A few more seconds and they walked offstage. You couldn't hear the crowd over the music, but I saw their surprise and amusement as they covered their mouths and pointed.

By the time Daniela noticed what had happened and finally lowered her pom-poms, the Angels were gone, and she was alone. The queen bee of Harbor Village High had finally fallen.

Ten

Nowhere to Run

Standing in the middle of the cafeteria with my tray and not knowing where to sit wasn't unfamiliar to me. It was the part where I had *options* that was freaking me out. So many people waved and called out from so many different directions, I didn't know where to begin. At least in the days when I was unknown, it was quiet, and there weren't expectations.

"Aaliyah! Yoo-hoo!" Sonam waved from their usual table at the epicenter of the madness. The burgundy headband in her shoulder-length black waves matched her plaid, high-waisted miniskirt, and there weren't many things that sparkled like the gold necklaces complementing her cropped, off-white sweater. She crossed her thigh-high boots and grinned like a wolf.

"Sit," commanded Piper, pointing one manicured finger at the empty seat before them. Her baggy tracksuit—mauve jogging bottoms with a white oversized hoodie—were couture, paired with large, gold hoops and pristine Balenciagas. Her long, high ponytail was snow white, but her dark, sculpted brows were the same color as her roots. And probably her soul.

"Hey, girls." I rubbed my palms nervously down my jeans. This was weird. Really, really weird. "Where's Dani?"

"Who knows?" Piper shrugged.

"Probably somewhere *spiraling* with a center–point guard sandwich." Sonam rolled her eyes.

Piper chuckled. "Congratulations on bagging Mr. Billboard Music Award. Dani swore it was all rumors—didn't know you had it in you." She winked one of her sly brown eyes, and I felt queasy.

"Tyler's so hot. That's one merry-go-round I'd love to take a ride on." Sonam bumped knuckles with Piper, laughing.

"Just so y'know, Aaliyah, we do *not* condone what happened back at the lake house," said Piper. "We're on your side." She took an innocent bite from her bacon-cheese fries, batting her lash extensions.

They sounded like they were pitching a campaign for some evil agenda I wanted zero part of.

"Look, guys, I really appreciate your, um, *support?* But isn't this, like, a major conflict of interest?" I shrugged. "You two are Dani's best friends—I mean, you're performing with her in the talent show."

"*Former* best friends," Piper stated, genuinely insulted.

Sonam nodded, playing with the metal straw in her Red Bull.

"Dani's been off the rails since Tyler came back," she said. "But *swear ta gawd*, we didn't think she'd actually take things that far. I mean—calling your dad? And then telling you in front of everyone how he doesn't love you—pretty wild."

"Yeah. *Wild.*" I picked up my fork, jabbing aimlessly at my baked potato.

"Chin up, Preston." Piper flashed a cold-blooded half smirk. "Your daddy issues came through. Dani ruined her streak, making herself look like an *idiot* throwing herself at Tyler. But after she blitzed you at the lake house, Quinn pulled us aside."

"She gave us an ultimatum." Sonam sat back in her chair, legs crossed, face pinched like she tasted lemons. "Our social annihilation or Dani's." She looked like she needed a stiff drink.

"And Dani's actions didn't give us much of a choice," finished Piper. "She alienated herself when she took on a pop star's girlfriend. And I am *just* starting to get subscribers on YouTube. I am *not* getting canceled for bullying."

"Do you *hear* yourselves? Sonam, Piper, you two are her *friends*. How can you just . . . drop her?" I shifted uncomfortably in my seat, realizing that not so very long ago I had done the same thing.

"Don't be such a Puritan, Aaliyah." Sonam's dark-brown eyes narrowed. "You should be happy, Daniela's been doing everything she can to get between you and Tyler. She said some freak named Aleksandr gave her the green light. But obviously her plan failed. And now that you two are official . . ." Sonam shrugged, exchanging a sly glance with Piper.

"Well . . ." Piper smirked. "Let's just say, we know how we're voting for prom court."

Hands down, Tyler would score a prom court nomination. And with Daniela's crown up for grabs, I knew I stood close to the queen bee's throne. But being popular wasn't high on the list of my life's aspirations. And neither was taking Dani's place on the social ladder.

"You won, Aaliyah." Piper offered me a devilish smile. "And it doesn't have to stop there."

"What do you mean?" I asked slowly, feeling the darkness in the air spreading like a virus.

"We're done with Daniela," replied Piper. "Which means So-So and I quit the band—Motivation is no more."

"Which means no more talent show." Sonam smirked.

"Which means you win," Piper added. "How much was the prize money again?"

The deranged Doublemint Twins were too busy cackling to notice the disgust on my face.

After the final bell rang, I spotted Eric in the hall and waved tentatively; he walked right past with his head down, pretending we hadn't made eye contact. But I didn't hold it against him. I could see how dating your ex-girlfriend's ex–best friend might put a damper on things.

That night, I was in the kitchen making popcorn (with pickles on the side for Trina) for family movie night when I heard the home phone ring. I was on my way back to the living room with our snack when Tyler stopped me, a finger pressed to his lips. I joined him, hovering on the opposite side of the door to the living room, eavesdropping on the heated conversation Trina was having over the phone.

"I don't give a shit how you feel—my sister is *dead*! Do you *know* what that did to her?" Trina's back was to us, but I could tell by the stiffness in her body and her rigid movements that she was upset.

"Well, you *would* know, if you'd been there—but you weren't, were you?" Trina exhaled loudly, nodding in anger. The cordless phone was glued to her ear as she planted a fist on her hip. "Well, of course she's not okay, Drake! What kid would be okay after their mom died?"

Trina turned and began to pace. Tyler and I darted back, sliding away from the door and farther down the wall as Trina turned her head as if checking to see no one was coming. Tyler's green eyes were wide with surprise, but not as large as mine.

"Damn it, I don't need some long-winded explanation about how many strings you can pull! I don't want your blood money, and I certainly don't need it. *Tuh!*"

Drake? Tyler mouthed. *Did she say Drake?*

I nodded back, holding the popcorn bowl against my racing heart.

"She's a teenage girl, Drake—something's *always* going on. But if she really is in danger, and you're not just high on whatever designer drug you're currently bingeing, *I* will find out, and I will handle it. I made a promise to Amelia before she died, and I intend to keep it. Aaliyah has too much going for her. She has a *future*—I won't let you take that away from her like you took it from Amelia. You made your bed, Drake—and I won't let that life *anywhere* near my niece. You stay away from Aaliyah. And the next time you call, it better be an emergency or you better be dead!"

Tyler and I both jumped when Trina slammed the phone down. We flattened ourselves against the wall in a panic, but Trina was so distracted she didn't even notice us as she stomped past. I breathed a sigh of relief, watching her storm up the stairs.

"When your aunt goes off, she *goes off,*" said Tyler, pushing his hair back in awe.

"Yeah," I said, biting my lip as I glanced at the empty staircase. "She seemed pretty pissed at my dad. It's been years since I've even heard from him. Why would he call now?"

Tyler snapped his fingers as the light bulb clicked. "Because of Daniela—remember? She called Drake and told him you were in trouble. I knew she was wrong, Ali. Your aunt's conversation proves it—your dad *does* care about you. Otherwise, he wouldn't have called."

I should have felt relief as Tyler drew me into a silent, comforting hug, but the more I dissected the parts of their conversation I had heard, the more I was ill at ease. All these years, I'd thought my dad stayed away because he wanted to, but that was a lie. My mom and my aunt had kept him away—now I was going to figure out why.

Tyler and I were sitting on the couch eating popcorn when Trina returned. She seemed more composed than when she was on the phone with my dad, but I could tell by the way her brows were knit that she was still upset.

"I heard the phone ring earlier," I said, casting Tyler a quick sideways glance.

"Oh, you know those telemarketers—always trying to sell you something you don't need." It was the first time Trina had ever lied to me. But, considering how many times I had lied to her over the past few months, I was willing to forgive her.

She plopped down on the couch, forcing Tyler and me apart as she made herself comfortable and grabbed the remote.

"So," she said. "What are we watching?"

I was still dissecting the phone call the next morning at breakfast, at practice that afternoon with the B-Team, and later that night when a bunch of us met up at our local bowling alley, Ten Pins. Usually, I couldn't get enough of the alley, with its neon lights and glow-in-the-dark pins. I loved renting the goofy shoes at the check-in counter, hearing the pins being knocked down, and feeling the smooth, heavy ball in my hand as I pulled back my arm and let loose. A strike always put a smile on my face, but the whoops of celebration as another X was added to my name sounded faint and tinny. My body was on autopilot; the rest of me was a thousand miles away.

I dropped into a seat at my team's table. With my head leaning against my fist, I played with the straw in a half-melted milkshake, waiting for my next turn. I stiffened as a pair of arms slid around me, relaxing when I recognized Quinn's sparkly blue manicure. She pecked my cheek with a few kisses and sat down across from me to sample my nachos.

"I thought Tyler said he was good at this," she complained. "What happened to being 'the world's greatest unknown bowler'?"

I glanced over my shoulder, chuckling as Tyler unleashed a colorful string of curses after throwing his fourth gutter ball.

"I warned you not to take him. You wanted him on your team—*captain*." I grinned, sipping my milkshake.

"That wasn't the goal, y'know?" Quinn bit her lip, looking down at her hands as she twisted them on the table. "I wasn't *trying* to take the captaincy from Daniela. After two weeks together stuck in detention, I thought maybe things could be different— maybe she'd back down. Not the first time I've gotten something majorly wrong. She got what she deserved—I guess I just wish it had been on fairer terms." Quinn didn't mind fighting dirty, but defeating Daniela had been more like a WWE handicap match than anything.

"Dani stepped down," I said quietly. "That was her choice."

"Was it, though?"

Like severing a rotten limb to save the body, the whole team had turned against Daniela. Quinn had come clean, explaining how Aleksandr had reached out to her the night of the lake house party, warning her that Daniela was a loose end that needed to be tied.

"He didn't even have to threaten me, Aaliyah." Quinn's clear blue eyes turned as stormy as winter skies in the Village. "I did it because I knew if I didn't, he'd find a way to make you suffer. And you have enough on your plate, with your dad and . . . everything else."

"Quinn, I'm so sorry you had to do that. I think about that day at the hotel with Aleksandr and Tyler's dad, and . . . I just wish I had never taken you with me." I shrugged. "Why did Aleksandr involve you, Q? Why would he ask *you* to take care of Dani?"

"You mean why me and not you? Don't know, don't care." Quinn drummed the table decisively. "Daniela had some nerve calling your dad, but reaching out to *Aleksandr?*" Quinn whistled like a nuclear bomb. "I'm sure he chewed her up and spit her out—which would explain why she wigged out at the party. Either way, the evil queen's reign of terror is over. Aleksandr is a menace, but at least he helped us get rid of the wicked witch."

"You shouldn't have had to do that."

"Ride or die." Quinn rolled her eyes, but her smile was affectionate. "Isn't that, like, the definition of best friends?"

I sat back in my chair, arms folded in defeat. "This isn't what senior year was supposed to be."

"It ain't over yet." Quinn stood up, extending her hand. I was on the fence for a second or two, more interested in sulking with my half-melted milkshake than pretending the world wasn't on fire. But if Quinn was willing to walk through flames for me, the least I could do was bowl with her.

I took her hand, and we crossed the bright, waxed floor back to our lanes. I met Tyler under the electronic scoreboard. His Versace shirt and gold chain glowed in the neon lights, but that gleaming smile always stole the show.

"Good thing you're better at singing than bowling," I said, glancing at the score with a smirk.

"Careful, Preston. Or I might pull you up there with me," he said, walking backward toward the stage. Every night was karaoke night at Ten Pins, but not everyone could sing like Tyler. He took the stage, and the bowling alley erupted in cheers and applause.

"I'm gonna need a partner," he said into the microphone, smiling bashfully at the audience.

"Quinn!" I ran down the wooden lanes, slipping and sliding right into her arms. "Q, get up there!"

"What?"

"Yes, *you*! Get up there! Now! If you don't go, I'll have to go—and I can't sing!"

I pushed Quinn toward the stage, and she joined him, nervous in the spotlight. But when the low lights dimmed even further and the music began, she opened up like a flower. Tyler borrowed a guitar from someone in the crowd and joined her at the mic, where they sang an alluring version of "Ring of Fire." Quinn's delicate, bubbly tone complemented Tyler's deeper, warmer notes as if they had written and produced it together.

Their voices captivated the alley, encouraging our friends and complete strangers to dance and sing along. Knowing a historic moment when I saw one, I took my phone and filmed the pair. I turned, smiling as Declan appeared, but my grin faded when I noticed his hands thrust in his pockets and the way his dark brows were knit with concern.

"Who is Aleksandr, Aaliyah? And don't lie to me, okay?"

"Okay," I said, lowering my phone. "H-how do you know that name?"

"Because Quinn keeps accidentally mentioning him—and so did Dani, at the lake house, and Eric lost it in the locker room, *ranting* about this guy. Wherever that name goes, trouble follows—and I'm just trying to look out for my girlfriend."

Declan switched his frosty gaze to mine; his usually friendly nature had been replaced by coldness. "Should I be worried?"

The last thing I wanted to do was get Declan involved in Aleksandr's world. So I did something that was beginning to feel a lot like second nature—I lied.

"No." I shook my head. "Aleksandr is . . . a ghost from my past—so he's *my* problem. You don't have to be worried, Dec. Quinn will be fine, I promise."

Declan nodded, seemingly relieved as he turned his gaze to his beautiful girlfriend. Lying about Aleksandr wasn't just about keeping things smooth between Quinn and Declan. This was about survival. If Dec kept trying to do the right thing and walked into the fire with us, he would only get burned.

☆ ☆ ☆

That night, riding in the back of Quinn's Jeep, Tyler popped the question.

I blinked at Tyler. "You want me to have dinner? With your family?"

He grinned. "Well, yeah. I told my mom we're official, and she's kind of excited about it."

I chuckled. "She wants to meet me?"

"She wants to celebrate," he said, raising his hand to weave his fingers through mine. His Southern accent was on point as he tipped his imaginary hat. "I don't blame her—I'm kind of a big deal around these here parts, ma'am."

"Lucky me," I said, draping my arms around his neck and kissing Tyler in the back seat until Quinn and Declan told us we were disgusting and commanded me to get out.

I hopped out of the Jeep and said goodbye to my friends.

"Pick me up for breakfast," said Tyler. "My treat."

Quinn was still backing out of the driveway when Tyler sent me a text with a silly string of emojis.

I wuv u

I texted back, a big, goofy smile on my face as I headed toward the house.

"Hi." I waved. Trina was sitting on the porch swing, wrapped in a blanket. "It's cold, you shouldn't be out here this late—especially not—"

"*In your condition*," she said with me, rolling her amber eyes. "I know, I know. It's just . . . I can't shake this *feeling*." She clutched the blanket tighter, eyes wide in the moonlight.

"What feeling?" I asked, stopping short at the bottom of the porch steps.

"Like when you know a storm is coming," she said quietly. "My granny used to get those feelings. She was never wrong."

I swallowed, following Trina's gaze as she scanned the street behind me.

"We should get you inside—"

Trina stood, her gaze still glued to the street. "There's this car I've never seen before—it keeps driving down our street. An old gray sedan. Wonder who he's looking for."

"He's probably just lost." I swallowed; my mouth was suddenly dry as an old well. "C'mon. It's past your bedtime, young lady."

I made the mistake of glancing behind me as I ushered my aunt into the house. I felt my heart in my fingers as I shut the door, fumbling with the bolts and locks. And when I laid my head on the pillow and closed my eyes, I could still see the headlights of the gray sedan.

The next day, I used my free period to clear my head, dancing through my drama in the gym. In the old days, no one would have looked twice in my direction, but by the time the last song ended, I had garnered an audience. Blushing at the eyes and phones aimed in my direction, I scooped up my duffel bag, waved, and hurried out.

Usually dancing cleared my head. But as I leaned against the wall outside the science lab, eyes closed, it felt like the walls were caving in. My phone playing the Darth Vader anthem was just more confirmation the world was ending.

I pressed the phone to my ear, stifling a weary exhale. "Yes?"

"It seems your leak has sprung again." Astrid's greeting was dry as stale bread.

"What now?"

"You never thought it pertinent to mention you were related to *the* Drake Preston—the songwriter-slash-producer?"

"He never thought it pertinent to show up for my birthday, so no—I *didn't* mention him. Why is that important?"

"Because *Canceled* discovered the connection, and they're running a story." Astrid exhaled. "Drake—your father—has . . . history in New York. And some of that history is about to come out."

"It would be bad for Tyler's image, wouldn't it?"

"Maybe. *Canceled* reached out, and I was able to buy Tyler's name out of the article, but that doesn't mean the public won't make assumptions. About you as well, Aaliyah."

"But I'm not even in contact with my dad. I—I don't even have his number."

"That doesn't matter, luv." That was the first time Astrid had ever shown me open kindness, so I knew things were serious. "Tyler said you and he are official, but you haven't formally announced it. I understand—you want to be your own person, and one day your own brand. And so far, you're headed in the right direction. The public likes you, you're the new 'it' girl. The connection to your father could either tarnish that image or strengthen it. That depends on how *you* react—and who you choose to associate with. I'll do what I can to protect you and Tyler from my end. Be careful, Aaliyah."

I rang the doorbell at the Vega residence and stepped back, impatiently shifting my weight from one leg to the other. Just as I was going to press the bell again, Daniela answered, looking pretty haggard for a girl of seventeen.

"What do you *want*, Preston?"

"Is it you?" I demanded. "Are you the one talking to the press, feeding them stories about me and Tyler? Did you give them my dad's name?"

Daniela scoffed, wrapping her cheetah-print robe tighter around her pajamas. "Why would I do that?"

"Oh, I don't know, because you hate me? Because Aleksandr told you to ruin my relationship? Yeah, Piper and Sonam told me *everything*." I stepped closer, sparks and laser beams shooting from my eyes. "Rule number one—*never* trust the press. And rule number two—keep my family's name out of your mouth!"

"Or what?" Daniela folded her arms, her chin stubbornly raised. "You already took everything from me, *puta*. Aleksandr was right—you curse everyone you cross paths with. That's probably why he likes you so much—you're both the same. And now that you're Little Miss Harbor Village, you have an entire kingdom to ravage. And Tyler will help you do it because he thinks he's in love. He can protect you from idiots like Eric, Aaliyah, but he can't save you from Aleksandr. Good luck."

Daniela slammed the door in my face so hard the wind blew my hair back. I banged the door with my fist and kicked it, leaving scuff marks behind. Blinded by tears and rage, I stomped back to my car, throwing the door shut and crying into the steering wheel.

After a few minutes of wallowing in self-pity, I fished my phone from my pocket and dialed a number I knew by heart. After so many weeks of silence, he picked up on the second ring.

"I need to see you," I said, wiping my face. "It's important."

"After the first hundred missed calls, it didn't cross your mind that I might be, I don't know, *busy?*" Aleksandr's strained question ended with a grunt, like he was preoccupied and maybe this *was* a bad time.

"*I don't care*," I hissed back. "I have questions, and you have answers—you owe me that much." The odd noises continued. "What are you *doing?*"

I heard his wheels turning in the pause that followed.

"Changing a tire."

"Liar!" He was probably having someone chopped into little pieces as we spoke. "Where are you? Tell me where you are!"

"You are very bossy for a seventeen-year-old girl with no authority whatsoever. What do you want, Aaliyah?"

"I wanna know about my father." My voice was hoarse from tears and desperation—the words felt like knives coming out. "I want you to tell me *everything*."

"And if I don't? What will you do, *pchelka*? Boo-hoo, will you cry some more and stamp your little foot at me?"

"No." I was tired of crying—all it ever gave me was a headache, and I wanted the truth. "Either you talk to me or I start talking to the police."

The seconds wound down like the timer on a bomb. I swallowed; I had gone too far to turn back now.

"That would be a very bad idea, Aaliyah."

"So we're agreed."

It was the dead of night when Quinn's Jeep pulled up outside an old, abandoned stretch of buildings on the edge of town. This area had been deserted decades ago, and it would have been ghostly quiet if not for the roar of the Harbor Dam beyond. I gazed at the empty parking garage ahead, noting how eerie and desolate it appeared in the moonlight.

"We do not tell Dec about this," Quinn said, cutting the engine.

I nodded. "Or Tyler."

"Ali, you can't go in there by yourself."

"I have to. Come alone—that was the deal. Besides, if something goes down, one of us needs to be on the outside—just in case."

"Just in case," she repeated, releasing a mega exhale as she gripped the steering wheel. "Oh! Almost forgot!" Quinn dug in the pocket of her sparkly bomber jacket and passed me something small and heavy. "Pepper spray. Aim for the eyes. If I honk three times, that means run, okay?"

I nodded, hopping out of the Jeep before doubling back for a fist bump. Then I turned on the flashlight on my phone, pulled up the hood of my jacket, and crossed the frost-covered lot before entering the dark mouth of the building ahead.

I ducked underneath the boom barrier, brushing off the cobwebs in disgust. The garage smelled like the dust and dirt littering the cracked concrete floors. It was silent, apart from the steady drip of moisture. I navigated around small stacks of rubble, using the light from my phone to reach the red cherry dancing in the dark.

The outline of a smoking man appeared ahead, his glowing gaze like phantom lights in the dark.

"Let's go." Aleksandr motioned with his cigarette, and I followed him up to the third floor.

We stopped near an old elevator, where the doors were cracked open. Aleksandr leaned against the balcony, gazing out over the dam, where the sky was still blue with night. I had never been this close to the dam—a concrete waterfall rushing hundreds of feet down toward death. I swallowed.

"Why here?" I asked, rubbing my arms.

"It's out of the way. The little stunt your boyfriend pulled has angered some of my investors. One of them is not so forgiving—I've got some heat."

I groaned. "You're being *followed*?"

"Well, I did try to warn you earlier." Aleksandr shrugged and blew a smoke ring. "But you were too busy calling me an asshole to pay attention." He formed a talking mouth with his hand, pestering me until I lost my patience and shoved him.

"You *are* an asshole!"

"So we're agreed."

We glared at each other.

"An old gray sedan's been driving through my neighborhood. Are you having me watched?"

"I have no need to follow you when I know exactly where you are. Besides, Bortnik is on holiday. Bad guys have families too, Aaliyah." Aleksandr smirked. "And honestly, I'm offended—do I dress like I drive an old gray sedan?" He glanced at me. "But if you are so worried—"

"What? You'll look into it? Don't bother. It's not like you care—which is why I can't figure out why you got involved with my friends in the first place."

"Your little friend got involved with me first. Daniela knows too much, and she was targeting you. She needed to be put in her place."

"So you had Quinn handle it—but why her? Why not ask me? Daniela is *my* problem."

"In ant hills, does the queen dig her own tunnels, find her own food?" Aleksandr offered me his cigarette. "You have bigger problems."

Furious, I knocked the cigarette from his hand.

Aleksandr laughed. "Wishing you could put me in my place, *pchelka*?" He leaned against one of the garage's supporting columns, arms folded. "I knew you were strong like your mother, not a coward like your father."

"What do you know about my family?"

The jarring sound of screeching tires interrupted us. Aleksandr and I flew to the balcony, gripping the rail as we watched a black Lexus come speeding down the road. It didn't stop for anything; I flinched at the distant crash as the boom barrier was destroyed, followed by three sharp honks—Quinn's signal.

"I'm probably stating the obvious, but I think we should leave." I backed away from the rail, knowing the mace in my pocket wouldn't stop the person on their way up.

"There is nowhere to run." Never one to lose his cool under pressure, Aleksandr let his icy gaze sweep across the garage.

But we were trapped like mice. Any second now, that Lexus would come barreling up the ramp onto our level—and then what?

Aleksandr strode to the elevator, wedged one of his shiny Oxfords in the gap between the doors, and used his strength to heave them apart.

"Get in," he ordered.

"Are you *insane*? No way!"

"I can't protect you out here, Aaliyah!" Aleksandr grabbed my arm and forced me toward the elevator. "Get in!"

Heart pounding, palms slippery, I took Aleksandr's hand as he knelt and hoisted me down into the shaft. I dropped four or five feet into the darkness, landing on the elevator's carriage. I wobbled and steadied myself, trying not to think about the acrid, stuffy air I was breathing, or falling down the shaft, or being crushed, or—worse yet—being trapped in here forever . . .

Neck craned, I gripped the wall of the elevator shaft and called up to him.

"Don't leave me down here, Aleksandr, *please!*"

"I won't. I promise, Aaliyah, I will not leave you—trust me."

Trust *him*? It was impossible, but what choice did I have?

Aleksandr straightened. Trying not to hyperventilate, I watched through the narrow crack between the doors as he pulled a gun from his pocket.

He disappeared from view, and for a few tense seconds the silence was crushing—until that agony was replaced by the bedlam of squealing tires and gunshots. I covered my mouth so I wouldn't scream. Then, suddenly, there was a horrific crash, like the sound of thunder, and the whole building seemed to tremble. A car horn sounded, stuck on a loop, ringing desperately in my ears.

Eleven

The Ringmaster

Of course, there was no cell service down in the shaft.

I pointed my phone light upward at the doors, hopping in vain as I shouted Aleksandr's name, fighting to be heard over the Lexus and its never-ending horn. I flashed the light around the small, dark space, searching for an exit that didn't exist. Because after so long alone in a lightless room, with only your worst fears for company, you'll do anything to escape.

I fought the ugly thoughts circling inside my head, reminding myself that even if my battery died and left me in the pitch black, I wouldn't be trapped down here forever. Quinn knew I was here; once she realized I wasn't coming out, she would call the cops and they would find me. Sure, I'd be grounded for the rest of my life, but at least I'd be alive. But, just in case, it wouldn't hurt to scream for help in the meantime.

"Hey! I swear, if you're dead I'll kill you!" I banged on the walls, pleading. "Aleksandr, *answer me!*"

I jumped, holding my thumping heart, when Aleksandr sagged against the door. He lowered his arm, instructing me to grab his hand. I breathed a sigh of relief then backed to the opposite side of the elevator. Taking another deep breath, I dashed forward, running up the wall high enough to grab Aleksandr's hand. My stomach dropped as he hauled me up through the air. I wriggled through the opening and collapsed, my face pressed against the cold, dirty concrete. I turned on my back and sat up, thanking my lucky stars that I had survived.

"We have to go." Aleksandr stood over me, one hand extended, the other pressed to his side. I gasped at the blood seeping through his fingers. He spat, and the saliva was mixed with pink.

"You've been shot!"

"We have to leave, Aaliyah—*right now*."

The sound of shattering glass validated the sense of urgency. My gaze snapped to the far wall of the parking garage, where the Lexus was a smoking ruin. The driver had lost control, hitting the wall fast enough to crush the hood. And judging by the banging coming from inside, whoever had shot Aleksandr was attempting to break out of the wreckage. I had tunnel vision, wondering what would happen to us both when they escaped.

Aleksandr called my name. He was winded and sweating, his blue eyes hollow underneath. I took his hand, and he pulled me to my feet, wincing as blood droplets hit the floor.

"Go. I'll stay behind. Finish this."

"Let you die and become a martyr? Yeah, right! No one's kicking the bucket today, jerk-face." I grabbed his arm and threw it over my shoulder. We hustled across the parking lot and into the stairs. The adrenaline that kicked my heart and feet into overdrive made everything seem unreal, like none of this was really happening and I was just a character in some fucked-up video game. But Aleksandr's blood on my hands and jacket was my anchor to reality and the pressure I needed to keep going.

The farther we walked, the weaker Aleksandr grew. On the

second-floor landing, as I tried to heave the heavy, rusted door closed to buy us more time, Aleksandr stumbled and fell down the steps, half-dead. I ran after him and shook him awake, gasping when I heard a door slam overhead. The faint, tinny sound of Quinn's horn followed, like a lifeline in the dark—the encouragement I needed to save Aleksandr.

"Get up, get up, get up!" I bullied him onto his feet, and we kept going—racing across the lower level toward the large, gray rectangle of dawn light ahead, the finish line to our mad dash for freedom.

We broke from the building, flying into the cold morning air. Time seemed to slow when Aleksandr slipped from my arms, falling facedown, motionless in the parking lot. Quinn jumped up and down beside the Jeep, screaming and waving her arms.

"Come on, come on! *Run! Run!*"

Sensing the assassin behind us, I hauled Aleksandr to his feet one last time, dodging the bullets flying overhead as we ran for the Jeep. Quinn threw open the back door before jumping in the driver's seat. Aleksandr and I dived inside, covering our heads as the Jeep's back window shattered and glass rained down. Quinn threw the Jeep into drive, and we held on, tires screeching and white smoke billowing she stepped on the gas and pulled a U-turn.

Aleksandr and I stayed hunched down in our seats until the shots faded. For a few tense moments, the only sounds were my own harsh breathing and the wind whipping in the air. Then Quinn whooped, pounding the steering wheel as she told the assassin to screw himself, along with a few other choice phrases. Eyes on the steel-gray skies overhead, I didn't relax until I saw the trees whipping past and knew we were close to the off-ramp.

Aleksandr's groan drew my gaze just as his red-rimmed eyes

fluttered closed. I sat up when his head drooped, instructing Quinn to drive faster.

"You're still freaking out—why are you still freaking out?" she demanded, her anxious blue eyes connecting with mine through the rearview mirror. "Is the Lexus following us?"

"No." I removed the bandana I was using for a headband and pressed it against Aleksandr's wound. "Aleksandr's shot. He might be dying."

But the curse he released when I pressed down seemed like a good sign.

"Okay, we're going to the emergency room—"

"No hospitals." Aleksandr's voice was a breathless wheeze.

"Good idea!" Quinn shot back. "Let's swing by the dock and finish the job ourselves."

Aleksandr's laugh turned into a cough.

"Alek, shut up! Quinn, keep driving! We'll go to my place." I exhaled, repositioning my hands, relieved to see the pressure was working and the bleeding had slowed down. I scowled at Aleksandr—this was all his fault. "What are you looking at?"

He smiled. "You called me Alek. Don't get soft on me now, *pchelka.*" Those were his last words before he passed out.

Quinn pulled into our driveway and left the Jeep running to fling open the back door. Our neighbor, Mr. Schulze, paused in the middle of stuffing letters in his mailbox, watching, mouth open, as we dragged Aleksandr's lifeless body across the lawn.

Quinn and I screamed for Trina as we hauled him through the front door.

"Aaliyah, where the *hell* have you been!" I heard her shout from the second floor, followed by the thunder of her footsteps as she raced down the stairs and into the foyer. She stopped short, already dressed in her blue maternity scrubs. "Aaliyah, you're covered in blood—what happened!" She strode forward, gripping my face in her hands. "Where are you hurt?" she demanded, checking me for wounds.

"It's not my blood—it's his. Please, Aunt Trina, you have to help him!"

Trina took a knee at Aleksandr's side, checking the pulse in his neck. "He's alive—barely. What he needs is a hospital!"

"We can't. I'm sorry." I shook my head.

"This man is bleeding out on my rug—*why the hell not?*"

"H-he, uh, he doesn't have insurance!" Quinn blurted.

"He can afford Italian leather shoes, but he can't buy insurance? Don't you lie to me, Quinn Davis!" She rose to her feet, amber eyes flashing as she planted her hands on her hips.

"Aunt Trina, *please.*" I grabbed her hand in earnest. "I know you and Mom didn't want Dad's world to find me, but it did. His name is Aleksandr, and he saved my life—"

"*Aleksandr?*" Trina squinted, like his name was familiar.

I nodded. "You *have* to help him—*please.*"

Trina shook her head, lips pursed, then released a heavy, reluctant exhale.

"Oh lord, I'm gonna lose my license! Aaliyah, get my medical bag from under my bathroom sink!" Trina pointed at Quinn. "And you, grab his feet," she instructed. "Help me get him into the kitchen. We don't have much time."

☆ ☆ ☆

As our classmates were getting ready for a normal day at school, Quinn and I sat near the bottom of the stairs at my place, listening to Aleksandr cry out in pain as my aunt stitched him back together. Eventually, when Quinn couldn't stand it any longer, she jumped up, declaring she needed a shower and was going to borrow some clothes. I watched her charge up the stairs, and I was thinking about going after her when Tyler texted.

where are you?

It was the middle of first period. I was sure half the school had noticed my absence by now. I chewed my thumb, knowing he would be pissed when he found out what had happened.

at home. sick day.

ok aaliyah. must be pretty contagious if u and q r sick togethr . . .

I rolled my eyes, shutting off my phone before he called and found out Aleksandr was bleeding out in my kitchen.

Quinn hadn't left me a lick of hot water.

I sighed and removed my hand from under the faucet, shaking off the cold water. I walked to the bathroom sink and stripped. I didn't recognize the girl in the mirror. Her curls were a mess. Her face and hands were smeared with blood and dirt. This wasn't the image of a girl holding out hope for an acceptance letter to the Conservatory. I had no idea who this girl even was.

She couldn't be me.

After a cold shower, I met Quinn in the driveway, where we stood side by side, inspecting her busted Jeep.

Quinn dragged her fingers through her hair and shrugged, helpless. "Once my mom sobers up, she's gonna *flip*."

"Don't worry, she's not gonna find out," I said firmly. "We'll clean it up and take it to Hudson's shop. I'll pay for the damage."

"Really?" Quinn's face brightened with hope. "Is that totally selfish of me? Aleksandr is in there dying, and I'm out here, worried that my mom is gonna kill me too."

"Considering your mom's aim actually improves with alcohol, I'd say your fears are pretty valid." I laughed with Quinn, wrapping my friend in a warm, tight hug as she wiped the tears from her eyes.

"I thought you were gonna fucking die," she said.

"Me too." I stepped back, wearing a lopsided grin. "C'mon. You grab the vacuum; I'll grab the cleaning supplies. By the way, do you and Declan still keep those furry handcuffs in the glovebox?"

Quinn frowned.

Quinn was vacuuming up the broken glass and I was scrubbing blood out of the back seat when we heard a car pull into the driveway, right behind the Jeep.

Quinn and I popped our heads up, watching through the busted window as our boyfriends stepped out of Declan's cherry-red BMW.

"Oh, shit," we said.

We scrambled to remove our yellow rubber gloves and rearrange our hair, knowing it wouldn't cover up the mess we were struggling to clean. We got out of the car as Tyler and Declan strolled up, staring at the Jeep's busted window.

"What the fuck is that?" asked Tyler, pointing at the red-stained rag hanging out the door.

"Uhhh . . ." Quinn and I stared wide-eyed at one another, each frantically motioning for the other to hurry up and say something.

Declan opened the Jeep's back door. He and Tyler exchanged dark looks as they observed the bloody mess.

"Are you hurt?" Tyler demanded, green eyes inspecting me for damage as he took my face in his hands.

I shook my head. "We're fine."

On the outside . . .

"Bro, *what* is *happening*?" Declan raised his hands then planted them on his head, his brown eyes filled with a mixture of shock and disbelief. "This is so messed up . . . I don't even know what to say."

"It's no big deal, Dec," Q insisted, eyes watering, chin trembling. "Everything's gonna be okay—I promise." She started toward him, stopping in hurt surprise as he backed away.

"Quinn, we aren't even in the same stratosphere as okay," he replied, fists clenched. My heart sank to the bottom of my boots—I had never seen Declan this angry.

"Wait! Declan, I can explain—"

"You always have a good excuse, Quinn—but I'm tired of those. And honestly, I don't care." Declan shrugged, jamming his hands into the pockets of his jeans as he gazed forlornly away. "I don't know what's going on here, I just know I don't want any part of it." He walked past Quinn, pulling away as she sobbed his name and reached for him.

"Shit." Tyler sighed, lifting his chin to the gray afternoon sky.

"Tyler, you should go with him," I said sadly, watching Declan slam the driver's-side door behind him.

"What about you?"

"I'm fine, really. Go with Dec. I'll take care of Quinn."

We both cringed when she let out a wordless shriek.

"Fine! Leave!" she shouted. "I didn't want you to come to Vegas anyway—I'm better off without you!"

She picked up a pebble, striking Declan's windshield, then broke down in tears and stomped back toward the house.

I pinched the bridge of my nose, frowning at the headache that was forming. Everything was falling apart, fast.

"Hey." Tyler lifted my chin until I looked him in the eye. "You know why the walrus got away with eating the oysters? Because the carpenter had his back." Tyler pressed a soft, reassuring kiss against my cheek. "You look tired. Get some sleep."

He returned to the BMW; I was glued to the spot as they backed down the drive. The assassin's bullets hadn't fazed me, but Declan's aim had been straight and true. That murderous glance he shot through the windshield said this was my fault and that he blamed me for everything.

Well, so did I.

Trina met me in the foyer, on her way out as I was heading in. She had on a fresh pair of scrubs, her large Coach purse slung over her arm.

"How's the patient?" I asked, closing the door behind me.

"Stable." Trina exhaled, hoisting the purse strap higher on her shoulder. "But he's not out of the woods yet. I'm off to score him some antibiotics—the untraceable way."

I raised my brow. "Untraceable how?"

"The less you know the better. And I think I'm going to take my own advice and *not* ask why this man almost died in my kitchen." She walked to the door and grabbed the handle, then changed her mind and turned around. "Aaliyah, why did this man almost die in my kitchen?"

"That is kind of a long story . . ."

"Aaliyah, how long have you been running with him?" The narrow eyes and folded arms meant she was not to be messed with.

"I'm not running. It's more like a light jog—"

"*Aaliyah.*"

"Since Tyler came back." I chewed my lip, studying the floor in shame. "But it's not Tyler's fault."

"Your mom said the same thing when she first started dating your father. I'm not saying Tyler is like your dad, but Pete is—you have to stay away from him, Aaliyah. Men like Pete and your dad and Aleksandr—they're like quicksand. They'll suck you in, and then you'll never get out."

"Mom did," I said, lifting my chin.

Her large amber eyes softened; she nodded. "Yes, and it cost her everything, Aaliyah. It almost cost her *you*." She took a deep, heavy breath and straightened, preparing to face whatever lay outside that door. "Back when your dad was still around, sometimes he would bring along this cute little boy with blond hair and big blue eyes. His name was Aleksandr." Trina folded her arms, watching as I processed this new information. "Y'know, I asked your dad once why Aleksandr was always with him and not his own dad. He said Aleksandr's father had a bad temper. Clearly that cycle of violence has continued, because he's dying from a bullet wound—*in my kitchen!*"

"Aleksandr is going to die?" My heart leaped in dismay.

"If I don't get him those antibiotics, he will." Trina turned toward the door, then turned back once again. "You said he saved your life—which means *you* almost died. I'm not going to ask if you're okay—because who would be—but I need to know that you're safe, Aaliyah. After I get those antibiotics, we are going straight to the police and filing a report—"

"And then Aleksandr's dad will ruin us. I didn't listen to him once, and he took his anger out on you and Hudson. Auntie, he's the reason we lost the house—"

Trina gasped, clutching her belly in panic.

"I'm sorry," I said, with a sad, empty shrug. "The police can't protect us from people like him. You can't keep me safe, Aunt Trina. Not from this."

One day soon, our little suburban neighborhood would be steamrolled to make way for a business complex named in the Vitali family's honor. There were people like our neighbor who were going to lose everything because of one stupid mistake I'd made. If Trina went to the police, or if Aleksandr died on our countertop, I didn't want to think about what his family would do.

"Well, Aaliyah, if I can't protect you, then that means I can't protect my son. Every minute you're here, he's in danger too."

I nodded. "I understand."

In a few months, I would be eighteen and off to college. Tyler had started his life's journey years early. I could handle a few extra months on my own, especially if it meant keeping my family safe.

Trina swiped the tears from her cheek. "I love you, Aaliyah. But I have to think about Michael too. I hope you understand."

"Michael—that's his name?" I chuckled, wiping the tears from my own eyes.

"Yeah." My aunt nodded, eyes wet, as she smiled back. "Michael Hudson Espinosa." She glanced down at her stomach. "He's kicking. Here, feel."

When she took my hand and pressed it against her belly, and I felt the little flutters of life against my palm, I was overcome by the need to love and protect him. But when I looked in my aunt's eyes, I knew those feelings were only a fraction of what inspired Trina to protect him too. She was his mother, not mine, and he deserved to come into a world full of peace, not the chaos I lived in.

"You're gonna be a great mom—you're the next best thing I ever had," I said. And because there had been a few times that day that I thought I would never see her again, I hugged her, just in case.

☆ ☆ ☆

At Hudson's repair shop, I paced back in forth in the garage, watching him study Quinn's poor, violated Jeep. I chewed my nails, in silent agony as he removed his ball cap and scratched his head, mystified. Hudson was the only person I knew who could help me out of this mess. Well, part of it anyway.

"You can fix it, right?"

"*Por supuesto*, definitely. I guess I'm just . . . surprised." His brows rose in concern. "*Eres tan . . . buena, simpática.*" He turned, motioning at the damage on Quinn's Jeep. "And *this* is . . ."

"Not?"

"Uh, sí. That's one way to put it."

I sighed. "I know how this looks—"

"It looks like bullet holes! Ay, *mija*—what have you and Quinn gotten into? Do I even *want* to know why you're not at school today?"

I shook my head.

"Does your aunt know, at least?"

I nodded, and Hudson visibly relaxed, no longer struggling to uphold the constant balance between his friendship with me and his loyalty to Trina.

Hudson shook his head at the Jeep one last time. "Find a ride here after school tomorrow, and you can take it home."

"Okay. Should I pay now or later?"

"You've got the money for this?"

"My mom had life insurance. Most of it's going toward my tuition at the Conservatory, but I can use some of it for emergencies. Like this." I made to grab my purse—but Hudson stopped me.

"Save your money for the Conservatory—and other 'emergencies.'" He offered a commiserating pat on my shoulder.

I was thanking Hudson when the shop's door gave a merry tinkle, and an all-too-familiar face entered. I had never seen

Pete with a gun on his hip, but the fresh bruise under his eye was a good indication of his sudden change of heart. Pete was intimidating on his own, but after the showdown in the parking garage, it was the gun that paralyzed me with fear. I felt Hudson's gaze and knew that he connected the panic in my face to Pete.

Hudson took a rag from his back pocket, wiping the motor oil from his hands. "We're closed. *Lo siento.*"

"The sign says you're open," said Pete, cocking his thumb over his shoulder. That knowing smirk said he was well aware we wanted nothing to do with him. "Anyway, I'm just here for a tune-up. My car's making funny noises. And when you have a problem . . . you fix it. Right?" I broke out in a cold sweat under Pete's hawklike gaze, and though I tried not to fixate on the gun, I was spiraling.

It didn't matter how much he sounded like Tyler when he was pretending to be friendly or whether his presence in Hudson's shop really was just a coincidence, the gun was too obvious to ignore. A gun sends a message, and this one was loud and clear. A passing mechanic dropped one of his tools. I jumped as the bang ricocheted across the shop. Panting, heart racing, I was overcome by a flashback of flying bullets . . .

Hudson reached out and steadied me with his hand, then seemed to grow another six feet as he turned his flashing gaze on Tyler's dad. Hudson was slow to anger—until you poked the bear.

"I can't help you, Mr. Moore," he said firmly. "You need to leave."

The tension was palpable; it hung in the air, spreading across the shop like a virus. Pete's gaze darted around, noting the half dozen mechanics who had paused what they were doing and were ready to square up. All they needed was Hudson's signal.

Hudson raised his brows, calmly casting his rag aside as he waited for Pete to put up or shut up.

"I see." Pete's lip curled into an ugly sneer. "That's too bad, Espinosa. Business is looking a little slow. Probably get more tumbleweeds than customers."

"I don't want your blood money. Leave my shop, *pendejo*."

Pete finally took the hint and backed down. He sucked his teeth, spitting on the way out. The door closed behind him, and I sagged against the counter in relief, holding my chest as I fought to catch my breath.

Hudson crouched before me as one mechanic pulled up a chair and another passed Hudson a paper cup and a pitcher of water.

"Here." Hudson poured the water, extending the cup.

I took a few grateful sips, breathing deep as I waited for the dizziness to pass. Now I just felt sick to my stomach.

"I'm fine. Thanks, everyone, really."

Hudson gave the nod, and the mechanics went back to work—but he wasn't satisfied, not by a long shot. "He's been giving you a hard time, hasn't he? Since you started dating Tyler?"

I grabbed my arm and glanced away, which was all the answer he needed. Hudson cursed, raining fire on Pete in Spanish.

"These problems, they didn't start until *he* arrived. And I'm sure, in some way, he had everything to do with *this*," said Hudson, pointing at the Jeep with his chin.

And that was true, in a way. Pete wasn't the hitman who'd shot out the Jeep's back window, but he *was* the reason I wound up in the parking garage in the first place.

"You can't make this your problem, Hudson. He's *dangerous*."

"Some men are dangerous, and some men are smart." Hudson walked past me into the shop office, closing the door behind him.

Jared was happy to swing by the shop and pick me up in his gold '96 Impala, with a hula girl on the dash and dice hanging off the mirror. From there, we swung through the Mickey D's drive-through, where I sprang for an early dinner. Too cold to sit on the hood and watch the town lights flicker to life, we sat in the parking lot and chowed down. I didn't realize my phone had been stuck on silent until I was halfway through the meal. I gasped, seeing a string of missed calls and texts from Quinn, Declan, and Tyler. I choked on my iced coffee, listening to the angry voice mail Tyler had left. Not only had he found out what had happened to the Jeep, he also knew I was harboring the comatose criminal who had nearly gotten me killed.

Tyler and Declan pulled up into the driveway seconds after Jared dropped me off. I raced Tyler across the lawn, darting ahead of him just in time to block the front door.

"Aaliyah—move! I know he's in there!"

"You're not getting inside, Tyler!" Suctioned to the door, my limbs were splayed in a giant X.

"Seriously, Aaliyah—after everything he's done to you?" Tyler was so close I felt his warm, minty breath on my lips. "You're really going to protect him?"

"I'm not protecting him, I'm protecting you, genius!" I pushed him back. *"Go home."*

"Aaliyah, wait, don't leave—"

Tyler smacked the door when I closed it in his face.

I was sitting in a chair in the guest room, brushing up on Spanish verb tenses, when I received yet another phone call. I rolled my eyes, assuming it was from Tyler, until I saw the number was listed as private. I *hate* private numbers.

"Hello?"

"Hi. Am I speaking with Aaliyah Preston?" The female voice on the other end of the line was smooth—and careful. Right away, I could tell her friendliness wasn't genuine, it was professional.

"This is her—maybe."

She chuckled. "Nice to meet you, Aaliyah. Lina Fuller—*Sugar* magazine. Could I ask you a few questions? About your relationship with Tyler Moore?"

"Um, no? I'm still waiting on that apology for the article you guys wrote telling everyone I'm getting married."

"We issued a retraction—"

"That's not an apology." I waited, annoyed by the silence on the other end of the line. "All right, fine. At least tell me who's been feeding you information about my life. All those pictures and tips being submitted—they're coming from somewhere."

"I'm sorry, Aaliyah, all our sources are confidential—"

"Except for the most intimate details of my personal life. Thanks for that, *Lina*." I hung up with a sigh, done with tabloids for life.

Beside me, Aleksandr rested easy in the guest bed, on a steady drip of fluids and antibiotics. He had passed out in the middle of Trina's procedure and had been unconscious ever since. Trina said that if he survived, she wanted him gone as soon as he was back on his feet. I heaved a heavy exhale, turning the page in my Spanish book.

"I'm alive?" Aleksandr smirked without opening his eyes. "You must be devastated."

"That's one word for it," I said dryly, taking the glass of water from his bedside and bringing the straw to his lips. "My aunt saved your life. You're welcome."

"I never asked for favors," he retorted, wincing as he lifted his head from the pillow then tried to lift his arm. Aleksandr stared at the fuzzy pink cuffs that shackled him to the bed, listening to the clink as he gave them another shake. "What the hell?"

"You have answers—about my father," I said, closing my Spanish book with a snap. "And you're not going anywhere until I get them."

I caught up to Tyler at his locker the next morning, shooing away the giggling gaggle of underclassmen. Judging by the look he gave me, Tyler would rather have taken on an entire horde of fans than listen to what I was about to say. Of course, he had every right to be upset with me for getting mixed up with Aleksandr.

"So? Where is he?" said Tyler, giving me the side-eye as he shoved his books in his locker.

"Handcuffed to the guest bed."

Tyler dropped his calculus book on the toe of his Gucci sneakers, so to say he was hopping mad was fairly accurate.

"What?" I shrugged. "I left him a bucket and some food—I also took his wallet and his phone. He's not going anywhere."

"Oh my god, am I dating a *serial killer*?"

"Aleksandr's not leaving until I find out what happened between his family and my dad—I'm *this* close, Tyler."

"You realize this is insane, right?" Tyler exhaled. "What about the B-Team—don't they have practice this afternoon? You can't be with them and babysit Aleksandr at the same time." He sighed. "I'll cover for you."

I kissed his cheek. "I owe you one."

"Damn straight. Look, I forgive you for almost getting killed the other night, but I don't think D's gonna let this go any time soon. He's pretty pissed at you for taking Quinn to that parking garage. And honestly, Ali . . . I can't say I blame him."

I leaned against the gray bank of lockers, chewing my lip in guilt as Tyler cupped my face in sympathy. Sure, I could fix Quinn's Jeep, replace the broken window, but I couldn't mend her relationship with Declan. And that was on me.

After school, with Jared's help, I rounded up a few boxes from the dumpsters and headed home to find the rest of the B-Team camped out in my front lawn as we pulled into the driveway.

"What's all this?" I asked, raising my brow at Jared, who wore a crafty grin as he put the car in park.

"I mean, c'mon, Preston. You didn't *really* think we'd let you go through all this alone."

Chinara met me on the front lawn, wrapping me in a tight, warm hug that smelled like Chanel.

"Quinn says you're moving out! You should have told us!"

"But what about cheering at the basketball game?" I laughed, wiping happy tears. "And the B-Team has practice—"

Quinn stepped forward, her red, puffy eyes offset by a resilient smile. "We're here for you, Ali. Always."

"Even though I messed things up with you and Declan?"

Quinn took a short, deep breath, gathering her strength. "It was my choice to go with you to that parking garage. If Declan wants to be mad, he should be mad at me."

"I'm still sorry," I said, hugging my friend. I stepped back, taking her hands. "Thank you for always being there—all of you."

As my friends helped me tote the boxes from Jared's car into the house, I didn't feel nearly as alone as I had the moment that I realized it was time to move out.

☆ ☆ ☆

It only took a couple of hours to strip my room, boxing up memories, throwing out the ones too faded to take with me. By the time I taped up the last box, I could see the full moon through the window. I stood and sighed, glancing around the bare, unfriendly space. I walked to my bedpost, rubbing an old, familiar chip in the wood.

"Hey, you." Tyler leaned in the doorway, arms folded. "After the B-Team bailed, my mom called, freaking out."

"Oh no, what happened?"

"My idiot father stood Emma up at the mall. Who forgets to pick up their own kid?" Tyler straightened, stuffing his hands in his back pockets. "Sorry I wasn't here to help you pack."

"You had more important things to do. Anyway, you're here now."

"I'm here now," he repeated with a smile, pecking me on the cheek before grabbing the last box. "It really was a nice room, Ali-Cat."

"Yeah, it was." I smiled, turning off the lamp for the last time.

☆ ☆ ☆

Saying goodbye to my mother at her funeral was the hardest thing I had ever done. Saying goodbye to my aunt was the second. I'll never forget the sadness in her eyes as she stood on the doorstep, holding Hudson's hand on her shoulder as she watched me drive away.

"Is this really necessary?" Aleksandr drawled from the passenger seat, indicating the handcuffs that linked his arms.

"You just let me know when you're ready to start talking," I said and turned up the radio, drowning him out so I could concentrate on the drive to my new home.

Ten minutes later, I set my bag on the doorstep of a beautiful, fully furnished guesthouse. Aleksandr remained shackled at the wrists, hunched over and sweating as he clutched his side in pain.

"Kidnapped by a seventeen-year-old girl," he rasped, leaning against a pillar. "Didn't see that coming."

"That makes two of us," I said and rang the bell.

Daniela Vega opened the door, still not her usual sparkly, villainous self, but at least she appeared well rested, which was more than I could say for me.

"Hey, *chica*. When you called and said you needed a place to stay, I thought you were joking. This him?"

I nodded, then reached in my jacket and removed Aleksandr's black card. "One shopping spree to Nordstrom, as agreed. In exchange, I get a place to stay."

Aleksandr smirked.

Daniela studied the card for a few seconds, then snatched it from my hand, turning it between her manicured fingers.

"I still hate you," she said. "The only reason I'm doing this is because I hate him more—and the sooner he's out of the Village, the better."

Daniela stepped back and opened the door wider, her dark eyes unreadable as I entered my new home.

"You sure your parents won't mind that I'm crashing?" I asked, removing folded clothes from the suitcase on my new queen-size canopy bed, placing them in the matching ornate ecru dresser.

"My parents are on vacation in Dubai," she said, nosing

through my suitcase. "Even if they were here, they wouldn't care. They've been icing me out since I dropped the team—but they *love you.*" The way she dragged out the words *love* and *you* and spritzed my perfume, I knew Dani's beef with me had yet to be squashed.

"I'll be out of your hair by next summer—then we never have to see each other again," I said, plucking my perfume from her hands and setting it on the dresser.

"You said Aleksandr has to stay until he tells you about your dad—but what's stopping him from leaving? It's not like there's bars on the window in the guest room." She grabbed one of my shirts from the suitcase, checking it against her reflection in the white-framed full-length mirror. "You're like those ringmasters, leading bears around by a rope, thinking they're the ones in charge . . ."

"I know." I removed a picture of my mom from my suitcase, running my thumb across the glass before setting it on my new bedside table. "But he owes me, and he knows it," I said, turning back to Dani, our eyes connecting through the mirror. "Funny thing is, Aleksandr's a cold-blooded monster, and he still has more loyalty than you. You *betrayed* me, Dani—multiple times."

"You betrayed me first, Aaliyah!" She raised her hands, growling in frustration as she squeezed them into fists. "My entire world has collapsed—and no one cares . . ." She seemed to deflate as she glanced down, the shirt dangling from her silver-ringed fingers. "I know I deserve it—Dad says you have to be made of iron to make a name for yourself. Let's just say, I didn't get to the top of the pyramid by shaking hands and baking cookies."

Neither had Quinn.

"Your dad's wrong, Dani."

"Is he? When it's men like him and Aleksandr who are in charge?" Daniela's laugh was short and bitter. "Well, even the pyramids will turn to dust one day. I've lost everything, Aaliyah—my friends, my reputation, my team—and to top it off, my parents are threatening to cut me off because I keep falling short of their *psychotic* expectations. And after *everything* that's happened between us, I *still* let you stay here. Why did you even call—I thought you were done with me, like everyone else." Daniela balled up the shirt, casting it aside in anger.

"Dani, I called because the more people I expose Aleksandr to, the more people I hurt, and *you*—"

"Are already damaged goods," she finished, folding her arms, her glossy lips pursed as the truth went down like lemons. "Y'know, for a minute, I thought maybe you called because you cared. Guess I was wrong."

"Dani . . . Dani, wait—"

Daniela left the room; a few seconds later, the front door slammed closed behind her.

Aleksandr poked his head in the door, smug as a cat with a bellyful of goldfish.

"Trouble in paradise?" He laughed, ducking the pillow I chucked across the room.

"Asshole! Why would you ask Dani to break up me and Tyler? I thought you liked us together."

He smirked. "What, Aaliyah? Are you searching for my approval?"

"No!"

"Look. I like you together—I really do. But you and I, we walk a different path. I see where you're going, Aaliyah, and it's a place he can't follow. The sooner you make peace with that, the sooner you will heal and move on."

Aleksandr left. Glaring at the empty doorway, I growled and threw another pillow. He was supposed to be *my* prisoner, but it would always be the opposite.

That night, I tossed and turned in unfamiliar sheets beneath an unfamiliar ceiling, then eventually fell into an uneasy sleep. It seemed like only seconds had passed before I was being shaken awake in the dark. I heard a click, and the large, airy space was flooded with light. I sat up, blinking back the spots and confusion.

"Why are you in my room?" I demanded, hurriedly wiping the sweat and tears from my face.

"I woke up—there was a noise outside my window. I thought someone was sneaking around the property. Then I heard you calling in your sleep." Aleksandr pulled up a white rocking chair and sat down gingerly. Whatever Trina had done, he was recovering quickly. His color had returned, he was eating solids, and he was taking his antibiotics in pill form now.

"You were telling me to run," he said quietly, his cool blue eyes surprisingly soft as they met mine. He looked almost . . . suburban, in Tyler's basketball shorts and plain T-shirt.

I drew my chin to my knees, trying to recall the nightmare that had slipped away the moment I opened my eyes. My heart was still pounding.

"When I was a boy, I would watch the men in my country go off to war. The ones who survived were not the same when they returned. The lucky ones had nightmares . . ."

My throat was too tight to speak; I glared at Aleksandr in silence.

"I can tell you the truth about our families, Aaliyah, but

I can't guarantee you will like what you hear. And frankly, the fact that you saved my life changes nothing between us. It only proves your loyalty, which is *exactly* what I need."

"Screw you." I swallowed, realizing Daniela was right. The ringmaster's power is a façade; they never really have control over the bear. "Just tell me the truth. You owe me that much."

"I will tell you what I know," he said. "But I'm afraid Bortnik is going to be a problem . . ."

Twelve

The Sky Is Falling

Even though my head was still reeling from the late-night conversation with Aleksandr, I started the school day with my head above water. It was Friday; HVH was abuzz with gameday excitement. Rumor had it, Eric was back on his grind. It was peak awkwardness when the two of us bumped into each other early that morning—me as I was coming from the guesthouse, and Eric as he was leaving the mansion. We fell naturally into step, walking the garden path that separated the beach home–style guesthouse from the pool and the rest of the manor.

Before we could round the bend where the mansion ended and our descent toward the gate began, Eric darted in front of me.

Hands thrust in the pockets of his letterman jacket, the basketball captain with the steadiest arms in the game was suddenly unsure of himself as he stared down at his Jordans.

"That night, on the boardwalk, I panicked. I left when I should have tried to save you. And when Tyler ran past me, I knew he was looking for you. I'm an idiot, but I'm not out to get you, Aaliyah."

But someone was. Just that morning, in the middle of getting dressed for school, I'd gotten an alert from *Sugar*'s online blog. Splashed beneath a picture of me in sunglasses, loading boxes into my car, was a whole list of conspiracy theories on how my life was spiraling and why I had been kicked out for dating Tyler.

"So you're not talking to the blogs about me?" I asked, folding my arms.

Eric looked me in the eye as he shook his head.

"What about Daniela? She only gave me a place to crash 'cause I twisted her arm."

"Honestly . . ." Eric glanced over his shoulder toward the blank, white mansion. "I don't know if she sold you out, Aaliyah. But that night at the lake house, I think she just wanted to make you hurt as much as she's hurting."

"She told you that?"

Eric grinned. "More or less."

I smiled back. "Good luck at your game, Eric." He called my name again as I walked past him. His smile had vanished.

"There's something else I have to tell you, Aaliyah."

But after the things Aleksandr had told me last night, nothing would surprise me.

Tyler slid into the passenger seat of my car, removing one of his AirPods to slip me a slow, minty kiss.

"Really?" I asked, pulling back and removing a wad of gum from my mouth.

"What, I was in the moment," he said, popping the gum into his mouth and blowing a bubble with a grin.

"Do you want the bad news or the really bad news?"

"Well, good morning to you too, Aaliyah. My night was wonderful, thank you so much for asking." Tyler clicked his seat belt in place with more than a hint of annoyance. But I didn't have time for him to be angry with me.

"Remember back in October, when I was chased in the mansion?" I asked. "Well, Eric told me it was someone on the basketball team. Apparently, some guy with a camera paid him to do it. He told Eric what happened, but Eric couldn't do anything about it. His hands were tied. This guy's family is part of the booster club—they basically paid for the gym, and they even help renovate the school every year. The best Eric could do was warn him not to bother me again."

"How is that bad news for me? Sounds like bad news for Eric and his friends." Tyler's eyes flashed with anger as he gazed down the long road ahead. "Eric's known for this long—why's he telling you now?"

"Guilt, maybe? I think he just wanted to finally clear the air. Maybe it's good he sat on it. Astrid would lose her mind if you were on the Internet for beating up the basketball team."

"Maybe I will. Counselor Vasav did say I needed another extracurricular activity. Who is this guy anyway? The asshole that chased you—what's his name?"

"I didn't ask because I knew you would make me tell you. And anyway, it doesn't matter who he is."

"Of course it matters, Aaliyah!"

"He tried to scare me, and it didn't even work. The cops would call it just another dumb Halloween prank, and you'd go to jail for assault. Booster club parents do *not* fuck around, Tyler."

He thumped his head against the seat, releasing his annoyance through a long exhale.

"Then what *can* we do?" he said, his green eyes turning to mine, looking to me for the answers.

"We focus on the guy with the camera. He drives a gray sedan, and he's been harassing our friends for stories about us to make our lives *miserable*. He's got to be Lina Fuller's source at *Sugar* magazine, he has to be. I just need to figure out why."

"Why?" Tyler repeated, brows arched in confusion.

"Driving past my house? Sneaking photographs in the middle of the night? Never wanting to be seen? Hiring some kid on the basketball team to scare the shit out of me? All of this seems so . . . targeted for just some random paparazzo."

"I take physics, and even that shit doesn't make my head spin as much as this. C'mon, Ali, let's just get to school before we're late."

If this conversation was a prelude to tonight's dinner date with Tyler's sister and his mom, then it couldn't have been a worse start to the day.

After school, I jetted back to the guesthouse to get ready for dinner, calling Aleksandr's name as I hung my jacket on the coatrack in the foyer. The guesthouse was more like a luxury apartment, with a spare room for Aleksandr. But when I knocked on his door and watched it swing open, I realized he was gone once again. His bed was made, his medication missing from the nightstand. The only thing he had left behind was a plain white card on the dresser. I flipped it open, reading the short message scribbled inside.

Sorry things have to be this way. See you soon, pchelka.

I wasn't about to let Aleksandr's cryptic warning ruin the night I had planned. I spent an hour choosing my outfit, and another ten minutes picking the right heels and earrings. Tyler rang the bell at seven sharp, and I opened the front door to a teenage dream, snipped from the pages of *Teen Vogue* and delivered right to my doorstep. His dark plaid shirt was rolled at the forearms and unbuttoned, exposing the white V-neck beneath. His slim-fitting jeans were blue black, his Adidas as sparkling white as his smile. Some girls had posters. I kissed the real thing.

Tyler had obviously had some time to cool off since that morning. He handed me a large bouquet of roses and complimented my dress. I led him into the kitchen, where I found a vase for the roses and the perfect spot to place them. I set the vase in the little window above the sink, taking a moment to admire the flowers. But the real stunner was in the kiss that I turned and walked into, as Tyler swept me off my feet and into his arms.

"My life lost all direction," he said, taking my face in his hands. "Then I found my way back to you. I just wish my dad and Aleksandr and this fucking leak would all just fucking disappear."

"I know. Let's not think about any of that tonight. Let's just think about us."

Tyler slipped his fingers through mine, and I followed him to the white Jaguar stretch limo he had rented for the evening. The driver opened the door, and we climbed inside, tangling ourselves in the back seat.

He extracted his lips from mine with a heavy sigh when "U Can't Touch This" started playing in his jeans.

"Emma, I already told you—I can't just DM all your favorite boy bands for concert tickets. It's embarrassing . . . *What?* Why would she do that? That's the worst idea *ever* . . ."

Watching his face during his conversation was like watching storm clouds gather on the horizon. Tyler said goodbye to his sister and hung up the phone, lowering the partition just long enough to give the driver a new set of directions.

"Emma says we're all having dinner at my dad's place—not my mom's. Which means . . ."

"Your dad will be there too. Great." My stomach sank in disappointment. Whatever Madilyn had made was bound to be amazing, but I had zero appetite now. "Who cares? Let him throw a temper tantrum and ruin dinner—it wouldn't be the first time."

I was deadly serious as I slid into Tyler's lap, and he chuckled as I draped my arms around his shoulders.

"Ali, my mom doesn't know about Aleksandr or my dad—or any of it. And it has to stay that way. For Emma's sake. Our mom is the only person left in our family who makes her life feel normal. I have to protect that."

I nodded, smiling in reassurance. "As long as we're not eating shellfish, I'm pretty much down for anything."

"You make the world a better place," he said softly. "My life would be so much darker without you, Ali."

Tyler kissed the gold Cuban chain at my neck, then his fingers traveled to the rose in my hair before he swept my waves aside. The loosened curls now cascaded down my back. He brushed them from my shoulders, his gaze devouring my satin cami dress, which was nearly the same shade as his famous green eyes.

"I'm trying to be positive, Tyler, for you, my aunt, Hudson, our friends—but the truth is, I would be terrified if I didn't have you with me tonight. Your dad's getting desperate. I'm worried he might do something."

"He's off the rails. It's the perfect storm of drugs, debt, and pressure. I keep thinking that someone needs to end this. If writing a check is all it takes, then maybe I can talk to Astrid. I won't tell her everything, just enough details to help her pull a few strings. Maybe if I just give in, do things the easy way, we can end this, Aaliyah. Be done with Aleksandr and my dad for good."

"Are you sure? None of this is your fault or your responsibility. You shouldn't have to be the one who pays for your dad's mistakes."

"The label wants me to go on tour after I graduate, and I know my dad only agreed because he wants the money. But maybe this time he's right about something. If Astrid won't help, then I'll go on tour, and I'll pay off Aleksandr that way. I'll do whatever it takes to protect you, Aaliyah."

After all the beautiful things he'd said, how could I tell him the truth and be the one to take his hope away? It wouldn't hurt to pretend that the clock wasn't ticking for just a little bit longer.

We raided the minibar, extracting a bottle of champagne the company had forgotten to remove, and returned it half-empty. I was still giggling when Tyler and I emerged from the back seat of the limo. Tyler gave the driver instructions to meet us in ten minutes, then changed it to an hour when I pinched his leg. On the sidewalk, he sorted my dress and straightened my hair, smiling with pride. I loved his enthusiasm at taking me home to his family. We would be almost ordinary for a night.

The winter sea breeze ruffled our hair as the queen palms and live oaks dipped and waved. The stars were a white glow scraped across azure skies, yellow streetlights gleaming in the evening twilight. Pete's apartment complex was in view up ahead, a gray thumb in the sky. We looked both ways, crossing the street hand in hand.

In this upmarket section of the neighborhood, a stranger with unkempt clothes and an expensive camera around his neck certainly stuck out. Tyler didn't seem to notice when I squeezed his hand, pressing closer to him as the stranger walked toward us, leaving the apartment building. The silver parts on his camera glinted in the streetlights. Something about it was as jarring as seeing a ghost—or running from one.

He stepped aside as we walked by, flowing past us like a deadly current as Tyler and I continued toward the building's entrance. I glanced back, heart jumping into my mouth when I realized I had the man's attention. The way he stared at me, twisting the toothpick in his mouth as he snapped a picture, it was like he knew me, intimately—even though I had never seen him before. I still had goosebumps in the elevator as I thought about the camera and wondered whether he drove a gray sedan. Why was he leaving Pete's apartment building? The answer forming in my head wasn't pretty—but I would keep it to myself . . . for now.

On the fifth floor, Tyler pulled a key from his pocket, unlocking a door labeled 5C. I followed him inside, taking immediate note of the cool air and masculine furnishings. The bluntness and sparsity of the decor and the lack of family photos strongly declared this a bachelor pad, missing the softness of a partner's touch.

"Ali Ali oxen free!" Emma popped up from the couch, darting across the living room to the front door. We gave dap and mimed explosions, then threw our arms around each other. I hugged the shorter girl tightly, kissing the top of her head.

"Are we staying out of trouble?"

She matched my playful grin with one of her own. "Absolutely, sis."

"She's crossing her fingers behind her back, isn't she?"

Tyler nodded.

Besides stealing cars and telling lies, Emma had also begun wearing makeup in the last year or two, the blush on her cheeks and the shimmer on her eyes a step up from Lip Smackers and chunky plastic heels. The more Emma grew up, the wilder and more beautiful she became, like her brother.

Tyler tapped his sister on the shoulder. "No hug for me?"

"You're on TV, loser. I see you all the time." But there was really no hesitation when she placed her arms around him.

"Where are Mom and Dad?"

Emma's sweetness soured like milk.

"Where else? In the back, *fighting*. This weird guy showed up and totally nixed Mom's vibe. They've been arguing ever since." Emma and Tyler shook their heads in unison, interrupted by the oncoming din of raised voices.

"—can't *believe* this! Can't believe this!"

"*Calm down*, Madilyn. It was *business*."

"Then keep your 'business' away from our family, Pete! That's not the kind of people I want you bringing around Emma!"

Madilyn and Pete entered the living room still arguing. They didn't realize they had an audience until Emma cleared her throat.

Pete flung his hands in an outraged greeting.

"Welcome to the goddamn funhouse!" He strode from the room; Madilyn stormed after him.

Tyler snorted. "Funhouse my ass. More like the Tenth Circle of Hell."

Madilyn had roasted a chicken, seared vegetables, rolled homemade biscuits, and baked an apple pie that was golden all over. Reluctantly, Pete brought out his good dishware, while Madilyn lit the candles as Tyler and Emma set the table. It was nearly picture perfect, watching the four of them crowded round the dinner table, beckoning me to join them, as if I belonged.

Pete made a big show of pulling out my chair. Tyler rolled his eyes in understanding, dropping into the next seat over. I sank into my seat, wincing as Pete slid my chair uncomfortably close to the dining table. I adjusted, glaring as he sauntered back to his throne. To hell with the consequences, I had half a mind to spill his beans right on Madilyn's plate—until Tyler's knee shook to life, bouncing against mine in steady, rhythmic waves that convinced me to do better. For his sake.

The food was spectacular; I took small bites and chewed slowly. Keeping my mouth full meant that whenever one of the Moores asked me a question, they were usually too impatient to wait for me to swallow and carried on with their lively debates. Pete and I were the only ones more invested in the food than the conversation. I caught his gaze and swallowed hard, dragging my fork across my plate as the staring contest ensued. We were kings, each battling for territory, our silent war in ugly contrast to the white scented candles flickering between us.

"Aaliyah, we are *so* glad you're having dinner with us." Madilyn smiled, pausing to sip from her water glass. No wine for her, though Pete's flute was filled to the brim. "It's almost like old times, isn't it?"

I smiled and nodded. Old times was all of us together, sharing laughs and a meal, plus my mother and minus Pete. Old times were no longer here.

"C'mon, Maddie." Tyler's dad leaned back in his chair, smiling and glaring at the same time. "Cut to the chase, huh? The formalities are excruciating."

"It's called being polite, Dad. You should give it a try sometime."

"Eat your food, Tyler."

Emma dipped her head, snorting over her plate.

Madilyn drew herself together, ignoring the chaos, as dancers are trained to do.

"Aaliyah, I hope that in coming here tonight, you saw this as a *family* dinner—"

Pete snorted, earning dirty looks from his ex-wife and children.

"Because that's what you are, you're family, Aaliyah. You're special—to *all* of us. You're like my second daughter—"

"Oh, this is *rich*."

"Dad!" Tyler glared at his father, but Pete was on a roll.

"No, this is more than ridiculous—it's a slap in the face."

Madilyn's eyes flashed as she calmly set down her silverware. "Then, Pete, feel free to leave."

"I *live* here."

"Yeah, well, I keep the lights on. I also send a lady to wash your dishes, clean your toilet, and put food in the fridge," Tyler said as he leaned smugly in his seat. "The only reason we're even doing this here is because a pipe burst at Mom's place. Plus, Mom wanted this to be a *private* moment—otherwise, we'd be having this conversation at La Maison. Without you."

Across the way, Emma exploded in another fit of nervous giggles that were quickly stifled by her father's Medusa stare. Poor Emma turned to stone.

"Am I missing something?" I glanced around the table, mortified but curious.

"Go for it, Mom. Tell her, she'll love it." Tyler's smile was perfect because it was genuine. My heart flipped when he did the little things, like show appreciation for his mother.

"Tell me what?" I forced a lousy grin, hands twisting beneath the table.

"Ali, at the end of next summer . . . Emma and I are moving."

"What?" I couldn't believe Madilyn. I didn't dare.

"Yep." She nodded across the table, exchanging happy smiles with Emma. "We're going overseas . . . to London."

"You're moving to *Europe*?" Emotion swelled in my chest, so hot and tight I could barely breathe. What a terrible human being I was, that my knee-jerk reaction to big news was to be so desperately miserable for myself instead of happy for the people I loved. But Madilyn and Emma were moving on—to bigger, brighter, more exciting things. As they should. *Isn't that what we all deserve?* I thought, glancing at Pete. Well, most of us anyway.

"Guys, that's *incredible*. What made you decide to leave?"

Emma grinned. "Tyler's not the only one with a dream. I wanna play soccer in London. Why not? If he can win a Grammy, *I* can win an Olympic medal."

"Go, Em!" I said, high-fiving her across the table. "You know I'll be sitting in the stands at your first game."

Madilyn had all the pride and joy a mother could have, but Pete hardly moved. He should have been happy for his daughter, but generosity was beyond his nature.

"Ali." Tyler's fingers skipped across my knee; I jumped, shooing them away. "There's more good news."

"Really?" I glanced nervously between mother and son.

"The studio . . ." Madilyn cleared her throat. "I have to leave it behind. I could sell it . . . or I could give it to you."

"No way—no *freaking* way. Are you serious?"

Tyler shifted his chair closer to mine. "Being a choreographer, having your own studio, it's what you've always wanted. Well, here's your chance, babe."

"Guys, I . . . I don't know what to say. I . . . I *love* the studio. Thank you, that's so kind."

"Don't worry, Ali. I don't expect you to make up your mind right away." But already Madilyn seemed relieved, as if she knew my answer would be yes. "Why don't you take some time and think about it? No pressure."

"Sure, but . . . this is really okay with you? *All* of you?"

Everyone nodded. Everyone except Pete.

"No, it's not okay—it's *insane*. Damn it, Maddie!" Pete pounded his fist on the table. "You're talking about giving away the studio away—for *free*. Not only that but to someone *outside* the family."

Emma cast her silverware aside, glaring ferociously at her father. "Aaliyah is family, Dad."

Pete's laugh was short, made cruel by his disdain.

"More than you know." He turned to his ex-wife. "Ironic, isn't it? How close to being family she *really* became. Why didn't you sign those adoption papers in Amelia's will? What stopped you, Maddie? Huh? Was it guilt? Or was it because she just looks too much like her mother?"

I stiffened, numbed by his scalding gaze. With every ugly word, Pete had sucked my feelings away until I was cold and empty.

Emma pushed back her chair, food half-eaten, her head shaking in confusion.

"Mom, what's Dad talking about?"

"Ignore Dad, Em." Tyler shot his father a dark, meaningful glance. "He's had too much wine. Or *maybe* he's just jealous Mom won't give him the studio because she knows he'd sell it and blow all the money."

Pete was the spitting image of Tyler when he smirked; it made me sick to death just looking at him, imagining Pete as Tyler's future self.

Pete's grin widened and crumbled. "Or maybe it embarrasses me to see your mother hand over her life's work to the very symbol of her infidelity. Cheers." Pete raised his glass, draining his wine in one swallow.

I was fed up, but it was Emma who had had enough.

"This family *sucks*." She fled the table, ignoring Madilyn and me as we called after her.

"Wow." Tyler clapped slow and hard, smiling in his fury. "*Stellar* parenting, Dad. Really well done." He pushed his seat back and stormed from the table, disappearing after his sister.

"I don't understand." I sighed at my plate, wishing I could vanish too. "What is going on?"

"Honey?" Pete smiled sideways at his wife. "I believe your *daughter* asked you a question."

"What happened to you, Pete?" Madilyn's lips went white with fury. And hate. "You have become so cruel."

"Says the woman who shamed her wedding vows?"

"We were *separated*, Pete! God, you know that!"

"Did *you* know, Aaliyah?" Pete wasn't asking a question; he was making a demand. "Did you know we were legally married when my wife started *screwing* your dearly departed mother? What would you say to Amelia now, Aaliyah? Would you be able to look at her the same?"

"Wow," I said, pushing back my chair. "Out of all the celebrity dads, Pete, you are definitely the worst." Standing up to men like Pete and Aleksandr was torture. I went into emotional debt plucking up the courage to face him now. "Never say my mother's name again." I stood and made to go, then turned back to the table. "That was a photographer who left your apartment earlier, wasn't it? I'm just curious, 'cause I'd really love to have my picture taken."

From the table to the living room, I shook with rage, savoring the memory of the anger and humiliation in Pete's face as he realized I had cottoned on to his scheme. I found myself gravitating to the hallway, calmed by the quiet and the dark. I could see the soft orange glow of light beneath a door ahead, and I heard the low murmur of voices. I hated that I was the reason for Tyler's and Emma's pain.

"You ever think bad things happen to bad people, Aaliyah? I do. But you know what's worse than ruining your family's dinner?

Cancer, hands down. What do you think she did to deserve that, Aaliyah? Because I think she tried to take something that didn't belong to her. And the apple doesn't fall far from the tree, does it?"

I rounded on Pete, fists clenched. He hovered in the mouth of the hallway, the husk of something cold and empty—a thundering shape, something you would run from in a hall of mirrors.

"My mom was *not* a bad person. But I get why you hate me so much, Pete. It's obvious—Madilyn loved her more than she loved you, and since you can't punish my mom . . ." I shrugged and folded my arms. "Why not me? Well, guess what—I didn't even *know* about the affair. But I do know that you hired a photographer to make my life a living hell—why?"

Pete crossed the hall, closer and closer, until I was so uncomfortable I stepped back, feeling cornered, like an animal.

"Because you need to stay away from my family. For your own good. My son has responsibilities, he has a future—and you have *nothing*. Girls like you are a dime a dozen, and he'll figure that out once he's on the road, away from you."

I took a deep, shuddering breath, the sob hitching, tangling like thorns in my throat. "Hypocrite."

"Excuse me?"

The door opened. Emma poked her head into the hallway and was quickly ushered back inside. Tyler stepped out, closing the door behind him.

"After everything you've done, you think *I'm* the problem? Seriously?"

"You watch how you talk to me, Aaliyah, I'm still your elder."

"You're a *cokehead*—Aleksandr told me all about you. You're a washed-up, mooching addict so miserable at the way his life turned out that he takes it out on his own family. So yeah, you're my elder . . . but you are definitely *not* my better.

If anyone's the lost cause, Pete, it's you. But pretty soon you won't be able to hold anyone hostage any longer. Bortnik is coming for you."

It felt good to say. Dangerous, but good. My chest heaved, my pulse ticking like tiny bombs in my heart and wrists, ready to explode at any second. I had expected Pete's wrath—but I think it surprised us both when he struck me. I had been hit before, but never with such spite and vehemence. The attack was over as quickly as it happened, but the sound of that slap rang in my ears long afterward. I held my burning cheek, watching, stunned, as Pete stared at his hand, horrified. But the worst was yet to come.

The worst was right behind me.

Tyler lunged past me before anyone else could react. It wasn't much of a fight—he hit his father, and his father hit the ground. Pete sat up, groaning, with that god-awful smirk, wiping the blood from his jaw. But Tyler wasn't finished—he grabbed his father by his shirt, hauling him closer.

"Dad, what the hell do you think you're doing!" He shoved Pete, hard enough for his head to hit the ground.

"Look at you, Tyler—throwing your life away for a *girl*." Pete rose to his feet with a groan, nose to nose with his furious son, who refused to back down. "Drop her. Go on the tour—do what makes you happy."

"*Aaliyah* makes me happy, Dad! Aaliyah! The only person upset about what Mom did is *you*, so for everyone's sake just let it go. I won't let you drag Aaliyah into the past! I was going to ask Astrid to let me pay your debt, but . . ." Tyler stepped back, lifting his arms wide as he shrugged. "It's your problem. Not mine."

Pete shook his dark head, hands raised in defense, clearly the victim in this awful crime.

"*You're* right, I should just throw in the towel, huh, Tyler?

Let you be a disappointment like me and my old man, and his before him. Because let's face it, son, you're a dead end. I was wrong, it's the other way around—you're the problem. Aaliyah will *never* be happy with you."

Tyler had held back when he'd hit Pete the first time. He raised his arm, fist clenched—and I could see it in his eyes that this time there would be no holding back.

"I wanna leave—*now!*" Emma stood in the hallway, her skin pale, large eyes wide with fright.

Emma had stopped the mayhem, but not the madness. Tyler turned back to Pete, whispering something only I could hear.

"We're done. You're *fired*. I don't want anything to do with you. And if you ever, *ever* hit Aaliyah again, it won't be Bortnik that kills you. It'll be me."

Tyler walked away, calling over his shoulder for Emma. She followed her brother, face crumpling, trying her hardest not to cry as she darted past her father. He watched her run away from him, and suddenly his steely gaze had all the toughness of a hard-boiled egg. He was cracked in half, and regret washed from his wounded shell, but all it did was remind me of my stinging face as I turned my back on him too.

Tyler left me on his couch in search of Tylenol and an ice pack, but not before he told Alexa to keep the silence at bay. I sat back, listening to his favorite songs, one after the other. Like his girlfriends used to, the songs changed every week.

I took the medicine with the bottled water he offered when he returned, wincing as I stuck the compress to my cheek.

I sighed. "How's Emma?"

"Fine. She crashed in the guest room. She's gonna stay here

this weekend, take a vacay from our parents. Tonight just made me *really* glad my mom has full custody."

"Me too." I repositioned the ice pack, but the ache was nothing compared to the guilt.

Not to fear, the Love Doctor was here. Tyler took my chin in his hands, inspecting the damage. "Just a welt. How's it feel?"

"Better now."

"Ali, if any guy ever hits you like that, you better damn well tell me."

"Roger that." I smiled the best I could.

Tyler took that as an invitation to ease close, his arm on the back of the couch, playing with my dress strap.

"You know you did nothing wrong, right?"

Tyler didn't know how much I needed to hear that. I took his hand, careful to avoid the fresh scrapes on his knuckles.

"There was so much more I wanted to say to your dad. But I couldn't hurt your sister more than I already have." I covered my face and groaned. "It's him, Tyler. Your dad's the leak. He hired the photographer—the one who's been taking our pictures and selling information. Aleksandr thought someone was snooping outside the guesthouse. Maybe he wasn't wrong."

I didn't say it out loud, but part of me knew Tyler's dad was capable of so much worse than this.

Tyler pulled back in disgust. "Ali, that means my dad basically hired some guy to stalk us—it's harassment. They should both go to jail. We should call the police, let him learn his lesson for once—" Tyler moved to grab his phone from the coffee table, but I stopped him.

"He'll learn, but it doesn't have to be today." My only concern was Emma and shielding her from the consequences of her father's bad decisions for as long as possible.

"Earlier, you told my dad that Bortnik is coming for him. That was the other bad news, wasn't it?"

I nodded. "I'm sorry, Tyler. Bortnik has pretty clear instructions about what to do if your dad doesn't pay up, and Aleksandr can't stop him. I already asked."

"Yeah?" Tyler leaned forward, elbows on his knees as he looked down at his hands. "What else did Aleksandr say?"

"Too much." I tucked my legs beneath me, biting my lip as Tyler turned his dark gaze on mine. "He said that back in the day, my dad and his dad used to be business partners. Long story short, my dad double-crossed his. Drake stole from Andrey, and he's been enemies with the Vitali family ever since. But my dad also stole from Aleksandr. Drake befriended him and betrayed him. Aleksandr wants revenge."

"Is that why your dad stayed away all those years? To protect you?"

"Maybe. Aleksandr says it's safer for me to work with him than against him. Whatever that means."

"It means you have to stay away from Aleksandr, Aaliyah. No more mysterious phone calls and secret rendezvous." Tyler rubbed his face with his hands, drained. "If your dad ever did anything right, it was keeping you away from that family."

"I expected my dad to have secrets, but not my mom." I set down the ice pack, ignoring the injury for something more painful—the truth. "You knew what was going on between our moms, but you never said anything. Why?"

Tyler blew a raspberry as he sank in the couch cushions. "I wanted to tell you, Ali, but it seemed like there was never a good time. I mean, your mom wasn't just *with* my mom—Amelia wanted my family to adopt you. That's big."

It was major.

"Madilyn said I'm like a daughter. If that's true, why didn't she adopt me?"

Tyler exhaled. "Because I asked her not to."

"Okay . . ." I shifted. "Should I feel hurt by that?"

Tyler's face was flaming red. He rubbed it with both hands, too embarrassed to look me in the eye.

"I told my mom I didn't want her to adopt you, but I never told her the reason why. I never told anyone. But the truth is . . . I just didn't wanna fantasize about banging my stepsister. Do you know how *weird* it would have been for me, seeing you walk out of the shower every day? Knowing that every night you're falling asleep, ten feet away, and I couldn't be next to you? All right, you're laughing, but when you really think about it, it's not that funny."

I wiped the tears from my eyes, sagging against him with a dramatic sigh. Tyler's arms snaked around my shoulders; he lay back, and I nestled my head on his chest, listening to the orchestra of his heart.

"I don't know what to do, Tyler. I thought I knew everything about my mom. Now it feels like I never knew her. Maybe the person I thought she was didn't exist." It was like waking up from the loveliest dream and remembering it wasn't real.

"You knew her, Ali. You still do." Tyler's fingers, large and rough where mine were soft and small, traced the back of my hand. "Just because Amelia didn't involve you in every detail of her life doesn't mean she didn't love you. I should know."

"Yeah, but this was important—this was her *relationship*. Why didn't she feel like she could tell me? Why didn't Madilyn? Why didn't *you*?"

"They asked me not to. I only found out because I walked in on them once. Please do not ask me to relive that experience with details."

"Actually, that's the comforting part—knowing my mom had your mom, that she wasn't alone. But now . . . now I have all these questions. There are things I need to know, but I can't ask because she's gone. It's not fair."

Tyler kissed the top of my head, sifting my curls through his fingers. "They were happy. And they were best friends before the relationship, so when you think about it, them being together wasn't much of a stretch."

"Were you mad? When you found out?"

"My mom was really . . . *depressed* when she was with my dad. You see how they are now. When they were married it was even worse. So, was I upset when my mom found someone who treated her like she deserves to be treated? Never crossed my mind." He kissed me again. "They didn't want you to know because you already had a *lot* on your plate. Your mom was sick, and you were taking care of her while busting your ass to keep up your grades. Our moms thought it would be easier for you if they didn't bring it up."

"But your dad knew." I sighed. "No wonder he can't stand me. I said some pretty messed-up things at dinner—"

"You didn't deserve to be attacked for that." Tyler was firm, uncompromising. "Pete hit you because he's a coward, and because what you said is true and he knows it. If Bortnik is his karma, I can live with that."

But I wasn't sure if I could, so as I looked at Tyler's stony face, I hoped he didn't really mean that.

"Are you sure you don't wanna go on tour?"

Tyler turned his face aside. "Yeah. I'm *not* going."

"Why? It can't just be because of your dad. Going on tour is a big deal; you don't just walk away from that."

"I guess you thought I was kidding when I said I'd change my life for you."

"Tyler! I'm not asking you to do that!"

"Yeah, because it's *my* decision. Can I make it?"

I groaned, so frustrated I could hardly gather my thoughts. "But if you give up the tour, I would feel terrible for not dropping the Conservatory. Because that's exactly what I'll have to do if I run your mom's studio—which I know *nothing* about, by the way. And that kind of defeats the purpose of everything—dropping school for something I *need* school for."

"Ali, I really think you're overthinking things. Degree or no degree, you're smart enough to do anything. And anyway, I thought this was endgame—you *told* me this is what you wanted, remember? You said—"

"I *said* I wanted to do things my way. And the studio—"

"Is a handout. Right. I get it." But he pulled away nevertheless. I hadn't just disappointed him; worse, I had hurt him. "Look, Ali, I'm not asking you to feel guilty here."

"I know, but that's exactly how I feel. If I run the studio, then I can't go to Boston. I'd be stuck here—"

"Yeah, with me."

"That's not how I meant it."

"I know how you meant it. Still sucks."

My shoulders sagged. I felt so horrible and selfish. Honesty is supposed to be a good thing, but these days it just seemed like a giant wrecking ball, destroying everything in its path.

"Is this really how it's gonna be in the end, Ali? Either we pick our careers or we pick each other?"

"Maybe," I said, pushing Tyler on his back and straddling his waist. "But right now, in this moment . . . does it matter?"

Tyler shook his head.

"I just want you." He stood, his lips pressed to mine as he carried me down the hall to his room. The sky was falling—all we could do was watch and hold on.

Thirteen

A Pound of Flesh

Quinn and I opened tiny windows between the red silk curtains, aahing and oohing over the size of the crowd. The Harbor Village Coliseum was the perfect venue for tonight's show. A normal talent show would hardly fill the school auditorium, but Tyler's name had drawn people from far and wide. The hall was packed, the judges' panel front and center. Tyler was sitting between Mr. Woods and the principal. He looked like he was having trouble finding a balance between being polite and ignoring their animated conversation.

"All these people . . . they're here because of Tyler, aren't they?" Quinn retreated from the view, clutching her stomach like she might ralph down the front of her costume. "Oh boy, I don't think I should've had that burrito . . ."

"Quinn." I gripped my bestie's shoulders and looked straight into her frightened blue eyes. "You've got this. You're amazing— you're *way* too badass to let a little stage fright stop you."

"Easy for you to say. You've been onstage a million times already, plus you're totally channeling Beyoncé in that sexy leotard and jeans—how am I supposed to compete with that?"

I laughed, though I felt sorry for Quinn. She was right: I had experience performing for large crowds, and she didn't.

"Q, you and I are not competing against each other. We're a team, and you're gonna be fine. Everyone gets nervous before a performance, even the vets. All you have to remember is that trying to imagine them naked never works. It's much easier to picture them gone."

"Gone as in . . ." She drew a slicing motion along her neck then jumped right into hanging herself.

I shook my head. "Whatever floats your boat. I forget how weird you are sometimes."

"It's a talent." Quinn shrugged.

"Maybe you should be onstage for that instead."

"*Psst!* Guys!" A tech student motioned near the exit.

Busted, Quinn and I headed back to the dressing room, where all the night's acts were waiting. In ten minutes, those red curtains would rise, and the talent show would begin. Some students paced, others muttered beneath their breath or practiced their performances. Daniela had been right—tonight was important, maybe not so much for *my* future but for anyone else who needed the trophy for transcripts. Tyler's stamp of approval had a magical ring to it, one that businesses and colleges would be silly to ignore. This wouldn't be like winning *Epic*, but it was the next best thing.

"Guess what?" I decided to use my remaining time warming up, crossing one arm over the other as Quinn inspected her makeup in a nearby mirror. "Tyler has the chance to go on tour again."

Quinn paused in the midst of fluffing her golden curls as she gazed in the mirror. "Um, free concert tickets? Yes, please. Tell me he said yes."

I switched arms, shaking my head. "He won't even consider

it. He has the chance to travel the world for *three months*, but he'd rather spend the summer with me. Can you believe him?"

"I can't believe *you*." Her arms were crossed when she swiveled to face me.

"What?"

"Look, I totally wrecked things with Declan—I don't wanna see you go down the same road with Tyler. A hot, famous dude wants to spend the summer with you, and you're complaining. Who does that?" Quinn cut me off before I could answer. "Stop selling yourself short. If Tyler thinks you're worth more than the fame and the cars and the clothes and the money and the free merch—"

"Quinn—"

"—and the adoring fans and the super-hot girls and the *bitchin'* parties—"

"All right, *Quinn*, I get it!"

"Then why not support his decision?"

I sighed. "Because Tyler's making decisions based on his anger at his dad. It's complicated."

Quinn hunched her shoulder. "Is it?"

Saved by the whistle. The call was clear and sharp, issued by a tall, lanky tech student wearing a headset and holding a clipboard. "Showtime, folks! Let's move it to the hallway!" He glanced down at his board. "Next act—Quinn Davis, onstage in ten!"

Quinn just about fainted. "Ali, he didn't say your name— why didn't he say your name?"

"Don't panic. It's a clerical error. Just focus on your breathing."

Quinn nodded, shaking her hands as she breathed through the jitters. We made our way back to the narrow hall offstage, where we stood in line with the other performers.

"Seriously, Q, you look like you're about to faint. Are you okay? Do you need some water?"

"I love to sing and write songs, Ali. That's my passion. But let's be realistic—I'm not the next Tyler Moore. And I'm not ever gonna be able to dance like you—"

"Q—"

"This might be the last stage I perform on. I don't know . . . I guess maybe that's why this stupid talent show is so important to me. Tonight might be the last time I get to do the thing I love the most." Quinn threw her arms around me. I hugged her back, wondering if we shared the same fate.

"Quinn, you're an amazing performer. Whatever happens onstage tonight won't change that."

"Thanks." She sniffed, patting her face. "Be right back. Can't go onstage looking like a raccoon."

Quinn slipped away to adjust her makeup. My heart started the dance early as I thought about all those filled seats in the audience and how slowly but steadily the line was shortening. *If I dance with Quinn tonight, will I be taking the spotlight from my friend? Is it fair for me to even be onstage, knowing that Tyler might be biased when judging?*

Was a first-place trophy worth more than my integrity?

"Oh no, is Harbor Village's new queen bee suffering some sort of moral dilemma?" Daniela was front and center, minus her groupies, whom I had no doubt were sitting in the crowd, eating popcorn as they enjoyed the fireworks. I never realized that being popular meant that the same people who fawned over you would buy front-row tickets to watch you fall.

Daniela smirked. "Heavy is the head that wears the crown."

"You want it back, Dani? Take it."

"I already am. Don't think because you're living in my back-yard, and because my girls and my team abandoned me, that I've lost my edge."

"Without the doo-wop chicks to sing backup for you, the spotlight's all yours." Crossing swords with my landlord wasn't the smartest idea, but being nice to Daniela also left a horrible taste in my mouth. "Good luck," I said, smiling tightly.

I stuck out my hand, waiting for her to give in and finally end this stupid feud once and for all.

"I'd say the same to you, but who needs luck when you have a pop star?" she said, ignoring my hand. "Although, I don't know how'd I feel knowing that everything I get from here on out isn't because I earned it but because my boyfriend *thinks* he's in love."

"Tyler does love me—and I love him. You have to accept that, Dani."

"Everything has an expiration date, Aaliyah." She strutted past me and turned in her ankle boots. "Just between us girls—your first time, did he buy you a pretty necklace and tell you he loved you before he screwed you on some random couch in a basement?"

"Actually, it was at the lake house in the woods, and it was beautiful. I don't know what to say, Dani—except I'm sorry that Tyler didn't love you the way you needed him to. I mean that." I made the mistake of placing my hand on Daniela's shoulder, which she immediately pushed away.

Because Dani wasn't in a forgiving mood, and she definitely wasn't feeling the holiday spirit.

"You've got some nerve feeling sorry for *me* when you're the one dancing under Tyler's *ginormous* shadow. You'll never be seen again. Not by Tyler, not by anyone. Now if you'll excuse me, I'm up next."

Mouth dry, palms sweating, I watched Daniela go, wondering how she'd gained access to my worst nightmares.

The time had come. The techie with the clipboard opened the door that led backstage, poking his head around before stepping all the way through.

"Quinn, you're up!"

"Wait, what?" Quinn and I exchanged confused glances. "*We're* performing. Together. We're performing together!"

"That's funny." He checked his clipboard. "I crossed off all the names on my list. Hold on a sec . . ." He pushed a button on his headset, waiting for the click and the brief buzz of white noise. "Hey, Flores, you got a copy? How come Aaliyah Preston isn't on my list? . . . Oh damn, really? . . . Shit. Okay, well, I'll let her know." He flashed a small, apologetic smile that none of us would remember except for me. "Sorry, Aaliyah. I guess somebody forgot to tell you—you're off the schedule."

"What? But *why?*"

He hesitated. No one liked to be the bearer of bad news.

"Apparently, Mr. Woods got a few complaints. Some of the other students were concerned you might get special treatment—y'know, since your boyfriend's one of the judges? My bad—someone *really* should've told you sooner. Good luck, Quinn."

He gave an awkward wave and disappeared.

"Looks like you're up, Q."

She shook her head. "No, Aaliyah. I—I can't do this on my own. We're partners. This—this is what we've been practicing for."

"Q, you never needed me up there. You're a star. You shine all on your own, without anybody else. And he's right—I shouldn't be allowed to go out there, not with Tyler judging. That's not fair."

"Aaliyah, I don't have a chance in hell. Do you really think Tyler is gonna vote for *me?* Without *you?*"

"Once you start singing, he won't have a choice. Now go out there and kick Daniela's ass. Do it for me."

Quinn wrapped me in a fierce hug, hesitating one last time before hustling away with a final wave.

I rushed backstage, joining a throng of tech students watching the performance. I was just in time to watch Quinn's spectacular opening notes before she brought the house down.

After the talent show, Tyler slid into the back seat of the Uber, right into my waiting arms.

"The vote was unanimous," he said, cupping my face in one hand. "I didn't even give my input until the rest of the judges had already spoken. Quinn would have won, hands down, even if I hadn't voted for her."

I sighed in relief, feeling lighter than I had in weeks. I still had bad dreams and I still looked over my shoulder, but as long as I looked in those dark green eyes, none of that mattered.

"Here." Tyler pulled an envelope from his pocket, instructing me to open it. Inside was an enormous check, with a blank space following "pay to the order of."

"*Ten thousand dollars?* Tyler, what is this?"

"Quinn's winnings from the talent show. She asked me to give it to you. She said you'd know what to do with it."

"I do." I smiled, tucking his hair behind his ear before I kissed him.

The next morning before school, I swung by Pete's apartment building, knocking on his door with a coffee and the envelope in hand. Pete opened the door a crack, one bleary, suspicious eye peeking into the hallway before he closed the door and undid the chain. He was in his bathrobe, looking hollow and disheveled, with circles under his eyes and a five-o'clock shadow. Guess I wasn't the only one finding it hard to sleep.

"Here." I handed him the envelope and the coffee. I didn't expect a thank-you, so I didn't wait for his reply.

"Why are you giving me this?" he called.

I halted, sighing at the elevator waiting up ahead before thrusting my fists in my jean jacket and turning to face Pete.

"I'm doing this because even though Tyler hates you, he would only end up hating himself more if you died. The coffee is so you can sober up and call your daughter. The check is for Aleksandr. Maybe if you give him the money, Bortnik will hold off a little longer."

"It's not *nearly* enough."

"Actually, it's more than you deserve."

"Aaliyah, if you really want to help, then accept the studio as a gift and sign over the rights to me. I can sell Perfect Form to pay off my debt. You have to do it this way—my ex-wife will never give me the studio."

"And in what world do you think *I* would?" I walked to the elevator with a laugh, pushing the button for the lobby before popping my shades back in place. "Stop having me followed, and stop selling pieces of my life—or the next time it'll be Hudson knocking on your door," I warned, letting the elevator doors close behind me.

Something about Pete's life hanging in the balance had me thinking about my own future and all the ways I was wrecking things in the present. If running for my life with Aleksandr had taught me anything, it was that life was short. So I vowed to keep dancing for as long as I could.

I danced in the living room with my family during Thanksgiving break as we put up the Christmas decorations. We danced on Turkey Day and again when Emma, Madilyn, and Pete joined us for Christmas. Pete was the only one who chose not to wear an ugly sweater, but that was the only problem he dared cause with Hudson under the same roof. That evening, after a full day of sneaking spiked eggnog, stuffing our faces with cookies, and opening gifts, I pulled Tyler aside. I led him beneath the mistletoe, with Trina's giant Christmas tree and a beautiful fire in the background. The whole house was warm and inviting and smelled like gingerbread. I was happy and grateful that nothing had changed since I'd left.

"I took some time to really think about my decision," I said. "I *love* Perfect Form. It's been part of your family for so long, and it's brought so many people together and changed so many lives—yours included. It's a special place." I exhaled, trying to ignore Pete's dark, insidious gaze as he nursed a full glass of whiskey across the room. "Even though I'm not ready to run the studio, I don't want Perfect Form to close. So . . ." I took Tyler's hands, sliding his ringed fingers through mine. "Trina helped me find a good lawyer who said I can have someone run the studio for me while I'm at college. I can take back the reins whenever I want. The studio doesn't have to close."

Tyler was so excited he spun me in a circle and kissed me under the mistletoe. Dizzy in his arms was exactly where I wanted to be. And we kept on dancing.

In January, everyone gathered in solidarity when Tyler finally earned his driver's license. The milestone was celebrated under the Sunset, where we danced with our friends all evening. That night, when Tyler drove me back to the Vega mansion to kiss me between the sheets, the guesthouse finally felt less like an exile and more like a retreat.

February came, and it was finally time for the Angels to show what they were made of at nationals. I went to the parking lot to say goodbye as Quinn, the other Angels, and the B-Team boarded the school bus to the airport. I would have loved nothing more than to join them in Florida at the Walt Disney World Resort, competing for the title, but I would just have to cheer them on from my living room . . . alone.

Tyler dropped his duffel bag to sweep me off my feet and kiss me.

"I'm gonna miss you," he said, sliding the curls from my forehead.

I smiled. "It's one weekend—not forever. Besides, the B-Team needs you for moral support. Especially since Quinn asked them to join the Angels at nationals—that's monumental."

Aleksandr's rule about leaving the Village still stood. Of course I didn't want Pete to die, but until the debt was paid I would be tossing and turning with nightmares of being stuck in the Village forever. But any chance I got to look in those green eyes was worth it—even if every day I teetered between giving Tyler part of me and losing everything for him.

After the bus left, I found myself opening a tab at the bar under the Sunset. I was nursing a virgin Cosmo, alone, on a Friday night, waiting to go back to the guesthouse and watch *The Office* while I studied for the SATs, when someone walked up to the bar and asked for a job application.

"Daniela?"

Dani snatched the application, red-faced. "Anyone finds out about this, and you'll be homeless—*entiendes?*"

"Yeah, I got it. Jeez . . ."

But I didn't have to tell anyone Daniela's secret. After the Angels returned with a silver trophy and ribbons, it wasn't long before the rumors were circulating that Daniela was scrubbing tables at the Sunset. Ever since she had quit the Angels and lost the talent show, right was left, up was down, and boys were being nice to me. As for Daniela, there was no doubt the Angels had lost gold without her—and she was lost without them.

Things had blown over by Valentine's Day. Though it was weird not coaching the B-Team, I devoted my spare time to helping Madilyn out at the studio. Transitioning ownership was a process, and I had a lot to learn. But the one person I needed to have faith in me never left my side. That night, Tyler and Quinn teamed up for a duet at the '50s sweetheart dance. There was no need to feel jealous of their chemistry onstage when there were so many sparks between us. We danced cheek to cheek at the sock hop, me in a poodle skirt and Tyler in a polo shirt and loafers with his hair slicked back. And of course we slow danced again that night in Tyler's bedroom, listening to "I Only Have Eyes for You" by the fire.

And then, suddenly, it was March, and time for the SATs—our last chance to impress the colleges before they made their final decision. Some of us, like me and Chinara, were buckling down, while others, like Quinn and Tyler, were more likely to blow on a set of dice and leave their scores up to chance. But either way, no matter what your plans after high school, conquering the SATs was a victory for everyone and yet another reason to keep dancing.

April was the senior trip. While most of our friends would have said there was nothing like spring break in LA, I wouldn't have traded park days and movie marathons with Tyler for anything. Missing the senior trip because of Aleksandr's petty rules meant, for once, I had the green-eyed Adonis all to myself.

Tyler might be a world-famous musician, but being a pop star didn't absolve him from missing out on some of life's golden moments too. Rather than celebrate another name day in the spotlight, Tyler requested a quiet, intimate get-together for his eighteenth birthday. Our closest family and friends joined him for an elegant candlelit dinner at La Maison, followed by a heart-pounding exit from an escape room, drunk karaoke at a local bar, and all the dancing you could do in one night.

Tyler acted like it didn't bother him that Pete never showed, but he looked so unhappy as he scrolled through his social media, as if searching for some special words between the videos and gifs and messages from the thousands of fans who wanted to celebrate his birthday with him. Pete had Twitter, but he didn't have time for his son. So when Tyler was sad, I kissed him, and when he cried, I pretended not to notice.

I marked off the months that slipped by on my calendar, counting the days in study groups and make-out sessions. They passed in the blink of an eye—until suddenly it was senior week in May—five days of juvenile pranks, crazily themed dress-up days, and all-around delinquent behavior. Thursday, the school held a ceremony in the gym, which Tyler opened with a stunning rendition of "The Star-Spangled Banner." Then the senior class officially passed the school torch to the juniors.

Friday was senior skip day, and the day of the *real* torch ceremony. That evening, the juniors and seniors invaded the beach, bypassing the CLOSED UNTIL SUMMER sign, slipping right through the low-slung metal gates, which didn't quite meet in the center. It was there, down by the water, that we lit the bonfire for the annual end-of-school/beginning-of-summer celebration. Every year, the seniors gave the juniors the same test—supply the beer, earn the torch. They never failed.

Pop music serenaded the night, blending seamlessly with

shouts and laughter. The bonfire licked at the navy sky, and waves of steel blue lapped gently at the curving shore. Summer was nearly upon us. Tyler and I strolled contentedly up the beach. One arm was slung around my neck, while his free hand gripped a water bottle filled with beer. We were closer and happier than we'd ever been, even though our time slipped by faster and faster.

Aunt Trina had spent weeks scrambling to prepare for her last-minute wedding—checking and re-checking that the ball-room at La Maison was still available for the big day, booking appointments for hair and makeup—and scheduling for the movers to come and pack the house. Hudson had put a down payment on a home in Daniela's neighborhood; they were moving right after the wedding ceremony at the end of May, when the baby was due. The wedding might be the last time I saw some of my friends, and one of the last times I would dance young and free at seventeen.

Sitting in my lawyer's office, I had never felt more important as I waited for her to return with the ownership papers for Perfect Form. The day was finally here for Madilyn to hand over the reins, and all we were waiting on was my signature. Tyler leaned back nonchalantly in the high-backed leather wing chair like he had built a tolerance to earth-shattering moments. But I was nervous—tapping my foot, adjusting my curls, picking fluff from the hem of my sundress . . .

Tyler glanced over his shoulder then leaned close and asked if I was okay.

"Tyler, I don't deserve this."

He exhaled. "Ali, we've been over this."

"It should go to you—why didn't Maddie give you the studio?"

He sat up, shoulders straightening beneath his Gucci bowling shirt. "I grew up there. Perfect Form will always be part of me . . ." Tyler trailed off, gazing into the distance as he summoned old ghosts from the past. "But the studio wasn't always the sanctuary for me that it was for you. Honestly, Ali, the place is better off sold than in my hands."

I nodded in understanding, sliding my fingers through his just as the lawyer swept back into the room.

"Are we ready?" she asked with her bright, cheerful smile as she sat down behind her glossy, wooden desk.

I smiled. "Where do I sign?"

I came home from a rave a few nights later covered in glitter and body paint, a tipsy Tyler on my arm. We kept the lights off, maneuvering through the darkened guesthouse into the living room. Tyler tripped over the couch, falling face-first into the cushions, laughing like an idiot. I grabbed the afghan from the back of the couch and draped it over him, kneeling at his side to say good night.

"Ali-a-go-go, you're, like, a total businesswoman now," he slurred. "I'm so proud of you, G."

"Thanks, *G.*" I laughed. "It still feels surreal—like none of it's really happening. Like I'll wake up tomorrow and this will all have been a dream. Even you." I pushed the hair back from green eyes half-lidded from weariness and alcohol.

"Nothing's going to happen," he murmured, tapping my nose in reassurance. "Unless you fuck shit up."

We burst into laughter, foreheads touching.

"But really, though—my family trusts you, Ali. You just have to trust yourself, and everything will be fine."

I told him I loved him, and seconds later Tyler was snoring. I doubled-checked the locks, then finally dragged myself to bed—only to be shaken awake hours later, in the middle of the night. I swam from sweat-soaked, terrifying dreams to see Tyler standing wide-eyed over me.

"Ali, it's the cops!"

"What?" I squinted through the yellow harshness of the lamplight, wiping the sleep from my eyes.

"It's the cops! Aaliyah, something's happened!"

Understanding clicked, and I flew out of bed, throwing my bathrobe over my pajamas and rushing to meet the official-looking pair standing in the foyer.

"Hello, officers. Is something wrong?"

The look of hesitation they shared before they answered told me everything.

The next day after school, I pulled into Perfect Form's parking lot, hesitating before I opened the door.

"You don't have to do this, y'know," said Tyler gently.

"It was my responsibility," I said and stepped out of the car.

Tyler closed his door, and we joined his mother where she knelt in the wreckage, sifting through the studio's charred, still smoking remains for whatever memories had been left intact. So far, her arms were empty.

"I can't believe this place is actually gone," said Tyler, thrusting his hands in his jeans pockets as he gazed in bitter dismay.

It must have been a sight for those who'd witnessed the once magnificent building toppled by searing heat and flames. Gray rings of smoke still wafted from the studio's blackened skeleton. The whole scene smelled like a giant campfire or barbecue—but those things were nice and comforting. *This* was horrifying and awful.

"Was anyone hurt?" I toed a fallen beam singed by the fire, recoiling from the scorched, melted remnants of a dance trophy.

"It was the middle of the night, so no one was here—thank goodness." Madilyn dusted her gloved hands before rising to her feet. Her jeans and sweater were stained with soot; I could still smell the smoke and flames. I couldn't imagine how painful that must have been—having to stand in the crumbling ashes of your life's work.

"It was arson," she said, wiping the sweat from her brow and the tears from her eyes. "The firefighters told me this morning."

"The police filled us in last night," I replied, clutching my twisting stomach. "What *happened?*"

Madilyn shrugged. "There's an open investigation—no leads yet, but I'm sure the police department will sort it out. For now, there's nothing we can really do. Since it's arson, insurance may be tied up for a while . . ." Madilyn shook her head, shrugging helplessly. "I'm so sorry, Ali, Tyler." This wasn't the way things were supposed to be. Losing Perfect Form felt like a death in the family. Madilyn was clearly heartbroken and devastated, but if she were thinking the thoughts inside my head, she would probably be feeling murderous.

"Feel free to keep anything you find," she said, squeezing my shoulder as she passed.

Hands in my hair, I stood and surveyed the rubble as Tyler paced.

"He did this, I *know* he fucking did this! There's only one person who'd steal from his own family!" Furious, Tyler kicked at the ruins, sending up a cloud of dust and debris. Hands on his knees, he laughed bitterly as he fought to breathe through the anger. "No wonder he's dodging my calls—Pete burned down the studio out of spite. If he can't have it, no one can."

"Madilyn doesn't know," I said quietly. "Should we tell her?"

"No. It would only make her feel worse—she's been through enough."

Tyler kicked something else, and I released a tiny breath, trying to keep it together. I'd known Pete was desperate to get his hands on the studio, but I never thought he would take it this far. And maybe that was the problem—seeing people for who I wanted them to be, instead of accepting them as they were. Play stupid games, win stupid prizes. I should have known it wouldn't be this easy—companies don't just fall into your lap. Neither do pop stars.

Once people discovered the town's most beloved dance studio had burned down, the community came together to show their support. Friends and strangers came out to clean up the space; Chinara even offered to start a fundraiser. But Tyler was rich—money wasn't the issue. The problem was Pete, who had done something unforgiveable, and it looked like he'd get away with it scot-free.

One day, as Tyler and I were having afternoon bowls of cereal, I happened to turn on the news. Madilyn was giving an interview, offering a reward for any information that could lead to the capture of the arsonist.

I slowly chewed and swallowed the last bite of my Corn Pops, watching Tyler's face turn red from feelings probably similar to my own—anger, frustration, *guilt*.

"This dance studio was bigger than me—for many of my

students, it was a lifeline," said Madilyn, looking earnestly into the camera. "If you know something, *please*, don't be afraid to speak up."

Tyler's spoon dropped in his bowl with an angry clink. Apparently, he had lost his appetite.

"It's not your fault," I said, watching him get up and storm from the table. I called after him again, sighing in disappointment when the door slammed in response.

To try to take his mind off things, that night I took Tyler dancing at the Sunset with our friends. The days when all of us would be together in the same room, or even the same zip code, were coming to a close. As we stood in a circle and toasted senior year, the sight of Declan with his arm around Quinn, and the happiness on her face, gave me hope for the future. Declan caught me staring, offering a tiny grin of reconciliation as we each tipped our champagne glasses.

"I'm sorry about the studio," he told me later that evening as I joined him outside, behind the Sunset. We were having a beer, reminiscing over our sickest rides at the Airwalk, a conversation that drifted into silence until awkwardness compelled us to speak now or forever hold our peace.

"And I'm sorry about you and Quinn," I replied, tucking my hair behind my ear then twisting the beer bottle nervously between my hands. "Really, Dec—I should never have asked Quinn to come with me to that parking garage. And I should've apologized to you a lot sooner."

"You tried." Declan grinned. "I just wasn't ready to hear it."

"You and Quinn were getting kind of close downstairs," I said, wearing a sly grin as I raised my beer to my lips. "Does this mean you're back together?"

Declan's smile wavered, and I immediately regretted my question.

"Oh, Dec, I'm sorry. I didn't mean to intrude—"

"No, no, it's okay, Ali. You're good." Declan's smile was sad and wistful as he studied the ground. "Actually, we're not together—more like, together for a night. In a few months, Quinn's life will be in Vegas, and mine will be here. And we decided that following her south was about as practical as asking her to stay. I love her enough to let her go. You okay, Aaliyah?"

Declan reached out, grabbing my arm in concern.

"Yeah." I cleared my throat, forcing a smile to my face. "No, I'm fine." His words had just hit a little too close to home, that's all. "Hey." I frowned, pointing over Declan's shoulder. "Did you see that? Someone's behind the dumpster—I think they're watching us."

"What?"

Together, Declan and I circled the dumpster until the culprit was in view. The wave of recognition on Declan's face mirrored my own as we stared at an older, balding man with a camera around his neck. It was the same man whom had I had seen leaving Pete's apartment building.

"Hey, aren't you that weirdo that's always taking pictures and asking questions about Tyler and Aaliyah?" said Declan, his lip curling in disgust.

"It's called freedom of the press, pal." The man backed off, hands in the air, like he hadn't set out on a predestined course to ruin my life and Tyler's.

"Yeah?" I replied, hands balled into tight, angry fists. "Is it legal to stalk people? I bet you have pictures of me on that camera right now, don't you!"

"Maybe—but you'll never prove that in a court of law!"

Declan and I lunged at the same time, wrestling for the man's camera as he fought to keep it from reach. Declan and I were so preoccupied with what we were doing, we paid no heed to the black car that came screeching up to the Sunset. The only thing on my mind was getting that camera and destroying whatever was on it.

I managed to grab the strap, yanking it from the photographer's neck. As Declan held him back, I dashed the camera to the pavement and ground it beneath my heel, feeling immense satisfaction as I listened to his angry protests.

He managed to break free, pushing Declan aside before rounding on me. I knew I was in trouble when he pulled a pocketknife from his jacket. Seeing the rage and panic in his face, I stepped back, lifting my hands to protect myself as he brandished the knife, prepared to slash.

There was a loud pop, like a car backfiring, and the photographer stopped in his tracks, staring open-mouthed at the red flower blooming on his chest. He fell, motionless, on the cement, and there was Bortnik standing behind him, his gun still smoking.

"Declan, *run!*"

But it was already too late. Bortnik smashed him in the face with the butt of his gun, knocking him to the ground. I screamed, reaching for Declan as Bortnik's pie-sized hand clamped down on my arm like a vise. He dragged me away and threw me in back of a blacked-out Town Car. Pete was already sitting by the window, thin-lipped and bleeding, red rivers of blood streaming from the gash over his eye.

I banged on the glass window, shouting for help as Pete commanded me to be quiet and shut the hell up. The car lurched forward, hope slipping away as Bortnik accelerated. My last image of the Sunset fading behind us was patrons spilling from the back door of the diner, gathering in horrified throngs as they witnessed the dead body and Declan, on his knees, drooling blood on the pavement.

It was dim inside the warehouse. The only light came from a bare bulb that cast a weak glow from two stories above. The moths dancing in its light were the only free things in the room. The warehouse was lined with cracked glass windows, all of them smeared with grime, dust, and cobwebs.

The darkness beyond was broken up by the distant lights of the village I might never see again, not while bound to this chair with a piece of duct tape over my mouth—Bortnik had eventually gotten tired of telling me to shut up. Now, my ever-surly captor paced the dusty concrete floor, striding back and forth between me and the warehouse doorway—the only exit.

Time passed painfully slow; the moon sank inch by inch. I twisted in discomfort, trying to fight the tingling spreading through my stiff limbs. My wrists were bound behind me with tape, my ankles strapped to the chair legs. Taped into a metal folding chair across from me, Tyler's dad was in much the same position, but Bortnik hadn't bothered to tape his mouth. Pete hadn't said a word since we'd arrived. Bortnik had had to pick me up and toss me over his shoulder like a sack to get me across the field and into this chair. But Pete never struggled or tried to run. I guess we all have our own ways of coping with the end of the world.

When the yellow beams of headlights swept across the glass panes, my heart jumped at the new chance for escape. I watched the black mouth of the warehouse entrance, waiting to be saved. But the pit in my stomach only deepened when Aleksandr materialized. Outside the shadows Aleksandr walked on two feet, but I swear in the darkness he drifted.

Bortnik approached him, and the two initiated a heated exchange in Russian. Eventually, Bortnik retreated to a corner of the warehouse, lighting a cigarette and sipping from a flask as Aleksandr approached Pete.

"Good evening, Mr. Moore." Aleksandr's honeyed tone belied his steely gaze. "My father sends his condolences. Unfortunately, he will not be joining us tonight because he has more exciting things to do. I believe he was being audited when I left . . ."

"I was gonna pay you—I told you I could get the insurance money for the studio!" Tyler's dad nodded emphatically, as if that proved he wasn't lying. "Listen, the insurance company is just working out a few things on their end—and then the money is yours, I swear! C'mon, Aleksandr, she's just a kid! You didn't have to involve her in this!"

"But I didn't involve her, Mr. Moore, you did." Aleksandr walked behind me; seconds later, I cringed, recoiling when I felt his hands in my hair. "Look at her," he said, tucking my curls behind my ear as he lowered his face next to mine. "Does she deserve to die for your mistakes?"

"I—I—I'm sorry. I didn't mean for it go this far . . ."

"I would disagree, considering Bortnik was forced to dispatch the man you hired to follow Aaliyah. Do you know what I found inside his home when I followed *him*? Down in his basement, dozens of *pictures*—of Tyler and Aaliyah . . . and Bortnik . . . and me. It would be a shame if the fire that burned down his home was ever linked to the arson you committed . . ."

I could see by the dark light in his eyes that Aleksandr truly enjoyed torturing Pete Moore.

"Look, you made your point, okay? You can ruin my life, do whatever you want, just let the kid go."

"*Nyet.*" Bortnik strode forward, his voice the low, guttural snarl of an animal barely tamed. "Everyone stays." The Armani giant removed a cell phone from the inside pocket of his dark suit and dialed a number one-handed, never taking his eyes, or his gun, from Pete. He spoke briefly in his native tongue and hung up.

Aleksandr asked him a question in Russian, which Bortnik returned with a solemn nod.

"A moment, comrade."

Bortnik hesitated but lowered his gun and stepped aside once again.

"Aaliyah . . ." Aleksandr squatted before me, my furious shouts muffled by the tape. "Aaliyah, please, try to listen. Bortnik knows I have grown rather fond of you—he worries that my attachment to you will prevent me from doing what needs to be done. So he did not tell me before he took you—for that I apologize. I know you're afraid, but you're also brave, considering the state of Bortnik's eye." Aleksandr chuckled at Bortnik's dark scowl. "I'm going to remove the tape, and you are *not* going to scream. Understood?"

I nodded, and he peeled off the tape. The second my lips were free, I tipped my head back and called for help as loudly as I could. Aleksandr sighed and reapplied the tape. Head hung in defeat, shoulders racked with dry sobs, I fought to keep myself together in a place designed for falling apart.

"Aaliyah, you are a witness—you've seen too much. Bortnik has brought you here to kill you." I thrashed in panic until he silenced me with a finger. "But I explained to Bortnik how you saved my life. Honor compels me to return the favor. You will live—provided you never speak of this night to anyone. Understand?" I nodded my head emphatically, willing to say and do anything to survive the night.

"As for you, Mr. Moore . . ." Aleksandr straightened, turning to Pete. "Our business ends here. You will die tonight."

Once again I lost my cool, struggling uselessly in my chair with nowhere to go, like a fish flopping on the beach.

"I told your father I'd get him his money! It's all sorted out; I have a plan—"

"Forget the plan. It's over. Unless you can pull two hundred thousand from your ass right now, on top of the ten thousand dollars Aaliyah trusted you with—"

Pete and I gasped at the same time. Bastard! What had Pete done with the check I had given him? The talent show money Quinn had given up—money she could have used for her Vegas fund—had been no small sacrifice. And Pete had spat on it.

"H-how did you know about that check?" stuttered Pete.

"Because your apartment, and the hallway outside it, is bugged. After Aaliyah gave you the check, I followed you to the bank and watched you deposit the money." Aleksandr stuffed his hands in his pockets, smiling down at Pete as though he were simply listing off the amusing whims of a child. "And then I followed you to the casino and watched you gamble it all away."

Pete was so ashamed he couldn't even look at me.

Aleksandr tutted. "My father has run out of patience with you." Bortnik seconded this by cracking the sausage fingers in his gloves. "No one steals from my family. Tonight, you will pay back everything you owe in full; I will ship a pound of your flesh to my father."

"Wait! *Please.*" Pete's voice trembled, the sweat collecting on his bloodied brow as he licked his lips in desperation. "Even if the insurance money falls through, my son is going on tour this summer. In just a couple more months, I can pay back everything."

Aleksandr exhaled and rolled his eyes. "I have a business to run. That means no more loans and no more extensions. Time's up." He gave the giant a single nod. "Shoot Moore; knock the girl out, but don't touch her. We are still gentlemen."

Bortnik pulled out his gun, and I cried out, jerking violently against my restraints. All it took was a raised hand from Aleksandr for Bortnik to lower the weapon.

"Looks like our beautiful companion has something to say.

Perhaps a eulogy for Mr. Moore?" Aleksandr exchanged smirks with Bortnik and squatted before me once again. "Shall we give this one more try?" he asked and removed the tape.

"Please don't kill him!" My words flew out in a breathless rush, my heart pumping fire and adrenaline. "I can give you what you want, Aleksandr—I have money."

"People kill for reputation. So do I. If I allow Mr. Moore to live, how will I send my message?" He had me there. Aleksandr cast Pete a dark look. "I'd receive more pleasure making an example out of him than twiddling my thumbs waiting for champagne money."

"Let us both go or you'll have to kill me too." I shook with fear. The strength I had left was barely enough to keep my voice steady. "And I know you don't want to kill me, Alek."

"Do you know what I really want, Aaliyah?" Aleksandr reached in the pocket of his suit jacket; I squeezed my eyes shut and flinched, as if somehow that would stop the bullet. "Your autograph."

I opened one eye first and then the other, staring blankly at the pen and napkin in his hand. "You're serious?"

"Are you right- or left-handed?"

"Um, right?" He undid the tape on my hand, and I obediently scribbled my name on the napkin. "A hundred grand— that's what I can give you."

Aleksandr tucked it all away with a frown. "After everything he's done—why do you want him to live? If you knew this man as I do, you might end up pulling the trigger yourself."

"I'm not doing this for him. I'm doing it for Tyler. I love him enough to give up everything—even my dance career."

"Because that's what you'd be giving me, isn't it, Aaliyah? You'd be giving up your future."

I nodded. "You like taking invisible things, right? Well,

here's your chance. If your father hates my father as much as you say he does, I'm sure he'll take pleasure in knowing you destroyed his enemy's daughter. Because that's what this will do. I'll never dance again." I swallowed and lifted my chin in resolution, waiting as Aleksandr considered my offer.

"Fuck me." Aleksandr sighed and shook his head. "Once again, my plan—*foiled* by a beautiful woman. Do you suppose the universe is trying to tell me something, Bortnik?"

Bortnik retorted in Russian, and the two men shared a hearty laugh. But it was with all seriousness that Aleksandr's gaze returned to mine.

"Aaliyah, I will accept your offer, for two reasons. One—I like the way you do business. And two—for reminding me of people whom I love very much." I tried not to let my relief show in case he went back on his offer just to teach me some warped lesson. "Someone once said women are never more beautiful or dangerous than when they're in love. I would have to agree."

It wasn't Aleksandr that left me speechless, it was his strange, unexpected capacity for kindness. How many had crossed paths with a shark that swam from the scent of blood?

"However . . ." Aleksandr took out a cigarette and his signature golden zippo, signaling for Bortnik with a quick motion of his hand. "I'm going to need more insurance than just a pretty girl's word. Besides, Mr. Moore still has a lesson to learn—doesn't he, Bortnik?"

Bortnik grinned at Pete, showing all his teeth like the shark's second-in-command, the rabid dire wolf. He raised the gun, and just as there had been no mercy when he'd killed the photographer, there was no hesitation when he fired.

Fourteen

Bad Reputation

I entered the sliding glass doors of the emergency room, dazed by the bright lights and whirl of activity. The murmur of voices on the intercom, the steady flow of scrubs, gurneys, and clipboards, and the overpowering scent of cleaners and antiseptic took me back to the past. The first time my mom collapsed, I had walked her through these doors, calling for help as I did now.

Pete's arm was slung over my shoulder as he limped slowly along, his face strained and sweating as he walked on his injured leg. Bortnik swore the shot was clean—Pete wouldn't die from his wound. Still, he had lost a lot of blood on the way; most of it was on our clothes.

A nurse took one look at us and shouted for aid. From then on, we were surrounded by a flurry of hospital staff, questions tossed at us from all directions. I answered what I could, forced to repeat that the blood wasn't mine. Finally, Pete was deposited in a wheelchair and a clipboard was shoved in my hands. I stood at the edge of the hallway, watching as they wheeled him to surgery. He turned and caught my eye, his gratitude palpable through the silence. I walked away.

By the time the police caught up with me in the waiting room, I was ready. Pete and I had perfected our story on the way, repeating exactly what Aleksandr had told us to say.

"A man abducted me from the Harley Sunset. The same man shot and killed a photographer and then injured my friend, Declan. He wore a mask; I—I never saw his face." I described how my kidnapper had taken me and Pete to an abandoned warehouse, where he'd threatened to kill us if Tyler didn't pay an obscene amount of money. "Somehow, Pete managed to get free, and we escaped. He saved both our lives. I . . . feel safe with him." The two police officers left me their cards and a promise that this would be fully investigated. My stomach shrank into a knot the size of a pin.

Somewhere down the line, someone decided it was a good idea for me to be admitted. I changed into a blue gown and was ushered to a bed. Aunt Trina and Hudson burst into the room, coats over their pajamas, arriving just in time to watch the nurse draw blood. Needless to say, it was an emotional moment for everyone.

"Oh my god—Hudson, there's *blood* on her face!"

"I'm fine, Aunt Trina. It's not even mine, I'm okay—just some bumps and bruises."

She cried anyway, almost breaking a few bones with her fierce hug as Hudson peered over the nurse's shoulder to inspect her work. The nurse finished up, and when they were sure I wasn't in any present danger, they left to speak with the police. I was finally alone, long enough to watch old reruns of *Jersey Shore* as I cried myself to sleep.

I opened my eyes, weary, disoriented by the dimness and unfamiliar surroundings. For a few tense seconds I was back in the warehouse, tied up and helpless . . .

"Aaliyah?"

Groggy from sleep and pain meds, I rolled over, squinting at the door. Someone on the hospital staff stood there.

"Guys, I don't think I have any more blood left . . ."

As the door closed behind him, the person lowered the surgical mask he was wearing and removed the blue bonnet, letting them drop.

"Tyler?"

He didn't speak; maybe he couldn't. I swung my feet over the bedside, using the empty flip-tray to steady myself. Tyler saw this and flew across the room, where the pressure of his love hit like a cannonball. I would have fallen if I weren't wrapped so tightly in his arms.

He squeezed harder, kissing my forehead.

"I thought I'd never see you again . . ." His voice was husky with emotion. He didn't pull away, and I didn't try either. I nodded, my face buried in his sweater, inhaling the familiar scent of his cologne. "Once I found out you'd been admitted, it was too late for visitors who aren't relatives. Apparently, I'm not family."

"Yeah, right. C'mere."

Tyler's face crumpled as he hugged me again. The tearstains on my gown were still warm when he let go.

"This is my fault—all of it, Ali. I never should have come back to the Village."

I shook my head. "You didn't do this, Tyler. It's just something that happened."

But we both knew that wasn't entirely true. This hadn't just happened. Tonight had been coming for a while—months of mind games, deceit, and betrayal culminating in the perfect storm.

"Tonight felt like the end of the world." Tyler swallowed hard, the tears in his soft green eyes in danger of spilling over. "When Declan said someone took you, Ali, I lost it . . ." He closed his eyes, turning into my embrace as I pressed my hand against his cheek. "Calling your aunt, telling her you were missing . . . it was the hardest thing I've ever had to do."

Trina, naturally suspicious, had waited for a private moment to ask me if Aleksandr had had anything to do with tonight.

"He saved my life, Aunt Trina." She'd understood when I'd told her I had to repay him with my silence. But that did little to ease her fear.

I exhaled, closing my eyes against phantom images of my friends and family, terrified at the tragedy that had rocked our small town. I would never forget the photographer's final look of horror or his glassy eyes as the life seeped from his body. I didn't even know his name . . .

"How's Declan?" I asked, remembering there were two of us who had to live with the memory of his death.

"Actually, he's a few doors down. He's doing okay for a guy who got his teeth knocked out. A few stitches and some caps, and Dec'll be good as new. Still, he feels pretty guilty for not being able to save you. Truth be told, I don't know how to save you either, Aaliyah. What can I do? Please, tell me how to make this better for you."

I smiled. "You already are."

My fingertips dipped down his neck to his collarbone, his peach skin responding in goosebumps. Tyler removed his sweater and tossed it aside before striking me with a lightning kiss. I had felt alone in the warehouse and in my last moments at the Sunset. Now I had never felt safer, basking in his warmth and solidness. Tyler's lips weren't the cure, but they numbed the pain.

We kissed on the bed until my heart monitor beeped in protest. Tyler groaned and laughed, sliding from the bed and tucking me in.

"We probably shouldn't get you too excited. They told me you were okay—I just wanted to see for myself." Tyler reached out, pulling a broken leaf from my curls, shocked by the evidence of my struggle. I plucked it from his hand, tossing it aside.

"What *happened* to you?" He shook his head. "No, wait, I'm sorry—you don't have to answer that. We don't have to talk about it—"

"I made a deal with Aleksandr," I said quietly.

Tyler pulled up a chair, listening as I recounted the night's awful events, starting with discovering the photographer with Declan and ending with finally escaping the warehouse with Pete. I finished my story, and Tyler blew out a heavy breath, letting his head sink as he clasped the back of his neck.

"I know this is upsetting, Tyler. But I wanted to protect you—and Pete. If I do this, if I pay Aleksandr, this all goes away—"

"No, it doesn't, Aaliyah!" Tyler threw himself back in his seat. "Declan was hurt, a guy was murdered, my dad is going down for arson, my mom lost her life's work, and you . . . you almost *died*. None of that just goes away." Tyler's soul-piercing gaze was as hard and sharp as emeralds. "You said I wasn't responsible for my dad's mistakes, remember? So why does it have to be *you*?"

"Because those are the rules," I said firmly. "To help cover up Bortnik's involvement in the murder, Pete has to give up his freedom, and I have to give up mine. My dad double-crossed Aleksandr's dad. In a way, both our dads owe a debt to the Vitali family. So I have to be the one who pays back Aleksandr. It's part of the arrangement."

I would never forget the parting words Aleksandr had whispered before he let me go.

"I'm going to tell you a secret, Aaliyah—I hate my father. I despise him. And I hate yours even more for abandoning me to him. He abandoned you as well, didn't he?"

I looked away.

"One day, I'm going to destroy them both, Aaliyah. And you will help me do it . . ."

"The 'arrangement'—please." Tyler scoffed, rolling his eyes in disgust. "Fuck Aleksandr *and* his bullshit fucking rules!"

"Tyler—"

"No, Aaliyah, someone has to say it—you're being brainwashed by this guy, okay? Wake up! He's grooming you—"

"I'm not an idiot, Tyler! But what choice did I have? He was going to *kill* your dad! Do you understand that? You would never have seen Pete again."

"Yeah, well, I can live with that—but I can't live without you, Aaliyah. I won't." He sighed, softening as he looked at my face. Tyler brought his chair closer; he took my hand in both of his. "Don't worry, okay? I've already worked things out with Astrid—I'm going to take care of Declan's hospital bills and yours. And Astrid's going to work her magic, try to spin this whole thing so none of the fallout lands on you. Your future is safe, I promise. I'm not going to let anyone find out the truth, especially not the people at the Conservatory." Tyler kissed my hand. "All you have to think about is getting back on your feet—and deciding how we're going to celebrate when you get that acceptance letter." He grinned.

At this point, a rejection letter from the Conservatory would be ten times better than the look on Tyler's face when he found out I had given all my tuition money to Aleksandr—and I would never dance onstage again.

"You should get some rest," said Tyler, planting a soft kiss on my forehead.

"Will you stay with me? Until I fall asleep?"

Tyler nodded. He cut the lights and climbed into bed, wrapping his arms around me. I closed my eyes, resting my head against his chest, lulled by the rhythm of his heartbeat.

"Will you sing me a song?" I whispered.

"What do you wanna hear?" he asked, stroking my hair, his voice a gentle rumble in his chest.

"'Joy to the World.'" I grinned. "On repeat."

I fell asleep listening to him whimsically singing about a bullfrog, and fish in the sea. Tyler must have fallen asleep too because that's where he stayed until a nurse shooed him out the next morning.

As I waited for Trina to sign me out of St. Cyprian, I took a walk past the nurses' station through the recovery ward. Pete's door was half-open; I spied him through the crack, dozing, his injured leg propped in the air—his wrist shackled to the bed by a shiny pair of silver cuffs, courtesy of the Harbor Village Police Department.

I turned and walked away, humming "Joy to the World," my new favorite song.

By confessing to burning down Perfect Form, Pete also set fire to the Village. Stories about the kidnapping, murder, and arson were all over the news. Half the town called Tyler's dad a hero, the other half said he was a devil. Maybe the judge would shave a few years from his sentence for "rescuing me" from Aleksandr, but I knew it would be a long time before I saw Pete Moore again. When his lawyer reached out on the hopes that Tyler and

I would write letters to the judge asking for a lighter sentence, we politely told him to fuck off.

The *Harbor Village Herald* was the first to leak the news about the arson and what had happened at the Sunset. Our little paper hadn't seen that kind of steam since the roaring twenties. Not to be outdone, within days of each other, *Sugar* and *Canceled* also released scathing stories featuring my dad—just as Astrid had predicted.

Reading those articles, I learned more about Drake Preston than my mother had ever intended me to know. He wasn't just a music mogul, launching the careers of talented artists. He worked in the shadows, making secret deals, skimming profits, putting entertainers in a chokehold with the contracts he drafted. After all the rumors and speculation in those articles, and the fact that no one would go on the record to speak for him, I knew Aleksandr and his father had every reason to hate mine.

One popular blog called me the daughter of a kingpin. The author wrote that it was no wonder Tyler was attracted to girls like me. *She's dangerous*, they said. But after everything that had gone down, maybe that was true.

With Bortnik still at large, and Declan and I unable to provide many details about our attacker, the police offered to assign a security detail. But I refused. Every time I was called to the police station, Bortnik's warning rang inside my head.

No police, solnishko. *Or I will know . . .*

I also refused to move back in with Trina. She only agreed to my decision because she had wrangled herself early maternity leave. With the excuse of dropping off a casserole or baked goods, she managed to keep an eye on me anyway.

After leaving the hospital, I spent a few days on the mend, trying to heal my body and my soul. I camped out in my bedroom, watching the world bloom and fade from the window.

Daniela took pity and delivered my homework; she even stopped by some evenings to play cards and gossip like we used to. Some of my friends acted weird and awkward after the kidnapping, but Daniela treated me like a favorite prima she hadn't seen in a while.

One sunny afternoon, Tyler and I hopped in my car to wrestle an astronomical check out of the bank. We sat in the parking lot, the engine idling as we stared at the money in my hands. The ink was still wet on the paper.

"It's not too late, y'know. You don't have to do this, Aaliyah—not for anyone. We could tear this up right now. Or cash it and go to the Bahamas."

"No, we can't. If I do any of that, people will die, I know it. This way is better."

We went to the post office and mailed the check, just as I'd promised Aleksandr. And then I sat on my aunt's porch, with her, Hudson, and Tyler, drinking iced tea as we watched the sunset. It was the perfect opportunity to tell them about the Conservatory, but it was the first time I had seen them this happy since before the kidnapping. And I wanted to keep it that way for as long as I could.

The countdown had begun. May graduation was just around the corner—and Aunt Trina was in near hysterics. A few weeks shy of her due date, her belly grew rounder by the day, the baby keeping her mood swings on constant highs and lows. I decided to wait until after the wedding to tell her about the Conservatory, limiting her tears to wedding planning and stretch marks.

But Aunt Trina wasn't the only one dealing with the blues. I went back on a prescription I hadn't needed since my mom passed—one pill a day so I didn't lie awake counting sheep at night or have flashbacks in the middle of class. By prom week, there were fewer tears soaking my pillow and fewer nightmares about Bortnik killing the photographer.

Trina knew about the meds because she signed for them; Tyler found out because he walked in on me taking them. But I didn't tell anyone else. Not even Quinn, who was one of a handful of people who knew the real story about what had happened after the Sunset. I didn't need her to have another reason to worry about me. I just needed her to be my best friend, the person I could go shopping for prom dresses with.

"Earth to Aaliyah? Hello? Come in!" Quinn waved a hand in front of my face, asking my opinion on a sequined mermaid gown. We were dress shopping at the mall. Quinn was restless, zigzagging from one rack to the next while I took my time with each gown, savoring the rainbow of fabrics and patterns.

"Does this dress say dazzling, or does it say I have zero taste?"

I grinned. "It says you will be stunning no matter what you wear."

Quinn smiled back, running her hand across the dress I was eyeing. "You *are* buying one, right? Red is totally your color. You would *rock* this."

I exhaled, letting the skirt slip from my fingers. "It's pretty, but it's way too short. Better for homecoming."

"So try . . . *this* one." Quinn plucked a stunning coral number from the rack. The perfect length, with a neck and waistline to die for . . . and I would never wear it.

"I wish. I still can't believe how many guys and girls asked me to prom this year. I turned down every single one; even the ones I would've said yes to."

Quinn pushed my shoulder. "Why didn't you say yes?"

"Q . . ." I exhaled, preparing for the explosion when the grenade landed. "I'm not going to prom."

Quinn's blue eyes widened in panic. She shoved the dress back on the rack then grabbed me by the forearms and shook me good.

"Are you *insane?* We have been waiting for this moment since we were *freshmen*. Is it a brain injury? Were you body-snatched?" Quinn gasped. "Did the new president of Tyler's fan club *threaten* you?"

I laughed. "With everything that's happened, it's just a lot, y'know? Honestly, I'd rather just stay out of the spotlight for once."

At school, I was getting my wish. People treated me like I was contagious and kept their distance as if what had happened to me and Declan was something you could catch. Our first day back at school, I took a seat next to him outside the counselor's office. He had a black eye and a huge bandage on his cheek. After everything that had gone down, I thought he would hate me, but when I asked for permission to hug him, he didn't even say yes. He just stood up, and we held each other until the counselor poked her head out and asked him to come in. But not everyone at school was as understanding as Dec. Because of who my father was and what he'd done, some people even thought I'd brought the kidnapping on myself. The last thing I wanted was to be a pariah on the dance floor too.

"Besides . . ." I shrugged. "I'm not even in the running for court." And as far as I was concerned, it was better this way. My popularity ship had sunk, but Daniela's was on the rise. Not only was her name on the ballot, so was Tyler's. I sincerely hoped they survived the first dance after they were both crowned.

"Damn it, Ali!" Quinn returning to the rack, shuffling through dresses with a vengeance. "This can't be how it ends! You sound like Declan—I have to drag Scrooge to the prom too!"

"You guys have fun at the dance," I said, placing my hand on Quinn's arm. "Tell me all about it at graduation."

It wasn't an easy decision, missing the most important dance of my youth. I knew what I was giving up. Prom was this Saturday; Monday we would receive our diplomas, and then one by one my high school days would unravel until it all felt like a dream.

Ever since I was a freshman, I had imagined how I would end senior year. Skipping prom was never in the program; neither was dodging bullets, having my picture taken by paparazzi, being chased by thugs, getting kidnapped by gangsters, or falling in love with a pop star. But if I had to do it all over again, for just one kiss . . . I would.

The attention of my classmates finally seemed to shift as seniors began receiving their college admission letters—and some didn't. Eric made the mistake of opening his letter in front of his friends and ended up punching a dent in his locker. Daniela opened hers at lunch. Sonam and Piper had decided to forgive her for nearly ruining their reputations, but Dani hadn't forgiven them. Murder and kidnapping have a way of putting things into perspective, and an unspoken truce had been struck between Dani and Quinn. So Dani wasn't alone when she proudly announced she'd been accepted to Penn State—and then burst into tears after admitting she couldn't afford tuition because her parents had cut her off. If I hadn't been such a coward, I would have told her we were rowing in the same boat.

Tyler and I were sunbathing by the Vegas' pool the next day when I decided it was time to finally come clean. We sat poolside in our swimsuits, warm sunshine on our backs as we kicked our feet in the cool, crystalline water.

"Ali, before you do this . . ." Tyler took my hand, the gold Cuban chains at his neck and wrist as bright as his smile. "I want you to know that no matter what it says in that envelope, you're amazing, and I'm proud of you." He reached out, fussing with my damp curls. "The Conservatory is where you belong. And this summer, I just wanna have some fun with you before you go. I'm not going on tour. I'm staying with you."

"And I'm not going to the Conservatory." I ripped the letter to shreds, tossing the pieces in the pool. I'd thought I would cry when this moment came, but what I felt was relief.

"Ali, what the hell—"

"Even if I had gotten in, Tyler, it wouldn't matter."

"Why not? I thought Boston was a sure thing."

"It was. Until I gave Aleksandr the money for my tuition— and promised I wouldn't dance."

"Ali . . ." Tyler shifted away, hurt, surprised, angry. "You should have told me sooner."

"I haven't even told Trina." I took his face in my hands, brushing the freckles on his nose that always got darker in the summer. "I don't need the Conservatory. Just you. And maybe a dog named Baxter."

"That can be arranged." We kissed. Then he wrapped his arms around me and took me overboard, where we were adrift but not alone.

I rose with a dreamy sigh Saturday morning, my late-night conversation with Tyler fresh on my mind. He'd talked my ear off about Astrid and how upset she was at his decision to pass on the tour—even though Drake and Taylor Swift were on the list of openers. Furious, Astrid demanded Tyler appease her, and the label, by packing up shop and returning to New York first thing that summer.

"That's because Astrid doesn't know how badass summer in the Village can be. Tourists blow their vacations on the docks for a reason," he'd said. "I don't care what Astrid or the label has to say—I'm gonna spend every day on the water, skinny-dipping, writing songs . . . and kissing you."

It wasn't hard to imagine Tyler shirtless, the wind in his hair as he jogged in surf shorts down the beach . . .

"It doesn't matter what we do this summer, Tyler. I care about you. That's all that matters," I'd replied. And just like that, I'd traded my prom wish for summer dreams instead.

I took a shower, threw my robe over a clean pair of pajamas, and was on my way to begin a *Supernatural* marathon in the living room when the doorbell rang. I sighed, pasting a smile to my face as I opened the front door, prepared to give whatever excuse was needed to make whoever was outside leave as soon as possible. Moping was always a solitary affair when a pint of Ben and Jerry's was involved. But the smiling pair of strangers standing bright-eyed and bushy-tailed on my doorstep clearly had other plans.

With millions of followers and billions of hits, Mark and Tracy were a sensation on their YouTube vlog, *Makeup and Madness*, where they documented their (mis)adventures in NYC, styling celebrities. Mark was hair, Tracy was makeup, and apparently they had flown all the way from the Big Apple for *me*.

I watched in amazement as a troop of movers marched single file from the front door to my bedroom. They toted racks of dresses and shoes, along with two heavy carts of makeup. Mark directed traffic with the grace of an orchestra conductor, while

Tracy stood off to the side, popping her gum as she asked personal questions and shared equally personal stories in turn.

Despite the verbal diarrhea, the beautiful brunette with fierce lipstick and killer curves seemed like she knew her stuff. The red on her lips matched the bandanna in her 1950s ponytail. Tracy was friendly despite her invasiveness, cordial where her tall, narrow-eyed friend was more sour than sweet. Mark's dark hair was swept back in a low-key pompadour, his arms folded in concentration. His brown eyes were flecked with amber you had to get up close and look past the rudeness to see.

Tracy directed me to the swivel seat they had stolen from the kitchen. She observed my reflection in the dresser mirror, turning her head from side to side in masked concentration.

"So, is this for your vlog?" I asked, watching as she began to match my foundation shade.

She laughed. "Nope, consider this a favor."

"A *big* one." Mark appeared behind me, comb and scissors at the ready.

Tracy bent to eye level, her false lashes in pleasant contrast with her natural grin. "Tyler's one of our best clients. When he called and asked us to help you get ready for prom, we jumped on a flight. And now we're here to *fix* you!"

Tyler's taking me to prom. I *knew* he was up to something.

"All right, ladies, let's get started, shall we?"

I raised my brows at Mark, who clearly viewed my hair as a complex puzzle we both had trouble solving. "It's nine in the morning. Prom doesn't start for another ten hours."

"Oh, honey." He plucked at my curls and sighed loudly. "I'm gonna need at least six hours for this . . . nest." I shrank lower in my seat as Mark raised his scissors. "Snip-snip."

"Just a little longer, Cinderella. We'll get you to the ball, don't worry." Mark sectioned off another piece of hair to straighten, glancing at my reflection with a knowing smile.

I shifted carefully in my seat. "It's not that, it's just . . . I can't believe this is really happening." I was talking about more than getting a celebrity-style makeover. I was talking about every amazing, terrifying thing that had happened since Tyler had dropped back into my world. Chance, fate, repayment for a past life—I accepted him and the inevitable broken heart in full.

"I felt the same way when Trace and I started our channel."

Tracy laughed at her partner. "Our first thumbs-down knocked the wind out of him; he cried like a baby."

Mark cleared his throat, shooting a glare at Tracy that suggested she zip her lips at once. "The point is, when we think we don't deserve something is usually when we deserve it the most. I don't know you, Aaliyah, but I know Tyler, and he has good taste, usually. If he thinks you're worth it, then you are. Now hold still or I'll singe your neck hairs."

Tracy's reflection nodded, eyes wide. *He will.*

"Well. How do I look?"

Mark smirked. "Ever seen the videos we do for charity? The before-and-afters for the homeless?"

Traci fluffed my hair on my shoulders. "You're *beautiful.*"

Until today, Terani Couture had been nothing more than the obnoxious pop-ups on my computer screen. Now I was dressed to the nines in a silver trumpet gown with off-the-shoulder sleeves and a flared skirt. Mark had given my hair a good trim, straightening it before using his iron to mold soft waves with his fingers. Tracy fastened a silver hairpin behind my ear, the petite tassel chains that dangled from it attached to a spiked ear cuff. I reached down, raising the hem of my dress to admire a pair of matching Jimmy Choos.

"Guys . . ." I turned to Mark and Tracy, searching for the right words. "I don't know what to say; this is amazing. Thank you—thank you so much." I hugged them both, one arm around Tracy, the other holding Mark firmly in place so he couldn't run.

There was a knock at the door. Aunt Trina, who had stuck her nose in every inch of the transformation process after I'd called her and Hudson, poked her head inside.

"Your date's here. He's waiting in the foyer."

I left the room with my heart drumming to a strange, wonderful symphony of beats. I rounded the corner into the hallway that led to the foyer, where Tyler awaited, tempting as the forbidden fruit that damned Eve.

His hair was slicked back from his face, revealing those gorgeous green eyes in a completely new way. His tuxedo was dark and slim fitting, and his bow tie matched my dress. Between his hands was an extravagant silver corsage made from iridescent crystals, tied in place by a string of pearls. Comparing its beauty to anything else in the world seemed impossible, but he found a way.

"It shines in the light like you." All I comprehended were peach lips and white teeth in a movie-star smile. So vivid and lovely, Tyler and his beautiful words had to be a dream come true. So, naturally, I pinched him.

Tyler laughed, batting my hand away. "Why?"

"Had to be done." I adjusted his bow tie—a totally transparent attempt to feel him up. "Sometimes you're so epic, it's hard to believe you're real."

"Takes one to know one," he teased, and then he kissed me until Hudson pried us apart.

After Tyler slipped the corsage on my wrist and we posed

for pictures in the foyer, Hudson whispered directions in my ear as he walked me out the door. "Have fun, *mi corazón*—and be safe." One was imperative, the other impossible.

The driver closed the door behind us, and my world collapsed until it was just the back seat of the limo and the darling boy whose arms were wrapped around me. Nestled against his side, I thought the giddy mixture of Tyler's cologne and shampoo smelled like the cold sea spray. I had goosebumps again, like that night on the beach during senior skip day.

"Look, Ali, I know you said you didn't want to go to prom, but I couldn't let you miss this. You've already given up so much. I won't let Aleksandr and Bortnik take this from you too." Nose to nose, he slid my wrap from my shoulders with expert fingers. "Tonight is your night, Aaliyah Nichole Preston, and I want to enjoy every second of it by your side."

"That's all I needed to hear," I said, grabbing him by the lapels and pinning him to the seat.

Every year, the HVH prom was held at La Maison, the large ballroom decked out in whatever theme the dance committee voted for. Once again, Chinara and the committee had come through. This year's theme was Neon Nights—as surreal as waltzing in a lava lamp. Black lights transformed the ballroom to a bright jungle of ever-changing colors; anything white glowed in the dark. A black foil curtain fell from the glowing arches above the dance floor's entrance, tickling your skin as you walked beneath. Multicolored balloons waved from the walls, climbing the giant columns up to the ceiling, where there were rows upon rows of chandeliers in pink, green, and blue. At the rear of the ballroom were the tables and refreshments; on the stage at the front, a DJ spun the latest popular tunes.

No matter where you went, the dance floor or the supermarket, sliding out of a limo with a pop star on your arm was like stepping onto the red carpet. Tyler had anticipated the news vans ahead of time, so the driver delivered us to a rear entrance, where a hotel employee was waiting to guide us to the ballroom. They fended off the nosy reporters and paparazzi who snapped pics on the way.

"Tyler, after the arson, are you still in contact with your father?"

"Aaliyah, you're gorgeous—tell us what you're wearing!"

"One question: where's the after-party?"

"Aaliyah is the after-party." Tyler kissed my cheek and grabbed my hands, leading us from the chaos to the dance floor.

We caught up with Declan and Quinn, who sparkled in a midnight-purple mermaid gown. The tips of her blond hair were dyed a matching shade and piled in double buns, two locks framing her stunning face. She handed me a pink glowstick necklace, a party favor she'd snagged from the tables, then stepped aside so her boyfriend could hug me.

"Glad you could make it, Preston."

I smiled back. "Ditto. You clean up pretty nice in that suit, Skater Boy. How are you feeling?"

"Better." Declan's bandage was gone, revealing the angry stitches in his face where his teeth had passed through the skin. "I wish people would stop worrying about me," he said, rolling his eyes at Quinn.

"She's good people. So are you." My chin wobbled, and Quinn swooped in, dabbing at my eyes and commanding me not to ruin my makeup. After Quinn helped me fix what I had smudged, Tyler walked me backward toward the stage, where the music was loudest.

The DJ was on fire, and the crowd was decked out in sparkly outfits and glow-in-the-dark jewelry. Perfectly in time with the beat, Tyler's body fit me even better than my designer dress as we danced to the music.

The song ended, and the DJ turned to the mic.

"Are we having a good time?" Cheers erupted in the ballroom; Tyler hugged me from behind, swaying gently from side to side. "I'm gonna take five—but don't worry, I'm leaving you in *excellent* hands." She gave the thumbs-up to someone offstage, and the lights dimmed. Tyler's hands slipped away before I was ready.

"Save me a dance?" He kissed my cheek and set off for the stage. A teacher handed Tyler a guitar, and he took center stage, adjusting the mic. "Damn, y'all are short." The crowd chuckled. A spotlight bathed him in all white, fresher than falling snow—a devil in disguise. "New stuff, different sound. I wrote this song for my girlfriend. Hope you like it—I'm sure you'll tell me on YouTube." Another laugh from the crowd. I stared, transfixed, rubbing goosebumps raised by the opening notes of Tyler's guitar.

little oyster, little oyster, come downstairs
little oyster, little oyster, don't be scared
little oyster, little oyster, tell me your name
little oyster, little oyster, play my game
all that I want is with you
all that I want is with you
all that I want is with you
all that I want
little oyster, little oyster, take my hand
little oyster, little oyster, don't be scared
little oyster, little oyster, take my hand.
little oyster, little oyster, don't be scared . . .

Later that night, I found myself holed up in the bathroom stall, inadvertently spying on two girls touching up their makeup as they discussed Tyler's set—and me. Because obviously putting on a dress and dancing with my boyfriend and trying to feel normal for once didn't absolve me from judgment—not even for one night.

"Can you believe he picked Little Miss Girl Next Door?"

"He'd pick anything in that slutty dress. Just goes to show money can't buy class."

They laughed as though our lives weren't more than what they saw on a screen or read in a post. It felt like the air was thinning, my insides turning like forgotten milk in a hot car.

"Look at who her dad is. Can she really be that innocent?"

"Y'know that studio that burned down? Well, *I* read it was in *her* name, and Tyler's dad nuked it for the insurance money. Isn't that weird? Like, Tyler's rich—why not just *ask* him for the money?"

"I bet she had something to do with it. People say she became this different person after her mom died. Then Tyler ditched her and became famous. And guess what? I snuck into this party once, and Dani V outed *all* her shit. She said her father doesn't even love her. That's probably why he's not around—she *did* bring her uncle to father-daughter dances."

They burst into snorts of laughter.

My eyes burned. Anger urged me to open the door and start swinging—then embarrassment forced me to let the handle go. Gangsters *paled* in comparison to the wrath of high school girls.

"Wow. That's so many Ls."

"Maybe she deserved it."

"Ooh, you're *bad*."

"Promise you won't tell anyone? I heard through the grapevine that she didn't get kidnapped for no reason. That's just a cover-up. No one knows the real story . . . yet. *Sooo*, if you're wondering whether or not she deserved it, she was also there when that guy kicked the bucket. Declan Westbrook deserves a medal."

"For being hot?"

"No. I see now why you took pre-algebra twice. Declan was just an innocent bystander who she nearly got killed! He's practically a hero. So, she gets kidnapped, *and* some guy just happens to die at the same time? Then, after the guy dies, his house burns down. And that's not all! The cops found pictures of her and Tyler and a bunch of other people in the dead guy's lockbox. Like maybe he was saving the pictures, holding them over someone's head. *Two* arsons, and she's the, uh, what's that thing you call it in math? The common something?"

"Denominator?"

"Yeah, she should totally be demonetized. Those fires aren't a coincidence, but not enough people at the department care."

"Or maybe they're being paid off."

"Maybe. But you didn't hear any of this from me."

"Who did *you* hear it from?"

"My dad's a police officer, and my brother's a detective. I hear cop talk all the time. That's how I know they're interested in Aaliyah."

I didn't make a sound until the girls finally left. With shaking hands, I pulled my phone from my clutch and texted Aleksandr *911*.

I pushed my way through the dance floor until I found Quinn. Apologizing to Declan, I took his date by the hand, leading her to a dark corner near the refreshment stand.

"Quinn, have you seen Tyler? I have to warn him! He has to get out of here—"

"You're leaving the dance? No! You can't do that!"

"I wasn't talking about leaving the dance, I was talking about leaving the Village. Quinn, what were you talking about?"

Quinn bit her lip the way she always did when she was caught in 4K.

"I can't tell you, Ali, it's a secret. You're just gonna have to trust me, okay? *Don't* leave the dance." Quinn put a firm hand on my arm, leading me back to the dance floor just as the DJ resumed the spotlight. It was time to announce the prom accolades—silly awards that represented nothing meaningful but summarized us well.

Eric was Star Athlete, Chinara was Best Dressed, Declan was Class Clown, Piper was Most Likely to be Famous, and Tyler was Already Famous. Dani was the Cellphone-a-holic, and Quinn won an award for using the most bathroom passes to skip class. The awards went down the line until the only ones left were for the royal court.

Those who were nominated took the stage, honored with applause as they stood in line beneath the bright stage lights. Some prepared to take home their second award of the night.

"It's kind of weird, isn't it?" said Declan, nursing a glass that smelled a whole lot stronger than punch.

"What?" I asked, trying to act normal while my mind still raced with thoughts of the conversation I'd overheard in the bathroom.

"Quinn and Tyler up there. You and me down here. They were made for the stage. And we . . ."

"Are just supporting characters in our own story?" I smirked. "Yeah, I know what you mean."

But at the end of the day, it didn't matter how much of the spotlight I had to give up to protect Tyler. I would do it every time, again and again, no matter the outcome.

Chinara stepped forward, and the DJ handed her the mic. Chi was a goddess in a flowy purple gown with a ruched waist, spaghetti straps, and a spicy slit up the side. Her date, Christian, waved from the crowd and blew her a corny kiss.

Chi adjusted the microphone, cracking a joke about the feedback. She then proceeded to inaugurate the junior prince and princess with glow-in-the-dark crowns and scepters. They jittered with puppy-love excitement; the seniors kept it cool. Tyler winked from the stage; I did my best, but I couldn't even pretend to smile back. I knew that handsome grin would disappear after I told him what had happened in the bathroom.

I winced as more feedback sliced our ears.

"Bloody microphone . . . Anyway, this prom, the senior monarchs wanted to do something a little different in honor of two very special Ravens." Chinara's smile widened. "Though at times we are divided, it's the kindness, compassion, and loyalty of these two brave students that reminds us what unity means. These Ravens have not only dedicated time and energy to making this school a better, more positive place, they are also proof that even in Harbor Village's darkest hours, there will always be light in our little town. This year, will our student body and staff help us recognize two Ravens whose pictures will be proudly displayed in the school commons as well as in this year's time capsule?"

I clapped meekly along, glancing over my shoulder to see who Chinara could possibly be talking about. I had to admit, faith in my fellow Ravens was severely lacking at the moment.

"This year, your Harbor Village High prom king and queen are . . . drumroll please . . ." A teacher obliged, the anticipation swelling as everyone wondered who the senior monarchs could possibly be.

Chinara ripped through the envelope with the joy of

Christmas. "Declan Westbrook and my girl, the *fly-est* chick in the building—*Aaliyah Preston*!"

Whatever Chinara said after that, whatever the crowd cheered in reply, was drowned by the deafening white noise of shock. But I'm sure the ballroom exploded in cheers as Declan and I, dumbfounded, stared at each other with our mouths open until we were hustled onstage.

☆ ☆ ☆

After we were crowned, Declan and I were gifted our final surprise.

"As the king and queen enjoy their first dance, we would like to close this year's ceremonies with a very special performance by none other than Tyler Moore and this year's winner of the Battle of the Bands—Quinn Davis!"

I never thought I'd see anything as wild as slow dancing with Declan while being serenaded by Quinn and Tyler on my bingo card. And yet, there we were. Nervous, I danced with Declan at a polite distance, listening to our friends nail a killer rendition of "Don't Stop Believin'." I knew everyone meant well, but the spotlight was the last place I wanted to be—especially after hearing my reputation trashed in the girls' restroom.

"What's wrong?" Declan grinned. "Am I a terrible dancer?"

"No." I shook my head. "I'm just a terrible person. You didn't deserve what happened to you. I don't expect you to forgive me, but I'm sorry, Declan, for everything." I couldn't say it enough.

"You didn't deserve what happened to you either, Aaliyah. Maybe some people won't understand—I know I didn't. That night, at the Sunset, I saw how scared you were. And I know it may have seemed like it for a while, but you're not alone. There are people in this town who really care about you. Including me.

You don't need my forgiveness, Aaliyah, because none of what happened was your fault."

Declan didn't know he was my lifeline when I hugged him, but he saved me that night, in more ways than one.

There were a million after-parties to choose from, but a group of us gathered at Tyler's penthouse suite for dancing and drinks. For once, there was no fear of camera phones—Tyler let his guard down, and so did everyone else. Poolside with our friends, our feet dangled in the warm water as we watched the nightlife from Tyler's balcony and raised a toast to the memories we were leaving behind.

It was a prom tradition to have pancakes at the Sunset then camp overnight on the beach. Quinn and Declan and Chinara and Christian pitched their tents with the others, then Tyler and I joined our friends for a walk along the shore. Someone had Pandora going; one of Tyler's songs came on, and we all danced in the waves. Tyler had thrown on jeans and a hoodie before we left the hotel, but I was still in my dress, half-soaked. It twinkled like the stars and the shells in the sand under the moonlight. Tyler pulled me close, running his fingers through my streaming waves as he called me his little mermaid.

I threw my hands in the air and spun around, singing off-key at the top of my lungs. He lunged, laughing, trying to catch me as I sang out, but I dodged him, dress in my hands as I zigzagged away. I was caught fast.

I stopped singing at once as Tyler took me down into the sand.

"Don't sing."

I giggled. "Ever?"

"Never." His grin was bright as silver dollars in the moonlight. "Kiss me."

And that's exactly what I did as the tide rolled over us, his lips all the warmth I needed, tangled with him in the ocean spray.

We had skipped toasting marshmallows, but I got a taste of something sweet later that night in the limo.

"Why sleep in a bag on the beach when I can wake up to a five-star breakfast?" I'd said. Tyler had chased me across the sand with a crab, and that settled it.

"We're almost to the hotel." Naughty fingers gripped my waist as Tyler nuzzled my neck. "How long can you stay? Because I was thinking . . . after graduation, why not move out of the Vegas' guesthouse? I mean, why stay there when you can stay with me?"

"Um, Tyler . . ." I shook my head, glancing away in guilty discomfort. I still had to tell him what had happened at prom, and I wasn't sure how things would go when Tyler heard what I had to say.

"Hey, you don't have to say yes or no right now." Tyler smiled. "Just say you'll stay the night . . . pretty please?"

I mean honestly, how could anyone say no when he poked out his lower lip?

Laughing, giddy from alcohol and dancing, we raced through the marble foyer hand in hand. The timid clerk behind the desk looked too terrified to interfere. Tyler approached, tall, dark, and famous, and the clerk was instantly head over heels in love.

"Uh, Mr. Moore?" He cleared his throat. "The other Mr. Moore called for you. Again. Actually, he called four times. I wrote down all his messages—"

"Throw them out. Thanks, Aidan." Tyler turned to go, but I stopped him.

"Tyler, are you sure you don't want to at least look at them? He's your dad. He could go away for a long time."

"Aaliyah, my dad has been 'away' for as long as I can remember." He exhaled, looking down at my hands as he took them in his own. "A few phone calls aren't going to change that. And frankly, I'm done giving people like him and Aleksandr any more of my energy. You should be too."

I masked my sigh with a smile. If only letting go were really that easy.

We burst through his bedroom door, breathless, hearts racing, in the effort to be skin to skin. Tyler kicked off his Buscemi sneakers without a second thought. He lifted his hoodie, and his T-shirt went with it, his hungry green eyes a mirror of my desire and the longing to be devoured.

I turned and swept my hair to one side, shivering as Tyler ravaged my neck with kisses.

"Maybe we both need a break," I said. "From everything."

Tyler unzipped me, and the dress fell into a silver puddle at my feet.

"What are you saying, Ali?" He turned me around, admiring the Victoria's Secret with his eyes and hands. "You wanna leave the Village?"

"I want *you*." I draped my arms around his neck, standing on my tiptoes to kiss him. "You've made a life outside the Village. If that means I have to leave too, then I'll follow you wherever."

Our lips pressed together, which would have been the

perfect segue to moving things to his bed, but Tyler broke the kiss with a smile.

"Close your eyes."

I grinned. "If this has anything to do with worms or spiders, I'm out."

"We're not thirteen anymore, Aaliyah. Now close your eyes."

He poked my nose, and I did as he commanded with another sigh.

"No peeking."

"I'm not!" But I spied through the cracks between my fingers as Tyler rummaged through his bedside bureau.

"Okay. You can look."

It was the return of the velvet box, its familiar shape stretched invitingly in his hands.

"That better be the world's most expensive condom."

"C'mon, Ali. You know it's not an engagement ring. And you can't wear the corsage forever."

"Tyler, we've been over this—"

"I know, I know. But, Ali, this is a special occasion. Okay? Once in a lifetime. Humor me, please."

I exhaled. "Fine." I took the box with a tentative smile and cracked the lid, revealing the jewelry inside. The necklace was just as stunning as I remembered. Tyler removed an opal teardrop encased in champagne diamonds, glinting on a beautiful gold chain. It had to have been worth a fortune.

Tyler walked me to the full-length mirror leaning against the wall, where I watched him fasten the necklace in place.

"Tyler, it's . . . beautiful. *Thank you.*"

"Not as beautiful as you." His soft gaze filled with warmth as he watched me in the mirror.

I turned, tempting Tyler with a teasing smile. "Y'know,

moments like this are usually more memorable with chocolate syrup and whipped cream."

"Is that so?"

I nodded.

"Say no more!" I laughed as Tyler zipped from the room like the Flash, yelling for me to not start without him. He hadn't left a moment too soon. The smile disappeared when my phone flashed on the bed, Aleksandr's name printed on the screen. I snatched up the phone, answering in a rush.

"I have to admit, Aaliyah, I didn't expect to be hearing from you so soon."

"Trust me, I know, but we have a small problem," I said in a low voice. "Actually, make that a very, very *big* problem!" One hand on the phone, one hand in my hair, both eyes on the bedroom door, I hurriedly ran through the details of the conversation I'd overhead in the girls' room.

"Alek, I can't be sure exactly what the cops know, or what they *think* they know, but I have a bad feeling about this, okay? And honestly . . . I don't know what to do."

If Aleksandr was concerned about anything I'd said, he didn't show it. But the amusement in his voice was unmistakable. It reminded me of the days before I knew him, days when I was weaker than I was now.

"You called for advice? You're not actually worried about little old me now, are you?"

"The only thing that surpasses my hate for you is my love for Tyler. He's the only one I care about in any of this. And I just want to know how to save him from the fallout—when, or if, it happens. I covered for you and Bortnik, and now I'm paying the price. You have to help me."

"Do I?" His chuckle was infuriating. Once again, I had fallen down the Aleksandr rabbit hole. "You see, I knew you were loyal, *pchelka*. And it's your lucky day, because I'm going to reward your allegiance by giving you the solution to your problem."

"Okay." I swallowed. "Tell me what I have to do."

Fifteen

Sink or Swim

The next morning, I awoke in Tyler's arms, still holding a can of whipped cream. Tyler was snoring. Sunshine crisscrossed the room in layers, filling the space with warmth. Light fell across Tyler's face, illuminating his smooth skin and soft brown waves.

He smiled with his eyes closed as I pushed his hair from his forehead.

"Morning."

"Morning." I wiggled deeper under the covers, basking in the heat of his skin.

He opened his sleepy eyes and snaked his arms around me, tucking my hair behind my ears as I rose above him.

Tyler's smile was a coaxing invitation from this angle, an even more egregious temptation knowing I couldn't stay.

"Wanna get dirty in the shower?"

I groaned in disappointment. "If I go in that shower with you, there's no telling when I'll come out—and I have a bunch of stuff to get done before graduation. I'm going back to the guesthouse to get ready . . . but I would love to join you later."

"It's a date." Tyler sat up, and I leaned in, his lips sliding against mine in a tantalizing kiss that would have snared me once again if my phone hadn't beeped.

"See you at the ceremony," I said, rolling out of bed. Just to be safe, when he offered his lips for a goodbye kiss, I offered him a high five instead.

Even though I was leaving the hotel with racoon eyes in last night's dress, it felt like a whole new world. The sting of losing the Conservatory was cushioned by every kiss and every dance I shared with Tyler. I refused to let Aleksandr, or last night's conversation, be a death sentence to my relationship. Aleksandr was wrong about us, and I was going to prove it.

"It's not too late, Ali. Declan got accepted to the university here in town. You can apply to HVU with him. You're a total brain, I know you'll get in."

The Monday of graduation had arrived, and Quinn and I were sitting side by side at our favorite nail joint getting manicures. It had become something of a monthly ritual that might never happen again.

"I'm not staying in the Village any longer than I have to," I said, watching the cute designs being painted on my nails. "I have to get out of here. So does Tyler."

"Cryptic much?"

Quinn already knew more than I ever wanted her to. This time I kept my mouth shut, for her protection.

"Well, Ali, there are plenty of good schools out there. The Conservatory wasn't your one shot."

"Actually, it kinda was. I never considered a life without dancing."

"Hey. Remember that time Seth Greenleaf asked you out at the mall?"

"How could I forget?" I rolled my eyes. "That slimeball tried to feel me up at the arcade. I turned him down, and he was so mad he sent me a glitter bomb. I found random pieces of glitter on me for months—tiny, sparkly reminders of *him*." My lip curled at the memory of glitter exploding in my face, covering my skin for days, my hair for *weeks*.

"He'll never forget *you*." Quinn's smirk took me on a trip to the past—one fall night when Quinn and I had paid a senior a hundred bucks to sneak into the school. He'd spray-painted penises on a bunch of walls then planted the cans in Seth's locker. The next morning Quinn and I had high-fived as Seth walked past with his head down and his hands behind his back, escorted off the grounds by two officers. Notorious for harassing girls, Seth Greenleaf got exactly what he deserved.

"Actually, it was Dani's idea," I said, wincing at the truth. "And I almost didn't go through with it. But I never told you because I didn't want you to think I was just some loser who can't fight my own battles."

"That's the thing, Ali—you are strong. You made him *transfer*. And that same energy you use to put down bullies or build a cheerleading team—it's also why you're a good dancer, a good person, and my best fucking friend. So, this time, I want you to stop fighting other people's battles and start fighting for *you*."

Maybe Quinn was right. Maybe I should focus on me, but focusing on me was scary, because I didn't know what the future held for my relationship. I knew some people expected me to hitch my wagon to Tyler's star, but I had always been taught to pull my own weight. Even if I never danced onstage for the rest of my life, there had to be something else, something *more*, waiting for me. I couldn't let my life come to a grinding halt because one version of the future had slipped through my fingers. I had to think about what lay ahead, shape the future *I* wanted. It was time to dream new dreams.

"Maybe I'll join you down in Vegas," I said with a coy grin.

"You *will* come visit, right?" Misty-eyed Quinn was a rare sight to behold.

"You'll get sick of me, I promise."

But as we both looked away, I think we knew, deep down, life is as short as the wings of a hummingbird, and it flies by just as quickly. Maybe the next time we saw each other we would be old women with full lives, long memories, and gray hair. Or maybe we would never see each other again.

Nothing lasts forever.

Later that day, I sat on a park bench, twisting the necklace Tyler had given me in nervous fingers as Astrid listened to my story. The same one I had told Aleksandr, about the girls in the restroom discussing Pete's case. Some details I left out, like the ones about Aleksandr and Pete's gambling debt. My focus was the girls and how they came to possess the information they had. Other students and families were already gathering for the graduation ceremony. Like a superhero, I had T-minus one hour to save the world—or at least, the world as I knew it.

"Pete's already in jail," said Astrid, flipping her neat, shiny bob at the end of my story. "If he's the only who *could* be implicated should the police continue gathering evidence, I don't see what's the fuss. Tyler couldn't be arsed to send his father a get-well card in prison—what's a few more years to his sentence?"

"That's the thing—other people could be implicated. This

is bad all around, Astrid. There's a lot of variables you don't know—things I left out. For good reason, trust me."

"Probably just as well. It wouldn't help for me to know *all* the laws you and Tyler have broken."

My face turned red beneath her sharp gaze. But there was a reason I'd come to Astrid—she was the best at what she did.

"Astrid, despite what you or anyone else might think, I really do care about Tyler. That's why I'm coming to you—I want to protect him. There's a leak in the police department, and two girls are walking around with enough information to piss off some *very* bad people. Tyler says your job is to fix things. Maybe you can work your magic?"

"I have a feeling this affects you just as much as it does Tyler," Astrid said, passing me a wry glance. "Give me the names of the girls, and I'll hit their families with a cease and desist. Worded just right, and it'll put the fear of the goddess in anyone. Problem solved." She rose from the bench, and I stood, watching as she straightened her peach blouse and adjusted her dark pencil skirt.

"You can stop them? Make it all go away? Just like that?"

"Well, if your shadowy friends can shake down the police and keep them quiet, I can handle two little girls. It's good you came to me, Aaliyah. The kind of information those gremlins have could be very damaging for Tyler and his career. Thanks to you, I can ensure that it doesn't happen." Her head tilted, and her eyes narrowed, but when she spoke her tone was light. Almost casual. "You know, I never really succeeded in hardening that soft spot Tyler has for you. Maybe you are good for him after all."

"Maybe. Maybe not. Sometimes I worry we aren't good for each other. That we'll end up holding each other back." I exhaled slowly, blinking hard, even though I had worn the right makeup for the tears I knew this day would bring. "I just want Tyler to do what he was always meant to do. Sing."

"Well, there is a way you can make that happen. He can get out from under the roving eye of the HVPD and go back to doing what he loves. But for that to come true, he needs to go on tour. You're the only one who can convince him to do it, Aaliyah." Astrid exhaled as she straightened, as if her words were just as difficult to put out there as they were for me to hear.

Aleksandr had given me the same advice—far less tactfully. His version had included telling me to "save myself" and "pull the rip cord and jump free." He also thought it best Tyler put some distance between himself and the Village—and me. Hearing Astrid second his opinion only made the sting that much worse.

"This sort of thing doesn't happen to me often, but I *think* I was wrong about you, Aaliyah. You're different from other people Tyler is close to. Others take from him—in all ways, good and bad. But you *give*. Honestly, he needs more people like you in his life. You're not who I thought you were at all."

"Thanks, Astrid. That really means a lot, especially coming from someone with standards out to Mars."

She chuckled, pulling Gucci shades from a Gucci bag. Astrid was a completely different person when she smiled.

"I *am* hard on Tyler," she said, pushing her glasses in place. "I push Tyler to put his dream first, not because I'm his manager, licking her fingers for more crumbs, but because his dream is the only thing that I can make sure no one *ever* takes from him. It's how I protect him. And while I may not do it kindly or tactfully, I always see it done. Seems to me like you know what it means to be that person too. Happy graduation, Aaliyah."

I watched Astrid walk past me, wishing I had someone like her to do for me all the wonderful, terrifying things she could do for Tyler.

I made it to graduation just in time, dropping into my seat in the auditorium, still adjusting my black robe and matching cap. Tyler, whose seat was a row ahead of me with the Ms, turned and flashed me a look that said *Where the hell have you been, the ceremony's about to start!* I gave him a thumbs-up to let him know everything was fine. From that moment on, graduation was smooth sailing.

I'll never forget my feeling of accomplishment as I walked across the stage when the principal called my name, posing for a picture with Mr. O'Sullivan as he handed me my diploma. I turned my tassel from the right to the left and struck a pose. Then I walked proudly from the stage, smiling because even though the applause was thunderous, I could still hear Trina and Hudson over everyone else.

That night, Tyler and I joined our friends for a goodbye karaoke session at the Sunset. Declan and I hadn't been back since the shooting. It seemed fitting that we walked in at the same time, facing our fear of that night together instead of alone.

Only six hours had passed since we'd become high school graduates, but it might as well have been sixty years the way we reminisced. Half the booths in the Sunset had been commandeered by seniors in celebration. Not wanting to forget a single moment, I tried to memorize everything—from the smiles on everyone's faces to the lights, the music, the laughter, and the way Tyler's arm stayed looped around my neck, his fingertips rhythmically brushing my arm as he made conversation with our friends.

"Do you guys think we'll ever see each other again?" said Declan.

Our booth fell into a bittersweet silence as Declan's question went unanswered.

"We'll see each other at the wedding," I said brightly. "Well, some of you anyway . . ." My smile faltered as I thought of the friends who would already have left the Village by then, on to their new lives.

"Feels like we're already saying goodbye," said Tyler, circling the rim of his drink with his free hand.

"Not goodbye." Quinn smiled. "More like . . . see ya later."

"To senior year," I said, lifting my cup.

"Hear, hear!" they replied, and we clinked our glasses together for the last time.

We were cuddling in Tyler's jacuzzi that night when he started hashing out his grand plans for summer in the Village.

Disc golf and beach volleyball and bowling. Romantic movie nights and walks along the pier. Picnics on the lake, night trips to the museum. So many beautiful things to do and so little time to do them.

"This is totally our summer." Tyler tapped his beer glass with mine. "And we don't really have to stay in the Village. We could take a vacation—maybe three." Tyler smiled, playing with the wet tips of my hair that had escaped from my twin buns. "What do you think about Rome?"

"I think it's great," I said, sliding into his lap, staring tentatively into his bright eyes. "But I also think . . . that you should consider going on tour."

Tyler's brows knit as he mulled this over.

"But I thought you wanted to spend the summer together?" Wounded, he pulled away.

"Tyler, I want more than the summer," I said, using my finger to guide his face back to mine.

"Really?"

"Really really. But . . ."

Tyler rolled his eyes. "There's always a but," he grumbled.

"*But*, if you stay here with me, we might not get that chance."

"What do you mean?"

I sighed, twisting the beer in my hands. "The police might be looking deeper into what happened at the Sunset. And if that's true, things could get messy—for all of us. It's not good for you to stay here, Tyler. You have to distance yourself from this—"

"You mean distance myself from *you*." Tyler shook his head. "If it's not good for me to stay, how is it any better for you?"

Cat got my tongue. I had to admit, he made a fair point.

"Is this really what you want?" he asked after the silence had taken over for far too long.

I shook my head no. "But the alternative could be worse if you stay. And I can't watch you throw everything away—not for me."

"I would do anything for you," he said, wrapping his arm around me as I lay my head against his chest, melting against him in the warm water. "But I won't leave you behind, Aaliyah—not again. If I'm going on tour, then I want you to come with me."

I sat up in surprise, staring at the smile on Tyler's face, sure that I had misheard.

"You *what*?"

"I want you to come with me," he said slowly, enunciating each word so there was no room for misunderstanding.

"Is that a thing? Do boyfriends take their girlfriends on tour?"

"This one does." Tyler set our beers aside and conveniently pressed his lips to mine, leaving no room for argument. He was still smiling the next afternoon as we sat on his mom's front porch, drinking a round of sweet tea as we delivered the good news to Madilyn and Emma.

"We'll be leaving right after the wedding," said Tyler, his hand on my knee. "Aaliyah's coming with me."

"Wow, are you dancing backup?" said Emma, reaching out to bump my fist.

"Um, no," I said quietly, feeling the sting of regret—more at the indignity of not being able to make that choice myself than at the fact that I wasn't allowed to dance. And I couldn't explain Aleksandr's ridiculous rules without breaking them.

"But I'm still glad she's coming with me." Tyler smiled, speaking to his family while gazing at me. "The last time I went on tour was great—until I had to go back to New York alone. It's like going from having the world to having nothing. Some performers need therapy when they come back from the road, just to be able to make that switch. This time, Aaliyah will be there to help me."

"Well, it sounds like the two of you have made up your minds," said Madilyn. Her eyes were bright, and her smile was wobbly. "I guess you won't be needing this, but I'm going to give it to you anyway."

Madilyn reached for a thick manila envelope lying on her white wicker patio table and passed it to me.

"What is it?"

"The deed to the land where Perfect Form used to be," said Emma, smiling from ear to ear. "Since my dad confessed to the arson, that means you get the insurance money."

"Which means when, or if, you ever decide to rebuild the studio, the land will be waiting. Who knows—maybe you'll decide to build something different."

"Like a strip club," chirped Emma, earning a dark look from her mother.

"Guys, this is incredible," I said. "Honestly . . . I don't know what to say, except . . . *thank you.*"

"Just say you'll look out for each other." Madilyn smiled at me then cupped her son's handsome face. "Who am I kidding? You two have always done right by one another. No questions asked."

What could I say? Madilyn and my mom had raised us well.

Trina and Hudson's wedding was a few days later—a stunning ceremony at a beautiful chapel downtown. I wore my bridesmaid dress and held a bouquet of white roses, trying not to ruin my makeup as Hudson recited his vows to my aunt. Just by the way he looked in her eyes as they danced, I knew he would gladly spend the rest of his life making her happy. I could only hope the dance I'd choreographed for the ceremony was a worthy enough symbol of their love. My aunt worked so hard taking care of others. She deserved to be pampered and adored by her new husband.

After the ceremony, guests reconvened at La Maison for the reception. I sat at a table with friends and family, eating cake and sneaking champagne as I watched the newlyweds perform their wedding dance to "Human" by the Killers. Then the lights dimmed, and Tyler took to the stage for a final surprise, belting the lyrics to "At Last" by Etta James. Tyler surprised me too when he walked offstage to serenade me at my table, ending his song with a kiss that brought the house down.

The night ended with everyone waving goodbye to the newlyweds, sending them off in sprays of rice. Trina, too close to her due date to travel on her honeymoon, settled for a honeymoon suite the next town over. They drove off, tin cans rattling behind the car, a sign on the bumper that read JUST MARRIED.

And just like that, the world as we all knew it had ended, a new era on the horizon.

Tyler was one of the last to leave the ballroom. The difference between his goodbye and the farewells from our friends was that I knew he'd return. He had some last-minute errands before we left for the first destination on his world tour—we had two days to be in LA. Tyler kissed me goodbye, and I stayed behind to help the hotel staff with cleanup. Quinn and Declan stuck around to assist, but eventually, the night claimed them too. Declan was off to spend the summer overseas with his grandparents, and Quinn was headed to a summer job at a famous bar in Florida, singing and waitressing. The guests trickled out one by one until I was alone, trying not to cry from the loneliness and nostalgia as I chugged from a champagne bottle. I wiped my lips then picked up the last trash bag—and froze.

"That's a beautiful dress, *pchelka*. Would you believe this was my first American wedding?"

"What are *you* doing here?" I took another swig from the champagne, watching Aleksandr take a seat at one of the guest tables.

He wore a crisp suit with the dress shirt unbuttoned and the tie undone—and was still fit for a *Vogue* spread. He leaned back in his seat and shrugged, smiling like he knew something I didn't, which was pretty much always.

"I couldn't miss the big day."

"My aunt's wedding?" I asked, dropping the trash bag to plant my hand on my hip.

"I'm talking about your big day, Aaliyah. The day you go off to college to become an elite dancer and show the world what you're made of."

"What is this, some kind of sick joke? I *gave* you my tuition, remember?"

Aleksandr's grin was infuriatingly crafty. "Did you really believe I would clip your wings, little bird? How low you must think me."

"Absolutely," I replied, arms folded. "What do you want, Alek?"

"I want you to show up for orientation on August twenty-seventh," he said firmly. "I covered your full tuition and room and board. You'll have a private room and all the amenities. You're welcome." Aleksandr stood up to leave, not bothering to stick around for the fallout as he dropped yet another bomb on my life.

"Wait! Wh-why? Why would you do this? Take everything just to give it all back? Is this just to get me away from Tyler?"

"You're still thinking small. Tyler's not the big picture—it's *you*." Aleksandr made a big show of clearing his throat. When he spoke, the accent was gone. "Call me when you're ready. With my help, you're going to do big things, Aaliyah."

I gasped. "The New York talent agent! It was *you*!"

Aleksandr bowed with a flourish.

"You are sick," I hissed. "And you have seriously lost it if you think I would *ever* join forces with *you*!"

"But you already have." His blue eyes narrowed, sparking with the kind of live-wire danger that made me take a step back and assess the room for exits. "You proved your loyalty the night you saved me, Aaliyah."

"I should have left you to die!" I gripped the air around my head and growled when what I really wanted to do was scream—and destroy him.

"You forget I knew your mother. I know the kind of daughter she raised." Something passed over his face—a recollection, perhaps. He softened, and I knew my mother's memory haunted him. "You *will* help me, Aaliyah. You're in this too deep—without me you will *drown*."

"Yeah, because you'll hold me down or drag me under."

"So?" He spread his arms wide. "What will it be, Aaliyah? Will you sink or swim?"

"I'll tell you what I won't do—I won't do *this*. I'll never work with you, Alek. If that means giving up the Conservatory and never dancing again . . ." I lifted my chin. "So be it."

But Aleksandr was not so easily persuaded.

"You will change your mind. You won't have a choice." He shrugged, as if I weren't fighting him but fate itself. "Your father and mine—they are my greatest enemies. You and I are their greatest weaknesses. If you are going to be my champion in this fight, I need you sharp and determined."

"And strong," I finished, repeating the same word he had used that night at the drive-in theater. "Going against your father—it's a death sentence. You know that, right?"

Aleksandr sighed. "There are casualties in every war. See you soon, *pchelka*."

Aleksandr was almost out the ballroom door before I allowed my curiosity to get the better of me.

"How did you know that I was accepted? I—I tore up the letter they sent—I don't even know what it said."

"You want to know how I knew? I have faith in you, Aaliyah. You just have to believe in yourself the way I believe in you. Keep up with your studies, *pchelka*. The Conservatory awaits."

The next morning, I woke up thirty minutes late after sleeping through my alarm. I saw the time on the clock and jumped up, racing to get dressed. Tyler's people would kill us both if he missed his flight. So I hurried through my shower and breakfast, scribbled a goodbye note for Daniela's family and a separate note for her, then raced out of the guesthouse for the last time. My taxi was already waiting.

In the back seat, I made the mistake of dialing the Conservatory's admissions office. The perky lady on the other end of the line confirmed what I had feared—I was a registered student starting this year at the Boston Conservatory at Berklee.

"Congratulations, dear. We look forward to seeing you this fall."

I hung up, tossing my phone like it was a grenade. The driver eyed me suspiciously through the rearview mirror.

At the airport, I grabbed my bags, tipped the driver, and set off. It seemed like it took forever for me to check in, hand over my luggage, and pass through security—who treated me like I had something devious in every bag and container. Security had their fun with me, and I was released. Hands on my head, I searched above the crowd, spotting the giant screens listing flight times and schedules.

"'Scuse me—'scuse me—ow—sorry!" I dodged pointy elbows and bulky purses, weaving through the crowd at top speed until I was standing beneath the screens. I scanned the flights, searching for the one to LA, whooping out loud when I found Tyler's flight. I dashed through the airport, searching gate numbers until I found the right one. I arrived at the gate in record time, breathless and sweating while Tyler was fresh as a daisy.

"I know, I know, sorry I'm late!" I greeted him with a hurried hug and kiss, pulling his hand toward the door. We had only minutes to spare. "I really hope I have a window seat!" But the excitement of a seat with a view vanished completely when I saw the misery on Tyler's face.

"What's wrong?" I set my bags down to take his hand, but he wouldn't answer me or look me in the face. "Tyler, what is it?"

"Aaliyah, is there something you want to tell me?"

I frowned. "Like what?"

"Like . . . you got into the Conservatory? And your tuition's paid?"

"How did you . . ." I groaned in realization. *"Aleksandr."* I shook my head and grabbed Tyler's face so he could look me in the eye and see the truth. "Tyler, that doesn't matter, okay? None of it. The Conservatory is just his way of controlling me. He doesn't care about me."

"But I do." Tyler's gaze slipped from my face and down to the floor as he pulled my hands away, folding them in his. "And I really don't give a shit what his reasons are—he's giving your dream back to you, Aaliyah. You have to take it."

"Tyler, *no.*" The threat of tears choked any other plea I could make.

"We said we would never hold each other back. I won't break that promise now. Trust me, it's not easy." He smiled, straightening my opal necklace and wiping the wetness on my cheek. "I love you so much."

"I *hate* you!" But I threw myself in his arms, tasting the salt of our tears as we kissed until the flight was called.

"That's me." Tyler picked up his bags. "I'll make sure the airport sends your luggage back, okay? We'll FaceTime when I touch down. Wear something black and lacy."

I pushed his arm, succumbing to an involuntary laugh. Wiping my eyes as I looked into his for the last time, I almost wished he wouldn't call me. If saying goodbye was this painful, saying hello from different zip codes was bound to feel worse.

"Have fun," I said, while secretly hoping part of him would be tortured without me, like I would be without him. "You're gonna kill it."

He leaned down to kiss my cheek. "So are you, beautiful."

I watched Tyler until he disappeared through the tunnel. Then, feeling hollowed out and empty, I walked to the window, where I watched his plane take off. He was up in the sky, and I was stuck on the ground, but I knew deep down we would never really be apart. As I left the airport, twisting the opal on its chain, I imagined Tyler's face as he sat on the plane. I hoped when he looked out the window, daydreaming about what the future held, he was thinking of me too.

I was at St. Cyprian when Trina delivered baby Michael. It was three in the morning, and I had fallen asleep at a table in the room with the vending machines and microwaves. Hudson woke me up with a smile and a large coffee.

"He's here."

Having never seen anything so adorable in my life, I couldn't get over how tiny Michael's fingers were, how chubby and wrinkly his little brown face was or how wonderful his head smelled. He was perfect.

"He's amazing," I said, smiling down at him as I rocked him in my arms. "Can I steal him and take him with me?"

Sitting in the bed in her hospital gown, swollen, tired, and beautiful, Trina smiled. "Hell no, you can't take him. Give me back my baby, little girl. Come back here, Aaliyah! You better stop playing before I call the nurse!"

I got the chance to say goodbye to Michael too when Hudson and Trina saw me off at the airport. I wished the newlyweds farewell, kissed a sleeping Michael on his forehead, and grabbed my carry-on bags. I waved goodbye one last time, overcome by nostalgia as I promised to FaceTime when I landed.

I packed my bag away and took my seat on the plane, digging my earphones out of my purse, along with the letter Tyler had given me that special night at the lake house. I wiped away the tears that stained the page and blurred the words. He'd made me laugh and cry at the same time, and he'd also made me cherish every moment we had spent together. Our time hadn't been everlasting, but at least it had been real.

Later, after the plane had left the ground, ascending into a red and orange sunset, I turned on my favorite playlist. Swept away by a Tyler Moore song, I daydreamed about a captivating pair of green eyes and what could have been.

On a sunny afternoon in August, I joined a throng of freshmen on the sidewalk outside the Boston Conservatory. I couldn't believe I was actually standing in front of the historic brownstone building, gazing through its glass face, envying the students who traveled the stairs.

"Hello, everyone! I'm Riley, your tour guide!" A pretty girl with deep-brown skin and spiral curls smiled over her clipboard. "I want to welcome all of you to campus, and I hope that today, after seeing the Conservatory and learning more about its history, you'll feel more at home. Feel free to ask *any* questions along the way. Uh, you in the purple—cute dress—what's your name?"

"Thanks." I lowered my hand. "Hi, I'm Aaliyah. Is it true there's a bench on the grounds dedicated to a ballerina?"

"Ah, yes—what a wonderful question! That bench is one of

my favorite places to sit and think. It's special because it's dedicated to the Conservatory's first Black prima ballerina, Amelia Preston. We could add that to the tour, if you're interested?"

There was a general consensus of good-natured agreement from my fellow classmates.

I smiled. "I would love that."

School started, and suddenly I was caught in the whirlwind that was classes, dancing, and homework. In between the mad struggle to impress my teachers—without stirring the wrath of competitive upperclassmen—and studying, I also took a shift at a local café. I poured coffee, wiped tables, balanced the registers, and always smiled when I asked people if there was anything else they needed. It was that question that always invited people to ask for more—of me. They had questions about Tyler, about our relationship and why it had ended.

I gave a happy-go-lucky shrug, refilling the latest customer's mug. "Sometimes the stars align, and sometimes they fall. But it was fun while it lasted." I winked.

One semi-sunny morning a few weeks after I had begun to adjust to the chaos of school and work, I decided to skip the bus and ride my board. There was nothing like cruising the sidewalk in Boston in the early fall, with the sun on your face and your favorite artist in your ears. On my way to a shift at the café, I was distracted by a group of kids who had taken over a basketball court. But they weren't playing ball, they were dancing.

I stood behind the chain-link fence, watching them take turns breaking it down to Tori Kelly's "Should've Been Us." No classical training to speak of, but every move was slick and fierce, on point in their own signature ways. Eventually I was spotted;

someone whistled an invitation. I hesitated, then broke down with a grin. I slid through a gap in the fence and tossed my backpack and board aside, joining the fun.

Some pulled out their phones to record, but most of us were too into the music to do anything more than enjoy it.

"Hey, aren't you Tyler Moore's ex?" A tall girl with braces and her own skateboard came to bump my fist.

"Something like that."

"Can you teach us to dance like you?"

Looking into her sharp brown eyes, I realized I hadn't felt so much purpose and opportunity to make a difference since the B-Team.

I grinned. "Same time next week—that's your first lesson. We'll start with the basics."

The kids whooped.

Later that afternoon, I clocked out, said goodbye to my coworkers, then took a seat at the bus stop. I entered my private dorm—a sanctuary covered with pictures of high school friends, decorated with memories and mementoes. As always, Bernard the Bear was there to greet me, nestled against the stack of pillows on my bed. I took a seat at my desk and opened my laptop to take notes, my head buzzing with plans for my first recital.

I had only made it a few minutes into my notes when my phone buzzed. I answered Tyler's FaceTime with a grin.

"Did you miss me?" Tyler cheesed and waggled his eyebrows, his spectacular smile extra bright against the tan he had earned while touring. He was framed in front of an orange sky, someplace where the sun was setting.

He had been gone for three long months, then flown back to New York to take some time to decompress and get himself together. There had been late-night calls and early-morning texts sent from places like Bali, Japan, and the Gold Coast. Sometimes, when that wasn't enough, I would check the blogs and celebrity news shows to keep tabs on him. I would fall into a reverie, thinking about our last kiss, our last fight, and the first time he'd told me he loved me. Outrunning a person is one thing, but a memory can catch you anywhere.

I smiled. "How's New York? Is Astrid still on your case about your new contract?"

"Actually, I wouldn't know," he replied, biting his lip with a mysterious smile. "I kinda ditched her."

"Not again," I teased. "Where are you?"

"Why don't you come to the window and find out?"

I dropped my phone on the desk in shock. My heart skipped a beat as I crossed the room, lifting the venetian blinds to see a boy standing on the steps to my dorm.

Tyler looked up and waved.

I ran from my room, ignoring the RA's angry shout as I bolted across the hall and down the stairs, gripping my opal necklace in excitement. I threw open the front door and jumped into Tyler's arms. I guess it's true what they say—absence really does make the heart grow fonder. Tyler wrapped me in his warm embrace, lifting me off my feet, spinning me in a circle as he kissed me for what felt like the very first time. We didn't stop until we heard the catcalls and whistles from passing students.

Tyler cupped my face with his hand, tucking my curls behind my ear. "Happy early birthday, Little Miss Libra."

"I can't believe you're actually here," I said, sifting through the shorter, highlighted waves on his forehead, enchanted by the new gold hoop in his nose. "I thought you couldn't get away for a while?"

"I moved some things around. It's not even a four-hour drive from me to you." Tyler traced the opal necklace, and I could tell by his grin he was thrilled I'd never stopped wearing it. "I came for that tour of the city you promised."

"Good. Then we should probably start with my bedroom . . ."

I led him inside and up the stairs, where I put a pink sock on the knob and turned up the music. We laughed, ignoring the evil RA when he pounded on the door, demanding Tyler return downstairs to sign in. Tyler lifted his shirt over his head as he followed me to the bed, beaming like the sun as he settled over me.

His ringed fingers walked down my tummy, unzipping my jeans. "'The time has come,' the walrus said . . ."

But there was very little talking involved as we danced between the sheets, all night and well into the morning.

Acknowledgments

This book is for Wattpad, who believed in me and gave me my first big break. For my editor, Fiona, who believed in me every step of the way (no matter how many wrong turns I took). And for Sun and the rest of the team who brought *How (Not) to Date a Pop Star* from a dream to reality. Words cannot thank you enough!

About the Author

Jada Trainor joined the Air Force at seventeen, earned a major in English and a minor in psychology, and is currently a stay-at-home mom of four. Her work draws from her own life experiences and features inclusive and diverse characters and relationships. She lives in Indianapolis, IN. *How (Not) to Date a Pop Star* is her first novel.

Turn the page for a preview of
The Locker Exchange by Ann Rae!

wattpad books

the
LOCKER
EXCHANGE
a novel

ANN RAE

Available now, wherever books are sold.

CHAPTER ONE

IT SHOULD HAVE BEEN DARKER.

My foot crunched a fallen brown leaf as I left the school and headed toward an empty student parking lot. It was close to eight at night, which meant my white Jeep sat alone, sun reflecting off it at low angles. There was something odd about having the light over my shoulder just before it began its descent into darkness.

The fall air bit at my heels and cheeks, prompting me to quicken my pace as I drew closer to the Jeep and tugged open the heavy door.

My backpack slid off my shoulder as I tossed it into the passenger seat and collapsed, exhausted from filing paperwork for different classes. I was an office aide at my high school, which meant I had a "responsibility" to assist. It was still only the second week of classes, and I'd been filing student schedules, requests for class changes, and the like for hours. I hadn't signed up for helping after school, though, and vowed then and there to never do it again.

I shook my head at the memory of all the forms I'd dealt with

ANN RAE

that day and reached forward to start the Jeep. All I wanted now was to listen to some music and enjoy a peaceful drive back home. Just as my fingers barely brushed against the volume dial, an ear-splitting screech shot through the air, and I recoiled in shock, my head shooting upward.

Anticipation took hold of my heart.

I waited in silence for it to come again. Maybe I'd imagined it, or, more realistically, I hoped I'd imagined it. I wasn't equipped for this kind of situation, and my eyes skimmed my car for anything I could use just in case I wasn't hallucinating.

"Help!"

The desperate, distant scream shook me into motion, and I bolted up, scrambling for the phone in my car's cupholder. I knew I should've called the police, but there had been a few incidents on the news that didn't necessarily showcase their abilities, so I dialed someone I trusted.

"Hello?" a deep voice answered. My heart was thumping so loudly I was sure he could hear it.

"Thank God." I almost gasped. "Baylor, I'm in the parking lot at school, and no one else is here, but I heard a scream and then someone yell for help, and I want to go check—"

"Stop," my older brother said sternly. Even from miles away at college, he could still command and I'd listen. "Call the police and get out of there. It's not safe."

"What if I call them and it's too late? I need to go over there now, at least to check, or I won't be able to sleep tonight. I thought I'd ask you to stay on the line with me. You know, just in case."

"Are you wearing a hoodie?" he asked finally. "Cover your face as much as you can."

Luckily, I had a spare one in the car.

My arms trembled as I hurriedly threw it on and leapt out of the Jeep. Adrenaline coursed through my blood like I'd never felt before. I'd learned about this before, the fight-or-flight response, but I never thought I'd experience it so vividly. I crept in the direction of the noise, my breathing hitched, unconsciously treading on the balls of my feet.

When I turned the corner, it was still. The football field looked empty, but my hands still quivered.

"Do you see anything?" Baylor asked quietly. His voice was calm. I couldn't necessarily say his virtual presence was soothing, but it was still better than being alone.

As my lips formed the shape of *no*, a sudden movement attracted my gaze. A black figure loomed at the top of the bleachers before noticing my position and flinching. Sudden panic propelled my body forward in a desperate attempt to get a better look, but the man ducked down behind the bleachers, scurrying past the fence and out of my sight.

"I just saw someone—" I started, determined to get another glance as I stepped forward.

Then all my courage vanished.

I felt it against my shoe. Something warm. Wet.

"Baylor," I whispered, my eyes shut tight as I willed my lips not to tremble.

"What? What happened?"

"I . . ."

I didn't want to look. I didn't know what it was, but the guesses swarming my mind were enough to make me hesitate. Yet I knew I had to, and, with a daring I didn't typically possess, my eyes slowly swept the bleachers, then the cement, and finally the puddle of blood mixed in a whirlpool of soaked blond hair.

MY JEEP WAS NO LONGER ALONE. Red and blue lights flashed against the now consuming dark as Colorado police strolled around the scene of Westwood High. I crossed my arms around my chest, relying on my own warmth as I shrank into a body that shook.

"Did you find him?" I asked again as a man in a uniform walked past. I stood up from where I'd been leaning on the hood of my car; while being surrounded by the authorities wasn't necessarily the most comfortable situation ever, I needed answers. "The guy who was on the stairs."

He didn't seem to hear me.

"Hello?"

His eyes almost rolled as he turned in my direction. "No."

"No, you didn't find him?" I asked for clarification.

"We didn't find him. And we probably won't, but we're doing a sweep of the area just in case you really did see someone."

"What?" I gawked at him. "What do you mean 'really did see someone'? You think I made it up?"

"Look," he said, shadows outlining his glum face. "We got your report and all your information. Thank you for cooperating, but you should head home. It's late, and there's nothing else you can do. We have it under control."

"Wait!" I started, but he was already tilting a hat over his eyes and turning away. "I'm not lying! Wait!"

I tried countless others, asking them the same questions about the victim and the murderer, but all I got were impassive looks and short replies. My blood boiled as I finally sank into my car and slammed the door shut.

"I DON'T GET IT," I fumed, my hand clutching a silver fork. My parents sat across from me, both chasing their pasta around in an uncomfortable silence. "They said their 'early investigation' indicates she tripped and fell, but I literally told them what I saw! Why don't they believe me?"

"Honey," my mom started, finally meeting my gaze. Her irises were a smoky gray with smile creases sharpening the edges of her eyes. I'd always been told I looked like her, as we shared the same color eyes and full lips, but it was only recently that I'd begun to see the resemblance. "I know tonight was rough, and I'm sorry you had to experience any of it, but we should be thankful they don't consider you a suspect. Right?"

She looked helplessly at my father, who had just raised a bite of spaghetti toward his mouth. He lowered it and let out an awkward cough. "Right. I mean, it's lucky they caught you on the surveillance cameras in the school and the parking lot. It could have gone a lot worse than it did. Thankfully you've always been lucky, Brynn."

Lucky? They thought the fact that I'd stumbled upon a murderer and watched as he got away was lucky?

"What aren't you guys understanding? Do you think I just made it up too?" I accused, anger biting at my words.

"No, that's not it," my mom said hastily. She set her fork down and sighed. "Your dad and I have something to tell you, and we would've told you earlier, but the decision was very last minute. It's just . . . well, the timing couldn't be worse."

"What?" I asked. This was why they'd waited until I got home to have dinner. A hole began to form in the pit of my stomach as I waited for them to tell me their news.

"Well," she started, her eyes drifting aimlessly before coming back to me, "we're going on a business trip. I'm not exactly sure how long it'll be, but we were told it could last at least a month, maybe more." Her expression pleaded with me. "I'm so sorry, honey. We didn't think something like this would happen, and we tried to reschedule, but it was too late."

My parents worked in programming. I knew they used to do freelance stuff until Baylor and I came along, but now they worked for a corporation in the city that focused on creating websites and gathering intel. Trips weren't uncommon in their line of business, but I still didn't like it. Why did they have to leave now of all times? It was like the fates were laughing at me. "Where are you guys going?"

"California," my dad said. The circles under his eyes had gotten darker lately, and both my parents had hair that was starting to gray. My hair was a similar shade of brown to theirs, muted, dark, so sometimes I wondered if I'd look like them as I approached their age.

It was hard watching as they got older, and having them so far away always made me feel uneasy. I'd never really been left alone for long periods of time, mostly because Baylor would stay with me if they went on vacation by themselves. As a junior in high school, I didn't get too many opportunities for independence, but right now, it wasn't something I wanted. I was close with my parents, and, although I didn't want to admit it, I felt vulnerable after what had just happened.

And now they were leaving.

"You really have to go?" I asked in a faint voice. I didn't want them to, but it felt like I didn't have a choice.

"Unfortunately," my dad said, grasping my hand from across the table. His skin felt soft, fragile, and I gripped it tight. "Baylor will come up from school on the weekends to keep you company. We know you've missed him since he started college, so hopefully you guys can use this time to catch up." His smile didn't reach his eyes, but I could appreciate the forced optimism.

The part about Baylor visiting wasn't so bad. He was three years older than me, a sophomore in college, and we'd always been close. Baylor was adopted, which made it funny when people would say he looked like either of our parents because, of course, he didn't. Everything about him contrasted with me: his tanned skin, sandy hair, and bright golden eyes. The sun and the clouds, that's how I always imagined the pair of us.

Not that I was gloomy or anything.

"When are you guys leaving?" I asked.

They shared that look again. A look of uneasiness, like they were delivering news about something dreadful.

"Tonight."

I launched out of my chair. "*Tonight?*"

"After dinner," my mom said. "But we'll be back soon, I promise. It'll be like we were never gone."

Somehow, that seemed doubtful.

Dinner didn't last very long after that, even though I tried to drag it out as much as I could by taking small bites and asking for more water about ten times. Finally, there was nothing left I could do.

They brought their suitcases downstairs and gave me hugs so tight I thought I would break. My mother's knuckles turned white as her fingers laced together, and, when I caught her glance, she gave one more guilt-laden smile. With wistful expressions on their faces, they waved good-bye, but just before leaving, my dad looked back.

"We love you. Call us anytime."

I gave him a nod despite wanting to fight for them to stay. I'd done enough fighting tonight. "Love you."

Our eyes locked for a long second before I shut the door behind them and watched from the window as the bright lights of their car faded into black.

Then I stood alone in a house too big for a girl too close to tears.

I DIDN'T GO TO SCHOOL THE NEXT DAY.

I felt like my trauma from seeing a dead body was a good enough excuse to lie on my bed and stare at the ceiling for hours on end. Luckily, Baylor saw my point and called the school to let them know I was suffering from a "cold."

My friends, however, were a bit more relentless.

"Are you sure you don't want to just stop by? Maybe it'll help get your mind off things," Adalia, one of my best friends, said through the speaker on my phone. She had a high voice, but it was the type that soothed you, the type that made you feel like someone was listening to your problems instead of judging.

"Yeah!" a deeper voice chimed. "We miss you!"

"Whatever, Liam." I scoffed, but I couldn't help the smile forming on my lips. "You guys saw me yesterday."

"So, it's been a whole day! That's enough time to, like, I don't know, move to another state. Wait, ow—" he yelped, and I figured Adalia had given him a punch. "I didn't mean her parents! I was just giving an example!"

"Well, think of a better one!" Adalia said.

"You guys are way too energetic for me right now. I'll come to school tomorrow, so don't worry too much," I said, shaking my head. I wasn't that upset at Liam's choice of words, but it reminded me once again why I was feeling so dull inside. It was nice having friends who listened, and I wanted to be in good shape when I saw them again. At least, better shape than I was right now.

"All right. Text us if you're bored!" Adalia replied. After agreeing to her terms, I ended the call and plopped right back onto my comforter.

Only a few seconds passed before the screen lit up again, and I rolled to my side, bringing my phone toward my face. I'd expected it to be a text from those two, but the email notification caught my attention, and I opened a message from the school.

Brynn Hastings (and parents),
This is a final notice for gym lockers. Today is the last day
to get assigned a locker number, so please stop by the office

9

before 4:00 p.m. If not, you will be unable to use the lockers during and outside of PE.

I groaned. *Of course.* Of course, something like this would happen. I'd been slacking a little, sure, but why did my timing have to be so bad?

I recalled my dad's words: *You've always been lucky, Brynn.* Yeah, right.

By the time I got to school, the hallways were empty. Those who had stayed back were out on the field or practicing in the gym for school sports. I looked ridiculous pairing one of Baylor's old hoodies with loose sweats, but I didn't care. I was mourning the loss of a free afternoon.

The infamous **MAIN OFFICE** sign felt menacing as it stared at me from above. I'd been in that office until late last night, and I was anything but happy to be back.

"Excuse me?" I peeked my head into the room, hoping that everyone hadn't run away at the first sound of the bell. There was a woman perched at the main desk, but she made no reply.

I walked toward her, but I still had to stand there for a while before she finally noticed me.

"Excuse me," I said again, tired of having to convince people to listen to me.

The lady looked up, tilted her glasses down, then gave a vicious scowl. Her hair was in short, uneven curls, and her eyes squinted in an unamused manner. The lipstick she wore was too heavy and had smeared, since it was the end of the day. It was obvious we both wanted to leave.

"What can I help you with?" she asked, uninterested.

I tried to keep my expression calm. I wanted to get this over with as soon as possible, and starting a fight didn't seem like the best way. "I got an email telling me to come in to get a locker number."

"What's your name?" Her eyes drooped.

"Brynn Hastings."

The woman didn't respond, but the typing coming from her keyboard gave me hope that she'd heard me.

I didn't know if she was always like this, but I was guessing it wasn't personal. I mean, I didn't know her. She wasn't the one I worked with during fifth period, and though she always sat at this desk, she never seemed to look up unless she was called.

Finally, the keyboard pecking came to a halt, and she tore off a sticky note, jotted down a number, then slapped it onto the counter in front of me. "This is the last locker in there, so no changes."

I had never known how in demand school gym lockers were.

"Thanks," I said as I took the note.

Silence.

I figured that was all I'd get, so I quickly scurried out of the office, glad our odd interaction was over.

Glassy brick walls curved into two separate entrances for the locker room: one for the girls and one for the boys. It was a little different from the typical high school model. The only thing that separated the boys and girls was a wall of lockers, which basically meant we all shared a giant room split in the middle. Luckily, there was a thin, solid wall that rose from above where the boys' and girls' lockers divided the room all the way to the ceiling, which drowned out the noise from the guys' side of the room.

I had gym during my third period, but I always blocked out the memory. The only thing that made it bearable was Adalia's presence, though even I had to admit she was more athletic than I was. I liked dancing, but if there was a ball involved? Count me out.

The only reason I was even taking gym was because I could only use outside sources, like my past dance classes, for two years. Unfortunately, I needed three years of physical education in order to graduate, so here I was.

I glanced at the piece of paper and sighed.

Of course, I got a locker right in the middle of the dividing wall. At least I got the top half, which was about two feet wide and stopped just above my eye level.

I spun the lock to the numbers written on the note and pulled the handle toward me. The door came to a jolting halt, then rested on its hinges as I peered in.

Then I paused.

Was that a poster on the back of the wall? I reached my hand out, just a little, to see if it touched the back. But there was no back, just air. And abs.

I swear there were abs.

"Like what you see?" a deep voice asked from the other side of the locker. My feet stumbled backward before I caught myself and realized what was going on. With widened eyes, I bent forward to get a clearer view.

There was no back wall to my locker. It connected directly to the locker that opened on the boys' side.

And here was a boy.

"What?" I sputtered. I'd never been in this kind of situation before. Sure, I'd seen shirtless guys; I had an older brother. But this definitely wasn't my older brother. "Where's your shirt? Shouldn't there be a back to this locker?"

The voice answered, neglecting the first question. "There should be," he started to say, his body tilting down so I could see better. His face was tan, narrow, complemented with dark eyebrows that arched in amusement as his gaze locked with mine.

I recognized those eyes: the blue of the winter sky, glassy in its reflection through icicles, seemed trapped in the eyes of a boy with a conceited grin. "But there isn't."

I knew who he was. Almost everyone at Westwood did.

That was Kyler Fellan.